Ariel's Gift

Thomas Pullyblank

Square Circle Press
Schenectady, New York

Ariel's Gift

Square Circle Press LLC
PO Box 913
Schenectady, NY 12301
www.SquareCirclePress.com

©2020 by Thomas Pullyblank.
All rights reserved. No part of this publication may be reproduced or transmitted in any form or by any means, electronic or mechanical, except brief quotes extracted for the purpose of book reviews or similar articles, without permission in writing from the publisher.

First paperback edition 2020.
Printed and bound in the United States of America on acid-free, durable paper.
ISBN 13: 978-0-9989670-2-8
ISBN 10: 0-9989670-2-5
Library of Congress Control Number: 2020940384

Publisher's Acknowledgments
Cover: ©2020 by Square Circle Press. Cover design by Richard Vang, based on *Down Rent War, Around 1845* by Mary Earley, ca. 1939-1940. (Credit: Smithsonian American Art Museum, Transfer from the General Services Administration [Accession Number: 1974.28.367]).

Epigraphs: Part 1, Thomas Taylor, *A Dissertation on the Eleusinian and Bacchic Mysteries* (1790), in Patrick Harpur, *The Philosophers' Secret Fire*, p. 313. Part 2, Apuleius, from *The God of Socrates* (c. 150), in *The Works of Apuleius*, trans. Mrs. Henry Tighe, Hudson Gurney, Mary Blachford Tighe, pp. 357-358. Part 3, Thomas Traherne, *The Centuries of Meditations* (1660s), quoted in Philip and Carol Zaleski, *Prayer: A History*, frontispiece.

The author's acknowledgments appear in the Afterword.

*For Kristin and Bradon,
the loves of my life.*

Table of Contents

Part One, *3*

Part Two, *115*

Part Three, *263*

Afterword, *348*

Bibliography, *351*

Ariel's Gift Playlist, *353*

About the Author, *354*

Ariel's Gift

Part One

Clinton Falls
Mumford
Clinton Falls

And as to the philosophy, by whose assistance these mysteries are developed, it is coeval with the universe itself; and however its continuity may be broken by opposing systems, it will make its appearance at different periods of time, as long as the sun himself shall continue to illuminate the world.

—Thomas Taylor, *A Dissertation on the Eleusinian and Bacchic Mysteries* (1790)

Chapter One

IN MY DREAM I find myself in a garage, face down on the floor between a rusty oil tank and a hydraulic lift stuck three feet off the ground. The place stinks of stale gasoline, wet cigarette butts, mildew and rotting mice. My tuxedo, inherited from my father, is soiled with blood, cobwebs, dirt and who knows what else. A sticky dampness seeps through my pants as I slowly raise myself off the floor. I'm unsteady, even on both knees. I fall back to the floor with a groan.

Breathing comes with difficulty and brings with it a sharp pain across my ribs and down my back. Raising my head, I feel more pain pounding through my skull and down the left side of my neck. Up on a knee, I close my eyes and massage my brow and temples to clear my vision and ease the pain. I finally make it to my feet and steady myself against the lift. I concentrate on drawing one breath at a time. I feel my heartbeat slow to a pace approaching normal.

Slowly, my ears begin to register what's happening outside in the streets of Cape Vincent. I hear the wind scream over and around the building in which I've found shelter. Hail crashes onto the metal roof above, bringing a constant barrage of noise. Thunder shakes the cinder block walls of the garage and echoes through the air. With a horrific cracking noise, maples and oaks are splintered by lightning strikes, causing further havoc on the streets of this sleepy river town. Even inside, the electrically charged air makes the hair on the back of my neck tingle.

There are human sounds too, muffled somewhat by the concrete block walls but still audible. People shriek and shout the names of loved ones. They plea for mercy from God and God's only son. Merchants curse as their kiosks, set up with such great expectation on this tourist-heavy day, are blown to the ground by the wind and trampled under foot by people fleeing from the chaos. The voices are periodically silenced by the creak and thump of falling trees. Somehow, I've escaped the madness for a moment. I'm not the least bit confident that the thick walls of this old auto shop will protect me for long.

"You think it's all your fault," someone says from the direction of the doorway.

I turn and see Billy Masterson, my old friend who died to save the river back in 2001. He's thin and pale in my dream, like he was in real life. What surprises me is that he's here, on the river he loved, right now, at the time of the river's greatest peril. I shouldn't be that surprised, though, because Billy's ghost has a habit of appearing to other people, including my cousin Andrew, just when they need him.

"It is my fault," I say, articulating a simple truth from which no concrete walls can protect me.

Billy laughs. "What, you can control the weather now?" He moves closer and takes a pack of Marlboros from his pants' pocket.

Not a good idea with all the combustibles around, I think, even if you are a ghost.

"I know," he says. "You think you never shoulda done what you did. You think you actually had a choice, coulda done somethin' different."

Billy's right. Now, with the world loosed from its moorings, I know that the sum of my choices, returning to the Thousand Islands among them, was a huge mistake. Would I have done so had I known that the horrors of this day would be the inevitable consequence of my actions? Would I have done something different had I known that my chosen course of action would destroy so much of what I, and others, hold dear?

Something—a tree?—slams onto the garage roof. Stricken with fear and needing protection above all else, I gather objects to barricade the door. After a few minutes of piling up old tires and transmission parts and toolboxes and exhaust pipes, I'm bone-tired and breathing heavily. The pain in my ribs and back is worse than it had been before. I sink to the floor and rest against the tires.

Billy, laughing again, puts a cigarette in his mouth and lights it. "Buildin' yourself a barricade's a waste of time," he says. "Might not be your fault, might've been no other options back then, but that don't mean you can hide from what's out there now, or from what's comin'."

Billy gestures to the wall above the oil tank, where images appear of the destruction for which Billy tells me I'm not to blame. Heron's Nest, the summer home where my family had shared so much joy for so many years, is a pile of timber on the edge of a desolate island. Valhalla, the Ostend family castle and the most spectacular structure in the Thousand Islands, is a smoldering shell of stone.

"They're only buildings, ya' know," Billy says. "What really matters is the people."

"And where are they?" I ask.

Billy tells me that the River Rat Reporters, my father's friends and my friends, are either dead or, like me, in hiding. He says that my brother Patrick is who knows where. He says the same of a man he calls "the magician." Finally, he begins to tell me that my beloved, beautiful Mindy, who stood with me at the altar only moments ago as we exchanged wedding vows in the company of the people we love ...

"No!" I shout.

Billy stops talking and smiles.

I rub my eyes and feel the sting of sweat and dirt. If I refuse to acknowledge the truth of what Billy says is happening to Mindy, then perhaps all the other unthinkable events of this day will cease being true. I breathe deep, far past the pain in my ribs and back. I remove my coat and bow tie and hang them on the hydraulic lift. I breathe again and move to the door. The smoke from Billy's cigarette makes me cough.

If there's any chance at all of seeing Mindy again—if there's any chance of seeing anyone—I must leave the tenuous safety of this shelter and face up to the consequences of what I had begun. Slowly, with as much determination as I can muster, I begin to disassemble the barricade I had just built.

"Eff yeah," Billy encourages. He claps and the images on the wall disappear. "The only way to save her is to get out there and do it."

As I turn to ask him for help, the door bursts open from a ferocious blast of wind, which sends the remaining pieces of my barricade tumbling past me. The gust also blows Billy's cigarette from his hand into a pool of gasoline. Or did he flick it there? Either way, I awaken just as the explosion sends me through the door and into the street.

Chapter Two

LATER THAT DAY, still shaking off the dream's aftereffects, I looked out our kitchen window to see Mindy pedal up our driveway and lean her bike against our back porch.

She bounded up the stairs and through the door, and dropped her backpack on the chair next to me rather than in its usual weekend resting place.

She looked at me and said, in as calm a voice as she could manage, "Radisson's back."

I was smiling as I usually did when I watched Mindy arrive home, but my smile vanished, as if cued by the screen door's smack, the moment she dropped that information bomb.

"Which one?" I asked, trying to match Mindy's composure and very much hoping it wasn't the daughter.

"Martha," she answered, catching her breath.

I caught mine too, then sat back and unclenched the color swatches I'd been examining.

Mindy went to the refrigerator and removed two bottles of Snapple. She popped them open, handed the peach-flavored one to me and leaned her hip against my shoulder. I wrapped my arm around her waist and swigged my tea, relieved that it wasn't Julianne who had returned, yet very much puzzled as to why her mother had.

"Where'd you see her?" I asked.

"In my office. I was eating lunch and reviewing the semester's faculty activity reports. I almost gagged on my yogurt when I saw her at the door." Mindy giggled. "Wanna guess what she said?"

"No." I waited. "Are you gonna tell me?"

"Wait 'til you hear this," she said, and took a deep drink of tea. "Martha looked around my office, ran her finger along a bookshelf like she was checking for dust and said that New York State should hang a blue plaque outside the door to mark the office's historical significance."

"What did you say to that?"

Mindy's smile broadened. "I reminded her that I've been department chair for only two semesters, and thus had a little bit more history to make before the office was truly worthy of a taxpayer-funded sign."

"Good answer," I said with a loud laugh. "Seriously, though, what did she want?"

"She wanted you, darling." Mindy removed a business card from her shorts pocket and tossed it on the table. "I told her you'd call her on Monday."

I patted Mindy on the thigh. "Even better answer," I said.

She put down her drink, picked up the color swatches and fanned them out. "How's this going?"

"Teaberry green with sage tint trim, methinks."

"Satin and semi-gloss?"

"Semi-gloss for the trim. Satin only if I can patch up those cracks cleanly. Otherwise we'll go with flat like we did in the guest room."

"Flat's good too." She traded back the swatches for the drink. "Sure you're OK with all this?"

I gulped more Snapple. "With the return of Martha Radisson or with flat teaberry green and sage tint trim on our living room walls?"

"You know what I mean," she said.

I picked up the bottle and pretended to read the label. "I don't know," I continued. "Maybe we should try a blue."

Mindy saw the anxiety in my expression, heard the key

change in my voice. She grabbed the bottle from my hand and read my eyes. "Another dream?" she asked.

I nodded.

"Bad one?"

"Storm on the river knocked down a bunch of trees. I found shelter in an old garage, but it wasn't going to hold for long. Billy was there, Mindy. He was telling me things. Showing me things … " I looked away. I didn't tell her that my ribs and back still ached. I also kept quiet about the disturbing fact that my dream took place on our wedding day.

Mindy stroked my hand. "Maybe you should go up to the river early. Get some extra rest."

I shook my head. "Not a chance, hon. You've got graduation. I've got the painting to finish. We'll go up together and enjoy it." I added as an afterthought, "Like we always do."

She continued stroking my hand and touched my cheek. "I'm sorry. I know part of you wishes there was more time. The pressure of that's probably what's causing your dreams."

"Just part of me wishes there was more time," I explained. "A smaller and smaller part every day. Besides, pressure's not the same as temperature. I don't have cold feet, Mindy. I'm as committed as you are."

"I know," she said.

What I was committed to was our upcoming wedding, which we'd already postponed several times over the past four and a half years. We used as excuses the multitude of redecorating jobs in our Thousand Islands summer cottage, called Heron's Nest, and in the small bungalow we'd bought in Clinton Falls. Once I finished painting our living room teaberry green with sage tint trim, there would be no more projects left to do, and thus no more reasons to delay the nuptials.

We had used redecorating as our excuse, but the real reason for the delay, and, no doubt, another breeding ground for my dreams, was our search for my brother Patrick, who had gone missing when my father and mother died in a boat crash on the Saint Lawrence River on Labor Day 1996, soon before I became involved in Martha Radisson's life.

At first, my response to that fatal crash tore us apart. We were in graduate school then and I had no idea how to navigate my way through the emotional and spiritual land mines that such loss placed in my way. But Mindy remained steadfast. She wrote me a note once promising that she would always be there for me, although she would not chase me. She kept in touch when I moved to Brooklyn for a time to get away from Upstate New York and to immerse myself in historical research. In 2001 she accepted my invitation to visit me in the Thousand Islands, a visit which led to us growing closer than we had ever been before.

Giving priority to the search for Patrick was Mindy's idea. We were at Heron's Nest when both our engagement and our search for my brother began. On the last day of 2001 we sipped coffee and wine, made love and enjoyed an excellent dinner at Castello's in Alexandria Bay. After the breathtaking fireworks display over Boldt Castle, in the early minutes of the new year, Mindy had accepted my proposal of marriage. Later that morning, she suggested we spend as much time as we needed searching for Patrick. I cried as she assured me that official ceremonies can wait. I held her tight as she explained how we had already given each other our hearts, and how that was all that mattered.

Each year we planned to get married we sent save-the-date cards. Each time we postponed the wedding we telephoned our guests and told them they could have the date back. This year, knowing that painting the living room was the last job on our list, we sent genuine invitations. All fifty of our invited guests said they were coming.

Was Mindy angry with the delay? She was, and we'd argued about it a few times in the past several years, especially right after making the you-can-have-the-date-back phone calls. Was she jealous of Patrick, feeling that I was putting the brother I barely knew ahead of the woman with whom I promised to share my life? She was, and justifiably so since we both believed that marriage was an act of creating a new family that should at least equal in priority the families we were born into. Did the delay of our wedding day and the search for my brother threaten our relationship? From my point of view it had not. If there was one thing I knew about our relationship it was this: that we were blessed with the healthy habit of honesty in matters of the heart, a practice we'd developed over the span of a decade, first as lovers, then as friends, now as something more than both.

We were not married in the eyes of either church or state, but we had redecorated. In the summer of 2002 we tore down wallpaper and painted the interior of Heron's Nest throughout, choosing bright, bold colors that, in Mindy's words, would "keep us happy when that old blue mood starts coming on." The following year we replaced the wood casement windows with vinyl double-hungs. My cousin Andrew Hibbard, an island contractor with whom I had worked before I started my own business, was pleased to announce that our glazing days were over.

We bought our Clinton Falls bungalow that same year. We worked through the place room by room, making it our own. We painted walls and hung wallpaper borders. We pulled up the wall-to-wall carpets and refinished the pine floors. We bought furniture to suit our tastes and fulfill our needs for the nine months of the year we lived there.

We considered ourselves fortunate, even with our failed search for Patrick lurking in the background of our lives. Mindy was tenured by then and ready to take her turn as history department chair. I had my new business, Upstate Historical Services, LLC, up and running. My office was comfortably and conveniently located in a two-room suite above The 357, a bar and grill owned by Louie Fratello, my oldest and closest friend in Clinton Falls.

We were ready for married life, were *de facto* living it already. But the one missing element was the wedding itself, or, more accurately, the prerequisite presence of the only living member of my nuclear family at that wedding. So we put the wedding off, and kept putting it off, using job changes, the cottage renovations, the home purchase and its redecorating as our delaying tactics to cover up the real reason for our hesitation. "Ordering our lives together" was how we explained it to Mindy's parents. They knew better but silently played along.

Back in our kitchen on that warm, sunny May afternoon, Mindy held my hand and prompted me to rub her hip and outer thigh. "You know, sweetheart," she said hesitantly, but with a smile waiting on deck," we could get a puppy when we finish painting."

"What?"

"Make the phone calls again. Milk another year to house train the new arrival."

I stood up and moved closer. "Stop," I said, readying my fingers to tickle her.

"What? You don't want to make the phone calls again or you really do want to get a dog?"

"Not another word!"

Mindy laughed. "Can we get a labradoodle?"

"Stop! You guessed my wedding gift! You ruined the surprise!" I moved in on her. "I already named him Bojangles!"

She screamed as I tickled her, and we both laughed harder.

A moment later she placed her outstretched arms on my shoulders and looked me in the eye. "I don't want a labradoodle," she said, her smile in full bloom now. "I don't want whatever it is that Martha Radisson brings. I want you, darling. Only you."

She pulled me tight and rested her head on my shoulder.

I breathed deep despite the ache in my ribs. I could have held her there, just like that, for the rest of the day.

"Nothing will change," Mindy said after a few moments. "I promised you that we'll keep looking for as long as it takes and that we'll always be together."

"I know," I said, failing to hold back tears, irrationally fearing that finding my brother would make the worst of my dreams come true.

She kissed my forehead twice just above each eyebrow. "All shall be well," she repeated with each kiss. She looked me in the eye and smiled.

I nodded as we said together, like we had so many times before, "And all manner of things shall be well."

Chapter Three

MY BROTHER DISAPPEARED after the 1996 boating accident that killed my father and mother. At first I thought the accident was caused by a drunk speedboater, only to learn in 2001 that my parents' boat had been sabotaged by a man obsessed with using the power of the Saint Lawrence River to harm others.

Also in 2001 I learned that claims of my brother's death in the accident were mistaken. My father's final instruction to a friend who was at the scene was to let Patrick be. After that, the bishop of our diocese buried an empty casket, covering up my brother's disappearance for reasons I could not discern. My brother was very much alive, and from the moment I acquired that knowledge I felt a pressing need to find him. Mindy more than indulged that need.

We started our search for Patrick with the assumption that he was still in the Thousand Islands. We placed ads in both American and Canadian newspapers. We inquired at post offices. On Sundays we attended Roman Catholic churches, Methodist churches, and, splitting the difference, Episcopal and Anglican ones as well. We went to bars and restaurants on both sides of the border. We displayed a painted sign on my Uncle Jack's Chris-Craft and rode the boat up and down the river. The River Rat Reporters, my father's old friends who had welcomed me into their group when I returned to Heron's Nest in September 2001, asked their friends about him, and asked them to ask their friends. We found no trace of him.

We reconsidered our original assumption and widened our search systematically. We placed more ads in the big upstate newspapers and even in a few of the smaller ones, and then on the newspapers' web pages. We placed ads in local penny savers. We perused old yearbooks and searched the internet and contacted Patrick's high school classmates. We checked police reports and missing persons databases. We set up our own web page. We met with a sympathetic captain from the New York State Police. We investigated in all the ways that two well-experienced researchers knew how to investigate. We had an entire banker's box full of information. None of it led to Patrick.

Then there were the dreams, which I'd been having for about a month. They all happened somewhere in the Thousand Islands, and they all displayed some variant of mass destruction. Sometimes the river flooded despite the Joint International Commission's assurances that they had the water level of the Saint Lawrence Seaway well under control. Sometimes the ice failed to melt, even in high summer, and rendered the river un-navigable. In one dream the river boiled, sending up wave after wave of noxious effluvia that sickened anyone who inhaled it. In another dream a western wind blew so hard that it moved the smaller islands downriver.

Until that afternoon, however, none of my dreams had ever had much personal meaning. This one happened on the day of our wedding, at the place the ceremony was to be held. I was a direct participant in the dream and experienced the disaster with my own senses and my own emotions. For the first time in one of my dreams, Billy Masterson was back from the dead, questioning my motives as he had often done in life. Finally, this dream was connected to the search for my brother. I had no doubt that, in the dream, the events that sent me into the cement block-walled garage were caused by my brother's return to the river.

Chapter Four

Mindy cooked fettuccine primavera for dinner that evening as I removed the curtains, sanded the trim and patched the walls. The joint compound covered the cracks more smoothly than I had expected it would, allowing us to use the satin sheen we preferred. On Saturday morning we ate breakfast out and shopped for paint, and returned home to move furniture and apply the first of three coats to the walls. We cooperated well as a team, staying out of each other's way as we discussed wedding plans and other topics and listened to a shuffle mix of our favorite songs. I edged with a brush and Mindy followed with the roller, making giant "W's" and "M's" and then filling them in. When we finished for the day I covered the brush and roller with plastic bread bags and tied the bags shut around the handles to keep the tools wet for easy application of the second coat. We napped, made love, showered together and decided to have dinner and drinks at The 357.

"Look who's here!" Louie exclaimed as we walked in and sat down at the bar. He looked at me and at Mindy, then smiled. "What's got you two in town and not up at your river love nest?"

"Painting the living room," I said.

"Go with that green we talked about?" Louis asked.

"Teaberry green with sage tint trim," I confirmed. "First coat on the walls is done."

"You following my advice, Tommy? You applying three coats?"

"We are."

"Good," Louie said. "The extra work'll be worth it."

Mindy, who didn't know I had consulted Louie about the job, smiled and ordered two Saranac drafts. "Tom must have also told you that the living room is our last job," she said.

Louie knew. "So you're going through with it?" he asked.

"July eighth," I said.

Louie raised an eyebrow. "Your parents' anniversary."

"It's a great way to honor their legacy," Mindy said.

"True enough," Louie said. But the look he gave me said that we should talk more about it later. "Still having it up on the river?"

"You bet," Mindy said. She sipped her beer and smiled.

"And?" Louie prodded.

"The ceremony will be part of the Cape Vincent French Festival," she explained. "Napoleon himself will officiate right after the parade ends."

"I've heard of ship captains performing weddings, but never generals," Louie said. "How'd you swing that?"

"A friend of ours is the festival's official Napoleon," I said. "He's also a town justice. Besides, Napoleon was an emperor, not just a general. Emperors can do anything they want."

Louie laughed, then turned serious. "No priests, huh?"

I shook my head vigorously. "Not for me. Not after what the bishop did."

"So you've lost your religion," Louie said, his voice tinged with disappointment.

"Not exactly," I said. "I'm still OK with God. But priests? No thank you. I guess you could call me spiritual but not religious."

"I guess one out of two ain't bad." Louie shook his head. "A wedding officiated by Napoleon. Your mom would certainly approve, with the family connection and all."

"She attended the French festival every year," I said. "She arrived early with her lawn chair and three more for the rest of us and got a spot right next to the judge's stand. Then she enjoyed her coffee and French pastries and waited for the parade. When Napoleon came by she stood up, saluted and shouted 'Vive la France!' Every year she did that." I laughed. "It became so embarrassing once I turned about nine! But she loved it. She loved Napoleon. She always told us we wouldn't even be here if it weren't for him."

"Then it's a good way to honor her," Louie said to my deep appreciation. "What about your reception?" he asked. "Get Beethoven to play for that?"

"Close," Mindy said, giggling. "Handel."

"Huh?"

"Handel's *Water Music*?" Mindy asked.

Louie nodded.

She continued, "Our reception will be like the original performance, but on a different river, obviously. Tom and I and our A-level guests will be aboard the *Archangel*. Everyone else will be on rented tour boats. There'll be open bars and buffet tables on all three."

"Am I A-level?"

"Louie! Of course you're A-level."

"So you'll have an orchestra?"

"Nineteen piecer," I said. "Same one that played at our first Ostend Ball back in 2001. From Cape Vincent we'll cruise downriver. Those who want to join us for the after-hours party can disembark at Valhalla. The rest will be dropped off at Alex Bay where shuttles will return them to Cape Vincent."

"Wow. That must have taken some serious planning."

I shrugged. "A few phone calls. A couple letters. A bit of international diplomacy. It wasn't all that difficult with the help of our river friends."

"They'll be talking about this one for years." Louie

shook his head. "Too bad you're going all hoity-toity with your orchestra, though."

"Why's that?" Mindy asked.

"I've got the perfect wedding guy. He's playing right here in this room next week. I've been meaning to tell you about him. I think you'll like him." As well as food, Louie had added Friday night music to The 357's offerings. He figured that the combined attractions would allow him to retire from the bar business and move to Florida five years earlier than he had planned.

"What's his name?" I asked.

"Lodi."

"Like Napoleon's victory in Italy!" I exclaimed.

"Like the Creedence song," Louie answered.

"What kind of music does he play?" Mindy asked.

"Mostly covers of the old songs, with a few of his own mixed in for good measure. He's quite a character, very entertaining. Very persuasive too. Wait 'til you hear his version of name that tune."

I looked at Mindy. "Some music at our after-hours party would be nice," I said. "And how can we lose with a guy named after a Napoleonic victory?"

Mindy stomped her foot on the brass foot rail. "I can't make it next Friday," she said.

"Why not?" Louie asked.

"Big weekend at work," she explained. "History department banquet that night. Graduate commencement the next day. Undergraduate ceremony the day after that." She looked at me and smiled. "My fiancé loathes history department banquets, though, and he's already graduated. I'm sure he'd much rather come hear Lodi. Tom, maybe you should talk to him about our after-hours party. Or in case our orchestra gets held up at the border."

"Seriously?" I said. "You'd let me do that?"

"Better walk through that door before it closes," Louie advised.

Mindy straightened up and got formal. "As department chair, I hereby grant Thomas Flanagan leave to forgo his alumni obligations at the annual history department banquet in lieu of wedding planning research."

I leaned towards her and kissed her on the lips.

"Good," Louie said. "Come see Lodi. You'll enjoy him. Very interesting guy." Louie returned to wedding talk. "Having cake?"

"Of course," Mindy said, "but minus the little bride and groom figures on top. No selling out to the wedding-industrial complex for us. We didn't even hire a wedding planner."

"And if a summer storm comes blowin' in?" Louie asked, again changing the topic.

I thought of my most recent dream and shot him a look.

"What?" he asked, probably thinking that I was in denial that bad weather was even possible on our special day. "It could happen. For example, the last outdoor wedding I worked was nearly ruined by Hurricane Frances. The wedding day itself was sunny and warm, but it had rained buckets the previous three days. The bride was two hours late because her limo got stuck in the mud. The first keg was kicked before the couple exchanged vows. Hell, even the priest had a couple pints before the service. He didn't slur his sermon, though, which was a good thing." Louie laughed. "The ring bearer and flower girl were soaked with mud from chasing each other through the puddles. My point is, always have a backup plan."

"That's one advantage of Valhalla," I said. "Large upstairs ballroom. The only glitch is that we'd be in Canada. We'd have to get someone to replace Napoleon."

"That's a loaded statement for a historian to make," Mindy said.

"Might even have to be a priest," I conceded.

"Sounds like you've got it all figured out," Louie said.

"Guess that's one good thing about a five year engagement. Plenty of time to plan."

"Four-and-a-half years," I corrected, sipping the last of my Saranac and handing the glass back to Louie for a refill.

"How 'bout those water things?" Louie asked as he poured. "Do you have a contingency plan if they show up?"

"You mean the undines?" I replied.

Louie nodded.

"Would it be a problem if they did show up?"

"Not for me. In fact, I was hoping there'd be a way we could summon them. A chant or a series of torchlight signals or something."

"There's no signal that I know of," I said with a laugh. "If there were, I would've tried it myself by now."

"I thought you saw one," Louie said as he handed me the beer. "Felt one. Back when you first returned to the river."

"I'm not sure. The more I think about it, the more I tend to rationalize it away. Maybe a rogue current carried me to Magdalena Island. Maybe it was the warmth of the water that made it feel more buoyant when I jumped off Malqari's ship. Maybe all I saw when we buried Billy was a shimmer of the sun."

"I thought you Flanagans had a sixth sense."

"My mother did. Andrew says he does. Jury's still out on me. All I've seen since then is a shimmer here and a glimmer there. And like I said, the more I think about it, the more I'm convinced it was only the sun playing tricks. Anyway, I haven't seen anything like it since then."

"That doesn't surprise me," Mindy blurted.

Louie looked at her. "You're a doubter?" he asked.

I looked at Mindy too, having asked her the same question several times over the past five years and having never gotten a satisfactory answer.

She stared into her glass of beer. She paused for an inordinately long time.

"Well?" Louie added.

Mindy shook her head and smiled. "I find it a good policy to withhold judgement until I have verifiable proof one way or the other."

Louie pointed to me then back to Mindy. "Your soon-to-be-husband's testimony isn't verifiable proof?"

"There's a difference between testimony and proof," Mindy said. "Testimony can be unreliable, no matter how well-meaning the witness is." She took my hand and gave me a smile.

"True enough," Louie said.

"Anyway," Mindy continued, "the season's in high gear by early July. Even if the undines do exist, they won't show themselves until the boaters clear out." She looked at me and smiled.

Louie returned the smile. "So what'll you have?" he asked, getting back to business. "The usual?"

Mindy and I nodded together. Our usual at The 357 was a bowl of lamb stew with basmati rice made by Louie's cook, a Bantu from Somalia named Ghedi, who studied pre-law at the university and lived in an apartment building down the road from our bungalow. Ghedi was a fine cook. He had reconstructed several of his dishes, including the lamb stew, from childhood memories of his grandmother's kitchen. His stew had become a hit since he came to Clinton Falls and started working for Louie about a year before. Since first trying it, Mindy and I were both hooked.

A few minutes after Louie placed the order, Ghedi himself brought out two steaming bowls of stew and rice, which he often did for diners at the bar. He offered us a smile and a slight bow while serving us the food.

"Thank you, Ghedi," I said.

"What would we do without you?" Mindy asked.

"What would we all do without cardamom and sage?" Ghedi replied. He smiled broadly. "Oops! I just revealed two of my grandmother's secret ingredients."

Mindy inhaled deeply and smiled. "It takes more than a list of ingredients to make something this good. It takes magic. Alchemy. Oh my, sometimes just the aroma is enough."

"I prefer the food," I said after the first spoonful, savoring the taste of the lamb and lentils as well as the spices and herbs. "Have we thanked you yet, Ghedi?"

"A thousand times," Ghedi replied. "And I appreciate each one."

Ghedi stayed with us for a while, sipping a glass of water as we continued to compliment his work and quiz him on his grandmother's cooking secrets. He started back to the kitchen when Louie gave him another order, but stopped halfway through the doorway. He pivoted around and said to me, "I nearly forget, Tom. A visitor came for you yesterday while I was making preparations for my weekend cooking. She called herself an old friend. I went upstairs to find you, but you were not there." Ghedi produced a business card from his apron pocket and held it out. "She asked me to give you this."

Mindy stopped eating and set down her spoon. "Let me guess," she said.

"Martha Radisson." I crumpled the card and let it fall to the bar.

Ghedi's expression fell with it. "This is not good news?" he asked. "She is not an old friend?"

"Acquaintance, yes," I explained. "Friend, no. Was she alone?"

"Yes," Ghedi said. "She also said she would return this evening."

"She did?"

"I told her you come for dinner on Saturday nights when you are not at the Saint Lawrence River." Ghedi looked at me and paused. "I made a mistake?"

Mindy shook her head vigorously. "No, Ghedi. You did not make a mistake. Martha Radisson also stopped by my office yesterday afternoon. She left the same message with me, along with her card. Tom already got it. He's going to call her on Monday."

Louie, who was serving a group of students at the other end of the bar, heard the tail end of our conversation. He moved beside Ghedi, reached up and put his arm around his shoulder. "Tell me, Ghedi, you ever know someone who claims to be one person and turns out to be someone completely different?"

Ghedi nodded. "I knew many people like that in Somalia."

"Then you also know why Tom's so nervous about being stalked by this woman. Tom's the one who deconstructed her family history and showed the world the person she truly is. Some think he's also the one who killed her husband." Louie pointed to a bound and signed copy of my dissertation that he proudly displayed behind the bar. "It's all in there. You can read all about it on your breaks."

"That was a decade ago," I said with a dismissive wave. "I'm sure she's not here for revenge. I did save her life, after all." I sipped my beer. "Really, Louie? Stalked?"

I returned to my stew, which was still hot, still delicious, still a welcome distraction from Martha Radisson's reappearance in my life and it's possible implications.

Ghedi wiped his hands on his apron and sighed. "I have other customers to serve," he said. "But I will wish good luck to you with this woman."

"Thanks," I said.

"If what happened ten years ago is any guide," Louie said, "he'll need all the good luck he can get."

Chapter Five

GHEDI WAS THE FIRST TO SEE HER. "Oh, shoot," he said from the kitchen doorway as he delivered cheeseburgers to a couple of undergraduates.

Mindy and I were savoring the first bite of our shared dessert, a chocolate mousse cake drizzled with raspberry reduction sauce. My eyes were closed as I enjoyed the wave of flavors that started with the berries and ended with nutmeg.

"At least now you won't be spending the rest of the weekend wondering what she wants," Louie whispered.

I opened my eyes and saw him nod towards the door. I turned halfway and looked quickly over my shoulder, then turned back and hunched over in a feeble attempt to hide.

"Buck up and take it like a man," Louie whispered as he slyly moved a jar of pickled eggs in front of my dissertation.

His words brought a giggle from Mindy that caught Martha Radisson's attention.

"Ah, Professor McDonnell," she said. Following Louie's advice, I turned completely around and nodded. "And Mr. Flanagan," Martha continued. She walked towards us and smiled. She offered me her hand, which I shook. She looked tired and sad, defeated even. I wondered if I looked the same way to her ten years after I, too, had lost someone I love. "It's good to see you again, Tom."

I swallowed the bite of cake. "*Doctor* Flanagan," I said. "SUNY CF, 1998. History. I wrote my dissertation on—"

"Thank you, yes, I understand." She smiled. "I'm well aware of your academic achievements. They were made at my family's expense, after all." She coughed. "It's not your degree I'm referring to, however, it's your job. I make it a practice to not use academic titles for those who work outside academia."

"Including yourself?" I asked. "Last I heard, you were working down in Williamsburg."

She nodded. "Yes, I was at the historic village. But I don't work there any longer. I'm in the process of relocating back to Upstate New York. I'm returning closer to home. Also, to your point, I go by Martha Radisson now. No doctor, no professor, just Martha."

"*Touché*," I said.

"To be honest, I feel much better without all that academic baggage on my shoulders. I feel almost free. Almost." She looked at Mindy and smiled. "I say that with no offense towards the current history department chair, of course."

"None taken," Mindy said, raising her glass. She turned away and rolled her eyes, which forced both Ghedi and Louie to hold back chuckles.

"A raised glass means we must share a drink," Martha said. She brushed back a strand of grey hair, which was much longer and a little thinner than what I remembered from her professorial days. "Mr. Fratello, may I please have a gin and tonic?"

"Julianne's favorite drink," I exclaimed, wanting the words back the moment they were out.

Mindy cleared her throat.

Martha Radisson raised an eyebrow.

Louie said, "I'll make that gin and tonic," and turned towards the liquor shelves.

Ghedi sensed immediately that I'd said something awkward and lowered his eyes.

"It's still Julianne's favorite drink," Martha Radisson said. "I haven't shared one with her in quite some time, however. She lives in Chicago now. She usually comes home for Christmas, but this past year she and her husband took their children to London for a Dickensian holiday."

"Husband and children!" Mindy exclaimed. "How many children?"

"A son and a daughter. Four and two."

"Congratulate her for us," Mindy added.

"I will."

I wanted to ask if Julianne ever asked about me, but I held my tongue this time. I also wondered whether Julianne ever told her children the story of Cornflower's ghost, the story that had haunted her in childhood and well into her adult years, the story that got me involved in Radisson family history in the first place. I remained silent on that topic too.

Martha Radisson glanced at Mindy's hand then at mine. "I assumed you two would be married by now," she said.

"We're setting our lives in order first," Mindy said. "Getting used to our jobs, redecorating. This is the year, though. In July."

Louie, humming the CCR tune which took it's name from either the Napoleonic victory or from the town in California, served the gin and tonic and returned to the students at the other end of the bar. I could tell he was keeping one ear on our conversation, though.

Ghedi, meanwhile, remained in the bar area next to the kitchen door, most likely trying to figure out why I should be so nervous about Martha Radisson who, I had to admit, seemed anything but trouble.

Martha raised her glass. "A proper toast, then. To you, Tom and Mindy. May your life together bring you much peace and a fair amount of joy."

We drank. It was, after all, a generous toast.

Chapter Six

AFTER WE FINISHED our dessert and drinks and Mindy finished sharing the latest history department comings and goings, I reminded Martha that I'd call her on Monday morning. I hoped she would leave so Mindy and I could enjoy a nightcap together in peace.

But Martha didn't take the hint, and asked if we could talk now, the three of us, since she had to return to Williamsburg on Monday to finish packing and would not be able to talk on the phone.

Mindy nodded her assent, and together we walked up the back staircase to my office.

To the left of my office door was a plaque shaped like New York State, engraved with my name and with the words "Upstate Historical Services, LLC." On the door itself was Sherlock Holmes' hat and pipe stenciled in silhouette.

"Lofty ambitions," Martha said, pointing to the hat and pipe. "Clever too."

"A gift from Mindy," I said as I opened the door and flipped on the light. "I like it because it helps people understand that every historical inquiry, even simple genealogy, has some element of mystery to it, some unanswered question."

"So very true," Martha Radisson said.

Mindy tapped Sherlock's hat with a finger. "I like it because it implies that every mystery has a logical explanation, if only we're clever enough to see it."

"Mostly true," Martha replied this time.

I sat at my desk and turned on a floor lamp behind me.

Mindy and Martha sat in the two upholstered chairs that faced the desk.

"What can I do for you?" I asked politely. "And, if you don't mind me asking, why didn't you just e-mail?"

"I'm techno-phobic," Martha said. "Besides, I knew I'd be in the neighborhood. I thought it best that we speak in person." She put her purse on the floor. "Tell me, what do you know about New York's Anti-Rent Wars?"

"Why do you ask?"

"I'll get to that." She waited for my answer, which I did not give. "Please, Tom, indulge me. When you hear my reasons for asking the question, I think you'll agree that my reasons are very good ones. So please, tell me, what do you know about the Anti-Rent Wars?"

I counted on my fingers. "One, they took place in the middle eighteen hundreds around Albany. Two, they proved a fatal blow to the old New York aristocracy, ruining the fortunes and political influence of families like the Van Rensselaers, Livingstons and Hardenberghs. Three, they formed one of the contributing elements to the Free Soil movement and the Republican party." I paused. "There was also some violence involved, wasn't there?"

"If you're referring to the August 7, 1845, murder of Undersheriff Osman Steele, then, yes indeed, there was violence involved."

"Murder?" Mindy asked, enthused.

"Yes, his dear Watson," Martha Radisson said. "Undersheriff Osman Steele was murdered by one of a company of disguised men. 'Indians,' they called themselves, or 'Natives.' They were actually thugs, hooligans of the most vile and despicable sort, who used illegal tactics in an attempt to intimidate landlords into canceling their rent. Today, they'd be in jail or on probation more often than not."

"Tell us how you really feel," Mindy said.

Martha ignored her.

"They were disguised?" I asked.

"Yes."

"How?"

"With gaudily decorated gowns of calico fabric and masks of burlap, leather or sheepskin that were often embellished with horns like a buck's or floppy ears like a dog's. The costumes were quite revolting. Vile, in fact, like the men who wore them."

"This murder happened where?"

"In Andes." She saw my uncomprehending look. "In Delaware County. Southwest of Albany. In the Catskills."

"OK," I said, vaguely aware of the lay of the land.

"The place has a complicated history. It was originally part of the Hardenbergh estate before the Hardenberghs sold it to the Livingstons and several other less prominent, but still respectable families. The murder itself happened on Verplanck land. Have you done any research on the Anti-Rent Wars? Perused any books? Taken any classes?"

"I think Professor McNally covered them in one of his graduate seminars," I said. "But that was a long time ago. I try not to remember too much of those days."

"Me either," Martha replied.

"Why are you asking about books? Do you want some recommendations?" I opened the laptop I kept on my desk with the intention of Googling Osman Steele and the Anti-Rent Wars.

Martha Radisson waved me off. "You don't have to do that now," she said. "As I mentioned earlier, I have something of an aversion to technology."

"Guess you got out of the archives business at the right time," Mindy said, referring to Martha's former position as director of the university's Center for the Study of American Revolutionary Culture and History.

Martha simply nodded. "There are several published books, and yes, they've already been read."

I caught her switch to the passive voice and prompted, "And …"

"There are certain shortcomings to the written history," she said, "the most significant of which is that the shooter was never conclusively identified. Several men were tried and sent to prison for the crime and two others were sentenced to hang, but in the end, all the convicted men were pardoned. In the end, no one knows exactly who killed Undersheriff Osman Steele."

"The disguises," Mindy said.

"Yes," Martha Radisson affirmed. "The disguises." She paused, then asked me point blank, "Have you been hired to find Osman Steele's killer?"

I glanced at Mindy, whose eyes showed obvious suspicion. "Not that I'm aware of," I said tentatively. "Do *you* want to hire me to find Osman Steele's killer?"

She ignored my question, saying instead, "Well, then, I can safely conclude that what I'm about to show you was not sent by you." She paused. "At first I thought it was a practical joke. Or, I thought, you might have sent it to welcome me back to the neighborhood. But you seemed genuinely surprised when I told you that I was moving closer to home. And your obvious ignorance of the Anti-Rent Wars supports your claim that you've not been hired to solve the murder of Osman Steele." She produced a card that was folded horizontally in half. She placed it on my desk, saying, "Therefore, I'm going to conclude that you have no idea where this came from."

I reached forward and picked up the card. Her name was embossed on the face of the card above the fold. I opened the card and saw the words, "WHO KILLED OSMAN STEELE?" written on it, and "FLANAGAN" just below that. Both the question and my name were written in a beautiful cursive script. The ink was thick, and was such a dark green that it almost looked black. I turned the card over. Nothing was written on the back side.

"Where did you get this?" I asked.

"As I've already mentioned, I'm returning closer to home. Last week I started work at the New York State Historical Association. Have you been there?"

"In Cooperstown. Of course. I've used their archives for several investigations," I said. "It's an outstanding collection."

"It is indeed." Radisson nodded towards the card. "When I walked into my office on my first day of work, this card was sitting on my desk."

I glanced at Mindy, who narrowed her eyes. I knew she was as incredulous as I was.

"Did it come in an envelope or just like this?" I asked.

"Just like this."

"And this is your personal stationary?"

"It is. I use about 250 cards per year. I have matching envelopes with my return address imprinted on the flap."

"Looks like you're one card short," Mindy said. "I hate it when that happens."

Martha Radisson shook her head. "As I said, I found this card on my desk on my first day of work. The odd thing is, I did not have any cards besides this one or any envelopes at all in the office on my first day of work. I had ordered a package of 250 cards with my new address on them about a month earlier. I received the cards in the mail on my third day of work and didn't open the package until that afternoon. After opening the package, I counted both the cards and the envelopes. There were 250 of each. I counted them again to confirm—250 of each." She paused. "I'm not one card short, Mindy, and that's exactly the problem. I have no idea where this particular card came from. Nor do any of my colleagues."

Despite my incredulity, the fact of the card's existence made me a little uneasy. I placed it on my desk and slowly slid it away from me. But I had a difficult time taking my eyes off the beautiful script, writing that seemed to be calling my name.

Mindy asked the questions that were also on my mind. "Are you sure your colleagues didn't know? Sure it wasn't someone else's practical joke? A hazing prank or something? And why did you think it was Tom?"

"I'm quite certain my colleagues didn't know," she answered. "And why would someone else play a practical joke like this on me?" She gestured towards the card and frowned. "How would associating the Flanagan family name or Osman Steele's murder with me be even remotely funny to anyone?"

"I have no idea," I answered. "I'm sorry I can't be of any help." I slid the card closer to her but she waved me off. "And I'm sorry my family name brought you grief, no matter how inadvertently."

"Keep it," she said. "It has your name on it, after all. Seems like it should stay with you."

"You didn't answer my question," Mindy said.

"Which one?"

"The last one. Why exactly did you think it was Tom who sent you the card?"

She looked at me for a long moment. Then she produced something else from her purse, this time a folded up newspaper marked with thick red ink. She started to hand it to me then drew it back to examine it. "I'd forgotten about this until I received the note card. I suppose I forgot about it because, for a long time, I didn't want anything to do with you or your family given what you did to me and mine. But here it is." She met my gaze and half-smiled. "And here we are."

When she turned the newspaper I saw one of our ads: "MISSING PERSON—PATRICK FLANAGAN—AGE TWENTY NINE—6' 2"—AROUND 200 LBS.—DARK BROWN HAIR." Underneath that was a black and white picture of Patrick from 1996, followed by my phone number and the number for our New York State Police contact. The ad was in the Rochester *Democrat and Chronicle* and was from the summer of 2003, a few months before I stopped placing ads in print newspapers and started putting them online.

Growing angry, I looked at her and asked, "Why do you have this?"

"I think I saw him," Martha Radisson replied. "Unless, of course, it *was* you that I saw. At first, I was quite convinced of the latter."

"Saw him? Unless it was me? What are you talking about?"

Martha looked me in the eye. "Three years ago in Mumford," she said.

"Where?"

"At the Genesee Country Village and Museum in Mumford. Just south of Rochester. I saw someone I thought was you and called your name. You turned, said something to the woman you were with and walked away with her. You almost ran away, in fact. I was quite puzzled."

"A woman?" Mindy asked, raising an eyebrow towards me.

"I thought it was you, Professor McDonnell."

My heart pounded. "This was where? When?"

"Three years ago at the Genesee Country Village and Museum in Mumford," she repeated. "I was attending the Association for Living History's annual conference. I was giving a series of lectures on Revolutionary Era women's clothing. I was—"

"I wasn't at that conference," I said. "I've never been to a living history conference."

"Me either," Mindy added.

"And I've never been to Mumford," I continued, starting to feel lightheaded.

"So maybe it was Patrick," Mindy said, looking at me wide-eyed.

Martha Radisson picked up the card with the green writing and slowly turned it in her hand. "I'd completely forgotten about that ad. I'd also forgotten about the man I thought was you and now suspect was your brother. Then I received this card. Then I remembered it all."

"And what exactly did you remember?" Mindy asked. "What happened?"

"Like I said, I was in Mumford for the Association for Living History's 2003 annual conference. There were all sorts of interpreters there that week. One group performed a town ball exhibition."

"Town ball?" I asked.

"Old-time baseball. They used the 1848 rules at the village, although different groups of interpreters use different sets of rules from later years. In their version of the game, the ball is leather and the bats are made of homemade wood. There are no gloves. The teams set up stakes in a big square, and the striker comes to bat between first and fourth. There are no strikeouts, nor walks. All hit balls are in play, no matter where they land. When the striker becomes a runner he must go from first to second to third to fourth in order to score a tally. Fielders get the out—only one out per inning—by catching the ball or by plugging the runner."

"My brother played this game?"

"Your brother was an excellent player. He could hit the ball a country mile. He could knock it backwards with such spin that the catcher couldn't pick it up. He could throw almost as far as he could hit, and with accuracy. One time, I saw him plug a runner in the heel just as the runner was about to score the tying tally."

"So you saw my brother playing town ball," I said.

"And at first I thought it was you. I approached you ... well, him when the game ended. I called your name. He removed his hat—it was a wide-brimmed straw hat—and turned around. He was quite startled at first. He paused for a moment, then took the hand of the woman he was with, said something to her and, together, they walked away."

"What did this woman look like?" Mindy asked.

"She was gorgeous! She was tall, with long blond hair, green eyes and perfect skin. I can't easily describe it, but she radiated health and warmth and perhaps even peace. I thought she must have been famous. I thought I couldn't place her name because I don't pay much attention to celebrity news."

"And you thought she was me?"

"I did at first," Martha Radisson said.

"I'm a brunette," Mindy said.

Martha shrugged, then folded her arms and swallowed. "What I just told you is only part of what happened," she said. "I remember it clearly and can probably back it up with evidence, with the interpreter troupe's roster for example. But … " She paused again.

"But there's more to your story," I said.

"Yes." Her face lost expression and grew pale. She breathed deeply and exhaled slowly. "What I just told you is memory. What I'm about to tell you is more along the lines of recollection."

"What's the difference?" I asked.

Martha picked up the card and turned it in her hand. "To put it simply, memory is intellectual, the act of recalling the facts of what happened. Recollection is more evocative of the original experience. Through effort, it brings into play the emotions and quite a bit more that was essential to what happened. Think of it this way: if you were to recite a timeline or a simple list of events you get history as memory, as just the facts. But if you visit a living history museum, a good one like the Genesee Country Museum in Mumford, you experience past events more in terms of recollection. You get the sights, the sounds, the smells. You get history that literally comes alive. That's what we aim for as interpreters, to be something more than history in a classroom."

"OK, fair enough," I said, although it was a bit pedantic for my taste. "So what do you recollect about your time in Mumford? What else can you tell me about my brother?"

"A day after the town ball demonstration, I attended a dramatic interpretation of the Anti-Rent Wars. Specifically, it was a dramatic interpretation of Osman Steele's murder. It took place on the village green, next to the gazebo. Most of the interpreters were disguised in calico gowns and sheepskin masks, of course. A few portrayed the sheriff and his posse, including Osman Steele himself. The group did their homework: the man playing Steele was a redhead. The demonstration was fairly straightforward, but interesting all the same. The Anti-Renters gathered, words and insults were exchanged, and shots were fired, first from the law enforcement men on their horses and then by the Anti-Renters. Steele's horse was hit, then Steele himself. He fell dead. More words were exchanged, and all but a few of the Anti-Renters disbanded. Those who remained removed their masks and carried Steele away, bringing the drama to an end."

Martha Radisson continued to turn the card in her hand. "When I received this card I remembered, recollected, what else I saw that day. It all came back to me—the fact of what I saw, the light and shadow of the scene, the smells of smoke and horse manure, my reactions." She looked up and caught my gaze. "And a rather uncomfortable feeling."

"What?" Mindy asked.

"Fear," she answered quietly.

"Fear? What made you afraid?" I asked.

"The man I saw playing town ball, the man who I thought was you and very well might have been your brother, was, in the Anti-Rent War interpretation I had just watched, the calico-clad Anti-Renter who shot and killed Osman Steele."

I looked at Mindy, both of us silent.

"Are you sure about that?" I asked a moment later. My

head was reeling, I was barely able to control my breathing. The voice I heard speak the words sounded like someone else's.

"Quite sure. His calico gown was tinted grey with orange and purple decorations. His mask was of sheepskin and had large eyes and a large mouth, all painted green. His mask also had two tremendous horns curling up from the temples. The horns were so large that I was quite astonished that they didn't detach and fall to the ground. The costume was quite horrendous and quite unforgettable."

"Did you see him with the mask off?" I asked. "Were you able to confirm it was the same person you saw play town ball?"

"I knew it was him by the way he carried himself, by the way he moved. His motions were fluid, lithe like they were on the town ball field. I knew it by the way he *looked* at me through that mask and seemed to dare me to identify him."

"But how did you know it was *him*?" Mindy asked with urgency.

"And what was it that brought about the fear?" I added.

Her face had turned pale and her hand was shaking. She swallowed before she answered. "The man in purple and orange, your brother, turned to face me immediately after he shot Osman Steele. His look caused a spasm of fear to run down my back. It was like someone slipped an ice cube under the collar of my shirt. It was that palpable. It was the exact opposite feeling to the feeling I had when I saw the woman he was with after playing town ball."

"What did you do?" I asked. Seeing how much the recollection affected her now, I couldn't help but sympathize.

"I turned around and hurried back to my car, then drove to the bed and breakfast where I was staying. I left Mumford the next day after I finished delivering my third and final lecture on women's clothing during the Revolutionary War. The first two installments went very well. The final session did not go very well."

We were silent for a moment until Mindy asked, "And you say you forgot about all this until you received the note card?"

Martha cleared her throat. "Yes. When I received the note card I revisited my file from that conference. I had placed the newspaper clipping in my file. Seeing what was written on the note card, seeing the advertisement, remembering the man I saw play town ball, kill Osman Steele and … and look at me like that—when I saw this note card it all came back."

Mindy continued to press. "You didn't make the connection back then between the man who scared you and the newspaper ad?"

"Of course I did. But I thought the man was Tom. Also, I was scared. Finally, look at the newspaper's publication date. I saw the ad some three months after the conference. By then I had already decided, quite emphatically, that I did not want to become involved with Tom's family, even if the man was *not* Tom and was indeed his lost brother. So I put the newspaper clipping in my file and willed myself to forget about it." She half-smiled again, unable to hide the underlying grief. "Sometimes it's best to forget, you know. Sometimes, as Tom indicated a few moments ago, it's best to not remember."

"Sometimes it is best," Mindy agreed.

Chapter Seven

MARTHA RADISSON LEFT with my assurance that I'd call her if anything relating to the note card came up. After Martha shut the door, Mindy walked around my desk and placed a firm, massaging grip on my shoulders. I exhaled and let her rub me for a few moments before asking, "Do you really think it was Patrick she saw in Mumford?"

Mindy moved to the door, opened it and looked in the hallway and down the stairs. She closed the door and locked it. "I don't know. Do you?"

"Obviously it wasn't me," I said.

"And this woman, who radiated health, warmth and peace! What's that all about?"

"I don't know," I admitted. "Should I go out there? It's the first real lead we have."

Mindy resumed the shoulder rub. "You're on your own, you know. I can't go anywhere until after graduation."

"What about the painting?"

"I can put another coat on the walls when I come home from campus. Then you can finish it up while I'm busy with the other festivities."

I nodded. "I'll go tomorrow. A quick day trip." A curious thought came to mind. "Do you think she knows more about him than she's letting on? About his disappearance?"

"How would she?"

"Maybe she's been in contact with Walter Maitland. They used to mingle in the same circles back in the day." Walter Maitland was the former United States Ambassador to the Kingdom of Jordan. He was also the man who had sabotaged my parents' boat in 1996 and, by betraying me and my friends, had tried to harness the power of Napoleon's gold in 2001. But he was thwarted by the work of the River Rat Reporters and the mysterious Naguib Malqari, and was convicted by a Canadian court of attempting to illegally raise two hundred year old timbers from the bottom of the Saint Lawrence River.

"Maitland was in prison until three months ago," Mindy reminded me. "Radisson saw your brother three years ago. Besides, we can't even be sure Walter Maitland knows that Patrick's still alive. He never said anything about it back when we encountered him."

"What other options are there? That Ben Fries told her? That makes even less sense. We've seen him at the Ostend Ball every year and he hasn't said a thing about being in touch with her." Ben Fries, another family friend, had also been close to Radissons, but many years ago and under very different circumstances.

"We even talked about her in November. Remember that? Ben was quite clear that she's on his short list of people he'd rather not see for as long as he lives." Mindy stopped rubbing my shoulders and lightly poked me between the shoulder blades. "That card on her desk was a rather pathetic ruse, wouldn't you say?"

"You think she's lying?"

"Of course. In one way or another I know she's lying." Mindy paused. "But why would she bring the murder of Osman Steele up in such an obviously fraudulent way? Seriously, an extra note card? I should look around and see if I can find a sample of her writing. Bet you a dollar to donuts the handwriting's the same."

"Could be," I replied.

"Maybe Osman Steele is her ancestor. Could you imagine that?"

I groaned. "Come on! Given what we learned ten years

ago about the Radissons and Cranes, that would be … I don't know, way too much drama for one family."

"But we also learned to never take anything Martha Radisson says at face value. Tell you what—I'll ask around on campus. See if I can find anything out."

"Thanks," I said, yawning now. "Willing to resume that massage at home?"

"Only with reciprocation," Mindy said with a kiss to the top of my head.

Chapter Eight

THE NEXT DAY, refreshed by an excellent back rub and a good night's sleep with unremembered dreams, I drove west on Routes 5 and 20. That day, as on most other days I drove west, I preferred the variety of the villages and small cities through which I passed to the monotony of the New York State Thruway. I especially enjoyed Auburn, where I had lunch at an old diner near the canal park, Seneca Falls, the birthplace of the women's rights movement, and Canandaigua, home to an outstanding outdoor amphitheater where Mindy and I had attended several concerts. I went through Avon and Caledonia and into the small hamlet of Mumford. I stopped at the boundary between the two towns to see the Caledonia fish hatchery, America's oldest, which was designed and built by Seth Green. In Mumford I turned left at the blinking light towards the Genesee Country Village and Museum.

The museum contained almost seventy buildings that dated from as early as 1797 to as late as 1870. As I walked around on that warm, bright Sunday I saw printers, blacksmiths, silversmiths, apothecaries, broom makers, coopers, even a preacher giving a sermon in an 1840's Methodist church. I listened to the preacher for about ten minutes, smiling as I considered that this was very much what my Methodist ancestor Billy Hibbard might have sounded like towards the end of his life. All in all, I appreciated the variety of the buildings and the thoroughness of the living history displays in them.

I didn't ask directly about Patrick, but I did get information from a young woman who was sweeping the front steps of an exquisite octagon house, painted a creamy-yellow with red trim.

"No corners for the dust to hide," I said as I approached up the cobblestone sidewalk.

She looked at me, then at the junction where the siding meets the porch floor boards. She resumed sweeping. "If you'll pardon the rudeness of my contradicting you, sir, your observation is of little relevance when one is out of doors. Nevertheless, this is quite an interesting house. My dear father tells me that, inside, where the dust does indeed collect, all eight corners of this house are haunted by the ghosts of the builders, Master and Mistress Hyde."

"Do you believe him?" I asked.

"I cannot but believe my father!" she exclaimed. "The Hydes were spiritualists, you know."

"Have you seen these ghosts?"

"My father tells me a young lady should never speak of such things," she said, starting to blush as she realized that she already was speaking of such things. She quickened her sweeping.

"My name's Mr. Flanagan," I said, perhaps giving her another reason to blush.

She held the broom to the side and curtsied politely. "And I am Miss Noelle," she said. "I am pleased to meet you, Mr. Flanagan."

"Have you perhaps met any other Mr. Flanagans around here?" I asked. "I'm researching my family history and I know that there were several Flanagan families in these parts of New York in the nineteenth ... uh, prior to the war between the states."

"I did know another Mr. Flanagan!" Noelle said. "I knew him my first year as a housemaid. He played town ball and once worked with my father in the blacksmith shop."

My heart quickened. "Is your father the tall, bearded man at work now in the blacksmith shop?"

"No, that man is Mr. Heitzenrater. My father is ..." Pausing and looking around, she discreetly held a hand over her mouth and whispered, "My father is William Hamilton. But he has the day off for the Sons of the American Legion clambake. You can find him down at Freeman's Park, grilling steaks and steaming clams."

She resumed sweeping, having imparted this historically inaccurate information quietly and quickly. Her smile, I thought as she recomposed her face into a more serious expression, might also have been an anachronism. "I know nothing else, however, about the Mr. Flanagan you seek. For more information you might inquire with Master Hamilton."

I removed my Yankees cap and bowed. "I thank you, fair lass," I said, bringing another smile and even a muffled chuckle from Miss Noelle Hamilton. "I shall find your father and discuss these matters with him." Then I whispered, "keeping, of course, the strictest confidence as to my sources."

BY THE TIME I GOT BACK to the intersection, cars were parked along the sides of the roads in all four directions. The fire hall at the four corners was empty save for the trucks inside the open bays. I parked my pickup behind the fire hall, got out and looked around. The library and the craft and antique stores were closed. The one bar in town was open, but devoid of customers. When I turned to the east I saw steam from the clams coming from the other side of the intersection and smelled the steaks on the grill. I followed my nose and entered Freeman Park, where a large crowd mingled around a well-constructed picnic pavilion.

"Got your ticket?" asked a fifty-ish man in blue jeans and a maroon "Cal-Mum Football Boosters" t-shirt. He had cash in one hand and ticket stubs in the other.

"I don't," I said. "I'm from out of town and I'm looking for William Hamilton. The other blacksmith up at the historical village, Heitzenrater, told me he'd be here."

"Bill's right over there at the grill," the man said. "Dinner'll cost you twenty dollars if you want it. Ten without the drinks."

"What's cooking?" I asked.

"Clams, steak, corn on the cob, salt potatoes."

"And to drink?"

"Genny from a keg, Lake Niagara, Cella Lambrusco. That's as high as our shelf goes, I'm afraid."

I handed him a twenty as we walked over towards the pavilion.

"Stamp him, Ann!" the man said when we reached a table where a pretty woman with short black hair sat.

"Hi!" said Ann as she stamped my hand with what looked like the image of a fighter jet. "Welcome to the annual Sons of the American Legion Clambake!"

"Daughters too," I said.

"It's coed and multi-generational," the man with the money said as he motioned towards the playground, where about two dozen kids were swinging, climbing on monkey bars, digging in the sandboxes and teeter-tottering. "I'm Mark Pearsall. Sons of the Legion President. This is my bride, Ann."

"Tom Flanagan," I said. "I came out from Clinton Falls, looking for William Hamilton."

"Then find Bill Hamilton you shall, right after we set you up with what, a beer? You look like a beer man to me."

"Genny's great," I said. A moment later I held a "Sons of the Legion—2006 Clambake" commemorative cup as Mark Pearsall poured cold beer into it.

My cup full, we walked over to a large man who was cooking dozens of steaks on a grill made out of both halves of a split metal barrel. His khakis and white t-shirt were covered with a maroon and white checkered apron. He wore a maroon hat that also said Cal-Mum, this time inside a football.

I had seen the congratulatory road signs while entering Caledonia from the east. I gathered that Cal-Mum was short for Caledonia-Mumford, the local school district.

"They've got nothing," the man said, shaking his head. "And you-know-who should've retired years ago, when his sons graduated. He's too predictable now! His bag has run out of tricks! How many more times is he gonna try that fake punt?"

"Bill, it's only May," Mark Pearsall said. "Practice doesn't even start for another three months."

Bill Hamilton reached out and shook my hand. "I'm Bill Hamilton," he said. "Cut Bill Hamilton open and you'll find maroon and white blood in his veins."

"And in his arteries," Mark Pearsall said. "Bill's president of the football booster club, although he's been doing a lot more bitching than boostering these last couple years." Pearsall continued before Hamilton could answer. "Bill, this is Tom Flanagan from Clinton Falls. He said he came here looking for you."

"Not another one of those guys from Nisswah, are you?" he asked.

"I don't think so ... " I replied, looking at Mark Pearsall for guidance.

"The New York State Sports Writers Association," Pearsall explained. "Every two or three years they come out here from Syracuse or Binghamton to write a profile on Cal-Mum football. Best program around, you know. Nine state championships. Eighth in the nation in total undefeated teams. The 1929 team was undefeated, untied and unscored-upon."

"That's impressive," I said, impressed.

Pearsall looked back towards Hamilton. "But as I said, Bill, it's only May. The NYSSWA guys won't be here until October or November, once sectionals start."

"So you're not here to talk football," Hamilton said definitively. He turned about fifteen of the steaks, pressed them with his tongs and set them towards the edge of the grill. "Lizzy, some rare ones are ready!" he bellowed. He turned towards me. "How do you like yours?"

"Medium-well," I said.

"Talk, then. You've got seven minutes."

I decided to play it completely straight. "Well, I also live up in the Thousand Islands, where my parents died and my brother Patrick disappeared about ten years ago in a boating accident. I haven't seen my brother since then, but I have reason to believe that he was here three years ago, working at the historical village. I went there this morning looking for my brother, and your colleague, Mr. Heitzenrater, told me I should come ask you."

Bill Hamilton smiled broadly. "Was my colleague Mr. Heitzenrater wearing his pretty bonnet? Was he playing with his new broom?" Hamilton laughed hard and took a sip of beer from his plastic cup, which he had nestled into a maroon coozie emblazoned with a white Cal-Mum football. "Oh, don't worry about it," he continued with a wave of the tongs. "Noelle loves, and I mean *loves*, to gossip! If your brother is who I think he is—and from the looks of you I think he's who I think he is—his story is worth every demerit she'll get for speaking out of character while on the clock."

Chapter Nine

WE TALKED OVER DINNER, Bill Hamilton having sworn-in a deputy grill master with all kinds of instructions and suggestions for cooking the remaining eighty-five steaks perfectly to order.

"The clams are a piece of cake," he said as he stuck a forkful of clam meat into a bowl of butter. "Cook 'em 'til they open."

"Everything's delicious," I said as I continued to stuff clams and butter, steak and A-1, salted corn and potatoes, with more butter, into my mouth. I was washing the food down with plenty of good, cold Genny too. "I mean really, really delicious."

I was calm. I felt confident that I'd be told all I needed to know about Patrick in due time. I didn't press Hamilton for his story. I simply ate and drank and waited.

He finally told his tale after finishing his own prodigious meal and refilling his coozied cup with beer.

"Patrick you say?"

"Patrick Flanagan," I affirmed.

"I remember him. I remember everything about that year because it was the last time we won a state championship. Beat LeRoy on opening day and never looked back. Man, I loved that team!" Bill Hamilton took a long swig of beer.

"So you knew my brother?" I asked.

"When I first met him he was a town ball interpreter."

"Old time baseball," I said.

"You know the game?"

"A love of baseball runs in the family," I said. "All of us but Patrick were Yankee fans. I still am. He liked the Mets. Still does, as far as I know."

"I'm a football man myself. Most of us around here are."

"I gathered that," I said, pointing to his hat.

"So town ball's how I first met him. But I really got to know him when he came to work for me in the blacksmith's shop. He showed up at the forge one day ready to work, already wearing his gloves and apron. He asked if he could join me for the season. It just so happened that my colleague, Mr. Heitzenrater, was away until the end of July recovering from knee surgery. I'd have high school kids with me on weekends and on internships beginning in late June, but until then I needed someone the other five days of the week. Someone strong to work the billows and someone steady to keep the temperature up where I needed it to be. Someone aware enough to remove the iron from the forge when I was ready to strike it, when it was hot, and not a second earlier nor a second later."

"What do you make?"

"Did you visit the smithy today?"

"Briefly. I saw quite a few nails."

"Good nails! Strong nails! Nails that stay put. We make about ten thousand of them per season for the village's use and for sale to local carpenters, mostly restoration specialists. We make hooks, horseshoes, candle-holders. We also work on one or two special projects a year. This year we're making a balcony railing. Last year we made a pistol. In 2004 we made a gate for a local big shot renovating his mother's mansion. In 2003 we made a good number of weather vanes. All kinds of patterns. Horses. Fish. Men with straw hats. Women in big dresses." Bill Hamilton laughed. "I even made one of a football helmet with a C and an M on it! A bit anachronistic, but what the hell! Weather vanes aren't as easy as you might think because you have to get them properly balanced. Try that while keeping your large-mouth bass looking like a large-mouth bass!

"Your brother walked in all ready for work on a day I was making an especially difficult vane with an image of Saint George slaying the dragon. Horse and rider, armor, lance. Snout, wings, long tail! We had it all, even fire coming out of the dragon's mouth! I was having a hard time of it, actually. At first I thought it was Saint George's lance throwing the balance off, but then I realized it was the dragon's fire. It made the whole panorama spin in a way that would make east look south, if you know what I mean. I had to thin the iron out, peen it down to get the balance just right. It's one thing if you're making a fence or gate—you don't have to worry about balance. True, a gate needs to swing properly, but that has more to do with the placement of the hinge than anything else. Those weather vanes, though, they're a challenge."

"What did my brother do to help?"

Hamilton laughed. "Exactly the opposite of what I expected he'd want to do, what most kids want to do! They—most kids, that is—come to my forge and want to smash, to hit, hit, hit, and do some drawing out too. It takes me weeks to get them to refine their technique. You know what they all think?"

"What?"

"That hitting the metal hard is all that's needed to shape it. I teach them control and accuracy. Takes about three weeks. There's a lot of anger in these kids that they don't know what to do with. Once they get a hammer in their hands it seems to come right out. You need to channel the anger, make it work for you rather than against you. That's probably the biggest lesson I've taught over the years—how to channel anger into something constructive."

"My brother picked up on it more quickly?"

"Your brother didn't want anything to do with hammering! He wanted to be as close as he could to the forge, as often as he could. He was fascinated by fire."

"Fascinated how? Regulating it? Getting it as hot as possible?"

"Studying it. Learning it's ways."

"Did he learn it's ways?"

"Did he ever! Your brother learned when the temperature's rising too high or dropping too low without even looking at the thermometer. He knew just how much coal to add if that's what was needed or just how much air to take away if that's what was needed. He could do in a month what took me years to learn!"

"Fire," I said after taking a sip of beer.

"Fire," Hamilton repeated. "He studied it the whole summer. He learned it's ways." He shifted in his seat and wagged a finger. "What he did most of all was learn to fear it."

I considered this for a moment before answering. "He was afraid of it? Afraid of getting burned? Afraid of burning down the smithy? But you just said he was good with fire." Then I had an insight. "He was trying to work through his fear by being close to the forge, by working with the fire. But why would he be afraid of fire? Given what happened to him, he should have been afraid of water."

"No, not that kind of fear. Not the modern meaning of the word. Not your pop psychology meaning, either!" Bill Hamilton shook his head vigorously as he said these words. "I'm using 'fear' in the Old Testament sense of the word, the ancient sense. I'm talking about respect and awe for something far deeper than what we can know with the mind alone. Your brother feared fire like the Psalms tell us to fear the Lord."

I sipped my beer. "I guess that makes sense," I said.

"Try wrapping your mind around it a little more," Bill Hamilton suggested. "Tell me what fire can do."

"Burn down buildings. Burn skin." My mind went back a decade. "Burn a wooden boat."

"What else?"

"Cook. Disinfect."

Bill Hamilton nodded. "Fire can be both destructive and constructive. It all depends on how we decide to use it, or whether or not we properly fear it. Fire itself has no moral direction one way or the other. You ever hear of Aaron's sons? Nadab and Abihu?"

"Not that I recall. Are they from the Old Testament too?"

"From a story in Leviticus, a strange story! Happens when the Israelites are wandering through the desert on their way to the Promised Land, after the stopover at Mount Sinai. Nadab and Abihu make a mistake in their offering to God. Some translations say the fire they offer is unauthorized. Others say it's strange. Others yet say it's unholy. Whatever the details, however you characterize it, God doesn't accept it."

"What did He do?"

"Sure you want to know?"

"Of course."

"He incinerates 'em on the spot! Leaves nothing but two small piles of ash!"

"Oh," I said. I paused for a moment and tried to sort through the story. "What does this have to do with my brother?"

"Well, it seemed to me that your brother was aware that such a possibility exists. He knew that fire, if you get on the wrong side of it, can destroy you just as easily as it can cook your food!"

"It will come to your aid if you respect it."

"Yes," Bill Hamilton agreed, "if you respect it! That's what I meant by fear. Fear the Lord, as the Psalms say. Fear fire too!"

"I'm curious—how hot does the fire get in your forge?"

"I stoke my working fire up to about fourteen-hundred degrees Fahrenheit and like to keep it there."

"With coal?"

He nodded.

"That's pretty hot."

"That's the working temperature. That's how much heat you want to get into your iron before you work with it. Inside the coal pile, inside the actual fire, there's a hot spot of about three thousand degrees Fahrenheit. The hot spot's only a few cubic inches, but in that small space it gets that hot!"

"Three *thousand* degrees? Is that as hot as you can get it?"

"Not quite. With the proper oxygen flow you can hit thirty-five hundred degrees, but that's hard to do, and not very useful for actual work. That gets the iron too hot. Burns it." Hamilton laughed. "Get your iron too hot and the white sparks start flying. 'Beard-burners,' I call them!" He rubbed his own beard. "Believe me. I know!"

"Do you respect fire?" I asked. "Do you approach it with awe?"

"I thought I did." He paused. "But I discovered from your brother that my approach was superficial. I learned to truly respect fire only after I saw what your brother did."

I stopped mid-swig. "Pardon me? What do you mean?"

"Before August 2003, to me, fire was just one part of the process. It was a tool to put heat into the iron so the iron could be shaped to my will. I'd add the fuel, adjust the air, watch for the correct color and use the fire's heat just like I would use a hammer once I put the iron on the anvil. Like I said it was a tool, one among many."

"My brother changed that."

"He did! After forty-three years of working my craft, something your brother did in late August of 2003 changed the way I understood fire."

Chapter Ten

BILL HAMILTON PAUSED, picked up his cup, looked at the inch or so of beer left in it and emptied it onto the ground. "Getting warm," he said. "How you doing? Want another?"

I drained my cup and handed it to him. "Cola, please," I said.

"Let me get a couple refills and see how the grilling's coming along. When I come back I'll tell you exactly what your brother did!"

As I waited for Hamilton to return, I thought more about fire, perhaps the most dangerous of the four classical elements. What had my brother done? Why had it made such an impression on Bill Hamilton? I was eager to hear the rest of his story.

"Thank you," I said as he handed me a cup of pop. "How did Patrick instill the fear of fire in you?"

"Strange as it might sound, he brought the fire alive."

I shrugged. "I often think of fire as alive, especially while watching a campfire burn at night."

"We use those metaphors, don't we? The fire breathes. The fire dances. The fire jumps." He wagged a finger. "That's not at all what I'm talking about, though. What I saw was in broad daylight. What I saw was your brother bringing the fire *alive*!"

For half a second my mind thought back to the night of my first Ostend Ball, the night I was introduced to ideas that had been inconceivable to me beforehand, the night that I, like my father and mother before me, became part of the story of Napoleon's gold. From that half a second onwards, I knew what Bill Hamilton would say. Mindy, Louie and I had been talking about the same ideas the evening before at The 357. They were ideas I was not yet comfortable with. I was about to be introduced to a new perspective on those ideas. I listened with a combination of expectation and of unease.

"He'd been up for days on end. Feeding the fire. Tending it. Not so much to make it hotter or stronger. Purer, I guess, is the way to put it. He was trying to make the fire more pure. It was first thing in the morning when I saw him. I was ready to work. He asked me to give him time before I put the iron in the fire. I was continuing my work on a weather vane that showed a group of hummingbirds gathered around a rosebush. It was a delicate project. I'd already gone through several rods trying to get those birds right. I was hoping to finish the birds and get to the rose blooms that day. I was anxious. I wanted to work on those birds. I didn't want to give him any more time on my forge for an experiment that I didn't understand."

Hamilton took a long sip of beer. When he resumed speaking, his voice was quieter, more intense, infused with an increased sense of urgency. "I was about to cut the air supply to reduce the temperature to my fourteen hundred degrees when your brother whisper-yelled for me to stop. When I did, when I looked at him, what I saw on his face was an expression of sheer wonder. He was in awe! He slowly motioned me over to where he was standing. Without moving his head he told me to look carefully into the hot spot. I did. I looked into that little cube of three thousand degrees, the fire's core no larger than a tennis ball. What I saw astonished me!" He paused again. "Put fear in my heart!"

"What did you see?" I asked, already knowing the answer.

Hamilton smiled. "A living thing," he said. "What I saw

was a living thing! It looked no bigger than a mouse, but at the same time it looked like it had been and would soon be much larger, like it was itching to burst from the flames and grow back to its normal size. It was orange and white, like the flame itself, and was outlined in red. It had a face, just the hint of a face." He shook his head. "I'll be damned if your brother hadn't somehow, someway, brought that fire to life!"

"It's called a salamander," I said quietly.

Wide-eyed, he nodded. "I've heard that elsewhere."

"One of the four classical elementals," I added.

"Yes! Creatures of fire, air, water and earth."

We looked at each other for a moment before Bill Hamilton smiled and said, "You've seen one, haven't you."

I nodded. "I think so. It was up on the Saint Lawrence River. It was an undine. A water being. I never saw a salamander, though, or any of the other ones."

"They change ya', don't they? Somehow, they change ya'!"

I knew exactly what he meant. "They do. Awe always does, I guess."

"Hmm. I still haven't wrapped my mind around it. Maybe we're not supposed to see them. Maybe there are some things in the world better left unseen."

"I can't argue with that," I said, recalling how my experiences on the river had changed my life, also recalling what Martha Radisson had said about how it's sometimes better to not remember. "What happened after the salamander appeared?"

"Your brother just kept looking at it. His eyes were wide, impervious to the sweat dripping right into them. His sense of concentration impressed me. I looked at him and then back to the fire thing and knew they'd made contact. He changed in those moments, Tom, differently from how you and I changed. I could see him change right before my eyes!"

"How did he change?" I asked.

"It's hard to describe. He grew more confident, I guess. More in touch with who he really was." Hamilton removed his hat and rubbed the redness where the elastic band had left its mark. "I didn't like what I saw in him, either," he added. "To me, that confidence looked an awful lot like arrogance. But then again, he did bring the thing into being! Maybe men like him earn their arrogance the hard way."

"I hope it hasn't turned into hubris," I said.

"It's hard to stop that ball from rolling," Hamilton replied.

I nodded. "What happened next?" I asked.

"The fire thing was looking right back at him with the same amount of attention that he was giving it. This went on for a couple of minutes. Then the fire started to burn down. I asked him if he wanted more coal and he said no, it might choke it. I asked if he wanted more air and he said no, it would blow it away. We stood there, backs bent and necks stretched forward, watching wide-eyed in wonder as the fire-being started to fade."

"How long did that take?" I asked.

"Five minutes? Eight? I don't know. I lost track of time. Time seemed all askew just like the size of the fire-thing did. When it was all over I asked Patrick how long the fire-being had been there. You know what he said?"

"What?"

"He said it still is here! He tapped his chest with his hand and said it's still here! I asked him what he meant by that and he didn't answer. Didn't say another word, in fact. 'It's still here' are the last words I ever heard him speak."

"What do you mean?"

Bill Hamilton paused a moment before he answered. When he did so, he answered with a question. "You know what Aaron said?"

"Who?" Then I remembered the story of how Aaron's sons had been divinely incinerated for offering a strange, unholy, unwanted sacrifice. "Right, Aaron from Leviticus. What did he say after God obliterated his sons?"

"Nothing! Not a word! After Moses offered him a half-assed explanation about God sticking to his word, the man fell silent." Bill Hamilton stood up and finished his beer. "Nor did your brother speak a single word after indicating that the fire thing was inside him. He closed the damper and let the fire get down to a working temperature. He helped me finish that hummingbird and rose weather vane, but in complete silence, a silence that I respected. The finished product was a masterwork—I still have it hanging on my forge wall. When the day was done your brother walked out of my smithy without a word. I never saw him again. And that, my friend, is the end of my story."

As I was running Bill Hamilton's story through my head, I was also thinking about Martha Radisson and her note card.

"Did my brother happen to mention anything about Delaware County? Delhi? Or Andes? Did he mention having been there or maybe going there?"

"He did not. As I said, I never saw him again after the day he brought the fire alive. But ... " Hamilton got his wallet out of his pocket and searched for something. He produced a picture postcard of Mount Marcy, taken from the air. "He sent me this a month after he left town."

I unfolded the card and read it.

Mr. Hamilton—

Thank you for your hospitality and generosity this summer. What we did at your forge was very meaningful to me and will be, I hope, very important for many people. I'm sorry for my quick departure, but there was somewhere I had to go, something I had to do. I hope that someday you'll understand.

    All my best,
    'Trick

I handed him back the postcard. "Trick?" I asked before I let go.

"Apparently, that's what he called himself."

"Not to my knowledge," I admitted.

"Don't know what to tell ya'," Bill Hamilton said.

"Do you have any idea why he went to Lake Placid?" I asked.

Bill Hamilton shook his head.

"Did you ever see Patrick with a tall, beautiful woman with long blond hair?"

"Can't say I have."

"So you've kept this card in your wallet? All this time?"

"Reminds me to fear fire like my wife tells me I should fear God," he said. He looked right at me. "If you find him, tell him Bill Hamilton said thank you."

Chapter Eleven

AFTER AN HOUR OR SO of polite conversation with Mike and Ann Pearsall, I returned to my truck for a short nap before going home. As usual, I dreamed about the river. This time, there was a shadow that crept along the Saint Lawrence as in the fading light of a late December day. As Wolfe and then Simcoe Islands disappeared into the darkness, the shadow solidified and clung like tar to tree and rock alike. In a few minutes, all eighteen hundred-plus islands were like floating lumps of coal anchored to the riverbed.

My watch alarm woke me up at eight. I drove home fast, via the Thruway, wanting to get back to Mindy and share with her Bill Hamilton's improbable story. I called her to tell her I was on my way, but for some reason she wasn't answering either her cell phone or our land line. Oh well, I thought, she's probably asleep, or perhaps applying a second coat of paint to our walls or cleaning up the brushes.

I saw the ambulance and police car lights the moment I turned the corner towards home. As I pulled into our driveway I also saw Louie Fratello's truck. He and Ghedi ran out of the house to greet me.

"She'll be OK," Louie said, reaching out, palms up, to place his hands on my shoulders.

"What happened?" I asked, looking him in the eye.

"I saw the lights on as I was walking home from work," Ghedi said, his face etched with anxiety. He checked his watch. "It was about thirty minutes ago. I looked in your front window and saw … saw the wall, and then saw

Mindy." Ghedi turned towards me, but could not look directly at me, his eyes darting this way and that. He was as uncomfortable and distressed as I had ever seen him. "There are no curtains. I saw Mindy. I called Louie right away. I only saw because there were no curtains."

"We took them down to paint," I explained. "What happened?"" I asked again.

"Come inside," Louie replied.

I found Mindy on the floor between the living room and dining room, her head on a molded foam pillow, an EMT above her taking her blood pressure.

She was conscious but obviously groggy.

"Tom!" she said, sitting up. "You're home early."

I looked at my watch. "It's after ten, Mindy," I said.

"Oh."

"Are you OK?"

"I think so. I had just finished painting. I did the second coat, just like I said I would." She smiled. "I didn't see them come in, didn't hear them. They knocked me out. Some kind of … I don't know." Mindy paused and looked puzzled all of a sudden. "Ten? Really? I thought it was around six. Seven at the latest."

The EMT hushed her and eased her head back down to the floor. "Her back and neck are sore from the fall," the EMT said. "She can move her legs and fingers fine. She's obviously lost track of time."

I leaned down to brush the hair off her forehead and give her a kiss. I caught a whiff of something sweet and a bit tart—no doubt it was a trace of the substance that the intruder had used to knock her out. I stepped back so the EMT could finish her examination.

The EMT gently pressed her hands on Mindy's abdomen, moving them up towards her ribs and down towards her pelvis, and also side to side. "Feel anything?"

"It tickles a bit," Mindy said. The EMT smiled. "But no,

everything feels fine." Mindy looked up at me. "Really, I'm OK."

The EMT returned the blood pressure gauge to her medical kit and stood up. "You have two options then. We can drive you to Wildwood, where a resident will do the same thing I just did, or we can save you three hours of waiting and a second round of prodding and see how you feel in the morning."

"I definitely prefer option B," Mindy said.

I nodded my assent.

Mindy nodded too and shifted her gaze behind me.

"Mr. Flanagan," said a voice that I recognized before I turned around and saw the man. "I want you to see this."

I looked behind me, towards Detective Lieutenant Steven Delaney, who stood near the south wall of our living room. The furniture was still in the middle of the room, covered in drop cloths. The wood floor was also covered in drop cloths along each wall. The curtains were draped over the stairway banister and covered in clear plastic. The can of sage tint trim was there, unopened. Everything was as Mindy had left it. Almost.

"Louie called me the minute he got here. I usually let the uniforms handle something like this, but Louie insisted I come see."

"Thanks," I said, and shook the detective's hand.

"Don't thank me yet," Delaney continued. "And before you do, maybe you can explain why someone would break into your house, knock out your bride-to-be and write the Little Mermaid's name on your living room wall." Delaney stepped aside.

I looked from the can of paint to the wall. Written there, in sage tint trim over the second coat of teaberry green, in script that was quite beautiful with its semigloss shine, was the single word "ARIEL."

Chapter Twelve

THE NEXT MORNING, after a short and fitful sleep for both of us and, as far as I could remember, a dreamless one for me, Mindy and I were back at our breakfast nook table. She had taken two naproxen for the stiffness in her shoulders and neck and was sipping a cup of chamomile tea. I had my laptop open and was drinking coffee by the quart. I had already told her Bill Hamilton's story about my brother Patrick. She had not shown much surprise, a non-reaction that I attributed to a combination of her innate skepticism and shock at her own experience. We had moved on to possible explanations for the writing on our wall.

"What've you got?" Mindy asked.

"First is the obvious reference, at least to Detective Delaney's mind. Ariel is the heroine in Disney's film production of *The Little Mermaid*."

"But it was a fairy tale first, right? Hans Christian Andersen?"

"Yes, Andersen. 1837. It was turned into a ballet long before Disney got their hands on it, though. Also before Disney, *The Little Mermaid* was a stage play, an opera, a comic book and several other films, including a Soviet one. Then Ariel appeared in the Disney movie, followed by a prequel and a sequel, and is about to appear in a Broadway musical." I scanned a couple more websites I had tabbed. "Looks like Ariel herself was Disney's invention. In the earlier versions, the mermaid was nameless."

"So on the one hand Ariel meshes nicely with most people's misconception of the undines as half human, half fish. But on the other hand, Ariel herself cannot be considered a classic mermaid, only a cartoon iteration. What's next? Shakespeare?"

"*The Tempest.* Ariel was a spirit, or sprite, who aided Prospero with his magic."

"I thought Ariel was Prospero's daughter?"

"That was Miranda. Ariel helped Miranda and Ferdinand, a shipwrecked sailor, fall in love."

"You know your Bard," Mindy said.

"Hardly. It's all right here on eNotes.com." I scanned the article. "Ariel's a he in Shakespeare. He helped Prospero create the storm that wrecks Ferdinand's ship and gives the play its title. Ariel owes Prospero his allegiance because, before the play's action, Prospero had released him from a tree where an evil witch had imprisoned him. In the play itself Ariel thwarts two assassination attempts, one of them Caliban's against Prospero. As I said, he hooked Miranda up with the sailor, and for that he got his freedom." My eyes were drawn to one of the long quotes from the play. "Huh. Listen to this:

> Full fathom five thy father lies;
> Of his bones are coral made;
> Those are pearls that were his eyes:
> Nothing of him that doth fade
> But doth suffer a sea-change
> Into something rich and strange.
> Sea-nymphs hourly ring his knell
> Hark! Now I hear them—Ding-dong, bell."

"That's Ariel?" Mindy asked.

I nodded. "He sings the lines to Ferdinand, the sailor who eventually hooks up with Miranda. Ferdinand's father had died in the shipwreck."

Mindy caught my meaning. She reached to the keyboard

and placed her hand on mine. "They found your father, darling. And your mother. Your parents are properly buried in the ground. They're not submerged in thirty feet of water."

Not so Patrick, I thought.

I deleted the series of v's that Mindy's hand on mine had typed into the search field. I gave her a wan smile. "Ariel sings the song to lead Ferdinand to Prospero's hut." I scrolled some more. "I don't see any other lines that might connect to our situation, though."

"Next then."

"Sylvia Plath," I said. "Ariel was a collection of poems released posthumously in 1964 and re-released a couple years ago with 12 additional poems."

"Depressing poems, right?"

"Not necessarily. An Amazon reviewer says that the 2004 collection is more optimistic and closer to what Plath originally intended. Her husband, Ted Hughes, had edited and re-arranged the 1964 version after her death."

"Do you know any of the poems?"

"One of the poems is titled 'Ariel.' It's about riding a horse. 'Lady Lazarus' is the one I remember from high school. It's about a woman who died and was reborn."

"We might want to look more closely at those."

"I'll pick up a copy of the reissued collection and see what's there."

"Moving on then," Mindy said.

I went to the next search item. "Ariel is Biblical. Hebrew for the city of David. That's one of the references Sylvia Plath uses."

"Jerusalem, right? From the Psalms?"

"Isaiah chapter twenty-nine."

Mindy moved behind me, placed her arms on my shoulders and wrapped them around my chest. "I'll read this one," she whispered.

I sat back and listened.

"Woe to you, Ariel, Ariel,
the city where David settled!
Add year to year
and let your cycle of festivals go on.
Yet I will besiege Ariel;
she will mourn and lament,
she will be to me like an altar hearth.

And then there's this—

Suddenly, in an instant,
the LORD Almighty will come
with thunder and earthquake and great noise,
with windstorm and tempest and flames of a devouring fire.
Then the hordes of all the nations that fight against Ariel,
that attack her and her fortress and besiege her,
will be as it is with a dream,
with a vision in the night—
as when a hungry person dreams of eating,
but awakens hungry still;
as when a thirsty person dreams of drinking,
but awakens faint and thirsty still."

Mindy paused, then asked, "What do you make of that?"

"Did you catch the fire references?"

"I did. Are you thinking there's a connection with Bill Hamilton's story?"

"That, and several other connections."

"Like what?"

"Did you catch the dream references?"

"Yes."

"My dreams share that same theme of destruction. Like

Isaiah said—thunder, earthquake, windstorm, tempest, flames. In my dreams, it feels like the river is under attack."

"But what about the next part? A hungry person waking up hungry after a dream about eating? A thirsty person waking up thirsty after a dream about drinking? Those dreams aren't at all like your dreams."

"True. They're not. What happens in my dreams isn't … well, isn't just a dream. I wake up and feel the dream's effects. I mean literally, Mindy—hot, cold, angry, afraid. I wouldn't be surprised if I woke up satiated after eating or drinking in a dream. Remember the one I had the other night, where the storm knocked down the trees?"

She nodded.

"In the dream itself, my entire body ached from something that happened to me before I found myself in the old garage, before I saw Billy. My body hurt even more when the door blew open, right before the dream ended. When I woke up from that dream, my back and ribs were killing me."

"Are you sure you didn't toss and turn more than normal and throw out your back?"

"Tossed and turned enough to leave bruises?"

"That's problematic," she admitted.

"Anyway, that passage from Isaiah makes me wonder even more where my dreams are coming from."

"There are more things in heaven and on earth," Mindy said with a smile. She took a sip of tea. "Which reminds me of a hunch I had while reading Isaiah." She reached down and entered "Ariel" and "angel" as search terms. She hit enter. There were over 40 million hits.

"Hunch confirmed," I said. "We'll both need sabbaticals to get through this list."

"Probably not." Mindy reached down and opened three of the top ten web pages in new tabs, glanced them over, then shook her head. "Look, honey. They say almost the same thing. What we're seeing here is cyber-plagiarism at its best." She put a hand on my shoulder. "Time to go to the authority," she said.

"Which one?"

She cupped her hand around my ear and whispered. "Wikipedia."

I turned towards her and smiled. "Seriously?"

"Desperate circumstances call for desperate measures." She touched a finger to my lips. "Don't you dare tell my students."

Smiling, I opened the Wikipedia article on Ariel. There was the Isaiah reference, of course, and the Shakespeare one. Sylvia Plath was mentioned. Although admitting that the "earliest source is unclear" for the angel usage of the name, Wikipedia did give several references back to the turn of the sixteenth century. Ariel was an earth angel, a water angel, a wielder of fire, an archon, an archangel and, to John Milton, one of the early followers of Satan in his rebellion against God.

"And look at that," Mindy said, tapping the screen a few lines below where I was reading. "Our angel Ariel is also governor of the world's elemental forces, of sylphs, gnomes, salamanders and undines. Maybe the good people at Disney aren't as ignorant as we made them out to be. Maybe Ariel is a very appropriate name for a mermaid after all. More importantly, maybe there *is* a connection between the word on our wall and Bill Hamilton's story about your brother."

"Elementals R' Us," I joked.

Mindy almost spat out her tea as she laughed.

"So we've got a Disney mermaid, a Shakespearean sprite, a collection of poems, the Lion of God and, finally, an angel, possibly fallen, who has some connection to the elementals, including, of course, undines and salamanders. Anything else? A woman's name, perhaps?"

"Angel names," Mindy said with a snap of her fingers. "Ostend family names! Is there an Ariel in the bunch?

Raphael's daughter or granddaughter, maybe? One of the ones who looks like Lady Ostend?"

"Possibly." I Googled "Ariel Ostend." I found plenty of hits for Michael, Gabriel and Raphael, and, of course, the ones for Lady Ostend that I had already encountered when I first researched her name back in 2001. There was nothing for Ariel.

I got up to refill my coffee. Drinking it black now, I leaned against the kitchen sink. "We'll have to ask Raphael when we go north after graduation," I said. "The million dollar question is: does anything we learned help explain why the name is written on our wall and how it got there?"

Mindy frowned. "Guess there's no winner on today's program."

I took Mindy's cup and mine to the sink and rinsed them out. I put the half-and-half back into the refrigerator and, with the door still open, asked her if she had talked to Detective Delaney at all last night.

"There wasn't much I could tell him. And I don't remember much of what I did say. Why?"

"I'm wondering if he mentioned the brush."

"What brush? Oh, the paint brush. It's right here." Mindy came to the refrigerator and removed a plastic bread bag, secured with a rubber band, inside of which was the brush and roller she had used to apply the second coat of teaberry green before she was knocked out. "Just like Andrew taught us. Keeps it fresh in case we need to do any touching up."

I shook my head. "Not the teaberry green brush. The sage tint trim brush. The brush that was on the floor next to the can of semi-gloss—the *unopened* can of semi-gloss. Delaney took the brush in for evidence, although he didn't expect to find anything."

"He didn't mention that brush. Why? What about it? Why didn't he expect to find anything?"

"Delaney didn't expect to find anything because the

brush was dry. The brush was dry because we haven't started the trim yet. Dry because we haven't used it."

"Then how ... " Mindy almost ran to the living room, with me right behind her. As I had done alone for at least an hour the previous night after tucking Mindy into bed, we looked at the writing that was a shade darker and a sheen shinier than the second coat of satin Mindy had applied to our living room wall— "ARIEL."

Mindy spoke as she moved closer to the wall. "No brush marks. No finger marks. No roller marks. It looks almost sprayed on. But with no drips." She looked behind her and down. "And no open can. Who did this? And why?"

Uncomfortable, I moved back a step. "Should I sand it down and paint over it?"

She whirled to face me. "Absolutely not!"

Her tone surprised me. "It doesn't creep you out?" I asked. "It creeps me out."

"I've been going over it again and again and no, it doesn't creep me out." Mindy paused for a moment and her eyes seemed to brighten, her face flush with a bit of color. "Sure it challenges my rational way of thinking, but there's got to be a logical explanation for it. A reasonable explanation." She was smiling widely now, her eyes soft and losing their focus. She reached out as if to touch the word, but stopped short and let her hand go limp. "I kind of like it," she said, her index and middle finger twitching ever so slightly. "In fact, I think it's quite beautiful."

"What's going on, Mindy?"

"Huh?" She turned. "Oh. I just caught a whiff of it again, that's all. It makes me feel ... I don't know ... good, calm, serene."

"A whiff of what? Of paint?" I inhaled. I smelled nothing.

She shook her head and breathed again. "Not paint. The smell from last night, the one I noticed right before I passed out. Sweet, naturally sweet, like stevia. There it is again. And lemon too." Mindy moved to the open window, moved close to the screen and gazed out at the world. "It's stronger," she said. She snapped her fingers. "Verbena. It's lemon verbena."

My heart racing, I moved to the front door and opened it. I looked up the street and down. I saw no one. But now I too smelled a distinct citrus odor in the air.

"It's OK, sweetheart," Mindy said, her eyes brighter than they had been all morning. Still looking at me, she reached towards the word on our wall, almost touching it, but stopping short. I must have given her a suspicious look because she quickly moved her hand to my cheek and smiled. "I'm fine," she said. "Better than ever, in fact. You know what? I think I'll take full advantage of this beautiful day and walk to campus. Have you noticed how many beautiful days we've had this spring?" She looked at her watch. "And you, darling, had better do some work. We have a wedding to pay for, after all."

Mindy brushed by me and stroked the back of my hair as she walked by. She turned onto the sidewalk in the direction of the university, without her bike and without her backpack. She turned and smiled again and waved. She was almost skipping.

I stood on the front porch, breathing in the aroma of lemon verbena as it faded away. The back of my neck still tingled from Mindy's touch. I moved out to the steps and looked around our yard. We were the only ones in a three or four house radius with a perennial garden; all our neighbors planted annuals. We had several varieties of daisy, lily and iris, along with clematis, a butterfly bush, hosta, and several other perennials whose names I had forgotten. Some of them were in early bloom, others were just starting to bud. We did not have verbena, however. And even if we did have it in our garden, or even if any of our neighbors had it in their gardens, the plant would not be mature enough to emit a fragrance for at least another month.

Chapter Thirteen

SEEKING SOME DEGREE OF NORMALCY, I followed Mindy's advice and biked to my office, where I had several active cases to choose from. One was to establish whether a Dutch landscape painting owned by a Schenectady businessman was part of a collection that Harmanus Vedder had brought to the city when he helped settle it in the late 1600's. Another was to prepare a genealogy of one of New York's oldest apple growing families for an October reunion. A third job was to derive a list of people who regularly attended séances at Timothy Brown's "Spirit House" in Georgetown, New York, in the 1870's and 1880's. Yet another was to follow up on interviews conducted for an oral history of the Buffalo Yacht Club on Lake Erie. Finally, I was hired by Alfred State College to research and write a commemorative history for their upcoming sesquicentennial. They were good jobs, interesting jobs that paid at least reasonably well. All of them would have more than held my attention in normal times.

But my thoughts kept returning to the murder of Osman Steele, the strange costumes that his murderers wore and the personal greeting card from Martha Radisson that bore my family name and had brought this historical mystery into my life. Reluctantly, I pushed aside my other work and started investigating a case that I did not want to investigate and, at this point anyway, was not getting paid for.

I commenced my research using the time-tested system I'd developed as a student and as a private historical investigator. I began with the background, with the volatile mixture of historical ingredients that exploded on August 7, 1845, in Osman Steele' murder.

The first and most important ingredient—the flour in the bread—was the system of land ownership in eastern New York that provided a few families with an almost unlimited access to power and wealth and denied most tenant farmers even the most rudimentary freedom. In graduate school, some of my classmates had called it slavery. I might have been parsing definitions a bit too thin to see it as only servitude. The system was based on the centuries-old European practice of royal government land grants, followed by landowner leases that created a subservient tenant class. In New York, a landed aristocracy had become established in the early 1700's when several colonial governors gave millions of acres of land to the Hardenberghs and Van Rensselaers, and smaller amounts to several other favored families. The landlords collected rents on their properties. They retained mineral and water rights on the land their tenants improved. They had the right to collect twenty five percent on any sale of the land to a new tenant. They used their income to finance their extravagant lifestyles in their Hudson Valley mansions and in their Albany and Manhattan townhouses.

By the 1830's, Anti-Rent sentiments had deepened among the thousands of tenant families who had cleared and farmed the land, but who received no financial benefits from their work. Passive resistance in the form of withholding rent payments began in the hilltowns around Albany, in what was then called Rensselaerwyck Manor. Resistance spread south and west from there, including into Delaware County, into land owned by the Hardenberghs, Livingstons, Desplosses and Verplancks. Tenants who opposed the oppressive rents chose the Boston Tea Party rebels as their models. In the late 1830's they formed Anti-Rent societies. Beginning in 1841 they dressed up in disguise, specifically, as

Martha Radisson had explained, in brightly patterned calico cloaks and sheepskin masks decorated with spots, stripes, long strands of artificial hair and, sometimes, horns. They called each other by secret names like Big Thunder, Black Hawk, Pompey, Red Wing, Jumbo, Potasi and Thunderbolt. They were mustered by the sound of tin horns normally used to call farm workers to dinner. They made resolutions against "feudalism" and "land-slavery." They promised to finish the work that the revolutionaries had begun in 1776. They took oaths of secrecy and brotherhood. They continued to withhold payment of their rents.

In response to the anonymous character of popular resistance, the state legislature passed a law forbidding the wearing of costumes and masks at public assemblies. Anti-Rent activists ignored the new law and continued to don their costumes, continued to resist. Several landlords' agents were harassed and threatened as they attempted to serve legal papers to the tenants who would not pay. In the Hudson Valley, a collection agent was inadvertently shot when he instigated an argument with a financially-strapped tenant family.

The landlords, meanwhile, upped the ante by sending warrant-wielding sheriffs into the hilltowns to collect the rents that were not being paid or, as a last resort, to order the forced sale of a recalcitrant farmer's property to pay those rents. A property sale was supposed to happen on August 7, 1845, at the farm of Moses Earle in Andes, New York, after Earle refused to pay Charlotte Verplanck the rent he owed under the terms of the lease. The sheriff and his men had Earle's cattle counted, tagged, fenced and ready for sale. Several interested bidders were inspecting the herd when two hundred calico-clad Anti-Renters emerged from the surrounding woods to disrupt the auction.

Undersheriff Osman Steele led a group of "law-and-order men" into the ranks of the disguised protesters. The protesters opened fire on the horses. Most of the Anti-Renters hit their mark, bringing horse and, with it, rider to the ground. Three shots hit Steele in the chest, abdomen and right arm. He fell to the ground. Whether the three shots were aimed at Steele or whether they missed their equine target is unknown. The shots were certainly fatal—after falling to the ground Steele was carried into Moses Earle's home, where he died later that night. Some accounts mentioned an unknown Anti-Renter at the scene, a detail I dismissed—but shouldn't have—as based on hazy memories of confusing events.

Upon hearing news of the fatal shooting, Osman Steele's brother and brother-in-law led posses from Delhi into the surrounding countryside searching for the men who had killed the undersherrif. In the name of vengeance and under the cloak of authority, these men engaged in searches without warrant and destroyed private property with impunity. By the end of August, the posses had captured and a grand jury had indicted almost 350 men, far more than had been at Moses Earle's farm when Steele was shot. Just under half the jailed men were indicted on murder charges, the rationale being that they had committed murder by their mere presence in disguise at Moses Earle's farm on August 7. In the end, only two men, Edward O'Conner and John van Steenbergh, were convicted of murder and sentenced to hang. Moses Earle pleaded guilty to manslaughter and was sentenced to prison for life. A dozen other Anti-Renters, including several who lived many miles from Andes and were not at Earle's farm on August 7, were also convicted of manslaughter and received long sentences. The rest were fined, mostly on charges of assembling in public armed and disguised, thus violating the law passed by the New York legislature earlier in 1845.

The case against the Anti-Renters was weak. Even Adjutant General Thomas Farrington, who had been appointed by Governor Silas Wright to oversee the pacification of Delaware County, admitted that the evidence did not prove the defendants were guilty of murder. All but one juror from the Van Steenburgh trial agreed. But Judge Amasa Parker, under intense pressure from the pro-rent faction in Delhi, demanded that the jury find O'Conner and Van Steenbergh guilty. Most New Yorkers expected that both men's sentences would be commuted, which they eventually were. No one knew then, and no one knows now, who fired the shots that killed Osman Steele.

Chapter Fourteen

AFTER DEVISING THIS INITIAL OUTLINE of events and themes, I decided to consult an expert in the field, Professor Emeritus Seamus McNally, who once taught New York State history at the university and who now spent his retirement between Clinton Falls and Myrtle Beach. I always liked McNally as a professor because he was fair and reasonable and treated students with respect. I called him and asked if I could come over for a visit. He said he would be happy to have the company.

McNally lived alone in a riverside condo on the outskirts of Clinton Falls. The five mile bike ride took me on a route that I very much enjoyed, especially on a warm, sunny day like this one. I rode though downtown on a paved rail trail that skirted Fort Montgomery and the new minor league baseball stadium. Then I biked through the old warehouse district and past the abandoned Ostend hat factory, and into the west end of Clinton Falls along Seward Street, a wide boulevard lined with mansions that housed the city's academic and medical elites. I crossed the river about a mile after Seward Street merged onto Route 5.

Just beyond the bridge was the spot where Route 5 crossed Westcott Creek, the spot where Peter Langley, my friend and mentor, had died ten years before by the hand of Congressman Harold Radisson. Once across the bridge I stopped and looked to the southwest and saw the ruins of the old Radisson house, once called Crane's End, where Harold Radisson had died, and Martha and I had almost died, during a frightening February storm. The house was supposed to have been bought by a couple from New York City and bulldozed to make room for a bed and breakfast. It was still there, though, a charred hulk of a building that served as both a scar on the landscape and, to me, a reminder of much worse times. I got back on my bike and made the half-mile uphill climb to McNally's condo.

Once there, I joined him in his living room, me in a creaky wooden rocking chair and he in a recliner that, with the press of a button, tilted forward to ease the difficulty of standing.

"I don't trust it," McNally said as the chair slid down and back into its seating position. "I'm just waiting for the day I push the damn button and get ejected as if from a jet fighter in free-fall."

"That would be quite a ride," I said, laughing.

"It would be the fastest ride I've had since Operation Market Garden," he said. He spoke slowly and just above a whisper that I barely heard over the sound of the television. He once had a booming voice that commanded attention from all his students.

"You were in the war?" I asked.

McNally smiled and nodded. "I appreciate your use of the definite article," he said. "I mean no disrespect to the veterans of Korea and Vietnam, of course, nor to the soldiers currently fighting in Iraq and Afghanistan. But our war was *the* war. We gave everything we had to win it. Perhaps we gave up too much of what was once good." McNally took a sip of water and sighed. "I remember thinking during the McCarthy hearings, and again during the Civil Rights crackdowns and yet again during Vietnam ... I remember thinking, 'We fought for *this*?'" He turned towards me and smiled. "My apologies. The misgivings of an old, tired liberal, somewhat but not completely disillusioned by what he's seen in his long life. Partial disillusionment is perhaps the most cruel fate of all, hmm?"

"Perhaps," I agreed.

"You're here to discuss another time of disillusionment, are you not? Another era of misgivings that followed in the wake of another great war?"

"The Anti-Rent movement," I said. "Those fearless farmers, following the footsteps of their famous forefathers."

"They may have been fearless, but they were also fools, if I might continue your alliteration," McNally said slowly. Then he abruptly looked to his left and right, and stuck his hands down between the cushion and arm of the chair. "Hell, I can remember what happened during the war, I can remember classroom lectures from three decades ago, but I can't remember what I did with the damn flicker."

I saw it on the cabinet next to the television, but I stood up and lowered the sound with the control on the console.

"Thank you, and turn it right off," McNally said. "We probably won't want the distraction."

I pressed the power button and returned to the rocking chair. "You called them fools," I said. "Why?"

"Because they thought they could successfully challenge the landlords' power with violence. It was impossible for that strategy to succeed."

"But others have succeeded both before and after them using much the same strategy," I argued.

"Succeeded only in the short term, though. This old, tired liberal has learned another lesson, Mr. Flanagan, perhaps the most important lesson of them all. It's a lesson in the ineffectiveness of violence." McNally coughed several times and cleared his throat. "I've learned that violence begets more violence, which in turn creates more violence. An act of violence begins an inevitable cycle of escalation that undermines the achievement of any noble goal that society or a group within it might wish to achieve. That's the only certainty of violence, and most of us fail to see it." McNally blew his nose. "You haven't forgotten your involvement with the Crane and Radisson family histories, have you?"

I gasped. Did McNally know that Martha Radisson was the one who had asked me to research the Anti-Rent wars?

"What do you mean?" I asked, playing it tight.

"In that sordid affair, the violence of long ago returned to poison lives almost two hundred years after it happened. It poisoned Peter Langley's life. From what I've heard, it also poisoned yours."

"That was different," I said.

"It was? How? How do you know that the Anti-Rent violence doesn't still poison the lives of those who live in what used to be Livingston, Hardenbergh and Van Rensselaer holdings? It wasn't too long ago that some of them still had clauses in their mortgages that required an annual tithe. Some of them may still, although I doubt anyone remains to collect payment. Be that as it may, how do you know people don't still live with that burden?"

I couldn't answer the questions, and McNally knew it.

"OK. Assume you're right," I said instead. "What were the particulars? Why was this strategy of violence doomed from the start?"

"Two conditions of this particular situation made failure inevitable. First, by controlling state and local governments, the forces of conservatism also controlled law enforcement. On a local level, it's extremely difficult to challenge law enforcement with violence. Later, much later, the Freedom Marchers proved that you could challenge it with non-violence, but that option wasn't even on the Anti-Rent radar."

"I see your point," I admitted.

"On top of that, several of the sheriffs and undersheriffs were heroes in the eyes of a large segment of the population. Men who are thought of as heroes and think of themselves as the same will rarely, if ever, back down."

"Was Osman Steele a hero?"

"Was and is, at least to some. Did you know he's prominently cited as one of the first American policemen to be killed in the line of duty? There were a few dozen Texas Rangers who died in the Mexican incursion of 1838, but that was war. Steele was killed during peacetime. His fellow law enforcement officers are much kinder to his memory than historians have been."

"From the limited amount I've learned, he seems to have been quite the arrogant preener."

McNally laughed. "Preener. I like that," he said. "He was a redhead, you know, and very proud of his coif. The stories say that he checked his hair and straightened his kerchief every time he walked by a mirror."

"I've read about that," I said.

"There's another story about him, this one from right before his death. He was having lunch at the Hunting Tavern in Andes before heading up to the cattle sale at Moses Earle's farm. A group of pro-rent men were with him, and expressed concern about Steele's safety amidst the calico-clad Anti-Renters. Osman took a bullet from his pocket, dropped it into his glass of brandy, and exclaimed that 'lead can never penetrate steel.'"

"Wits to go along with his looks," I joked. "Did he drink it?"

"The brandy? He had a reputation as a heavy drinker, so he probably did. If so, it would have helped ease the pain of his eventual passing."

"You say he was popular."

"More so after his death than before it, surely. Have you been to Delhi to visit his grave?"

"Not yet."

"You must go. It's no mere gravestone to mark his resting place for family or for amateur genealogists. Undersheriff Osman Steele has an obelisk that says something or other about his faithfulness and bravery and worth as a citizen. A hero in the eyes of the establishment," McNally said. He raised a finger and smiled. "But there's always a but in history, Mr. Flanagan, trailing behind and weighing down the establishment's version of events, always on the edge of the establishment's vision, always an annoyance."

"What's this but?" I asked.

"There's another memorial."

"To Steele?"

"To the men who opposed him. To the men who killed him."

"Where?"

"In Andes, where the murder took place. The memorial there refers to Undersheriff Osman Steele as a short, red-haired, bad-tempered, brutal, unfair man who enjoyed harassing Anti-Renters far beyond what the letter of the law prescribed." McNally shifted in his seat. "You must visit these places, Tom. You must see the sights and breathe in the air. Feel the land under your feet. These monuments will give you a sense of how each side interpreted and continues to interpret this very complicated affair."

"What was the second condition?" I asked.

"Hmm? Oh, yes. The second condition that made failure inevitable was the disguises. Dressing up might have worked seventy years before back in Boston, but by the 1840's, in rural New York, it was not an effective strategy."

"Why not?"

"Because everyone knew everyone in isolated places like these, even by voice if the face was masked and the clothing covered. Sometimes, it's said, Anti-Renters tried speaking with wool in their mouths to disguise their voices. I'm sure it didn't work."

"Why do you think they did it then? Wore the disguises?"

"There are several possible answers, but only one of them satisfies me. They were scared of the same violence they half-convinced themselves they could commit, and putting on those ridiculous masks and ugly robes fed their courage, a false courage. What they lacked was the real courage to stand and fight, man to man."

A fair assessment from a member of the greatest generation, I thought. "I've seen pictures of the masks and robes," I said. "There's something about them that bothers me."

"Ah, pictures—that reminds me of something!" McNally pushed the button that inclined his chair forward and continued to lean forward until he was standing and balanced on his walker. Then he shuffled out of the room and down a hallway. I heard him muttering, "There? No, not there. Where is it? Ah!" Then he yelled, "I found it!" When he got back into the room he handed me a cardboard tube. "Open it," he insisted.

I removed the print from the cylinder and unrolled it. It was a scene that showed, on the left, a man-on-horseback, on the right, a young boy blowing a tin horn and, in the middle, a group of nine masked calico-clad Anti-Renters. The Anti-Renters were fearsome with their grotesque masks and aggressive body language and weapons. The farmer in the center was dressed in a red calico gown and his mask had deer antlers sprouting from its top. He held a torch, the smoke from which curled above the grouping and into the cloudy sky, the light from which illuminated the men's masks in a diabolical glow. A farmer on the right wielded a machete. The farmer to the farthest left held a sign that read "Down with the Rent." The sign resembled a large hatchet ready to do damage to any up-renter that got in its way. Dogs scurried around the men's feet. The hills and sky of the background were ominous shades of grey. The few trees in the painting were leafless and dead. The scene reminded me of the mood of my dreams as of late, a feeling that left me more than a little uncomfortable.

"What is this?" I asked when we had returned to our seats.

"It's a print of a mural by Mary Earley that was paid for

by the Works Progress Administration. Can you guess where it is? Hmm? It's in Delhi of all places!" he said when I gave no answer. "It's in the post office, where people see it every day!"

"Wow," I said. "This is an amazing painting."

"I agree. But tell me why you say so."

"Well, first of all Mary Earley captures exactly what I meant when I said the masks and gowns bother me."

"Go on."

"This isn't the stereotypical Indian attire that prevailed in Anglo-America. The Boston Tea Party heroes dressed as eighteenth century Bostonians imagined Indians to dress, with the leather and face paint and feathers. The Anti-Renters, though ... I don't know, not so much. Look at these!" I pointed at the painting. "The masks look like real heads, like they grew on the men's shoulders. And the gowns are simply absurd. Where did they get the idea for these costumes?"

McNally sat up without the aid of his automatic chair. "Some historians have posited a connection with India, where the calico fabric was made. There's more than one group of Indians in the world, they say. And the men of Delaware County did call themselves Calico Indians."

"That seems tenuous at best, though, even with the name."

"Yes, I agree. Other historians claim an equally implausible connection to Anti-Rent riots that occurred in the Hudson Valley over a century earlier."

"That doesn't seem so implausible."

"True, those early protestors wore masks and gowns, but they were made of plain, undecorated fabric, probably burlap. The costumes worn by the nineteenth century Anti-Renters were quite elaborate in their decoration, real calico, with realistic, animalistic decorations on the masks. And the horns! Why did they wear disguises so elaborate, so ostentatious? I think you're correct about the disconnect with previous Indian costumes. The answer, it seems to me, is that the Anti-Renters needed to feed the courage they found necessary to commit their violence. It was, as I said, a false courage."

The question of where the gowns and, especially, the masks originated lingered in my mind. I had my suspicions, but they were still vague and I was not yet able to articulate them. What I thought at the time was that the answer probably could not be found in history, at least in history as I had been trained to understand it. This bothered me, so I rolled the print of Mary Earley's mural back up and returned it to its cylinder. I held it out for McNally to take.

"Keep it," he said. "I've got no use for it now that I'm retired from the classroom. Keep it, because maybe you'll need to see it again during your quest for answers."

"Thank you," I said.

"You're welcome."

"Professor McNally, I know what happened immediately after the shooting. I know that all the major sentences were eventually commuted and that the prisoners returned home to a hero's welcome. What happened next? It seems like the Anti-Rent movement just kind of, I don't know, fizzled out."

"It was swallowed up by lawyers," McNally said. "First, some New York legislators tried and failed to reform the rent laws when they revised the state constitution."

"Tried and failed?"

"Failed miserably. Oh, there were some small victories. For example, from that point on judges would be elected rather than appointed by the wealthy and powerful. Another small victory was the prohibition against new leases in perpetuity. But the lawyers who drew up the new constitution, even the lawyers with Anti-Rent sympathies, couldn't get past their obsession with the sanctity of private property and the inviolability of contracts. Obsession. Yes, it was that."

"So the lease agreements held?"

"The lease agreements held. Still, the landlords were losing money for other reasons, including a revised tax code, and could not maintain their grip on legislative power for long."

"And that was the end?"

"Almost." McNally breathed deep and quietly laughed. "You're fortunate too because I've just about reached the end of my energy reserves."

"I'm sorry," I said. "Do you want me to go?"

McNally lifted his hand about four inches off the armrest and waved it. "Not at all. I appreciate the company, and I appreciate sharing what I'm able to share. I'm tired, I can only do so much, but I'll do what I can to help you. Let's finish." He cleared his throat. "Where were we?"

"Almost to the end, after the lawyers swallowed the Anti-Rent movement up."

"Yes." McNally chuckled. "The lawyers swallowed it up. Then—pardon my language here—they shat it out into the new market economy that still gives lawyers so much business, even to this day. The only thing more sacrosanct than property and contracts, you see, was and remains money. Eventually, by the 1860's, men with power agreed that land, even the aristocrat-owned, tenant-farmed land of eastern New York, could be sold and bought by anyone who could afford it. Prices were set. Money was exchanged. Even though the Van Rensselaers and Hardenberghs didn't get as much as they hoped, they still got something."

"And the tenants?"

"Many of them got lucky, luckier than the landlords, in fact."

"How?"

"Simple geography. They moved west. True, a few of the tenants could afford to buy their New York farms. Most of them, however, were severely disillusioned with their New York experiences and left the state for greener pastures. Literally, I mean. They settled in Ohio, Illinois and Iowa, amazed at what they could grow in sod three foot thick where barely a pebble could be found. They got lucky to get out from under those leases. They got lucky to get away from that land."

"Not all of them moved, though."

"No, not all all of them. Others stayed and continued to scratch a living from the land. They said the land provided two rocks for every dirt. As far as I know, it still does."

McNally sat back with a thud and a sigh. He was obviously done talking. I thanked him for his time, promised him that I'd come back to chat about non-business topics and stood up to leave.

"Who are you doing this work for?" he asked.

"A downstate businessman," I lied, pretty sure that he did not know that his former colleague had returned to town.

"Ah, yes. He's probably paying you well. Well, let me know how it turns out. And before you leave, Tom, could you turn the television back on and hand me the flicker? I see it now. It's over there, on top of the television cabinet."

I complied, said goodbye and left.

Chapter Fifteen

I DIDN'T SEE MUCH OF MINDY during graduation week. She had loads of work to finish before the official end of the spring semester, everything from grading final papers and exams to writing department reports to finishing the fall schedule to making last-minute travel arrangements for special guests of the department's several graduation ceremonies. She worked furiously that week, getting to her office by seven thirty and staying there well into the night. We did most of our talking on the phone. But we did have dinner together on Thursday evening after meeting at the city clerk's to get our marriage license. At dinner we chatted about her work and about our hopes for our first summer together as a married couple. We did not talk about Martha Radisson or about the mystery that surrounded the death of Osman Steele or about the painted name on our living room wall.

I WAS BACK AT THE 357 on Friday night for our "wedding planning research" while Mindy fulfilled her professional obligations at the history department graduation dinner.

Lodi was already playing to a packed house when I came down from my office to enjoy the show. He struck quite an impressive figure—tall and sturdy like a lumberjack with a dirty blond beard and long blond hair tied back in a ponytail. He was outfitted in a green and black flannel shirt left untucked over his blue jeans. And he played the guitar like a lumberjack, sometimes windmilling his arm and tugging the neck Pete Townshend-style, sometimes chopping the strings with his pick (when he used one) as if whittling a piece of wood with a pocket knife. Yet his music was filled with a delicate beauty and an understated pain—filled with soul, that is—and Lodi's expression of these feelings through his guitar and voice had virtually everyone in the room mesmerized.

He was on the second verse of Mentor Williams' "Drift Away" when I got there. He sung with an edge that challenged us to mean it, really mean it, if we wanted to free our soul from all that ails it and get lost in the healing power of music. Most of the audience, myself included, obliged, swaying and clapping and singing along with the extended final refrain.

Lodi sang about failed promise, appropriately enough given the theme of the eponymous CCR song, which was an early highlight of his first set. He sang about pain and regret and about finding grace in the memories of relationships gone bad. He sang about love longed for, love found, love lost and love regained. He sang a beautiful, desperation-filled rendition of Tyrone Davis' "Turn Back the Hands of Time" and a surprisingly plucky version of "People Get Ready," both of which I deeply appreciated.

My favorite number, however, was Lodi's take on Bob Seger's "Travelin' Man/Beautiful Loser," an iconic example of spiritual rock and roll at its finest. Lodi closed his eyes and tilted back his head as the ghosts of relationships past came alive in his singing. As he concluded the song, he waved his hand in the air between chords, inviting us to come along and join him in his journey of musical introspection. By the time he silenced his guitar, all of us who said yes knew we had found a reliable guide.

He ended the set with a marvelous version of Bob Dylan's "You Angel You." Beginning with the second verse it sounded as if he performed the song with two voices. I figured out this much after the third verse: he repeated words or parts of words rapidly and in such a way as to give an echo effect. His guitar playing—complex chords plucked with his fingers rather than a pick—added to the effect and made it seem like someone else was singing harmony.

The crowd reacted to the song with a long ovation, to which Lodi responded with several deep bows. After that Louie called me over to the bar. He handed me two Saranacs and instructed me to deliver one to Lodi and keep the other for myself.

"He's hoping the orchestra can't make it," Louie hinted as I walked away.

Having made my way through the crowd, I handed Lodi the glass and clinked it with mine. I noticed that the fingernails on his right hand were long and manicured to a point. That must be how he achieved the echo effect on the Dylan song, I thought.

"From one traveling man to another," I toasted.

He downed half the beer. "Where you headin'?" he asked in a voice much quieter than, but just as mesmerizing as, his singing voice.

Why not, I thought, why not. "Wherever I need to go," I said. "I'm looking for someone I lost long ago. Someone I never had the chance to love." Besides Mindy, Louie, my cousin Andrew and Bill Hamilton, Lodi was the first person I had talked to about Patrick in almost two years. My comment was vague, but my heart still beat wildly at having shared something so vulnerable with a stranger.

He looked around me towards the bar, where Louie was laughing with Ghedi and his girlfriend, who had just arrived. "So you've got a restless heart," he said.

I shook my head and smiled. "My fiancee Mindy had to work tonight. She's sorry she can't be here. We're getting married on the eighth of July, as Louie might've told you. We have an orchestra booked for the reception. But we'd also like some music for our after-hours party on a private Canadian island. We're hoping you can make it."

Lodi looked me in the eye. He was silent for a long time, neither blinking nor shifting his gaze. His facial expression revealed nothing. I returned his stare as long as I could. After I blinked, it seemed that his pupils had dilated some, and that the energy coming from them had intensified.

"I always appreciate the chance to play for our northern sisters and brothers," he said without looking away.

"Will you do it?"

"My schedule's flexible," he said. "My passport should get me over the border." He handed me the empty glass. "Should."

"Thank you," I said, my heart racing again.

"You're welcome," Lodi answered. "And thank you."

"For what?"

He gave me another silent stare before he spoke. "For being here tonight. For bringing me that beer. Most of all, for not giving up on that someone you never had a chance to love."

I gasped. Lodi reached out his hand and placed it on my shoulder. His grip on my shoulder was gentle, he applied hardly any force, but I could feel the pinch of his fingernails on my skin. With the slightest bit of movement he turned me around and sent me back across the room. When I got back to the bar I handed Louie the empty glasses and told him that everything was just fine.

"Persuasive one, ain't he?" Louie said.

Chapter Sixteen

LODI BEGAN HIS SECOND SET with his name-that-tune game. I kept quiet and didn't play because I needed time to work through our conversation and what I felt about it. Bill Hamilton had told me a story about Patrick from the past which had given me hope. I suspected that Lodi knew more about him—he had thanked me for not giving up on him—and I was filled with even more hope that he could lead me to him. What would Mindy think of all this? I wasn't sure, but it would be a day or two before I had a chance to tell her anyway.

Lodi was well into his game by the time I returned my attention to his music. Ghedi's girlfriend Denise excelled at the game, nailing all the Van Morrison songs and Creedence songs, the Sam Cooke and Otis Redding songs, and even the ones by Leadbelly and other early American artists. Once each song was identified, usually within ten or a dozen notes, Lodi encouraged the crowd to sing along for a few measures, which most of us did willingly.

We all knew his final name-that-tune selection after just a few notes. We all knew the words, at least the words to the chorus. It was Lodi's way of drawing us out of the game and back into the evening's musical message.

> *This land is your land, this land is my land*
> *From California, to the New York island*
> *From the Redwood forests to the Gulf Stream waters*
>   *This land was made for you and me.*

The game done, we sang the refrain over and over again —it must have been ten or fifteen times—swaying, clapping, holding hands, hugging. Into it now, happy after Lodi's words had sunk in, I partnered with a grad student I knew and her boyfriend, singing into her beer bottle as we exchanged smiles and high fives.

Lodi moved from this crowd-pleaser into a Woody Guthrie medley consisting of "Lindbergh," during which he played a blistering six string solo, "Pictures from Life's Other Side," "Do-Re-Mi," and "Jarama Valley," which he filled with as much soul as he could pack into a folk song about a long ago war in a far away land. After another spellbinding solo reprising the songs' main themes, Lodi ended the medley just as he had begun it, reprising a few verses of "This Land Is Your Land."

He ended the medley with a verse of his own invention, a verse that sent a wave of shock up my spine, especially when he pointed the headstock of his guitar right at me as he sang it:

She's in the fire that's burnin' and the river that's runnin'
In the air we're breathin' and the soil we're seedin'
When she was talkin', my ears were listenin'; She said,
"This land was made for you and me."

I applauded along with everyone else, although I was probably the only one puzzling over what his mention of the four classical elements might mean, and who Lodi's "She" actually was.

Chapter Seventeen

AN HOUR LATER, at Louie's invitation, I was on the back deck of The 357 with Lodi and his guitar. We were joined by Louie, Ghedi and Ghedi's girlfriend Denise, a graduate student in history who worked the late shift at a local bookstore a few doors down from Louie's bar. We were sharing a pitcher of spiced sangria that Ghedi had made after closing down the kitchen. A warm breeze blew from the southwest and the stars were out. Louie, Denise and I listened as Ghedi and Lodi exchanged notes on the meanings of their names.

"Ghedi means sojourner," Ghedi explained. "But having lived in London, my family is also known as Gaal, which means foreigner."

"A little less complimentary than sojourner," Lodi said.

"Still, it is descriptive enough in a society as insular as Somalia's is," Ghedi said.

"You said there are no surnames in Somalia? No family names?" I asked.

"No family names like Flanagan, Fratello or Phillips," Ghedi explained, looking to me, Louie and Denise in that order. "Yet Ghedi is a family name in the sense that it is passed down from father to son. So too is Ali, my family's common Muslim name."

"So it's Ghedi Ali Gaal?" Louie asked.

"Or Gaal Ali Ghedi," he replied, taking a sip of bottled water. "It does not matter to me."

"I'll stick with Ghedi," Louie said. "Much less confusing

to my mind. And what about you, my troubadour friend?" He nodded towards Lodi.

Lodi played a few chords on his guitar, which rested on his lap. "Lodi would normally be a habitational name," he said.

"Like the town in Italy," I offered, "where Napoleon won his battle."

"Or the city in California," Denise added, "after which John Fogerty named the Creedence song."

"See," said Louie, poking me in the side.

"You don't look Italian," Denise said.

"And I'm not from California," Lodi explained, "although I've hitched up and down the Pacific Highway a few times. No, Lodi is a stage name, which I did, however, derive from the Creedence song, as Miss Phillips so acutely observed." Lodi played a series of chords from the song and mumbled a few of the words. "But this troubadour might change his name to Ghedi," he said as he continued playing. "Or Sojourner"—he spoke the syllables slowly, melodically—"I like that. I like it a lot. I also like the thought of being in the eponymous company of one Sister Truth."

"Amen to that!" Denise lifted her glass and smiled. "I missed your first set because I had to work," she said, "but from what I heard after intermission I'm sure Sojourner Truth would proudly share the name with you."

"I appreciate the compliment," Lodi said. "Thank you very much."

Lodi played a chord, then another, and, finding the right key, continued playing and sang.

There is a truth abiding,
won't ever go into hiding
that every human being must be free

Belle Baumfree did the fightin'

her message struck like lightnin'
her dignity's a gift to you and me ...

He played more and hummed the tune. He sang the second verse again. Then he ended it with a loud strum.

"Wow. Whose is that?" Denise asked.

"It's yours now," Lodi said with a shrug and to Denise's obvious satisfaction. "Made it up as I sang it. Wasn't all that difficult because Ms. Truth and I share a connection beyond the struggle for justice. A blood connection if you will. She was a tried and true upstate New Yorker, you know, born and raised not far from my neck of the woods."

Denise nodded vigorously. "She was! Belle Baumfree was born a Hardenbergh family slave. She was sold by the Hardenbergh family with a flock of sheep for a hundred dollars when she was nine. Sold again—without the sheep—for just over a hundred dollars when she was eleven. Sold *again* for one-seventy-five when she was thirteen. Escaped slavery at age twenty-nine, after which she learned how to read and write. And the rest, as they say, is history. Tom, you must have learned all about her in McNally's Nineteenth Century American Culture class."

Most of what Denise said didn't register because my mind was stuck on the first part of her lesson. "Did you say the Hardenbergh family?" I asked. "As in the Hardenberghs of Delaware County? The same Hardenberghs who sold their land to Gulian Verplanck?"

Denise scowled. "Seriously? We're talking about one of the greatest freedom fighters in American history and all you care about is the real estate transactions of the tyrant who treated her like chattel? Sold her like *sheep*?"

Ghedi placed a hand on Denise's lap before she could stand up.

"No," I said. "I mean, yes. I'm sorry I put it the way I did. I meant no disrespect to Sojourner Truth's life or legacy. But this is the second time in a week someone's brought up the topic of that land. The land the Hardenberghs used to own."

"And the first was?" Ghedi asked, keeping pressure on Denise's knee.

"Martha Radisson."

"So she *is* back!" Denise sat forward, then turned towards Ghedi and back towards me in a whiplash motion. "Wait a minute. What's Professor Radisson have to do with the history of Delaware County?"

"She wondered if I was interested in taking on a murder investigation," I said rather evasively. "A murder that happened on land the Hardenberghs sold to the Verplancks."

"Must be the murder of Undersheriff Osman Steele," Lodi said with a knowing smile.

"The very one," I said, surprised that Lodi knew.

Denise, also surprised, whirled to face Lodi. "How do *you* know about *that*?"

"It's the most famous murder in Delaware County history," Lodi said. "It, like Sister Truth's struggle for justice, is also in my blood. I grew up in those parts, just like Belle Baumfree. I first learned about the murder when I was a kid, in song. Listen to this." He looked around the circle, clicked his nails on the guitar's body, then added, "This is one I did not write."

Come all ye Anti-Renters true,
The Delhi Clique we will subdue;
Soon our liberty we'll gain,
And Silas Wrong will cease to reign.

The Sheriff was to Andes sent,
The Farmer to distrain for Rent;
And with him three tory hounds –
In Delhi they do much abound.

"Rast Edgerton and Steele in Co.,

> *To Hunting's tavern they did go,*
> *The more the Brandy passed around,*
> *The more their courage did abound.*
>
> *The brandy to them courage gave –*
> *The heroes grew most wondrous brave!*
> *Away they went to try their skill,*
> *The Anti-Renters for to kill.*
>
> *They fired upon the Indian band,*
> *To make them run they did intend;*
> *But dearly Steele paid for his fun,*
> *The Indians shot and down he came.*
>
> *Come all ye Anti-Renters true,*
> *The Delhi Clique we will subdue;*
> *Soon our liberty we'll gain,*
> *And Silas Wrong will cease to reign.*

Lodi stopped playing and set the guitar on his knee. "There's more to it," he said. "Much more depending on how much time and drink you have. It's called 'The Fall Campaign' or 'The Reign of Terror.' The title refers to the backlash that followed Osman Steele's murder. Never been quite sure how to fit it into my set list. There's power in the song, though."

"There's power in a lot of what you play," Louie said.

"Music's all about power," Lodi affirmed, "the power to take you somewhere else, to turn you, like my Somali friend here, into a sojourner." He winked at Ghedi and they both smiled.

After a pause, during which several of us nodded and others sipped sangria, Denise turned to me and asked, "So, did you take the job?"

"I did not," I said. "I'm far too busy for that." I drank some sangria, then some more. I was growing increasingly uncomfortable with the way Martha Radisson, her note card and the mystery written on it refused to leave me alone.

"You're giving up quite a paycheck," Denise said.

"Excuse me?"

"I've perused your website," she explained. "You don't come cheap."

"Ah."

"I have a question about your song," Louie said before Denise could ask me another question about either Martha Radisson or my personal finances.

"Fire away," answered Lodi.

"What do the reference to the Indians mean?"

"The farmers dressed up in patterned calico cloaks," Denise explained. "They wore painted war masks as well. They said they were the heirs of the Boston tea party patriots."

"It was more than that," Lodi said.

"What more?" Louie asked.

"There are two common explanations," I said. I looked at Lodi. "Sorry to interrupt," I said.

"No, go ahead. You're the historian."

"Thanks. The first explanation is that the calico robes were made in India. *Ergo*, Indians. The second explanation is that the Anti-Renters borrowed the idea from tenants who lived a century before and who also wore costumes, albeit not as elaborately decorated, when they protested against landlord oppression."

Denise looked at me quizzically. "You sure you didn't take the job?"

"I had a talk with Professor McNally about the larger historical context." I said. "I was curious."

"It was more than the cotton's place of origin," Lodi said, "although that's a good point, often ignored. The cloaks and masks also represented the farmers' connection with the soil, their ties to the earth. Think about it. The landlords were making claims on land that did not belong to them. The farmers, like the Iroquois who worked the land before them, insisted that the soil under their feet was owned only by those who properly nurtured it. They were right, more than they knew. Turns out, the land itself was just as angry as the farmers were. Land doesn't want to be owned, perhaps even by those who care for it."

"Yes!" Denise exclaimed.

"So the cloaks and masks represented the earth?" I asked. "Where did the Anti-Renters get the idea for that?"

We were silent for a moment before Denise offered an answer. "The Green Man," she said with a snap of her fingers. We all looked at her. "The settlers of Delaware County came from England, Scotland and Wales, right? Back in the old country, young men used to dress up as the Green Man, an Earth deity that stretched back to Celtic times, maybe even earlier than that. They dressed up and paraded through their villages on May Day and during other festivals. Even after they converted to Christianity they still dressed up and marched. And churches in the British Isles are filled with Green Man sculptures. Like Lodi said, these representations of the Green Man connected people to the earth." Denise looked to Lodi for affirmation. He nodded. She smiled.

"And it gave the young men power," Ghedi offered. "Whether it was as the Green Man in Medieval England or as Indians in nineteenth century America, dressing in costumes connected these young men to the original owners of the land—Celts and Indians—and thus bypassed the power of society's landed elites. Like the celebrations of Carnival, these young men, through their costumes, turned the existing power structure upside down, if only for a time. Young men in Africa do a similar thing."

"Sounds like a rational explanation to me," Lodi added, putting a slight but clear emphasis on the word "rational."

"Is there any other kind of explanation worth talking about?" asked Denise with a slight sneer.

"There are plenty of non-rational theories," Lodi answered, "but I'm sure you don't want to hear those."

"You're right," Denise said with a chuckle. "Most of us academic historians are severely allergic to non-rational theories."

"All I'll say is that you'd better be very careful when you start trying to over-intellectualize the Green Man or any of those other old-country deities, as you call them."

Denise laughed. "We're graduate students!" she said. "We're *supposed* to over-intellectualize things!"

"True enough," Lodi said.

Without further comment he reached into a zippered pocket of his shoulder bag and produced a small pan flute. He began to play a tune that started slow and sad, and picked up in both tempo and pitch to the point where all of us were tapping our feet or clapping our hands. The music rose and fell, peaked and dipped. And underneath the melody was a foundation of sadness that felt, to me at least, old and primal. Lodi slowed the tune back down to its starting tempo and ended it with one long, sad note. By that point, the rest of us were silent.

"Wow," I said. I caught myself breathing harder than normal, choking up even, and didn't want to say anything else.

Denise wiped a tear from her cheek. "That was beautiful," she said. "And odd!"

"Another one of my compositions," Lodi said. "It's based on some horn dances from Medieval England."

"Don't you dare play that on Friday night," Louie said, "or my customers'll be crying in their beer."

"I like it!" Ghedi exclaimed, his eyes welling up too.

"Thank you," Lodi replied. "Thank you very much. The song is supposed to speak to the land, to wake it up in a manner of speaking. My guess is that the Anti-Renter costumes were meant to do the same thing, visually rather than acoustically."

"What I want to know," I asked, looking at Lodi, "is how the Anti-Rent Wars are in your blood."

"Hmm, yes, back to me and my story. Very good idea. Back to the facts." He strummed his guitar. "I grew up on a family farm on the outskirts of Andes," he answered. "My ancestor, who cleared the land and built our house, was an Anti-Renter. Who knows? Maybe he was there, wearing one of those strange costumes you seem to have all the rational explanations for."

"Your ancestor was at Moses Earle's farm?" I asked. "As a witness to Osman Steele's murder?"

"Friends of freedom came from all over Delaware County that day," Lodi said. "Andes, Roxbury, Bovina. Many were arrested after the shooting, but that didn't mean much."

"Why not?" I asked.

"Because some of the men arrested weren't there, and some of the men who were there and were arrested were eventually found innocent."

"They ever find the killer?" I asked, deciding a direct question was worth a shot.

"Several men were tried and sent to prison for the crime and two others were sentenced to hang. But all the convicted men were pardoned. No one Marley-d up. No one but the rocks and soil and trees knows who shot the undersheriff."

Nothing I didn't already know, I thought with disappointment.

"The disguises," Louie said, making the same point Mindy had made in our conversation with Martha Radisson.

"Yes, the disguises," Lodi said. "It keeps coming back to the disguises, doesn't it?"

"Can you say more about your song's references to the reign of terror?" Ghedi asked. "Given my own people's experience, that interests me."

"There were hundreds of arrests," Lodi said. "Indiscriminate arrests. Warrantless arrests. The present isn't the first time people experienced the wrath of authority wronged, you know."

"Somalia isn't the only place to have suffered injustice," Ghedi added.

Lodi drained his last sip of sangria. "'Tis true, my sojourning friend. Injustice seems to be the way of our world. But as my good friend Pete Seeger likes to say, our job is to march farther and further. Tell you what—you all should come down sometime and check out the lay of the land. Take a road trip. I'll show you places where, if you ask them, the rocks and pines will tell you all you want to know, and some things you might not have known to ask. Some of those rocks and trees are as old as the Anti-Renters themselves. Some of them remember."

Most of us were tired by this point. Denise put her head on Ghedi's shoulder. Ghedi himself yawned. Louie stood up and said that despite how much he appreciated yet another history lesson, he still had to get up early the next morning and pay his taxes. Lodi put his guitar away and said that although he didn't want this gathering to end, he did want to make it home before sunrise. He said goodnight to Ghedi and Denise, who declined a ride in favor of walking home. I declined a ride as well and asked to join them.

But I had one more question for Lodi before I left. I told Ghedi and Denise I'd catch up, then counted to five to buttress my courage.

"Who's the 'she' you mentioned at the end of name that tune?" I asked.

"Whoever you want her to be," Lodi answered. "Mother Earth. A moon goddess. Ishtar. An angel."

"Ariel?"

"Who?"

"Never mind," I said.

"Tell me the real reason why you have a restless heart," Lodi said. "Who are you looking for?"

"I'm looking for my brother. He survived drowning in the Saint Lawrence River and he learned to control fire out in Mumford. Somehow, maybe because of what you sang earlier about the elements and what you said just now about the earth, I get the feeling you might know him."

Lodi's eyes flickered and he looked quickly to his left and right, perhaps to see if any of the others were listening. They were all gone, so he looked back at me and a smile crossed his face. "Water, huh? And fire? Like I said earlier, there's much more for us to talk about, Tom Flanagan. But not here. Not at this time of night. Visit me before I come up to Canada, though. We'll talk about earth, and maybe about air too. And maybe we'll ask those rocks and trees a few questions. Who knows? Maybe you'll solve two mysteries in one trip."

My heart skipped a beat as Lodi turned and walked away.

"Where can I find you?" I shouted.

"Just come on down to the scene of the crime," he said without turning back. "You won't have to look far."

I caught up to Ghedi and Denise. She apologized for getting on my case about the Hardenberghs. I apologized for not being mindful of her criticisms. Then she mentioned something so obvious that it seemed more important than it probably was. With all our talk about familial and habitational monikers, she said, with the way our conversation ended on the topic of Lodi's Anti-Rent ancestor, we still didn't know his full name. Ghedi added that he was quite sure there was more to Lodi than his name we didn't know.

Chapter Eighteen

My dream that night was another one in which the river was destroyed, this time by an earthquake that opened up fissures through which the waters of the Saint Lawrence, and all life therein, drained.

In the dream I am walking along the cracked mud and broken granite of the river floor, which is littered with glass bottles, metal barrels, decomposing fish carcasses, rotting seaweed, outboard motors, auto parts and a thousand other pieces of detritus that had been cast into the water over years of abuse. I am walking in my tuxedo, which meant that the dream was taking place either on the day of the annual Ostend Ball in early November or, like the dream I had a few days before, on our wedding day. I would've put money on the latter.

In the distance I can see a wrecked and abandoned tanker, still oozing oil onto the barren ground. The granite cliffs of the islands remain pink above the former waterline but are bleached white and pale green below it. There are no signs of life. What was once river is now desert.

As I approach the American span of the Thousand Island Bridge, which looms two-hundred fifty feet above me, I am again surprised by the appearance of Billy Masterson, who seems to float an inch or so above the ground.

"Whaddya think?" he asks.

"About all this?" I ask. He nods. "It sucks."

"Don't worry too much about it," Billy offers. "Things are always changin', even our river."

"Billy, did I do this? Is this my fault?" I ask.

"I've got someone for you to meet," he says.

"Who?" I ask, wondering who else would be out in this wasteland that used to be the river.

Billy doesn't answer, just points to someone walking our way. "Go meet her," he says. "No need to be shy."

And he disappears as suddenly as he appeared.

As I get closer I see that she's a woman, and an attractive one at that. Her long golden hair glows like silk, her emerald-green eyes gleam in the sun and her wide, moist lips turn naturally upward into a smile. She wears a long black gown that fits loosely around her breasts and waist and sparkles with embossed silver threads and studded gemstones. Her feet are bare. She moves effortlessly, almost gliding over the dry mud and rock of the riverbed as her arms and hips gently sway. Seeing her move towards me quickens my heartbeat and brings a flush of expectation to my otherwise grief-weary face.

"Why do you worry?" she asks as she opens her arms in a gesture of invitation and peace. "Why do you grieve on your wedding day?" That explains the tuxedo, I think to myself.

I look around me at the emptiness—the deadness—of my most favorite place in the world, a place that I knew as teeming with life and filled with an unsurpassed beauty. I turn back to face her and she is right in front of me, no more than a foot away. Her breath is minty and citrusy and sweet, like a freshly cut bouquet of flowers, and it overwhelms the stink of death. The sun shines through her dress and fills it with light. I can see the outline of her body underneath the fabric. As I look into her eyes I am filled with an emotion that I can only call love.

"This is no place for despair," she says. "This is a place of life, filled with grace. This is a place where life will always survive." She moves forward. The touch of her hand upon the side of my face sends a ripple through my skin and down my neck and back. She leans into me and kisses me on the lips, a long kiss that sends waves of pleasure flowing into every nerve.

She holds the kiss for what seems like a long time, but, to me, is not close to being long enough.

"Open your eyes," she says as she pulls away. "Open your eyes and see." I don't realize I had closed them.

When I do open my eyes, I am dazzled by the scene around me. The Saint Lawrence River, as I had known it all my life, is no longer there. But neither is the wasteland that had surrounded me just seconds ago. Instead, a stream of clear, beautiful water about eight feet wide and three feet deep flows over a smooth granite bed. Here and there, the water rushes around boulders of various sizes that protrude above the surface. Small, quick rapids flow over the smooth, flat rocks that sit just below the water. The stream soaks through my shoes, socks and pants. I reach down and fill my cupped hands with water. I drink it and savor the cool, refreshing tingle of the purest water I have ever known.

There is no mud in the water, but fertile soil on either bank of the stream gives life to fields of grass and flowers. I see daisies and cyclamen and yarrow and bluebells. Hummingbirds and butterflies feast on the flowers' nectar. Above us, birds of all kinds fly about in flocks and sing their songs. The walls and cliffs of what used to be islands are still there beyond the stream-side meadow. The granite buttes are all pink now, from bottom to top. Many of them are crowned with tall pines and maples and tamaracks. Rock, meadow and stream are all illuminated by a soft, whitish-blue light that seems to emanate from nowhere and everywhere at the same time. I know right away that I've never seen anything on earth like this.

I turn to look again at the woman whose astonishing beauty matches the beauty of the scene around me.

She's gone.

"Where are you?" I cry. "Hello? Where'd you go? Billy? Where is she?"

I spin and look in every direction, but cannot find either her or Billy. My heart beats faster, in pain this time as the feeling of despair returns. As I continue to spin, the colors around me slowly fade and the dry mud of a ruined river reappears. The sun resumes casting its harsh, unyielding rays on the dead landscape that surrounds me.

"No!" I scream, tears running down my face, and louder, "NO!"

My heart aching with the pain of loss and longing, I woke up to find myself on the floor of our bedroom. I was sweating and shaking. My socks and pajama pant legs were soaking wet. I changed into other clothes and used towels to swab up the excess water on the floor. I got back into bed with Mindy, who had apparently slept through the whole thing. I knew I wouldn't sleep again that night. As I lay there with my eyes wide open, I could still smell the minty freshness of the strange woman's breath, could still taste the clean vitality of the water she had given me.

Chapter Nineteen

MY PLAN FOR THE NEXT DAY—graduate school commencement day for Mindy—was to paint the living room trim, thus finishing the job we had begun a week before, the last job before our wedding. The semi-gloss "ARIEL" shone like a ghost through the coats of satin paint that covered it—or, I thought as I stood there staring at it for some time before starting the day's work, shone like a barely opaque undine in the gin-clear water of the Saint Lawrence.

But my mind wasn't on the river, where my dream had taken me the night before, where Mindy and I would be relocating in a couple of days and where we would be married in a few weeks. Instead, and despite the power of the previous night's dream, I was thinking about Delaware County, where Osman Steele had been killed and where, as Lodi had implied the night before, I might find my brother.

I opened the can of sage tint trim and noticed that there was no paint in the drip channel around the outer edge of the can—indeed, the can was up to that point unopened. I picked up the unused brush that Detective Delaney had left on our front porch after the tests for fingerprints came up negative. How had the word been written on our wall if not with this brush and this paint? Letting the question percolate, I stood on the ladder and began work on the crown molding.

I had three feet of it done and was about to move the ladder when a vague thought started to develop deep in my mind. It matured quickly, and when I finally understood its implications I dropped the brush into the can of paint and set the can on the ladder, spilling about a cup of sage tint trim onto the ladder's lower rungs. I ran into the kitchen and grabbed our digital camera. Back in the living room, I took about a dozen photos of the word painted on our wall from several different angles and distances. Then I ran outside, got into the car and drove to Louie's. I parked out back and dashed up the stairs to my office. My hands shaking, I retrieved Martha Radisson's card from my desk drawer and opened it. I turned the camera on view mode and set it down next to the card.

And there it was, visual confirmation of the fact that now exploded in my brain: "WHO KILLED OSMAN STEELE?" and "FLANAGAN", the words written on Martha Radisson's card, were in the same beautiful script as "ARIEL," the word written on our living room wall.

I texted Mindy that I was off on another road trip, this time to Delhi, where Osman Steele was buried, and to Andes, where he'd died. Once again, a mystery that belonged to Martha Radisson had somehow taken over my life.

Part Two

Delaware County
Thousand Islands Park
Delaware County

Besides, there are certain divine powers of a middle nature, situate in this interval of the air, between the highest ether and the earth below, through whom our aspirations and our deserts are conveyed to the Gods. These the Greeks call by name, "daemons," and, being placed as messengers between the inhabitants of earth and those of heaven, they carry from the one to the other, prayers and bounties, supplications and assistance, being a kind of interpreters and message carriers for both. Through these same daemons, as Plato says in his Symposium, all revelations, the various miracles of magicians, and all kinds of presages are carried on. For specially appointed individuals of this number administer everything according to the province assigned to each ... by means of which we obtain knowledge of future events.

—Apuleius, *The God of Socrates* (c. 150)

Chapter Twenty

I DROVE THE THRUWAY to Herkimer, then south on Route 28 through Cooperstown and Oneonta, over Franklin Mountain, through Meridale and into Delhi. The feeling I had as I entered Delaware County was of encountering old land, where dairy farms outnumbered shopping plazas and where people remembered, and some still practiced, the traditional ways of life that I had seen recreated at the Genesee Country Village in Mumford.

But Mumford was less than twenty miles from Rochester and was hardly isolated from the city to the north. Delaware County was a different animal altogether. Oneonta was a small city, not much more than a town itself if you subtracted the two colleges there, and all the villages and towns along Route 28 were clearly rural. Most of the side roads off Route 28 below Franklin Mountain were named either something-Hill or something-Hollow.

I found Woodland Cemetery easily enough when I got to Delhi. It was halfway down the hill, before the bend where Route 28 meets Route 10 to form the downtown business district and the seat of county government. The post office in the center of town was closed, so I did not get to see the original version of Mary Earley's mural, although I did catch a glimpse of it through the window. Osman Steele's grave was also easy to find, all the way up the hill at the center of the cemetery, commanding a spectacular view of the surrounding mountains. It was indeed an obelisk. It was about twelve feet tall, made of marble and topped with a blunt pyramid. Between the base and the column was a simple pediment. Inscribed on the east side of the base, to meet the rising sun, were these words:

> OSMAN STEELE
> BORN AT WALTON AUGUST 16, 1809
> WAS MURDERED AT ANDES
> WHILE IN DISCHARGE OF HIS DUTY
> AS UNDER SHERIFF AUGUST 7, 1845
> BY AN ORGANIZED BAND OF MEN
> DISGUISED AS INDIANS
> TO RESIST THE LAWS.
>
> THIS MONUMENT
> IS ERECTED AS A TESTIMONIAL
> OF HIS FAITHFULNESS AND BRAVERY AS
> AN OFFICER,
> AND HIS WORTH AS A CITIZEN.

It was yet another beautiful day, sunny and warm with a blue sky and a refreshing breeze coming from the west. I spent almost an hour at Osman Steele's graveside. I photographed the obelisk from several different angles and distances. I looked at the inscription, read it aloud and copied the words into a notebook. I contemplated the words' meaning, both to the officials who wrote them and to the farmers who suffered under the system that Steele died for.

"An organized band of men disguised as Indians," the inscription read. "Indians," I thought, as I had during my conversation with Professor McNally and again with the others on Louie's back deck. But no, I wanted to tell the worthies who had commissioned and built the obelisk, calling them "Indians" was an error of historical interpretation. I still couldn't say exactly why I knew this to be true, but I knew it, and could feel this particular truth digging it's claws deeper and deeper into my mind.

The obelisk's marble was cold to the touch. The words engraved on it seemed just as cold, failing to catch the spirit of the man they purported to describe. They were official words, establishment words. They were also defensive words, written in the midst of crisis, words that might have given the powers-that-be in Delhi and in Albany a confidence boost for the authority they wielded and the system they tried to sustain. But the words said nothing about the relationships Osman Steele had with the people he was charged to protect. Who were those people? What did they hope to achieve? What was the source of their anger that led them to murder a man so faithful, brave and worthy?

I gazed out at the surrounding mountains, taking note of how they formed natural barriers between one valley and the next. I was used to living on rivers, the Mohawk and Saint Lawrence, where the bonds between communities were strengthened by river and highway access and where authority was more easily asserted over a wide geographical area. How different it must be here, especially in winter, to be isolated from neighboring villages and to have life concentrated in a valley hemmed in by mountains. It was surely not quite as different in our age of paved roads, snowplows and all-wheel drive SUV's, but still, the visual barrier must also produce a psychological barrier between one community and the next.

The landscape made me feel a bit claustrophobic, but I could also see how the same hills and valleys could bring comfort to those of a different persuasion. Thinking back to how life must have been in the 1840's, I considered how people could gather in these valleys away from the eyes and ears of authority to commiserate and devise plots against those who oppressed them. As I listened to the breeze, I could almost hear echoes of men and women agreeing to oppose Osman Steele and defend all that they and their fellow Anti-Renters held dear. Lodi's words about how people came from all surrounding communities on that August

1845 day impressed me even more now that I understood something of the geographical context.

Chapter Twenty One

MY MUSINGS ON ISOLATION were confirmed when I got to Andes, also on Route 28 about twelve miles southeast of Delhi, twelve miles deeper into the Catskills. Andes, like many other isolated villages in rural Upstate New York, showed clear evidence of the old ways' persistence. There were several buildings in town that dated from the early 1800's, among them the Hunting Tavern, where, on August 7, 1845, Osman Steele drank his final cup of brandy before heading to the fatal showdown at Moses Earle's farm. The tavern was now the home of the Andes Society of History and Culture. I stopped in for a look, but the museum and gift shop didn't open until the following week. So I spent a few minutes walking up and down Main Street, past several small hotels and B & B's, about a dozen small stores and art galleries that peddled homemade products to downstate tourists, and a few good looking restaurants that advertised local ingredients and farm-to-table food. I browsed for a while in the local bookstore, leafing through some of the same books on the Anti-Rent War that I had consulted in my earlier research.

Looking for specific directions and feeling hungry, I went into the general store and ordered a slice of pizza with pepperoni and mushrooms.

"We've got pepperoni right here," the cashier said, pointing to three slices on a tray underneath a heat lamp. "Let me take one out back and see if I can dig up some mushrooms for you. Well, not *actually* dig them up. Or pick them. They're prolly in the fridge. Be right back!"

She brought me back a slice, for which I thanked her with a smile. The pizza was excellent with its crispy crust, well-done pepperoni and earthy mushrooms. When I returned my plate to the counter I asked the cashier if she knew where the old Moses Earle farm was.

"Huh," she said, snapping her gum, "I'm sure I've heard of it somewhere. Wait." She turned back towards the kitchen. "Lodi?" she yelled. "Hey, Lodi? You know where the old Earle farm is, don't you? The guy who ordered pizza wants to know. Isn't it in one of those songs of yours?"

"Hey!" the cashier exclaimed as I ran behind the counter and into the kitchen. "You ever hear of OSHA?"

And there he was, wearing a hairnet, spinning dough, singing a Van Halen song. The dough seemed to float just off the tips of his long, manicured fingernails. That, or the sound of him singing a song about dreams, sent a chill down my back.

"Lodi," I said.

"Tom Flanagan!" he answered. "Well, well, well. You don't waste time, do you?" He glanced my way but did not drop the dough.

"I never knew you made pizza," I said.

He laughed. "I make soup and several varieties of bread as well. Food for the soul, I like to say. It's my uncle's place. I've worked here on and off since I was about twelve. Still work here, whenever I need some cash." He spread the dough onto a baking sheet. "Your bride-to-be with you?" he asked.

"No. She's got graduate school commencement today."

"Giving out credentials for piling it higher and deeper, eh?"

"Mine's on my office wall," I said. "Real parchment."

"Nice. Will I ever get to meet her? I'm starting to wonder if she's a phantom."

"One of these days, I'm sure," I said. "Is there somewhere private we can talk?" I was ready to tell him everything, from my brother's disappearance and my parent's death to my introduction to the undines to recent events concerning the writing on our wall and Martha Radisson's note card. I felt an irresistible urge to blurt it all out right then and there. But I held my tongue because of the cashier and her customers. I hoped Lodi could get off work soon, before my patience cracked.

"Once this pie's done, I'm done," he said. "It'll take about twenty minutes. Have you been up to Moses Earle's place yet?"

"Not yet. I came here from Delhi."

"You saw the obelisk. Good. What did you think?"

"The powers-that-be gave him quite an honor. Not much life to it, though."

"That's right. Not much life at all. Just cold, dead stone. You'll get a somewhat different impression when you head over to Moses Earle's farm, I promise you that. From what Emma said, I'm guessing you don't know where it is."

"Emma?"

"My co-worker and cousin. Her dad owns the place."

"Oh. I Googled directions before I left home, but the lay of the land is somewhat confusing around here."

He gave me the directions and told me to look for the blue New York State history sign. "You really can't miss it," he assured me.

"Good."

"I hope you've got time."

"I've got all the time I need. Like I said, Mindy's busy with graduation all day today and tomorrow."

"Excellent. Go on up there. Take some time to walk around. Then come back here, and I'll listen to anything you've got to say."

"We'll talk about earth and air?" I asked.

"We'll talk about whatever you want," Lodi assured me.

"Thanks," I said, and hurried out to find Moses Earle's farm.

Chapter Twenty Two

THE BLUE STATE DEPARTMENT OF EDUCATION SIGN at the corner of Tremperskill and Dingle Hill Roads marked one mile to the "scene of tragedy" where the shooting took place and thus, like Osman Steele's obelisk, marked the establishment's interpretation of the event as an assault on law and order. I parked just past the sign and walked up the hill, enjoying the tart freshness of the air and the intricately woven songs of the birds. Once I got to the actual site, I was pleasantly surprised to see that it was shrine-like in layout and in the care taken by local historians to maintain it.

There was a brass plaque bolted to a large bolder. It said, in beautiful copperplate engraving, that "Undersherrif Osman Steele was fatally shot by Anti-Renters disguised as calico Indians while conducting a tax sale, August 7, 1845." "This event," the sign said, "prompted the end of the feudal land system in New York State."

There was also a large interpretive history display erected on a gravel porch. The sign was covered with a protective roof and surrounded by day lilies. The display featured several reproductions of paintings of the Anti-Rent Wars, including one of the shooting itself. Osman Steele and his entourage were easy to spot. The lawmen were at the center of the painting, on their horses and with rifles aimed into the crowd. About a dozen costumed Anti-Renters surrounded them and another dozen or so lingered in the background behind stone or split-rail fences. The Anti-Renters were engaged in a variety of activities which included arguing with the undersherrif's men, loading their rifles, aiming their rifles at the lawmen and fleeing from the developing chaos. The painting wasn't as dramatic as Mary Earley's mural, but it still captured the oddness of the Anti-Renters' costumes and the immediacy of their protests.

The text of the display expanded the story to tell about the original ownership and settlement of the land and about the escalation of tensions that exploded on August 7. What the display lacked in objectivity it made up for in vividness. According to the local historians, the poor immigrant farmers of Delaware County were lured into settling there through the deceptive advertising of unscrupulous landlords. Osman Steele was "a short, red-haired, hot-tempered man who ... had angered many by his unfair and brutal treatment of the farmers and those who opposed the tyrannical rent collection." The tenants' resistance was an act of justice. They wore the calico gowns and sheepskin masks to protect themselves through anonymity, not as a political statement or, as Professor McNally thought, due to a lack of courage.

The local historians offered the India theory as the reason for the moniker "Indians," but preferred to call the protesters "Calicos" instead. The essay said that several hundred protesters gathered right at this spot to resist Steele's plan of using Earle as a scapegoat for all recalcitrant tenants, even though Earle owed only $60 of back rent on a small portion of his land and was quite willing to pay it. Blame for the "mass chaos" that culminated in the shooting was placed squarely on Osman Steele's shoulders. The essay cited the undersheriff's "Lead cannot penetrate Steele" comment as evidence of his arrogance and disrespect for the people.

I shifted my attention to my surroundings. To the right of the display was a woodland dominated by maple, ash and pine. To its left, just past the boulder with the plaque and next to a large oak tree, was a fieldstone fireplace and chimney, all that remained of the original farmstead. As the interpretive essay explained and the fieldstone ruins confirmed, Moses Earle's house was located directly behind the display on a knoll. Beyond that was a field overgrown with brush.

I was taking pictures of the interpretive essay signs and the land beyond it when I heard a sound coming from the other side of the hill to my left, some distance beyond the fieldstone fireplace. At first I thought it was the call of a loon muffled by a thick fog on the Saint Lawrence. I must be looking forward to heading north, I thought, to be hearing river sounds in a completely different part of the state. Then I heard it again, louder and closer. After a third time I identified the sound as the blaring of a tin horn, the simple instrument used to call farmers in the field to dinner and, right here, used more famously in the middle of the nineteenth century to call calico-clad Anti-Renters to war. I put my camera away and climbed in the horn-call's direction.

I was sliding between two shrubs when I saw a large buck standing on a rise in the general direction of the tin horn blast. He was motionless. His large black eyes looked straight at me. There was something in those eyes that commanded my attention, something that beckoned me towards the beast. He tapped his front hoof on the ground and rolled his head to his left. When he bolted in the same direction, I couldn't help but follow.

What I saw when I reached the top of the hill was not a deer, but a figure running downhill towards a dip in the field. He was tall and broad-shouldered, but that's all I knew for sure because the rest of his body was hidden by an orange, purple and tan gown that covered his shoulders and stopped at his ankles. Calico, I thought, smiling and breathing harder with heightened expectation. His head was disguised by a green mask with a huge set of antlers protruding from it. I counted five or six points on each side. I couldn't be sure, but the antlers seemed to be the same shape, size and pattern as those on the deer that had disappeared after beckoning me to the top of the rise.

"Hey!" I shouted. "What's going on? Who's there?" I slowed my breath, trying to calm down. Reason told me that the buck I had seen had run away through the tall grass in another direction. My intuition offered a different, more disturbing explanation. "Lodi? You finish that pizza early? Lodi?"

I moved three steps down the hill and stopped. I recalled Martha Radisson's story about watching the interpretive dramatization of Osman Steele's murder in which my brother had worn a calico gown colored tan, purple and orange and a mask with a pair of massive antlers attached, antlers so large that Martha had expected them to fall off at any moment.

"Patrick?" I whispered.

The figure also stopped, then turned to face me. He rolled his head to the left, just as the buck had done, and continued to move in that direction. He ascended an adjacent hill, a bit higher than the one I was on. I initially thought the figure ran, but when I looked directly at him I saw that floating was a more accurate description of his motion—it was unmistakeable that his legs below the hem of the calico gown did not move.

I scrambled down and climbed up again in the direction he was moving. I hurried my pace, but each time I approached the cloaked and masked figure it remained just over the next rise, just out of reach. I continued my pursuit. Both time and space seemed to have lost their concrete reality.

I stopped when I got to a particularly deep hollow in the field because something in the air felt different there. Bent over, hands on my knees, I breathed heavily and started to notice some odd changes happening to my body. It began with my hearing. The breeze around me sounded deeper and fresher, more pure. The air was filled with birds, all of them singing. I listened carefully and heard each bird's song individually, as if each melody were being fed to me through a different channel of a very complex sound system. To my left, hidden by another dip and rise in the land, I heard a cacophony of voices coming from a frog-filled pond.

My sense of sight had also been heightened. The grass at my feet and the leaves above me looked greener and sharper. I looked beyond the trees and saw into and through the clouds that moved across the sky. The clouds became alive in my vision, growing taller and wider and shrinking back into themselves as if they were breathing the very air through which they moved. Like a child, I fell to the ground and rested on my back to get a better view of the living panorama above.

The clouds changed shape rapidly, and I recognized figures in those shapes. I saw arrowheads, maple leaves, cones, battleships, spheres, cat heads, wheelbarrows and the letter Q. Several of the clouds seemed to move against the direction of the wind. Other clouds seemed to bounce across an invisible floor in the sky. Each cloud seemed three dimensional to my eyes. Some were outlined by a thin golden border.

And when I shifted my attention from the clouds to the sky below them, I saw that the atmosphere was a thousand shades of blue, each one as thin as a knife's edge. I quickly realized that the effect was being caused by the diffusion of at least a thousand spears of sunlight. Ignoring my mother's instructions to never do such a thing, I followed the spears back to their source and looked right into the heart of the sun.

My eyesight seemed enhanced by the sun rather than blinded by its light. I saw fluxations of yellow, orange and red. I saw what I can only describe as the prime material of life—pure energy—falling onto the Earth like rain falling from a cloud. Sensations of both warmth and coolness flowed from my eyes into my brain and through the rest of my body. When I finally looked away I saw every object around me as if each thing was illuminated by its own inner light. The sun was everywhere, and everything was wrapped in its life-giving power. At that moment, the world seemed more beautiful to me than it ever had before.

It was then that I noticed my sense of smell had sharpened as well. The first scent I noticed was the primroses. They were still a few days away from full bloom in Clinton Falls, but here they were magnificent, the sweetness of their perfume filling the air and dancing on the breeze. Beneath the roses I also detected patches of mint and thyme interlaced with the grass.

I smelled the soil of the earth. There was a warm dampness to that smell, a mustiness and an oldness so deep that it seemed like a millennium's worth of decayed plant and animal matter was being lifted through virgin sod by the blade of a farmer's plow. I had seen life in the sky above—now I smelled life in the earth below. With each breath I distinguished a new aroma underneath that of the soil. I smelled and identified all the vegetables, fruits, nuts and legumes that grew from the land and fed the creatures that roamed upon it.

Out of this fecundity came one particular fragrance that brought me to a state of panic. At first it smelled like the primroses, only sweeter. Then it became citrusy, lemony. It was verbena, the same scent that Mindy had identified on our front porch the morning after she had been knocked out, the morning after someone, or something, had written the word "ARIEL" on our living room wall. Unlike that day, however, the redolence was much more than a whiff. It was in every breath, and my whole being was overwhelmed by it.

I tried to sit up but was unable to move my arms or legs, which seemed pressed to the ground by some unseen force. At the same time, I felt the ground press up against me from underneath. The ground moved, not shaking so much as undulating, as if the land had lost its solidity and had become a body of water, a land-lake into which I slowly, yet without the least bit of impediment, began to sink.

Chapter Twenty Three

I SINK INTO DARKNESS. I phase through grass and topsoil, red clay and rock. At the very moment I think my body can handle no more pain, I land on a flat sheet of bedrock that feels cold and damp against my skin. The darkness is so deep that I cannot even see my own body, much less anything else around me. The contrast between this darkness and the bright light of a moment before stuns me.

From somewhere in the darkness a hand grasps mine and lifts me up. When we touch, a soft light illuminates the space. As my eyes adjust I see that I'm in a cave about ten feet wide and fifteen feet high. I look at the hand that's holding mine. I reach out and touch it with my other hand and trace the arm up the shoulder and neck. It's the woman from my dream, the one who changed the river from a wasteland to a place rich in life and beauty. The light that fills the cave comes from her, I see, shining from her face and from her hair like the glow of the moon on snow. She's even more beautiful in the cave than she was in the sun. Holding her, I can feel the pain melt away from my arm and then from my whole body. I'm awash in warmth.

She holds me as I steady myself, then guides me forward into a long tunnel. There's a light at the end of the tunnel, but it's a diffuse, muted light that shimmers and undulates. As we near the cave's exit I see that it's underwater.

I turn towards my guide to ask what to do, but she is gone. I look back, squinting into the tunnel, and see her figure in silhouette, a retreating shadow indistinct in the enveloping darkness. I hear a door close behind me and I know there is no other way for me to go but forward.

I walk to the edge of the cave, inhale deeply, hold my breath and jump into the water. When I reach the surface I know exactly where I am: in the Saint Lawrence River just offshore from Heron's Nest. When I look around and see my father's Lyman coming towards me I also know exactly when I am: September 4, 1996, the day my parents die.

I also see that I'm wearing my tuxedo. Whatever happened to me at Moses Earle's farm in Andes, I'm quite certain that I'm now in a dream.

At first, events play out more or less as they had been described to me five years before by Martin Comstock, my father's friend and a witness to the crash. I see my father's antique Lyman burst into flame and, a second later, clip the edge of a dock, sending my mother into the river. From my vantage point at the water's surface I see my father thrown off the wooden boat by the explosion, which I know happened because of a sabotaged fuel line and not because of the collision with the dock. As my father struggles to stay afloat, he says the words "drunk speedboater," the code he and the other River Rat Reporters had invented to indicate that Napoleon's gold, the life-giving treasure of the river itself, was in danger. I hear my father instruct his friends to tell me nothing about the gold until I return to the river and voluntarily seek out its true nature and meaning, instructions that his friends would dutifully follow for five long years. Turning to my right, I watch my mother's strength falter as she inhales her final breath and sinks into the water she loved.

I'm completely immobilized in my dream. I can do nothing but observe as Billy Masterson—real-life Billy, not his ghost—courageously shoots past me and pushes my mother to the surface, albeit too late to save her. I can do nothing to assuage my father's shock as he watches his wife die.

"Leave Patrick be!" I hear my father shout to Billy as he dives back under to search for my missing brother, and say again to Martin Comstock, "leave him be!"

As I'm looking up helplessly at the rippling image of Billy Masterson lifting my dead mother onto Martin Comstock's boat and of Martin comforting my father, who's dying from the burns and wounds suffered during the wooden boat's explosion, I notice another figure trying to tread water just a few feet from the burning Lyman. Who is it? I can account for my mom and dad, and for Billy Masterson and Martin Comstock. Thinking it must be Patrick, I begin to swim in the figure's direction.

But then I feel something grab my arm from behind and pull me deeper into the water. I turn, open my eyes and, even in my dream, am shocked to see my brother behind me rather than in front of me.

"Get out of here," he says telepathically, the words shouting in my brain. "Dad's telling *you*, big brother, not them. Listen to what he says for once and LEAVE ME BE!"

"No!" I shout back, feeling an irrepressible need to find out who the person is near my family's wooden boat.

"Don't go that way!" Patrick responds.

I reach out to him and grab his shoulders. He pushes me away, his arms and hands strong against my chest. My fingers slip from his shoulders and slide down his arm. I panic and tighten my grip. He continues to push; I continue to hold on. Anger mixes with fear and I grab hold even tighter, just above his elbows.

But it's not Patrick's arms around which my hands are tightening.

Mindy's screams awaken me, and in an instant of shock and fear I release my grip from her arms and fall to the floor of our Clinton Falls bedroom, sobbing.

Chapter Twenty Four

MINDY DROVE US NORTH about an hour after I woke her up. She gripped the steering wheel with white knuckles, and her lips were pressed together just as tight. My fingers had left marks on her arms just above the elbow, marks which changed from red to a bright purple during the course of our drive. I sat in the passenger seat, sometimes sobbing uncontrollably, sometimes gasping for air. I moved in and out of consciousness, not sure if I was under the water or on dry land, above ground or below it. Later, at sunrise, as we approached the bridge to Wellesley Island, I realized that I had no idea how I had gotten home. I remembered the dream, but I recalled nothing else that had happened between the time I saw the deer transform into the calico-clad Anti-Renter and the time I awoke with my fingers around Mindy's arms. I didn't dare mention the lost time to Mindy. Not only did she have to contend with me being an emotional wreck, she was also missing undergraduate commencement, the most significant event of the year for university faculty, especially for a department chair. Her demeanor made it obvious that she needed to be left alone.

We spent the day preparing Heron's Nest for summer use. The work included turning on the electricity and priming the water pump, removing cobwebs from ceilings, washing windows, wiping down walls with a light solution of Murphy's oil soap, mopping floors with the same, rolling out carpets, making beds and checking the wood stove and chimney for dead critters. To me, the work felt like ritual, the same rites of seasonal initiation that my grandparents and parents had performed for decades before Mindy and I did.

But we worked separately, and we barely talked except to ask for the mop or for help holding up a window as one of us washed it. I felt nauseous and had a hard time concentrating. Try as I might, I could not stop replaying the previous night's dream. Just as bad was my complete lack of memory of what happened before that, from the time I saw the deer-man to the time I woke up from the nightmare. I could come up with no explanation for my amnesia. Nor had I mentioned it to Mindy. I simply performed the family rituals, hoping that doing so would cleanse my soul of whatever it was that had poisoned it.

Once the housework was done, I lit charcoal in my family's old Weber, and we shared dinner at the picnic table near the dock as the sun set in the west. Mindy had made a pitcher of iced tea to go along with our dinner of marinated steak tips, grilled flatbread and asparagus salad. The air was warm but getting cooler in the evening breeze. Small whitecaps topped the river like frosting, and the combination of wind, sun and trees made the shadows dance on the lawn. We said grace and ate our meal in an awkward silence.

"I'd better mow tomorrow," I eventually said.

Mindy waved her fork then pointed it at me. "I'll mow the lawn. You get your kayak out and do what you need to do."

I looked at her. "And what's that?" I said, unable to check the bitterness in my voice.

She motioned towards the river. "Get out there. Get back to where you need to be."

I hesitated before responding. "I'm not sure I can. Or want to."

"Why not?"

"I'm sorry," I said. "I just—"

"You don't have to be sorry about anything," Mindy angrily interrupted. "And you don't have to explain yourself."

I started to sob. It took me a moment to work up the courage to ask, "Mindy, are you going to leave me?"

She waited a moment, sighed, and came over to my side of the table and sat next to me. She put her hand on my back. Her breathing was heavy with frustration.

"I'm not going to leave you, Tom. I'm scared, really scared, and confused, but I'm not going to leave you."

"That's a relief," I said while attempting a smile.

"I know how hard it is for you," she said. I nodded and mouthed a thank you. "I also know how bad your dream was," she added.

You know because I hurt you, I thought. Embarrassed, sobbing again, I turned away and avoided her gaze.

"Listen to me, Tom. I know how bad it was."

"How?" I wiped tears from my cheek. "How can you know? You were sleeping until I … "

"I know how bad it was because I had the same dream," she admitted.

Now I turned to face her. "You what?"

"Your father's boat. Your mother's drowning. Patrick's instructions. I saw it all." She paused and nodded. "In my version," she slowly said, "I was about twenty feet behind you, also underwater—"

"You were *behind* me? Are you sure?"

"Yes. Why?"

"I saw someone else closer to the boat, dangerously close to the boat. You sure it wasn't you?"

"I was behind you. I tried to come to you. I tried to help you when Patrick pulled you down, but I couldn't move. I saw you reach out to him. I saw you grab him around his arms. Then you woke me up."

My heart beat faster and I could feel the tears coming harder. "Mindy, I didn't mean—"

She held up a hand. "No. Don't. In the dream you

reached out and grabbed him. In our bed, you reached out and grabbed me. That's what woke me up. That's how I knew I was having the same dream you were having. In my dream I saw you holding onto him. You had control in your dream. But what you did to me was reflex. You had no control." She poured herself more tea and took a piece of flatbread from my plate. She looked at the bread for a moment then returned it. "Something terrible happens in all your dreams, doesn't it?"

"Yes."

"After last night, I'm starting to suspect they might be more than anxiety dreams."

I took a deep breath. I felt my eyes drying. "I've suspected that for months," I said.

Mindy shook her head and offered a slight laugh. "Are shared dreams even possible?"

"I don't know. It seems like magic."

"Hmm." Mindy thought for a moment. "I vaguely recall Freud saying something about how dreams originate in the collective unconscious." Mindy paused. "Wait. It wasn't Freud, it was Jung. You ever read Jung?"

"I haven't."

"I remember it from a freshman survey course. The collective unconscious, Jung said, is something distinct from ourselves. It's almost like an actual place we visit in our dreams, a place with an objective reality of its own. What if your dreams come from there, from somewhere other than your overactive imagination? What if your dreams are, I don't know, more than just dreams?"

"I've told you about the after-effects," I said. "About wet feet and aching muscles. And now this. Now they're—now I'm hurting you." I paused and looked away again, not wanting to go any further with that particular line of thought, not wanting the tears to return.

"Why were you wearing your tuxedo?"

My gaze shot back to her. "What?"

"Do you have any idea why you were wearing your tuxedo in the dream? I mean, you … we were under water."

"I have no idea," I said, which wasn't quite a lie because there was nothing else in the dream to indicate that it happened on our wedding day. But I had something else on my mind as well. "Mindy, there's something I need to tell you."

"What?"

"I have … I can't … damn, I don't even know how to say it. I lost time last night."

Mindy tightened her lips and stared.

So I told her about matching the writing on our wall with the writing on Martha Radisson's postcard, information I had not shared in the text I sent her before I drove to Delaware County. I gave her a brief summary of my visit to Osman Steele's grave and to the monument on Moses Earle's farm.

"I can't account for several hours," I concluded, "from the time I saw the deer morph into a man to the time we woke up. I have no idea what happened during that time. The last thing I remember is feeling like I was slipping into another dream. At first, I even thought I was having the dream about the river while I was still in Andes."

"Were the deer and man part of another dream? Maybe that accounts for the lost time."

"It was real, Mindy, more real than anything I've ever experienced. The sights, the sounds, the smells. It was all so real."

"And the deer and the man?"

"They were as real as everything else."

"How long were you out of it?"

"I don't know. Five hours. Maybe six?"

"You drove home from Andes during that time?"

"I guess so."

"Then where's your truck?"

"What?"

"When you woke me up last night, the first thing I did

was pack our car with our boxes of summer clothes. Your truck wasn't there."

I went inside and returned to the picnic table with my set of keys, which had been in my pocket when Mindy drove us north. The truck key, stamped with the word "FORD," was right there, where it always was, between our house key and my office keys.

"Spare's in the kitchen drawer, as always. So where's my truck?" I asked as I jingled the keys.

"I asked you first," Mindy said.

I put the keys in my pocket. "Huh. I don't remember driving. I don't remember where I parked my truck. I don't remember anything. Were you up when I got home?"

"No. I was exhausted from all the graduation pomp and circumstance. I fell right asleep after eating some leftovers. I knew I'd better get plenty of rest for today's ... for what I was supposed to do today." She paused. "You weren't drinking, were you?"

I shook my head. "Not a drop all day."

"That's a relief," she said.

"Did the same thing happen to you when you were knocked out?" I asked. "Did you lose time?"

Mindy thought about that for a moment then shook her head. "No, it was different for me. I was at home on the floor the whole time. I wasn't traveling, definitely not driving. I was also knocked out, not a victim of lost time. And what happened to me didn't feel at all like a dream."

I paused and watched a tour boat pass by on the river. Sunset dinner cruise, I guessed. "I don't know what to do," I said a moment later. Saying the words made me feel more helpless than I had before.

"Me either." Mindy paused for several minutes. I respected her silence. Finally she said, "I don't think I like this Lodi character, Tom. I don't think I trust him."

"You haven't even met him," I said, which, I could tell right away, was not the appropriate response.

"I don't have to meet him to not like him," she insisted. "Or trust him."

"He's been helpful ... "

"Helpful? By refusing to tell you whether or not he knows your brother? By sending you up to that old farm?" She exhaled a breath of frustration. "What kind of mushrooms did he put on that pizza anyway?"

"What kind of mushrooms? You think he *drugged* me?"

"That would explain the hallucinations and the feeling of lost time," Mindy offered.

"That's absurd," I said.

"Is it? Think about what you saw, about what happened to you. Doesn't that sound like you were hallucinating?"

"And I suppose you think he drove me home."

"Why not. Happened to both of us more than once as undergraduates."

"Why would he do that?" I asked, yet unable to keep the seed of suspicion from growing.

"We can talk about that later," she said, not wanting to fight. "The immediate question is, are you going to do what your father told you to do? What Patrick told you to do? In your ... in our dream?"

"What, leave him be?"

"Yes. Him and the whole thing. Are you going to leave it all be, or are you going to ... I don't know ... are you going to keep prodding, repeat past behaviors and try to discover why your father would have told you to leave him be?"

"But we said ... "

"I know what we said! I'm the one who originally said we should make finding Patrick our number one priority! But that was before Martha Radisson. Before the word on our wall. Before Lodi. Before all this! Now I don't know. Now I just want it to go away. To be perfectly honest, I'm really, really scared."

I looked up to my father's crow's nest office, in which I hadn't changed a thing since I took ownership of the cottage ten years before. I'm scared too, I thought, but my father faced dangers much worse and never flinched.

I looked back at Mindy and tried to smile. "So what you're really saying is that I should go out and play on the water instead of doing something stupid after I give up on mowing the lawn because I can't restrain myself any longer."

"That's exactly what I'm saying," Mindy said, finally cracking a smile. "And tell me, what stupid things do you promise not to do?"

"Ransack my father's office looking for answers? Go back to Clinton Falls and do more research on Osman Steele?" I thought about it a little longer. "I especially promise not to drive back to Delaware County."

"Good," Mindy said. "Look, I just need some time to wind down. That's why we're here, isn't it? To get away from it all?"

I hoped she would hold me like she had that day in our kitchen, the day Martha Radisson let fall the first stone of this avalanche. Instead she got up, collected the dishes and pecked me on the forehead. She stood over me with the dishes in one hand and the other hand on her hip.

"One more thing," she said. "Your promise to not do anything stupid is a direct order from the woman who needs you mentally and emotionally competent when, in just over a month, you publicly agree to be her husband."

Chapter Twenty Five

SO THE NEXT MORNING, after breakfast, I prepared to do exactly what Mindy had ordered me to do. I had my PFD on and kayak in the water and was sliding the two-pieced paddle together when I saw a flat-bottomed fishing boat approach our dock from upriver. The driver of the boat wore blue jeans, a white tank top, sunglasses and a New York Yankees baseball hat. He'd lost a few pounds since I last saw him, which wasn't surprising since the last time I saw him was at New Year's during a visit Mindy and I made to Florida. My cousin's weight tended to fluctuate with the seasons.

"Tomás!" he said with an exaggerated accent on the second syllable. "Welcome back!"

"Good to see you, Andrew," I replied as I walked down the dock and motioned for him to throw me the rope.

"I can't stay," he said as his boat bobbed on its own wake. "I'm only delivering a message."

"You couldn't call? Text?"

"I'm supposed to ensure that you receive said message loud and clear. Face to face is the best way to ensure that."

I paused for a moment as Andrew removed his hat and ran his fingers through his hair, which was longer in back than I'd ever seen it before.

"You growing a mullet?" I asked.

He replaced his hat. "It'll be back in fashion before you know it. When it does, I'll be way ahead of the curve."

"Looks good on you. Looks summery." I laughed and

realized how much I missed him during the offseason. "What's your message?"

"You'll be home today, right? When you get back from your kayaking?"

"Yes."

"Where you going, anyway?"

"Thought I'd paddle through the Narrows and around Eel Bay," I said.

Andrew scanned the clear blue sky. "Nice day for it. But after that you'll be back?"

"Should be home in a couple hours."

"Good. We need to meet. All of us. Ostend says it's important."

We, I knew, were the River Rat Reporters, my father's friends who had helped me solve the mystery of Napoleon's gold back in 2001. Ostend was Raphael Ostend, the wealthiest man in the Thousand Islands and the owner of Valhalla, the most extravagant castle on the river.

"Meet where?" I asked. "At Jimmy's?" Jimmy's was a bar in Alexandria Bay, about eight miles downriver, where my father and his friends used to meet on Friday afternoons to discuss local happenings. The River Rat Reporters weren't as regular with their gatherings as they had been in the old days, but the round table near the door was still theirs, and Mindy and I enjoyed their company five or six times during the season.

Andrew shook his head. "Too many eyes and ears at Jimmy's."

"The Undees still around?" The Undesirables, to use their full nickname, were a group of locals, sharp of ear and loose of tongue, who had once mistrusted my father, still mistrusted his friends and took every opportunity to thwart their work through gossip, harassment and worse.

"They are. That's one reason Ostend wants us to come here."

"One reason? Why else?"

"Because you're here. Because you just got here. And, apparently, because what he wants to talk about has something to do with you and your side of the family."

I sensed an undercurrent of jealousy in Andrew's final comment. It didn't surprise me because I'd known for years that my cousin felt cheated by the fact that Heron's Nest was passed down the Hibbard family line through my mother to me rather than through his father to him. But my Uncle Jack Hibbard, and Andrew after him, had inherited our grandfather's construction business, which had made both Jack and Andrew wealthier than either of them would admit.

Andrew added, "Don't ask me what the topic of conversation is because Ostend wouldn't tell me. All I know is that he wants us to be here around noon for his council. He actually called it a council. What is this, I said back to him, Middle Earth?"

I laughed. "Not working today?" I asked.

"Do I ever not work?" Andrew shook his head and flashed a smile. He was fond of reminding me, explicitly or otherwise, that work was only real when done with the hands. Thus, in his perspective, I rarely worked. "I'm repairing a sea wall over on Grennell," he added before I could answer his question. "But I'll be back around noon with the others."

"OK," I said. "Hey Andrew, has Billy appeared in any more of your dreams lately?"

"No. Not since the one about the manatee. That was almost a year ago. Why?"

"Just wondering."

Andrew nodded. "I know it's short notice, but you got anything for lunch?"

"Hot dogs? Chips and pickles? I don't know, potato salad?"

"That'll do," Andrew said. He throttled the boat's motor

and backed away from the dock. "See you in a few," he shouted as he began to turn back the way he came.

Chapter Twenty Six

AFTER TELLING MINDY about the unexpected party that would commence in our backyard around noon, I got in my kayak and paddled southwest around the end of Wellesley Island and into the Narrows, a strip of deep water between Wellesley Island and Murray Isle. The cliffs rose high on the Wellesley side of the channel. I was sometimes in shadow, sometimes in sun as I slowly and deliberately made my way through that beautiful thoroughfare. It being a weekday morning in mid-May, there were few other boats, and no cruise boats, on the water.

As always, being on the river was a relaxing, even therapeutic, experience. I could feel the tension evaporate from from my shoulders and abdomen. My pulse slowed and my blood pressure dropped. As I filled my lungs with fresh river air I felt renewed, made whole again. Mindy was right. Being out in my kayak was exactly what I needed.

When I got through the Narrows and entered Eel Bay I decided to let 'er rip, as Andrew would say, and get up some speed. The water in Eel Bay was shallow, four to five feet in most places, two to three in some, so cutting across it at speed was not nearly as difficult as traversing the deep water of the channel on the other side of Wellesley Island. I paddled hard until my arms burned and my legs started to cramp. Then I stopped, pulled the paddle into my boat and laid back in my seat. I reached down and immersed my hands in the cool, clear water of the Saint Lawrence as my kayak continued to rush over it. My kayak came to a stop about halfway between the southern and northern shores of Wellesley Island, in the middle of the bay.

I was alone for the first time since my odd experience at the Moses Earle farm in Andes. I found it hard to believe it was only yesterday. As I lay there in my kayak, part of me wanted it to happen again—whatever "it" was—here in the Thousand Islands, where I had experienced so many significant moments of my life. But another part of me dreaded it happening again. I vividly recalled my dreams of the past six months and suspected that, given the right conditions, they might indeed come true. And I was growing increasingly unsure that I wanted to remember what happened in Andes after I saw the deer transform into a masked, calico-clad Anti-Renter. Then I recalled what Mindy had wondered the previous evening about the collective unconscious. I remembered the physical effects that the dreams had had on me and the ineluctable feeling that nothing in my experience had ever seemed so real. I knew there was no escape from my dreams, from this other reality that continued to creep into my life, whatever I might want or not want to happen.

Feeling equal parts expectant and scared, I slipped out of my kayak and into the cold water of Eel Bay. My feet sank into the sandy bottom of the bay, which was about two and a half feet below the water's surface. At the moment I didn't care about the possible presence of the creatures that gave the bay its name.

I cupped my hands and filled them with water. I gazed into it and saw the reflection of the sun and, through it, the lines of my palm.

"What do you want?" I said quietly. Then louder, "tell me what you want!"

But who, I asked silently, are you? I tilted my head back and looked up at the sky. I saw the clouds above me just as they were. The sky was filled with the blaze of the late spring sun. But it was only sky and the sun was only sun, unlike that day in Andes when, I began to recall, they had both assumed such an otherworldly appearance.

"Who are you?" I pleaded, asking the question more in terms of what had happened to me rather than what was happening—or, more accurately, not happening—now. "What do you want?" I paused. "Are you God? Some demon? Ariel? Ariel the angel? Are you my brother Patrick?"

I turned in circles. I stretched out my arms as I continued to look up at the sky, this time indeed blinded by the sun's brightness. I closed my eyes and lowered my head. Still circling, I lifted water from the river and poured it onto my hair. Twirling faster, I splashed my hands in the water of Eel Bay, then stomped my feet as well. After a while I felt like an impetuous child. I continued splashing and stomping for a few minutes until thoughts of cottagers potentially watching from the shore stopped me cold.

Remembering a bit more of what had happened to me the day before in Andes, it took me only a second to decide what to do next. I lowered myself into the water, first onto my knees and then, after taking a deep breath, further onto my back until I was completely submerged. I opened my eyes and the water stung them. I opened my mouth and the river rushed into my esophagus and windpipe. I sat up, coughing and gagging, and rubbed my eyes with my knuckles to better see how far away my kayak had drifted. So much for trying to force it, I thought.

Sick of asking questions, tired of trying to make something happen, I retrieved my kayak—it had drifted about ten feet—and got back in. Embarrassed at what people on shore might have seen, I quickly paddled back the way I came, back to Heron's Nest, back home to Mindy.

Chapter Twenty Seven

ANDREW WAS THE FIRST River Rat Reporter to arrive. Smiling, full of greetings for me and for Mindy, he got off his boat, walked up the dock and onto the lawn and tried to grab a hot dog from the grill. But Mindy slapped his hand with the tongs and Andrew, still smiling, opted for a handful of potato chips and a cold can of pop instead.

Mike Slattery came next. Slattery was Alexandria Bay's mayor for an unprecedented seventh term, and he was up for reelection—one last time, he insisted—in the fall. He was short and stout, and even though his grey hair had thinned these past few years, he still wore it tied back in a ponytail. He was a kind, cautious man who had been very close to my parents, especially my mother, and loved the river as much as she had. Mike Slattery was the self-appointed voice of reason among the River Rat Reporters, always skeptical and never quick to jump to conclusions.

Then came the two Canadian members of the group, Jim Pembroke, a tour boat captain and former river pilot, and Raphael Ostend, our convener, whose family fortune was earned in the hat-making business. They arrived together aboard the Ostend family yacht, the *Archangel*, one of the most impressive wooden boats from the river's glory days, now a hundred years past. But the *Archangel* was no antique —over the years Ostend had retrofitted it with a high-performance diesel engine, titanium frame supports, and secret compartments throughout. Ostend had loaned the yacht to Clayton's Antique Boat Museum after it had played an essential role in the Napoleon's gold saga, but he still took it out onto the river, and almost always invited Jim Pembroke to pilot it. Both men were well-dressed, Pembroke in Bermuda shorts, a white buttoned-down shirt and tie, Ostend in slacks and a linen shirt. Pembroke was an inch or so taller than Ostend but Ostend was in better shape and carried himself with an almost-regal posture.

Last to arrive was Martin Comstock. A bartender at Castello's, a fine Alexandria Bay restaurant, he was the man my father had once called the secretary, treasurer and historian of the group. Comstock was the first River Rat Reporter I met when I returned to the Thousand Islands in September 2001. He was also the one who told me the story of how my parents died on the river five years before that.

I was washing dishes and looking out the kitchen window when Comstock pulled into our driveway in the Oldsmobile Cutlass Supreme he had inherited from his mother and drove only in the summer. I was once again replaying the dream of my parents' death when my attention was diverted by Comstock's arrival, and by the two passengers who disembarked from his car.

The passenger in the back seat got out on his own and closed the door with a thud. He was short and thin with a thick mop of almost-white hair. He wore leather sandals on his feet and a long-sleeve purple shirt under denim overalls. The moment I saw him I had a vague feeling that I already knew him, but it wasn't until he reached up and placed a tinted pince-nez on his face that I identified him as a former graduate student classmate in the history department of the State University of New York at Clinton Falls.

"Ray Dale?" I asked out loud. "What the hell are you doing here?"

I was surprised that one of the men in Comstock's car was a former classmate that I hadn't seen in almost a decade. I was downright shocked when I recognized the second passenger, riding shotgun, who needed Comstock's help to get out of the car and needed both men's help to keep himself steady as he slowly walked towards our picnic table on the river's shore.

I was out of the house long before he got there. My heart raced and my breathing quickened as I bound down the stairs of the porch and marched towards him.

"Whoa, Tom!" Martin Comstock warned, holding out one hand, palm up, while supporting the frail old man with the other.

"How dare you show up here!" I shouted. "How dare you come to my family's home, now, after everything you did!"

I was just a couple feet away from the man and just a second away from striking him when someone grabbed my right arm, my punching arm, from behind. At the same time, the retired Roman Catholic Bishop of the Northern New York Diocese seemed to bob and swerve his head to avoid the punch he saw coming. I was so surprised at his quick reaction that I lowered my arm to my side. But Andrew didn't let go.

"Told you it could have been worse," Ray Dale said, calmly removing the pince-nez from his nose before smoothing back his white hair.

"Told you I'd be ready," my cousin Andrew said from behind me as he tightened his grip on my arm.

"I come on an errand of mercy," the bishop squeaked as he struggled to catch his breath.

"Let me go," I said to Andrew. I yanked my arm hard, but Andrew held on. "I'm not going to hurt a guy who can barely stand. Or speak."

"You were about to," my cousin said.

"Let me go," I said again. "Please?" After Andrew did so, I turned around to face him. I intended to tell him off, but kept quiet when I looked past my cousin and saw the surprise and confusion on Mindy's face as she came towards us from the grill.

"And why are you here, Ray Dale?" she asked. "My God, we haven't seen you in years!"

"It has been a long time, hasn't it?" Ray Dale said. He glanced at the bishop and wiped his glasses on a handkerchief he carried in his pocket. "I'm here for the same reason as the monsignor," he said. "Only mine would be, I don't know, an errand of enlightenment?"

Raphael Ostend stepped forward and gently held the bishop's arm. He led him to a sturdy chair at the end of the picnic table and spoke to me. "Tom, I thank you in advance for your restraint now that you are again in the bishop's company. If I can assure you of anything, it's that he is indeed sorry for what he put you through all those years ago when he betrayed your trust. I disagree with his reasons, of course, now as then, but I also understand how he might have believed that he had no other choice. Not all things were as clear then as they are now." Ostend bent down. "Are you comfortable, my friend? Would you like a pillow for your back? Something to drink? Water, perhaps?"

"Hmm? Water. Yes," the bishop said in a near whisper. "And a straw if you please?"

"Of course," Ostend said. "Water and a straw."

While Ostend was talking to me and helping the bishop, Mindy looked back and forth at Ray Dale and Andrew, connecting the dots. "You two talked," she finally said. "You two know each other?"

"We met a week ago at Jimmy's," Andrew said. He nodded in Ray Dale's direction. "This guy might not look like much, but he sure can handle his Cuervo."

"He can also bowl," Jim Pembroke added, referring to the shuffleboard bowling game that Pembroke excelled at more than anyone else on the river. "He almost beat me."

"I prefer cricket," Ray added, "usually without the tequila."

Jim Pembroke laughed. "Too bad about that. Laurie took the board down the day after your visit."

"What?"

"She had to when two idiot Undees started throwing darts at each other during an argument over a NASCAR race."

Raphael Ostend returned from the house and gave the bishop his glass of water, with a straw. "Lady and gentlemen," he said with a clap of his hands. "Might I suggest that those of you who want lunch get it now? Mike and I will gather enough chairs around the picnic table. Then we can sit down and talk."

Chapter Twenty Eight

YOU CAN'T CAP ANGER for long, no matter how you try. You can bury it deep. You can pave it over with rationalizations and forgetfulness, maybe even some degree of forgiveness. You can thus hide it for awhile, but it's never really gone. It eventually comes back, sometimes bursting forth like a geyser, sometimes seeping to the surface like a persistent spring under an asphalt road.

Such was my condition as the others sat around the picnic table and ate their lunch. I was back in the kitchen, looking out the window again, as I was when Ray Dale and the bishop arrived. I could feel that second type of anger welling up inside me—deep, poisonous anger to go along with the geyser of spontaneous anger that, a few minutes before, had led me to almost punch the bishop in the face. I tried to steady myself through controlled breathing. I tried to pray. My hand was still shaking, but not so much, when Andrew entered the room.

"He lied to me," I said. "He presided over the funeral knowing all along that my brother wasn't dead. After that he deceived me and double-crossed me to help Maitland control Napoleon's gold. Tell me how I'm supposed to feel."

"Angry," Andrew said.

I turned around to face him.

"I feel it too," he continued, "although probably not as strongly as you do.

I know what he did, cuz. He screwed over our family. Lied to all of us. Hell, I'd want to punch him too."

"Then why'd you stop me?"

"It was my job to make sure you didn't do anything you'd regret. If I were in your shoes and you were in mine, we both would've done the same exact thing."

"I wouldn't regret it a bit if I knocked several of his teeth out."

"What good would that have done? Make you feel better? Doubt it. Give you revenge? Maybe, but what's revenge besides rationalized anger? Hell, a punch from you in the condition you were in might've killed the old coot. Then where would you be? Besides, the old coot doesn't have any teeth left."

I couldn't help but laugh. "I don't think it would've killed him," I said. "Did you see how he dodged? What the hell was that all about?"

"I don't know, but I hope I'm that spry in my old age."

We stood there in silence for a moment. As I turned around to finish washing the dishes I could feel other sources of anger following along the channel that had been cut by my rage towards the bishop.

"It's not just him," I admitted. "Martha Radisson's return reopened old wounds. I'm more frustrated than ever at not finding Patrick. And all the crap that's been happening to Mindy and me—" I stopped short, remembering that I hadn't yet told Andrew about the strange events happening to Mindy and me. "Never mind," I said as I sprayed the sink clean.

Andrew moved over next to me and leaned his back against the counter. "Mindy asked me for advice," he said.

"About what?"

"About whether you're ready for this."

"Ready for what?"

"Ready to marry her."

I sighed and threw the sponge into the sink. "What, she doesn't know the answer to that already?"

"She's worried. She's concerned about you. I admit I'm

not a relationship expert or anything, but it seems to me she's right. You can't bring the kind of baggage you have into a marriage."

"You told her that?"

"No. I listened to her concerns. I told her everything'll be OK. But I am telling you that."

"What exactly were her concerns?"

Andrew shook his head.

I picked up a towel to dry the dishes in the strainer, but then set it back down. "OK. What would you do?"

"I'll go one better and tell you what I do do. When I feel the anger rising I practice being mindful. If I'm working I practice mindful hammering or mindful measuring or mindful sawing. Sometimes I stop working and do some mindful walking or stop altogether and find somewhere to meditate."

"You meditate?"

"For a few years now. Ever since I saw … ever since I started feeling bad about Billy's death."

"What did you do, take a class or something?"

"I've read the Swami's teachings. Borrowed them from the library."

"Vivekananda?" I asked. Swami Vivekananda, the founder of the Hindu Ramakrishna Order, was one of the Thousand Islands' most famous visitors, having lived in Thousand Islands Park for two months in the summer of 1895.

"You don't believe me?" Andrew asked.

"You don't seem like the type is all."

"He lived here, right? If his teachings are good enough for the Islands, they're good enough for me. Besides, they work. Mindful breathing makes the anger dissipate. If it comes back again I just double down on the mindfulness."

"How often does this happen? How often do you get angry?"

"Once a week, maybe more. You can't control it. You

can't bury it, like you're trying to do. It'll find it's way out one way or another."

I gave a quiet laugh.

"What's so funny?"

"I was thinking the same thing when you found me."

He smiled. "You were? That's good. Awareness is a good start."

I folded the towel in half and hung it over the sink. "For me, hard work, physical work, has always helped."

Andrew went to the fridge and poured himself a glass of water. "The only thing is, you've already tried that, haven't you?"

"What do you mean?"

He waved an arm around the kitchen. "Haven't you already renovated this place? Haven't you painted every room in your bungalow?"

"Yes, but ... "

"But it hasn't helped much, has it?"

"I haven't been doing the work to help dissipate my anger. I've been doing it because it needed to get done."

"OK," Andrew said with raised arms. "Whatever you say."

"I'll try mindful breathing," I finally said.

"Anger out with the exhale, calmness in with the inhale."

"Can I ask you something else?"

"Go ahead."

"Why's the bishop here anyway? You seemed to know he was coming, and seemed to know what I'd do when I saw him. Why's he here? Why's Ray Dale here?"

"Guess it's time for you to find out," my cousin said.

Chapter Twenty Nine

"HERE HE COMES," Raphael Ostend said as Andrew and I walked across the deck and descended the stairs to the lawn. "Have a seat, Tom, and we'll provide you with as much of an explanation as we are able to give."

I silently joined Mindy on one of the picnic benches.

"We'll begin with Melinda," Ostend said, "who, I believe, is prepared to admit that she hasn't been completely honest with you these past few days."

My heart sank. "What do you mean?" I asked, turning to face her.

"I'm sorry," she said, sniffling. She rubbed the marks my fingers had left on her arms. "I, um, I called Raphael on our way up here, the night before last. I was scared … I told him I didn't understand what was happening to you and to us. I called him because I didn't know what else to do. The dreams … Raphael was the first person I thought of who could help us understand."

"You didn't tell me this?" I asked. I could feel the blood returning to my face, my temper rising with it. You can't cap anger for long.

"I'm telling you now," she said apologetically, almost as a question. "You were sleeping in the car."

"Was this … this council your idea too?" I looked around at the men who were my father's friends and now my friends, and at the other two men who were here for reasons I did not yet know. "What, is this supposed to be an intervention or something?"

Ostend walked around the table and stood right in front of us. He reached out and took Mindy's hand and mine, his face soft with sympathy. "Do not be angry with her, Tom. Melinda did what she had to do. She did what was right and she betrayed no confidences by calling me. In fact, I had been expecting to hear from one of you for some time before I received Melinda's call."

"You were?" I asked.

"I started making preparations for this council some time ago," Ostend said. "Our discussion today was inevitable, and no, it is not an intervention. All of us, especially those of us who live on the river, knew this discussion was going to happen sooner or later. The only uncertainty was the timing. When I heard what Melinda had to say, especially when I heard about the content of your dreams, I knew that the time was now."

"What's the content of *his* dreams?" Jim Pembroke asked. His emphasis on the pronoun caught my attention.

"We'll get to that," Raphael Ostend said. "For now, suffice it to say that Tom has been having particularly odd dreams about the river." He pursed his lips and nodded to Mike Slattery. "We need to hear Tom's story. We need to here it in full. But first, we have a preliminary story of our own to tell."

"We'll begin with what we know," Mike Slattery said, circling his gaze around the table before he settled it on Mindy. "We'll begin with what we know, and from there move on to the uncertainties."

"Fair enough," Mindy said. "Tell us what you know."

"What we know," Jim Pembroke said, "is that Tom's not the only one having dreams. We all are. They're not normal dreams, either. They seem more real than reality itself and they share a common theme. They're dreams of strange things happening on our river, odd occurrences among our islands. They're not only dreams, they're premonitions as well." He paused to motion to Slattery, Comstock, Ostend, my cousin and then to himself. "The five of us know the Thousand Islands from one end to the other better than anyone else alive, and we've never experienced anything quite like this."

"Back in the winter," Andrew said as he cracked open another can of pop, "I had a recurring dream about river levels. In the dream, I came up from Florida and found the river as low as it's ever been. Then, later in the dream, the water got as high as I've ever seen it. Soon after that it was back down to what's normal for this time of year. In my dream, it was going up and down like that all spring. It seemed almost tidal. I started having the dream right after Christmas, right after you and Mindy visited us in Florida. Odd thing is, I came up to the river in late March to get a jump on a few jobs and found the river levels extremely low. The next week they were extremely high. Guess what's next?" Andrew looked around the table and answered his own question. "That's right. They fell again a few days later, as if somebody pulled a drain plug or shut a sluice gate. The fluctuations have tapered off since then, but still."

"There are always fluctuations," Mindy said.

"True, and most of the time the fluctuations are the result of excessive runoff, heavy rainfall, severe drought or the authorities tinkering with their dams. Not this year, though. Snowpack was deep, but it melted slowly and steadily. Rainfall has been average. French Creek didn't flood at all this year. And when I asked a friend of mine in the Army Corps of Engineers what the hell was happening to the river levels, he admitted that he was as baffled as I am. He also made it very clear that his answer was off the record."

"Surprised he gave you an answer at all," I said.

"He owed me one."

"So what's causing the fluctuations?" Mindy asked. "The real ones, not your dream ones."

Andrew looked at Mike Slattery and smiled. "Even our

resident rationalist can't explain it," my cousin said. Mike Slattery shrugged in response. "All I know is that I dreamed it before it happened."

Mindy said, "OK, so the river levels are mysteriously fluctuating. What else?"

"Should we mention the birds next?" Jim Pembroke asked.

"What about the birds?" Mindy replied. "Have they been attacking people?"

"Not yet," Andrew said with a hint of a snicker that caused several of us to turn his way and Mindy to frown.

Martin Comstock wiped his face and breathed. "Well, I had a dream that I was over in Westminster Park, priming a water pump for a friend, when I saw a large flock of seagulls, forty or fifty of them, slam into a cliff on the north side of Fairyland Island, right across from Wellesley."

"Slam into it?" I asked.

"Yes," Comstock affirmed. "They slammed into the cliff and fell into the water, dead."

"Ouch," Andrew said.

"Yeah," Jim Pembroke agreed. "Ouch. Granted, seagulls aren't the brightest of birds, but still. I've got another one for you. In my dream I was ice fishing near Ivy Lea. I saw a flock of mixed birds, all different species, making a beeline for the bridge. Intrigued, I went back to shore and drove down to Darlingside. I saw the birds flying above the river, round and round, in perfect circles, making all kinds of noise. Then they got quiet." Jim Pembroke paused and looked around the table. "Then they took the plunge."

"Into the river?" Mindy asked.

"Right into the river."

"How many?" I asked.

"Over a hundred of them. Sparrows, swallows, cormorants, ospreys, gulls. All kinds of birds. They dove right in. Broke through the ice. It was the strangest thing I've ever seen—well, dreamed."

"Is there anything special about that part of the river?" I asked.

"It's where one of the largest sources of Napoleon's gold is," Pembroke said.

"That's right," I said, then added, "Isn't the gold supposed to help people? And wildlife?"

"That's what we always thought," Raphael Ostend said. "That's what Grandmother thought as well."

"And my parents," I said.

"Are these dreams about suicidal birds coming true?" Mindy asked, barely able to hide the tremble in her voice.

"Well, sort of," Martin Comstock answered. "Since early spring I've been seeing birds flying in formation. Not all the time. And not all of them are. The starlings are doing it, but they're strange birds to begin with. Cormorants are too which, for them, is odd behavior."

"You mean flying like geese? In a giant V?" Mindy made the letter with her hands.

"Not quite," Comstock said. "That's natural. Beautiful, but not anything out of the ordinary. They're flocking. Going this way and that. Zig-zagging. Flying in great loops or in spirals. Making all kinds of noise as well. They seem to be very agitated. Murmuration, it's called when starlings do it, but what I saw is beyond anything you'll find in an Audobon guide. Mike, you want to take over?"

"Last week I was fishing in the Lake of the Isles near the Wellesley shore," Mike Slattery said. "I saw three herons, flying together in circles. After a while a couple more joined them. The five birds kept flying in circles, perfect circles, for about fifteen minutes. Then they started looping down to the surface of the water and back up, still in perfect circles. It was very similar to what Jim saw in his dream. After flying in loops for about ten minutes they went their separate ways without diving once to catch a fish." Slattery paused then added, "I don't know how to explain it. Herons are usually solitary birds, except for when they nest, and constant hunters."

Mindy shook her head and smiled. "Just because they're flying in formation doesn't mean they're going to slam into a cliff or commit hari-kari into the river," she argued.

"But those herons came awfully close in those loops," Andrew said.

Ostend nodded. "All we know for sure is that Martin and Jim both had dreams that may be in the process of coming true."

"Whether the dreams come true or not, they definitely mean something," I said.

"They always do," Mike Slattery affirmed.

"I'll concede that much," Mindy said. "Does Naguib Malqari have any answers? Seems like he's the one to ask for a reliable interpretation."

Ray Dale abruptly stood up. "Naguib Malqari?" he asked, then looked around the table. "You guys *know* Naguib Malqari?"

Mindy looked at me to answer.

"He visits the river periodically to assess its spiritual health," I said. "Visited, I should say. Past tense. The last time we saw him was about five years ago. He hasn't been here since, as far as we know."

"As far as we know?" my cousin Andrew questioned. "Come on! He's definitely not been here. Do you think we could miss him with that ship of his?"

"Wait a minute. He brought the *Ouroboros* here?" Ray Dale asked, astonished. "You know what I'd give to see that ship? To meet him?"

"You may yet get your chance," Raphael Ostend assured him.

"Seriously?"

"You might seriously get your chance," Jim Pembroke continued, "because the next item on our dream inventory is the strangest one of all. If this dream comes true, and if

Malqari gets the messages we've been sending him, he's got no choice but to investigate."

"What's the next item on your dream list?" I asked.

"How should I put it?" Pembroke said, looking to Raphael Ostend for guidance.

"Just tell it straight," Andrew said. Pembroke replied with a shrug, as if to indicate that such things were impossible to just tell straight. "Never mind then," my cousin added. "I'll tell it." He paused anyway and drained the dregs from his pop can. "We dreamed we lost an island," he finally blurted.

"You dreamed what?" I asked, turning to him, wide-eyed.

"We dreamed we lost an island. All five of us dreamed it, in fact. If the pattern holds, if this dream comes true like the others, then sometime soon we'll be down to one thousand eight-hundred sixty-three."

"But your other dream didn't come true," I argued, just as much to support what Mindy had said a few moments before as for any other reason.

"The river rose and fell just like I dreamed it," Andrew said. "In that case, there's a direct correspondence between dream and reality."

"And the birds are starting to act strange," Martin Comstock added. "I have no doubt they'll soon do exactly what we saw them do in our dreams."

"Worse yet," Jim Pembroke said, "the tourists'll start coming next week. What do I tell them on the tour? Heads up for falling birds?"

"The upcoming tourist season does present a problem," Raphael Ostend said.

"Especially if what we dreamed about losing the island comes true," Andrew added.

"Wait a minute. What do you mean you dreamed you lost an island?" Mindy asked. "You thought it was an island but it turned out to be a shoal? It had two trees but one blew down in a storm?"

Andrew shook his head. "No. It's an island, all right. Griffin Island. It was about three acres in size, shaped like a rhombus and mostly wooded." Andrew laughed softly. "It's there now, but who knows for how long."

"So it's big enough and has trees enough not to be mistaken for a shoal," Mindy said.

"Yes. Mostly pine and some larch. And pretty high cliffs on two sides."

"What do you mean you lost it?" I asked. "What exactly happened in your dreams?"

"We lost it. One day it was there, the next day it was gone. In our dreams, there's nothing left of it, nothing there at all. In our dreams we got diver friends of ours to check it out. Nothing. Not a single stone. Not a single branch. Not a single speck of island dirt."

"You all dreamed about the same island?" I asked.

"Yes," Andrew said. "We all dreamed about losing Griffin Island."

"Was there ... um ... was there anyone living there?" I swallowed hard after I spoke the words. "In your dream?"

"That depends," Jim Pembroke said.

"Depends on what?" Mindy asked angrily. "How can that depend on something?"

"The answer to your question depends on which one of us you ask, Melinda," Raphael Ostend explained. "Right now the island is on the northeastern edge of the Ostend Group. It became part of the national park system when my family donated it to the Canadian government in 1957. In Jim's dream and Martin's dream there were four campers on Griffin Island in what looked to be summer. We don't know who they were—Jim said they seemed to have kayaked there and didn't sign the registration book like they should have—and we don't know where to find them. In my dream and Mike's dream no one was on the island when it disappeared.

So whether any life will be lost depends on which one of us you ask."

"What about your dream?" I asked, looking at my cousin.

"What about it?" he said evasively.

"Was anyone on the island in your dream? We know about the others' dreams. What about yours?" I waited for an answer. "Andrew? Hello?"

He mumbled something I couldn't understand.

"Just tell it straight, Andrew. Like you said before."

Nothing.

"Andrew," Mindy said with an edge.

"You two were there," he blurted. "You and Mindy were on Griffin Island when it disappeared, and both of you disappeared with it."

"Oh," I said. I looked around at the others, but no one would make eye contact. "Did I happen to be wearing a tux?"

"Yes."

"Why would you be wearing ... " Mindy started to ask. Then, perhaps remembering a previous dream I had described, she said, "Oh. It was our wedding day."

"Yes," Andrew answered. "I think it was your wedding day."

Mindy and I locked eyes and she began to cry again.

I defaulted to a rational approach. "How can an island disappear without a trace?" I asked. "Even if we accept that the other dreams came true or are coming true, there's no way this one could!"

"We don't know," Ostend answered. "But we're keeping Griffin Island under constant surveillance nevertheless. I have some of my best people there, just offshore on a houseboat equipped with all sorts of sophisticated equipment. If anything happens, we'll know about it right away. If the four campers show up, we'll get them off the island as soon as possible."

"And you two better stay as far away from Griffin Island as you can," Jim Pembroke said. "Stay away from it, at least until we hear back from Malqari."

"Or at least until after our wedding," Mindy added through sobs.

Andrew turned away.

"So," I said, and counted on my fingers. "We've got water level fluctuations. We've got strange bird behavior. And to top it all off we've got an island gone missing. I assume you saved the weirdest dream for last? I assume that's it?"

"Well, not exactly," Martin Comstock said.

"But the other phenomena are quite common," Raphael Ostend added. "They're strange, of course, but relatively common nonetheless." Ostend turned to his left, where Ray Dale was seated. "Professor Dale, perhaps it's time for you to join our conversation."

Mindy and I turned to face our former classmate. We glanced at each other and smiled, Mindy through her tears. Both of us were eager to hear what Ray had to say, eager to learn why he was here.

Chapter Thirty

RAY DALE STOOD and began to pace as if he were in a classroom full of students.

"By way of introduction," he began, "let me explain that I currently serve as the third director of the Institute for Applied Philosophical Research, which was founded fifty three years ago by Raphael's grandmother, Lady Ostend, and remains fully funded through her endowment to the University at Clinton Falls for that purpose and that purpose only."

"Wait a minute," I interrupted. "The Institute for Applied Philosophical Research actually exists?"

"It does," Ray said, "and, as I mentioned, I'm its current director."

"I've tried several times to discover where it is, what it does, anything about it, in fact. So far I've come up completely empty."

"We've learned how to cover our tracks," Ray said.

"To cover them quite effectively," Raphael Ostend added.

"Are you on campus?" Mindy asked. "You'd think we would've run into each other somewhere."

"Yes and no," Ray answered. "I have an office on campus, but it's in the sub-basement, underneath the audio visual department. It's only accessible via a tunnel from the basement of one of the four towers outside the academic quadrangle. Which tower, I'm not at liberty to say."

"So you're more like under campus," Mindy said.

"Yes. And my office is quite self-sufficient, which explains why we haven't run into each other on campus. Along with my office equipment I have a coffee maker, a refrigerator, a microwave, and a dedicated generator in case the power goes out. That, plus a radio and a futon, is all I need."

"Ray, if you don't mind me asking," I said, "why are you in the sub-basement? They run out of room above ground?"

"The Institute for Applied Philosophical Research is underground because it has a library," he said. "Lady Ostend's library, in fact, which contains many rare and priceless volumes that would be impossible to replace. These books and manuscripts were once shelved in the library at Valhalla, but Lady Ostend, as she approached the end of her life, wisely decided that she did not want the volumes on an island, especially on that particular island. So she offered the Clinton Falls State Teacher's College a generous donation in exchange for housing her library and provided the bequest to permanently fund the Institute. When the Clinton Falls State Teacher's College was enlarged to become a university, Governor Rockefeller himself suggested that the Institute and its library be housed in a specially constructed, hermetically sealed room surrounded by walls of steel-reinforced concrete."

"These manuscripts," I asked, "are they philosophical treatises?"

"They are," Raphael Ostend answered. "That is, they are philosophical in the broad, holistic meaning of the word that you and I discussed on the day I invited you and Melinda to your first Ostend Ball. Do you remember our conversation that day?"

"Of course," I said. "You explained how your grandmother defined philosophy as a discipline that included but was not limited to rational thinking. You spoke of how she understood philosophy as the love of wisdom, as the work of the soul. You spoke of how she appreciated the spiritual unseen elements of philosophy as much as she appreciated its material aspects."

"Indeed. I assume you also recall what you and Melinda learned at your first Ostend Ball?"

"How could we forget?" I looked at Mindy and we shared a smile. "You and the others taught us about Naguib Malqari, about Napoleon's gold, and about the existence of the undines and other elemental beings."

"Yes. Grandmother, Naguib Malqari, Professor Dale and many others like them, including your parents, appreciated and continue to appreciate the existence of the unseen, including the rarely-seen elementals. The investigation of the unseen—the work of the soul—forms the living core of this particular philosophical tradition, a tradition that is as old as human thought itself. Grandmother's library, now in the care of Professor Dale, is the greatest collection of books on the subject in North America."

"Thus the steel reinforced concrete," Andrew said.

Ray Dale smiled and nodded.

"Who can access it?" Mindy asked.

"Only a select few," Ray said, cleaning his pince-nez yet again. "Seven to be exact. Always and only seven. All others who wish to see one of Lady Ostend's manuscripts can do so only by written invitation from and accompanied by one of these seven."

"And I suppose the list is secret," I said.

"It is," Ostend affirmed. "But you know four of us already."

"Let me guess. You two, Naguib Malqari and … " I looked at Mindy. "Any guess who the fourth is?"

"Ben Fries?" she offered.

Ostend shook his head.

I faced my cousin. "Not you," I said.

"No way I can afford that library card," he said. Then he added, "none of us here are in the seven, so you might as well stop guessing."

"Then who?" I said. When Dale and Ostend exchanged a glance, I continued, "You're not going to tell us, are you."

"Not yet," Ostend said, "for reasons that you'll someday understand."

"Seems to me that a library with such limited access isn't very useful," Jim Pembroke said.

"The knowledge contained in these manuscripts is dangerous," Ostend answered. "The manuscripts themselves are dangerous."

"Apparently too dangerous for simple folk like us," Pembroke commented.

"What are these manuscripts?" Mindy asked. "How many do you have?"

"Oh, thousands of them," Ray said. "We have Hermetic manuscripts, alchemical treatises, gnostic scrolls, theosophical texts, sacred texts in Hebrew, Persian, Greek, Latin, Arabic, Sanskrit and Chinese, various translations of Egyptian magical texts and ancient Babylonian cuneiform tablets. We have Olympiodorus' complete commentary on Plato and Apuleius' *God of Socrates*. We have dozens of maps, including an authenticated copy of the Piri Re'is map. We have transcripts of interviews with some of the greatest Native American spirit persons. We have the complete annotated works of Jacob Boehme. We have ... "

"Aren't most of these manuscripts available on the internet?" I asked, thinking he would've gone on forever if given the chance.

"The texts themselves are," Ray answered, forgiving my interruption. "But as historians, surely you and Mindy both can appreciate the difference between reading a digital text on a computer screen and reading the original text, or an early translation of it, on paper, parchment or vellum. There's something deep and profound about holding the original book and turning the pages, something inherently spiritual about seeing the words written in ink by the hand of the author or by a copyist. Lady Ostend knew this. She knew that the original texts she collected imparted significant insights to the mind and soul that are unavailable in words alone."

"Grandmother called them 'living manuscripts'," Ostend added. "She loved them, literally cherished them. She also respected, and at times feared, their power." Ostend glanced at Jim Pembroke. "That is why access to them is restricted."

"OK," Mindy said, "so maybe you'll tell us why the library is in Clinton Falls and not at Queens or McGill or somewhere else in Canada?"

I snapped my fingers as the answer to Mindy's question came to me. "The hat factory," I said. "The Ostends have always had a connection with Clinton Falls through their downtown hat factory."

Ray Dale nodded. "And that's where the rest of the Institute for Applied Philosophical Research is housed," he said.

"I though the hat factory was abandoned?" I asked, surprised.

"It was, for the purpose of making hats," Raphael Ostend said. "After my father arranged to move the haberdashery itself to Puerto Rico, the Clinton Falls building was, as some like to say, repurposed. It became a factory of ideas, you might call it, where data are collected, classified and stored, and where knowledge of the most significant kind is drawn from the scientific and spiritual study of the raw data itself."

"What kind of data?" I asked. "Data like the things happening here? The strange things you dreamed about, the things we were just talking about?"

"In part," Ray Dale answered. "We have newspaper clippings on unexplained phenomena like river levels that mysteriously fluctuate, tides that turn at odd times, currents that suddenly reverse direction and streams that suddenly disappear or relocate. We have hundreds of files containing documented cases of red rains, black rains, gelatinous substances of a yellow nature that fall from the sky, organic material that falls from the sky, mud-rains, rock rains, ice rains. We have eyewitness reports of clouds that move against the wind, of strangely-colored clouds and clouds shaped like faces or giant arrows, of clouds that seem to bounce across an invisible floor thousands of feet in the air …"

I stopped him with a raised hand. Ray looked at me with a slight smile, as if he already knew what I was going to say. "I saw that," I said. I looked wide-eyed at Mindy and then at the others around the table. "I saw clouds move just like that the other day in Delaware County. I didn't completely remember it until now, but I saw clouds just like you described."

Ray nodded gently. "We'll get to your story in a few minutes," he said.

I quieted down and let Ray resume his description of the Institute's collection.

"Part of what the Institute is, then, is a storehouse for media and eyewitness accounts of what we call Fortean phenomena, named after the great pioneer in the field of collecting unusual data, Charles Fort. In addition to the written reports and testimonies, we have hundreds of samples. We have thunderstones found embedded in trees and stones found deep in the earth that were inscribed with characters belonging to no known language. We have pieces of quartz with nails in them, pieces of granite with polished lenses in the rocks' cores. We have crates and crates of frog, fish and bird skeletons that fell from the sky. We have a dozen white frogs preserved in formaldehyde. We have a lizard with transparent skin. We have perfectly sharpened axeheads that are almost three feet long and weigh nearly seventy pounds. We have tiny crosses and the cockroaches that were crucified on them with minuscule iron nails. We have three inch long coffins of exceptional workmanship, with brass hinges to match. We have photographs, albeit blurry ones—*always* blurry ones—of a winged shadow on the moon, or of flocks of thistledown-thin creatures flying across the sky, or of lights hovering just above the horizon or just off the wing of airplanes in flight. We have photographs from this very river of sailing ships moving upriver above the water. We have, in sum, evidence of just about every uncanny phenomenon known to mankind."

"Any alien corpses?" Andrew asked with a more than a hint of childlike anticipation in his voice.

"No," Ray Dale said emphatically and with a shake of his head. "We do not have any corpses of extraterrestrial beings, be they little green men, little grey men or tall pale beings with long blond hair. I'm sorry to disappoint."

"A guy can hope," Andrew said.

"So these Fortean phenomena," I said, "they've been happening here on the river? Or you've dreamed of them happening?"

"Not all of them, by any means," Raphael Ostend said. "But yes, we have witnessed several of these other strange occurrences. For example, last summer, on a perfectly clear night, I saw a streak of lightning and heard a great crack of thunder. The next morning, on an island adjacent to Valhalla, I found a thunderstone in the shape of a pyramid embedded in the ground. The grass around it was burned to a crisp."

"Last fall," Martin Comstock said, "myself and a number of islanders in the Summerland Group complained of a sticky yellow substance that fell from the sky during a week of autumn rain. It smelled like rotten meat and caused our skin to itch on contact."

"Some say it was refuse from an airplane," Mike Slattery offered.

"I'm quite sure it wasn't," Comstock said.

"Martin, who'd you complain to?" I asked.

"Various authorities. A team from the CDC came in their suits to collect it."

"That wasn't the CDC," Ray explained, "that was us."

"Oh," Comstock said.

"Did you dream about the yellow goop first?" I asked.

"No. It just fell."

"Hold on a sec," Mindy said. "I'm completely lost. How do these white frogs and thunderstones and clumps of yellow goop relate to Lady Ostend's world class library of esoterica?"

Raphael Ostend said, "The most significant point about the items in Grandmother's collection, about any Fortean phenomenon, isn't the items themselves. A fairy cross, a giant's axe, a thunderstone, yellow substances, even an undine or a fire-being—the material thing itself doesn't matter as much as the place from which the thing originates."

Mindy's look of frustration deepened. Mike Slattery put a hand on her shoulder. "Don't worry," he said, "I too had —still have—significant problems with this part of the story."

"Perhaps I can help clarify the matter," Ray Dale offered. "As Raphael just indicated, one of the key ideas in the timeless philosophy to which Lady Ostend subscribed is this: in addition to our material, visible world, there exists another world, a non-material, usually invisible one from which the phenomena we've been discussing originate. The four species of classical elementals exist primarily in this Otherworld, as do demons, as do what we call the ancient gods, as does the being that the bishop and several others among us worship and call God." Ray paused. His lips were taut and his eyes were intense. He glanced at the bishop when he mentioned God. The bishop nodded.

"The Otherworld is home to these unseen beings," Ray continued. "It is, quite literally, another world, with another set of rules governing space and time. In our material world, animals, insects, plants and rocks exist in a hierarchy of consciousness. Likewise, beings in the Otherworld exist in a hierarchical arrangement. The elementals and some demons are in the lower realms. Other demons, the ancient gods and what the Greeks called *daemons*, known to us as angels, exist in the upper realms. We humans are in a unique position because we have the ability to access both worlds, the material world of everyday existence and the unseen Otherworld. If you were to draw a Venn diagram of the universe as understood in the context of spiritual philosophy, the Otherworld and the material world would intersect, and human beings would inhabit the region of intersection.

"Our existence in the material world is obvious and well-attested by science and experience. Our existence in the Otherworld is not so well known, but is no less real than our existence in the material world. Part of who we are as human beings relates to the Otherworld that surrounds us every moment of our lives. Thus, it is quite possible to communicate, interact, learn from, cooperate with and sometimes control the beings from the Otherworld, depending on where they are on the Otherworld's vertical plane. It is also the case that these Otherworld beings sometimes harass, manipulate, confuse and destroy humans."

"These interactions," I said, "are they part of what Lady Ostend meant when she spoke of philosophy as the work of the soul?"

"Yes. Materialist philosophy and science are concerned with the work of the senses. Spiritual philosophy, Lady Ostend's philosophy, with a lineage going back to the beginning of human history, is concerned with the work of the soul. One of the most significant fields of investigation in the discipline of spiritual philosophy is the Otherworld. This Otherworld is also the primary subject of study at the Institute for Applied Philosophical Research. It's been my subject of study for many years."

"Do Carl Jung's archetypes come from the Otherworld?" Mindy asked. She glanced at me. "Do we travel there in our dreams? Is that what Tom's dreams … everyone's dreams are about?"

Raphael Ostend answered. "Professor Jung—a correspondent of Grandmother's, incidentally—knew of the Otherworld and we all know at least something of it from our dreams."

Hesitant to delve into the meaning of my own dreams, I tried to change the subject. "I hate to put it so crudely, Ray," I said, "but back in school, the rest of us always thought you were something of a conspiracy nut."

"I was," Ray agreed. "And my interest in conspiracy theories led me into my current line of work."

"How?"

"I realized that many of the conspiracies I found intriguing were not human in origin. I discovered, rather, that the phenomena that I and others interpreted as conspiracies originated in the Otherworld."

"For example?" Mindy asked.

Ray glanced at my cousin. "For example, the widely reported abductions of people by little green men—more precisely little grey men—are probably not abductions of people by extraterrestrials. Rather, they are abductions of people by beings from the Otherworld."

"How's that?" Andrew asked.

"In the first place, modern day abduction stories are very similar to the fairy abduction stories of premodern Europe. Little grey aliens are our fairies, suitably transformed for our technological age. Furthermore, the lights and flying objects that the abductees see are very similar to the fairy lights of old. Finally, the men who visit abductees and witnesses, the men who warn them to keep quiet about their experiences, are not men in black from the government. They are men in black from the Otherworld, allies of the little grey men. Together, they collude to keep the true nature of their existence elusive, an enigma, a puzzle, just as fairies did in the old days. Fairies, aliens and men in black are perfect examples of how Otherworld beings can harass and annoy humans, can create, in a word, conspiracies."

"So there's no such thing as aliens?" Andrew said, a clear expression of disappointment on his face.

"There may or may not be," Ray answered. "But if extraterrestrials do exist, they probably are not like the creatures many UFO conspiracy enthusiasts imagine them to be."

"Damn it," Andrew said as he pounded his fist onto the table.

Ray Dale adjusted his pince-nez and continued. "Of all the details we know and think we know about the Otherworld, the most important one for our consideration is this: at some times, in some places, objects or beings from the Otherworld, or conditions present in the Otherworld, can break through into the material world. These occurrences of breaking through have been known to humans for millennia. People in ancient civilizations were generally more comfortable with the idea and experience of the Otherworld than we are. They paid careful attention to their dreams, for example, especially to the ones that led them on journeys of discovery. They called them big dreams, and they never dismissed the experience as just a dream, as we so often do. The dreams that you all have been having"—Ray gestured around the table—"would definitely fall under the category of big dreams.

"Moreover, the ancients worshipped beings from the other side and called them satyrs, centaurs, fairies, jinn, even gods. You might remember from the old stories that these Otherworld beings were not always beneficent toward humans. Nevertheless, we worshipped them. We offered them gifts and sought their assistance. We understood that the thin places between the Otherworld and our world were sacred places. We built monuments, temples, and cathedrals there. Mindy, what Jung called archetypes are the psychological manifestation of these Otherworld beings. Other depth psychologists call them by their Greek names: Zeus, Apollo, Athena, Hermes, etc., etc.

"But in our materialistic way of thinking, in which everything is made literal, these beings and their special places are frightening. We call the beings demons and try to exorcize them with prayers or with prescription medications. We cap their natural springs and cut down their forests. We dam and dredge their rivers. We test nuclear weapons at these places or bury our toxic waste there.

"Sometimes, less maliciously, we build tourist destinations at the thin places between the worlds because these places draw people to them like a magnet draws steel shavings. What's been happening in the Thousand Islands is, to put it quite simply, an example of a thin place between two worlds becoming even thinner. So thin, in fact, that beings and objects from the Otherworld have had little difficulty crossing over as of late, especially in your dreams."

I was starting to get an uncomfortable feeling about what I was hearing, and why I was hearing it on my back lawn. "Is it a coincidence that this particular thin place is becoming thinner? That we're the ones dreaming about and witnessing these phenomenon?" The inevitability of sharing my own dreams started to press hard upon me. I simply did not want to go there, but at the same time knew I had to.

Ray Dale and Raphael Ostend both shook their heads. Mindy furrowed her brow in puzzlement. The bishop's head nodded to one side. The others stared at the ground or into their laps.

"I don't think it's a coincidence," Ray finally said. He motioned around the table. "I think I'm here for a reason, as are all of you. As Raphael said, this meeting was inevitable. It was only a matter of time before we had to have it. Perhaps I should explain more precisely my involvement."

"That would be helpful," Mindy said.

"Raphael contacted me last summer when he found the

thunderstone and again when Mike and the other islanders witnessed the yellow rain. I came to investigate, and since then I've been in close touch with the men on the river via e-mail and telephone. I've heard one story after another about the occurrences we just talked about, and several others. As Raphael indicated, he's been planning this meeting for some time, waiting until the right moment. And as Andrew mentioned, my most recent visit to the river was last week, at which time we discussed the most recent occurrences, including the dreamed-about disappearance of Griffin Island. It was then, just last week, that I learned that you, Tom and Mindy, were also part of this group. We knew we would have to meet as soon as possible after you two arrived. Then, when I returned home to Clinton Falls, something quite extraordinary happened." Ray Dale cast a concerned glance around the table. "I have yet to share this with any of you."

"What?" I asked.

"Last week, when I returned home to Clinton Falls, I found an unexpected message on my phone from someone who wanted my professional help. Two days ago I met with this someone, who was, in fact, quite desperate for my help. She gave me this." Ray Dale reached underneath his overalls and produced from his shirt pocket a folded note card. He unfolded it, looked at it and looked at me. "This may seem like coincidence to you, Tom—listen carefully to what I say —you might want to dismiss this as only a coincidence, but coincidences are the way of the Otherworld. My advice when dealing with these matters is to keep an open mind— a *very* open mind—and to look beyond the coincidences. Understand, Tom, and you too Mindy, that there is a long chain of causes for every effect, some of which causes may not be readily apparent to us." He examined the card again, which I now recognized as one I'd seen before, and handed it to me. "Now she's quite convinced it's a practical joke," he said.

Chapter Thirty One

I GAVE MINDY A LOOK of utter shock, looked back at Ray, and opened the note card. Mindy, peering over my shoulder, read the card and grabbed it from my hands. She turned it over to inspect the back, then opened it again. Without saying a word she dropped it in my lap, stood up, walked into the house, and returned with another note card, almost identical to the one Ray had given me, and a photograph. She gave these two items to Ray, who examined them, nodded and set the items on the table.

"What's it say?" Andrew asked.

Mindy spoke slowly, trying hard to control her emotions. "It says, 'FLANAGAN KNOWS THE TRUTH.' Same writing as the other one. Same writing as on our wall. Where'd Martha Radisson find this card, Ray? On her desk in her office at her new job?" Mindy's anger was rising. "She told us the same lie."

"What lie?" I asked defensively.

"She lied about everything, Tom! *She* wrote the names on the note cards! *She* wrote on our wall! She's playing with you, just like she did—"

"Where'd she find the card, Ray?" I interrupted.

"A man in brown delivered it to her house," Ray Dale answered solemnly. "He was driving a brown van, but according to Martha it was too brown, like chocolate pudding in a TV ad rather than the real thing."

"I don't get it," I said. "UPS delivered it?"

"It wasn't UPS. There were no markings on the van, no

logos. Just a man in a brown uniform driving a too-brown van."

"A man in black?" Andrew said.

"A man in black, wearing brown," Ray affirmed. He turned to face me as Mindy huffed and turned away. "Tom, Martha Radisson said you were quite ignorant—her words—about the history of Osman Steele's murder. She said it seemed to her like you were going to ignore the historical angle and recommit to finding your brother. But you didn't ignore it, did you?"

"No I didn't. Well, I did ignore it at first, but a few days later I changed my mind and started working the case anyway."

"You never told *her* that, did you?" Mindy shouted the words. I silently shook my head. "How could she know?" Mindy asked. She searched the faces around her for an answer that didn't come. "How could she know?!"

"She doesn't know," Ray Dale said. "Martha Radisson has no idea that Tom's done some pretty extensive research into Osman Steele's murder. They, however, do."

"They?" Mindy shouted. "Who's they?"

"Tom—listen to me carefully. You need to tell me what you know." Ray picked up the picture of the "ARIEL" on our wall and held it up for everyone to see. "You need to explain this."

And so I did. I told how Martha Radisson introduced me to the story of Osman Steele's murder and how she told Mindy and me about the first note card. I explained how she had seen someone who looked like me at the Genesee Country Museum and how she had made the connection between my search for Patrick and the first note card. I related my trip to Mumford and Bill Hamilton's story. From there I turned the telling over to Mindy, who explained how she was knocked out and how we found the word "ARIEL" written on our wall. I resumed my part of the story, sharing my findings about the Anti-Rent Wars and my experiences in Delhi and Andes—or as much of it as I could remember. Finally, and with great difficulty, I related all my dreams, including the one in which I saw my parents die and, wrestling with my brother, gripped Mindy's arms instead. Mindy tearfully nodded her affirmation of this part of my story, and showed the three marks my fingers had left on each side of her arms, a bracelet of unintended violence, the purpose of which I did not understand. I also shared the setting of my other dreams, on the river, some on our wedding day. Mindy responded to that information with an angry glare and more tears.

Looking back on it, I'm not sure why I didn't mention Lodi. Was the seed of suspicion planted by Mindy germinating, starting to take root? Did I not trust him? Or worse, did I not trust my friends with knowing that I knew him?

"Well, I'm sorry you two had to go through all that," Martin Comstock said. His words meant a lot to me because he was the man who, five years before, had shared with me the details of my parents' death. Since then, he always felt a deep sense of regret for having been the one to bring so much pain into my life in the story's telling. That regret was heavy in his voice.

"Jesus," my cousin Andrew exclaimed. He eyed the bishop and added, "sorry 'bout that."

Mike Slattery and Jim Pembroke silently shook their heads.

Raphael Ostend and Ray Dale shared some wordless communication between them. Both men looked especially grave.

The bishop was mumbling something—a prayer, I guessed, since, with a shaking hand, he was also holding the crucifix he wore around his neck.

Mike Slattery asked, "My question is—or rather one of my many questions is—what does Tom's investigation into Osman Steele's murder have to do with everything else we've been talking about?"

"I have an idea," Ray Dale offered, "but it's only a tentative hypothesis. Let me put it this way. Tom's experiences in Andes may have a connection with the others' dreams about the river in that all of them share some relationship with the Otherworld, perhaps with the same being or group of beings from the Otherworld."

Andrew laughed. "From what you said earlier, doesn't most of human history share some relationship with the Otherworld?"

Ray nodded vigorously. "Very true, but so far this relationship, however tentative, is all we have to go on."

"So these things you guys are dreaming about and seeing," I asked, "these things that are happening to you, they're happening because of me?" I looked around the table. Only Jim Pembroke nodded. The others just frowned.

"I think you should take that thought, that connection, a little further," Ray Dale said.

It didn't take me long to complete Ray's thought. "My brother," I said.

Ray nodded. "As I said, this is only a very rough hypothesis, but I think your brother did something to draw the interest of a being or group of beings from the Otherworld. Tom, over the past few years I've investigated several alleged incidents like the one in Mumford that Bill Hamilton described to you. I suspect that all these alleged incidents involve your brother."

"What?" I asked. "What alleged incidents are you talking about?"

"At the Adirondack hot air balloon festival in Glens Falls, a rogue wind or a microburst of some sort blew one particular balloon in the opposite direction of all the other balloons. A light prevailing wind was blowing the other balloons towards the east, but the balloon in question was speeding westward at an impressive velocity."

"Was my brother on that balloon?" I asked.

"I don't know. All I know is that the balloon was moving in the wrong direction. I have several video recordings of the event on file. The pilot was not visible in the videos."

"How the hell could something like that even happen?" Andrew asked.

"Sylphs," Ray said.

"You mean fairies?" Andrew said.

"Spirits of the air, whatever particular name you choose to call them," Ray said.

"What was the other incident?" I asked.

"That one is more relevant to your story," Ray Dale said.

"How so?"

"It happened in Walton, at the Delaware County Fair."

"Oh," I said.

"It seems that, somehow, during the demolition derby, the earth itself rose up and extinguished a car fire. Unfortunately, I do not have any videos of that incident."

"The earth itself rose up?" Jim Pembroke asked. "That must have been something to see!"

"It must have been," Ray agreed. "Eyewitness testimony agrees that a large pile of dirt and rock rose up from the ground and, like a wave, fell onto the engine compartment of a car that was about to explode. Eyewitness testimony has no doubt that the driver's life was saved."

"Earth-beings," I said.

"I call them gnomes," Andrew added.

"Yes," Ray affirmed. "Based on what we've discussed today, the frequency of these strange events seems to be increasing. If the pattern continues, I'm not optimistic about what the results might be."

"Why not?" Andrew asked. "The earth-beings saved a guy."

"Because engaging beings from the Otherworld is a very dangerous thing to do," Ray said. "All four classes of elementals are extremely fickle, extremely difficult to control.

If Patrick let them into our world, once they're here … well, you can't put the toothpaste back into the tube."

With a grim expression on his face, Martin Comstock stood and spoke. "Well, I don't like the fact that Tom and Mindy here are targets of this Otherworldly harassment. It seems clear to me that something powerful is trying to harm them."

"And like a pebble dropped into a pond, the effects of this harassment seem to be radiating outwards," Mike Slattery said.

"Into our lives," Jim Pembroke added. "And into the river."

I stood up. "Let's stop them," I said with conviction. "Let's stop them like we stopped Walter Maitland back in 2001. We've got the *Archangel* right here. Let's get Naguib Malqari and his ship back on the river and stop them. It worked then. It'll work now." I grew more agitated as I spoke, but I also grew less confident as I watched the others frown, shake their heads and sigh. To a man, they all avoided eye contact.

I stopped cold when I saw Mindy staring right at me, tears flowing down her cheeks. Mike Slattery saw her reaction. He took Mindy's hand in his, put his arm around her shoulder, looked at me and put a finger to his lips. Mindy, her head resting on Slattery's shoulder, kept her eyes closed and continued to sob. I stopped talking.

"Let's not be hasty with our conclusions," Raphael Ostend said quietly, "at least not at the moment. We do not know who or what this being is or these beings are. We do not know if they are malicious or benevolent. Moreover, we do not know for certain what role Tom's brother plays in this story. You, Martin, and you, Jim, might share a sense of pessimism, but if Grandmother taught me anything, she taught me that the Otherworld, like the visible world, is divided between beings that wish to harm us and beings that yearn to help us. Remember, my friends, the elementals bestowed many gifts on Grandmother. Some of these gifts may have yet to be fully unveiled." Ostend paused and gauged our responses. When he was satisfied that his words were having an effect, he continued.

"For the time being, and until we gain some certainty, I advise all of us to stay put, to keep our eyes open and to record everything—*everything*—that happens to us. All of us should journal, in fact. All of us should take time during the day to reflect on what's happened to us during the preceding few hours. Encounters with the Otherworld can be confusing and disorienting if they're not intentionally recorded and examined. We should pay special attention to our dreams. Keep paper and pen underneath your pillow. Write down your dreams immediately upon waking, before your conscious mind has a chance to erase them. The more information we have, the better off we will be when the situation calls for action, and we are able to act. Perhaps Master Malqari will offer other, more proactive advice. But for the time being, and until he does, we need to be careful and not engage. Observe and record, but do not engage."

"And pray," the bishop added.

"That certainly can't hurt," my cousin Andrew affirmed.

"Wouldn't Lady Ostend have done something?" I asked. "Wouldn't she have acted?"

"She would have, no doubt," Ostend answered with a calming gesture, "and no doubt I will too. But another lesson Grandmother taught me is that taking premature action can be far more disastrous than taking no action at all."

Having completely deflated my argument for immediate action, Ostend turned to Mindy. "Melinda, you look like you need to speak. Do you have questions?"

"OK," she said hesitantly and sounding scared. She breathed deeply and exhaled. "Is Ariel one of the good guys? Or one of the good girls? Or things? I mean, there's so much conflicting information. The lion of God, the governor of the elements, a fallen angel that serves as a lieutenant of Satan." She paused and gazed at Ostend. "Does your family have an Ariel?"

"No," Ostend said. "A Michael, a Gabriel and a Raphael, of course, but no Ariel."

"There goes that theory," I said, disappointed.

Mindy continued. "OK. Assume Ariel's an angel, then. Did Ariel the angel write the word on our wall and the messages on the two note cards?"

"That would be a good working hypothesis," Ray Dale said. "But it's not the last word on the subject." Ray turned to his right and bounced down into a squatting position. "Bishop, can you offer some insight on the matter of angels?"

"The young lady is correct," the bishop said in a clear voice, but with labored breathing. "Ariel is an angel. Not one of the first rank of angels, to be sure, but a powerful one nonetheless, certainly powerful enough to write its name on a living room wall. It is also correct to say that Ariel has a special relationship with the four classical elements of earth, air, fire and water. Some branches of Catholic esoterica—branches, some say, of a near-heretical persuasion—claim that Ariel was an important figure in the creation of the world, setting the elements into their final form and separating them into their respective domains. Be that as it may, it was certainly Ariel who revealed to Hildegard of Bingen the great vision of the repair and restoration of creation. Do you know it? Hmm?" None of us answered, although Ray smiled and nodded his head. "It's quite beautiful. It should be shared.

"Hildegard said:

> After all these things, I looked again and behold, all the elements and all the creatures were shaking with horrible motion. The fire, the air, and the water broke open and moved the land. Flashes of lightning and claps of thunder clashed. Mountains and

forests fell. As a result, all mortal things breathed forth their life. But all the elements were cleansed, so that whatever had been dirty vanished in such a way that it was no longer visible ... Thereupon, all the elements of the world shone with great serenity, as if a shadow had been removed from them. Fire no longer held heat, air no longer held density, water raging, and land frailty.

When all these things have been accomplished and when all the filth has been carried away, the elements will shine with the greatest brightness and beauty. Fire will shine with a gleam as red as the dawn, but without boiling heat. The air will glitter as most pure and without any density. Water will stand clear and gentle, without flowing rapidly and without flooding things. The land will appear as firm and very flat without any frailty and torment. All these things will have been changed into a state of great tranquility and beauty."

The bishop paused for a moment to catch his breath, as did I. The similarities between Hildegard's vision and several of my own dreams bothered me deeply. I wasn't ready to share that fact, though, so I kept quiet and left the discussion to the others.

"That's quite a vision," Jim Pembroke said.

"And a unique one," Ray Dale added enthusiastically. "You know, Bishop, the Institute has a copy of Hildegard's *Scivias*, from which that description comes. It's an illustrated manuscript from the late fifteenth century. It's really quite marvelous."

"I must see it!" the bishop exclaimed.

"I can arrange that," Ray said with a smile.

"Thank you. As far as your other question is concerned ... ah, my apologies, what is your name again?"

"Mindy."

"Yes, of course. As far as your other question is concerned, Mindy, I do not know if Ariel is a benevolent angel or a malicious one. One of the more unfortunate consequences of modern secularism, and of the church's uneasy alliance with it, is a dangerous ignorance of the same profound spiritual truths we have been discussing all afternoon. At least in the western world, our ability to evaluate the nature and intentions of unseen beings is all but lost."

"Why's that ignorance so dangerous?" Mike Slattery asked.

"Because the war between good and evil rages on," the bishop answered with some urgency. "As human beings, we are caught in the middle of it, but fewer and fewer of us are able to discern which side is which. The situation could not be more dangerous given the fact that one side wants to save us and the other side wants to destroy us. I'm quite certain that the demons are winning, and that they are using us to destroy ourselves. Yes, the horrors of the past century are proof positive that the demons are winning."

"And I suppose you think the church is our last best defense," Mike Slattery snapped.

"Not at all," the bishop answered, shaking his head. "The church, at times, has fallen under the same demonic sway as any other human institution. Like government, Wall Street, Hollywood, and countless other sectors of society, the church is often filled with greed, ambition, lust, sloth, and every other evil under the sun. Some of us in the ranks of the clergy, a dwindling number of us, understand the precipice over which church and civilization lean. Most of us have no idea."

"But if Ariel gave Hildegard of Bingen that vision," Mindy reasoned, "can't we be reasonably confident that Ariel is a benevolent angel?"

The bishop nodded sadly. "Ariel may have been benevolent in the twelfth century," he said, "but quite a lot has changed since then."

I turned to face the bishop. "You said earlier that you came on an errand of mercy. What did you mean by that?"

"I did say that," the bishop affirmed. "I certainly did not come here to speak of angels and demons. I came here to tell a story of my own, a story that began many years ago, a story that I did not share with you, Tom, but perhaps should have, a decade ago when you began your frantic and hopeless search for the drunk speedboater who you believed killed your parents and brother."

Chapter Thirty Two

"THERE WAS NO DRUNK SPEEDBOATER," I said sharply. "I already knew that."

"Hmm. Yes. My story begins a decade before that. It begins when I was called to investigate certain peculiarities in the tenure of your family's parish priest."

"Father D'Agostino," I said. "No, wait, it was after him. Father Malone!"

"Yes. Father Malone. You were entering your teenage years and Patrick had just offered his first reconciliation and received his first communion. Tell me, what do you remember about your brother in those years?"

"Not much," I said. "He always seemed to be pestering me or Andrew to play with him. I do remember that he loved going to church."

The bishop nodded. "He did indeed. Father Malone often spoke of how your brother's eyes lit up during the dramatic liturgical moments of the high holy days. Christmas Mass, Epiphany, Holy Thursday and Good Friday, Easter Sunday, Pentecost. He especially enjoyed the Feast of the Immaculate Conception, which is hardly anyone's favorite. I asked Father Malone what Patrick found so thrilling about the Feast of the Immaculate Conception. He told me that your brother was comforted by the fact that God knew enough about what was to come to prepare Our Lady for the birth of the Christ child. I appreciated that answer as a sound bit of theological thinking, but as nothing more than that."

"I don't get it," Jim Pembroke said. "I thought the Immaculate Conception was the same thing as Jesus' birth, the same thing as Christmas."

"You're one generation off," Ray Dale said.

"Yes," the bishop confirmed. "The conception referred to is Mary's. Roman Catholic doctrine says she was conceived and born without the taint of original sin because our Lord himself had to be born without the same blemish."

"You don't sound convinced," Pembroke said.

"Let's just say that I appreciate some aspects of official church doctrine more than others," the bishop said.

"So my brother liked the certainty of it all," I said.

"He did," the bishop agreed. "Certainty provides comfort for many believers. Unfortunately, it is hard to come by, although your brother found a more reliable source of it than many others have."

"What do you mean?" I asked.

"I might as well get right to the point," the bishop said. "When he was a young boy, just after his first reconciliation and first communion, he started telling Father Malone on Sunday mornings who would win certain baseball games on those same Sunday afternoons."

"He made predictions?" I asked.

"They were more than predictions, more than just guesses. They were visions, premonitions of exactly how the games would end. The accuracy of his visions was quite extraordinary. I suppose a gambling man could have used Patrick's precognition to make a substantial amount of money."

"Did anyone else know about his ability?" I asked. "Did my parents know?"

"From the nature of your question, I assume that you did not know." I shook my head. The bishop continued. "Your parents did not know, either. In fact, during my investigation, Patrick himself asked me not to tell them, especially not to tell your father."

"Why not?"

"For the same reason I just indicated in my comment of a moment ago."

"He thought my dad would try to use his visions for gambling," I concluded.

"Yes," the bishop said. "Your father and his friends." The bishop, with a teasing smile, looked around at the remaining River Rat Reporters.

"Smart kid," Jim Pembroke said. He too looked around at the others and caught their unappreciative expressions. "What? We all gambled back then. I did. Billy did. Even you, Raphael, put a loonie or two down on an occasional horse race. Imagine what we would've done if we knew the kid could see into the future!"

"That's just plain wrong," Mindy said.

"That's why I said he was smart not to tell us," Pembroke responded.

The bishop cleared his throat and continued. "At first Father Malone doubted Patrick's abilities. At first he could not believe that anyone could see into the future with such accuracy. Even after Patrick shared accurate predictions of six or seven games, Father Malone did not believe that what he claimed to be able to do was real."

"Did he see all the games? There were, what, eight to twelve games a day back then."

"That would've driven him mad!" the bishop exclaimed. "He told me he saw one or, at the most, two per night and not every night."

"Well, I can't blame the priest for doubting," Martin Comstock said.

"Father Malone doubted until October 1986," the bishop said. "Then everything changed. Tom, do you recall that your brother was a Mets fan?"

"Of course. He was the only one in the family not to root for the Yankees."

"Need I even ask if any of you fail to recall the 1986 World Series?"

"I lost a fortune on that series!" Jim Pembroke said.

"My retirement account still thanks you," Mike Slattery added to Pembroke's chagrin.

"I think we all remember it," I said. "It was one of the most memorable Series' ever."

"Then you'll recall that the Boston Red Sox led the New York Mets three games to two going into game six on Saturday, October 26 at Shea Stadium. Father Malone saw your mother and your brother at the supermarket that Saturday morning. Patrick came running up to him and told him that the Mets were going to win game six. He asked Patrick how that was going to happen. Patrick replied that Ray Knight would score the winning run and would be mobbed by his teammates at home plate. Knowing that Patrick did not want your parents aware of his gift, Father Malone laughed and said that we all need to have our dreams."

"Turns out the kid was right," Martin Comstock said.

"Poor Bill Buckner," Andrew added.

"In all honesty Jim, I was ready to pay up," Mike Slattery said. "The Sox were up by two runs entering the bottom of the tenth. Hell, they were *still* up by two runs with two outs in the bottom of the tenth, only a couple batters before Wilson hit the ball that rolled under Buckner's glove. Tom, your dad liked to point out that half the Mets team was in the clubhouse after Keith Hernandez popped up for the second out. *Everybody*, even the Mets, thought the Sox were going to win."

"Everybody except my brother," I said.

The bishop nodded. "As I mentioned earlier, Father Malone had a difficult time accepting the veracity of Patrick's premonitions, even and especially as the game drew towards an end. As he watched the tenth inning unfold, as the Red Sox moved closer to victory, he grew ever more secure in his doubt. Then Gary Carter got a hit. Then Kevin Mitchell got a hit. Then Ray Knight singled Carter home. Then Mitchell scored on a wild pitch. Then Mookie Wilson, after fouling off pitch after pitch, hit that slow roller up the first base line. For whatever reason Bill Buckner did not field the ball. And just like Patrick described, Ray Knight scored the winning run and was mobbed by his teammates at home plate."

"So Patrick was right, and Father Malone started to believe," I said.

"He did." The bishop paused to catch his breath. "But there is another, more significant question—why did Bill Buckner fail to field the ball?"

"Well, it took a bad hop," Martin Comstock said.

"He couldn't get his glove down with those bad knees of his," Jim Pembroke argued.

"We went over this a hundred times back in the day," Mike Slattery said. He looked at me. "You ever hear how your father explained it?"

"How?" I asked.

"He said there was a significant amount of spin on the ball," Raphael Ostend answered. "The ball hit the turf and hopped, and Buckner didn't have a chance to stop it because of the spin."

The bishop nodded at each of these explanations. He was tired. He said softly, "Of all the games men play, baseball is the strangest. Golf is a close second, but golf is an individual sport. The interaction of nine fielders, the batter and up to three base runners makes for a game of almost infinite complexity. And complexity breeds strangeness. Each of your explanations makes a valid argument for what Aristotle would call the proximate cause of the event, but the ultimate cause was as clear as day in Father Malone's mind."

"And that is?" Andrew finally asked after a long pause.

"Father Malone believed that the ball went under Bill Buckner's glove because Patrick Flanagan saw it happen that way. Patrick not only predicted the events of that evening, he also brought that particular set of events into being. In a word, Patrick Flanagan made history happen."

Chapter Thirty Three

MINDY POINTED A FINGER right at the bishop. "Your implication," she said, "is that Tom's brother not only saw the future, but influenced the future as well? That's absurd!"

"It may be absurd," the bishop said, ignoring Mindy's rude gesture, "but that is precisely what Father Malone believed. The events of that game were shaped by what Patrick saw some hours before they happened."

Mindy whirled to face me. "Did you know anything about this?"

"I remember him being thrilled by the Mets' victory," I said. "He was a kid in love with a baseball team, after all. Other than that … "

"Well," Mindy said.

"Bishop," I asked, "what do you believe?"

"I believe that your brother has an amazing gift," the bishop said. "For what purpose he is able to use that gift is, in my opinion, a question that has yet to be answered."

Raphael Ostend asked Ray Dale if he had any insights to share.

"Perhaps I do," Ray answered. "Modern physics has shown that time is not a straight ahead, one-way process like most of us interpret it. Instead, time is more like a loop or, even better, like a three dimensional sphere. We exist on the outer surface of the sphere, and although it makes us comfortable to think that we're living our lives along a straight line of past, present and future, a line on which cause and effect relationships are clearly established, we are actually constantly moving to different points on the sphere, to different points in time. At the Institute for Applied Philosophical Research, we have several thousand accounts of precognition."

I asked, "That includes our dreams, right? The ones about river levels, birds, Griffin Island. My dreams about … well … "

"Your nightmares about our wedding day," Mindy snapped.

"We all have the ability to see the future," Ray answered. "We all have the potential to see glimpses of things to come in our dreams. However, most of us dismiss these precognitive dreams as just dreams. Most of us self-censor these dreams because we believe that to see into the future is impossible. When the events we dream about come to pass, we call the experience *dèjà vu* because, in our waking consciousness, we don't remember the dream. When we do remember the dream, when we become aware that the events were dreamed about before they actually happen, we are often shocked and dismayed. We protect our sanity by again telling ourselves that precognitive dreams are impossible. If my hypothesis that the Otherworld is breaking into our lives is correct, then it's more than possible that the dreams we've been talking about are indeed premonitions."

"Why?" Mindy asked. "How are those two ideas—the Otherworld and premonitions—connected?" She looked around the table. "I have better reasons than most of you for wanting to figure this out."

"We all want to figure it out, Melinda," Raphael Ostend said. "Please be assured that we all share your anxiety for what our dreams tell us might happen."

"Unlike us, beings in the Otherworld don't seem to be constrained by a straight and narrow understanding of time," Ray said. "They seem to be able—and very willing, by the way—to move around the sphere of time much more freely than we are. Our ancestors knew this quite well, and some of our ancestors, the true sages, were able to tap into this power. When one of us taps into the Otherworld, or when the Otherworld intrudes into our lives, it just might happen that time starts to do very strange things."

"And did time ever do strange things with Patrick!" the bishop said. "After the Mets won game six and consequently the World Series, Father Malone told Patrick that he was starting to understand his gift. Father Malone asked Patrick if he would feel comfortable sharing any other premonitions he might have. Patrick said he would. I think he was relieved to finally find someone who believed him."

"Ray," I asked, "can you help explain how my brother might have been able to influence future events?"

"There have been some experiments," Ray answered, "but the results are inconclusive. Again, I would say his talents were somehow influenced by the Otherworld."

"Hmm," the bishop said. "I'll come back to that."

"What other premonitions did Patrick have?" I asked.

"About a month after the World Series, he told Father Malone about a dream in which Mrs. Higginbotham, your church organist, was unable to play on Christmas Eve because she had broken her arm. A week after Thanksgiving, Mrs. Higginbotham slipped on a patch of ice and did indeed break her elbow. Following that incident, Father Malone got to thinking that he might be able to use Patrick's premonitions to help his parishioners. So when Patrick told him that he foresaw Mr. Jacobs get into an automobile accident, Father Malone advised Mr. Jacobs to take his car to the garage for a checkup. The mechanic discovered that the car's brake lines were severely corroded. The mechanic called Mr. Jacobs a lucky man, but Father Malone knew better than to ascribe it to luck.

"Father Malone acted on Patrick's premonitions for over four years. He helped a lot of people thanks to Patrick's foreknowledge. It was during that time that I decided to investigate. Father Malone's pastoral work was extraordinary, saint-like even. I wanted to discover how he was able to do it."

"What else did my brother see?" I asked.

"He helped Mrs. Boyd find a lost engagement ring. He helped the church avoid a water leak from a burst pipe. There was nothing spectacular in these premonitions, but they helped people, and they helped Father Malone become a very special priest."

"How do you know those incidents would have turned out differently?" Mindy asked. "I mean, you can't know for sure what the future holds until it happens, until it becomes the past. You can't know for sure that a water pipe will burst until it does."

"You are correct," the bishop admitted. "Patrick's ability cannot be replicated in an observable experiment. Certain knowledge is quite impossible in this case. But let me continue, please, and finish my story. I want to show you how Patrick himself came to understand his ability, came to understand it in much the same way as I just described it."

"OK," Mindy said.

"During the course of my investigation I discovered that Father Malone was using Patrick's ability to help many people. His flock loved him; his colleagues envied him. Nevertheless, when I completed my investigation I could not allow his relationship with Patrick to continue."

"Why not?" I asked.

"Because, in the course of my investigation, I discovered the source of Patrick's visions, or at least what he claimed to be the source. Tom, your brother told me that he received the ability to see into the future from what he called the invisible fish. I knew, of course, that he meant the water-beings, the undines of the Saint Lawrence River."

"And what's wrong with that?" Andrew asked a little too defensively.

The bishop sighed. "Unfortunately, over the centuries Christianity has polarized the spiritual realm, labeling the inhabitants of the Otherworld as either good angels or evil demons. The vast majority of Otherworldly beings, including the elementals, have been cast into the latter category and are thus enemies of the church."

"So there was no way you could allow a priest to build his pastoral success upon the abilities a child had acquired from demons," Mindy said.

"Correct. And yet, I was sympathetic enough to the perennial philosophy of the soul that I could not bring myself to expose and punish either Father Malone or Patrick Flanagan. But I arranged for Father Malone to be transferred to Cheektowaga and I strongly advised Patrick to keep his visions to himself."

"Awfully Christian of you not to punish them," Andrew said with a hint of sarcasm.

The bishop smiled and shook his head. "Actually it was just the opposite. Had I encouraged either Father Malone or Tom's brother, I would have been acting against nearly two thousand years of church tradition and teaching. I would have also put both Father Malone and Patrick in serious danger." The bishop turned towards Raphael Ostend. "Otherworldly beings are dangerous, even if they seem temporarily beneficent to people like your grandmother. They are dangerous precisely because they live according to a different moral code than we do."

"Perhaps they live according to a different set of physical laws than we do," Ray Dale added.

"Very true," said the bishop. "So even the most well-intentioned of men can be seriously harmed in any interaction with an Otherworldly being."

"I'm beginning to understand why you couldn't tell me," I said.

"Thank you, Tom," the bishop answered with a slight bow.

"Is that the end of your story?" Mindy asked.

"No. And the end of my story is the ultimate reason

why I could not share with Tom what I knew about his brother. Patrick visited me one day in 1995, right before Christmas. It was in the confessional. He asked me to keep what he told me a secret. To this day, I have honored that promise. Perhaps I was wrong in doing so. Perhaps I should have told you, Tom, or told your parents. I have come to regret my silence, but at the same time I hold the promise of confidentiality inviolable."

"Patrick foresaw my parents' death," I guessed.

"He did," the bishop answered. "He did indeed. Your brother had a recurring dream of seeing your parents die in a boating accident on the river. He didn't know when it would happen, but he knew where it would happen."

"In the channel, just offshore from Thousand Island Park," I said.

"Yes."

"Did he try to change that future?" I asked.

"He tried over and over again to conjure up an alternate vision, but he failed every time." The bishop's breathing became labored. "When he came to see me, he had had the same dream of your parents' deaths three or four nights in a row. Despite his best efforts, he was unable to influence any part of how the events of that day would proceed."

"Did he ask the undines for help?"

"He did, to his great peril. They insisted that they could not change this particular future, and they warned him that the consequences of him trying to do so could be very dangerous."

"Why?" I asked. "Why dangerous?"

"I do not know."

"Why did you promise to keep it a secret? I asked. "Why didn't you tell my parents? Didn't you realize you could've saved them?"

"I could not have saved them," the bishop responded, almost in tears. "What I learned in my investigation of your brother and Father Malone caused me to trust your brother's abilities completely and without question. When he said there was no way to prevent your parents' deaths, I believed him, again completely and without question. Granted, I did not expect him to ask me to help him fake his own death. To be honest, even he wasn't sure whether he would live or die that day. His own fate was never clear in his dreams."

"Well, he lived," Martin Comstock said. "I was there, and I heard Charlie tell both me and Billy Masterson to leave Patrick be."

I thought about my most recent dream and shuddered.

"He lived," the bishop repeated, "and he paid me one final visit the day after surviving the crash. Of course, he blamed himself for your parents' deaths. He had tried for months to create a different path for them, a different future, but he failed. He blamed himself for this failure, and, during his final visit, he shared with me a promise, a dangerous vow he had made to learn how to control his abilities so that he would never fail again."

"How would he learn that?" I asked.

"By calling upon more beings from the Otherworld," Ray Dale answered. "Elementals to be sure, as your story about what happened in the blacksmith's forge confirms. Perhaps angels, as well. Maybe even the being whose name is written on Tom and Mindy's wall."

"And maybe demons," I said. "Maybe my brother's on the wrong side of the bishop's war."

"Perhaps so," Raphael Ostend said, "and perhaps not. That is why we should bide our time until we discover whether your brother is an ally or an enemy." He stood and raised his arms. He turned towards each of us as he spoke. "I think we have heard enough for today. We are all tired and we have a lot of new ideas to process. Along with journaling, I have one more piece of advice: do not continue this conversation on the phone or via e-mail. If you need to discuss anything further, do so in person, face to face.

Above all else, we must be cautious. Prying eyes may be watching our every move, and unknown ears may be listening to our every word."

Chapter Thirty Four

I WAS BACK IN THE COTTAGE KITCHEN, watching Raphael Ostend and Martin Comstock help the bishop back into Comstock's car, when I heard someone clear his throat from the living room doorway.

"It was good to see you again Ray," I said when I saw his reflection in the window. "I admit I haven't done that well keeping in touch with my classmates. It was good to reconnect today."

"I know it's not the same as keeping in touch," he answered, "but I have been keeping tabs on you."

I turned to face him. "You have?"

"Yes. You're doing good work with your business. Valuable work. I think you made the right choice in setting off on your own and not getting bogged down in academia."

"Getting bogged down like Mindy?"

"Seems like she's been able to maintain her independence," he said with a grin.

"Like you then?"

His laugh was quick and high-pitched. "I've been lucky. The Institute has provided me with a degree of freedom that I couldn't have found anywhere else. I guess I have the Ostends to thank for that."

"I guess so."

"I have to leave soon because Martin wants to get the bishop back home while it's still early. But before I do, I want to offer you two pieces of advice."

"OK."

"First, to expand upon Raphael's warning, you might want to keep quiet about what you learned today. You might not want to talk to anyone outside those of us here today about the Otherworld or about your dreams or about the bishop's story. And when you do talk to us, don't do so in public."

"Let me guess. People will think I'm crazy if I tell them."

"Exactly. And depending on who's doing the thinking, such a perspective could have serious repercussions."

I laughed.

"I mean it. Loose lips might do more than sink you."

"OK. Mum's the word. What's your second piece of advice?"

"Be careful, very careful, with your new friend."

I played coy. "Which new friend is that?"

"The singer."

There was no hiding it now. "Lodi."

"Yes, although he's much more than a singer, believe you me."

"Did Mindy tell you about him? She hasn't even met him yet."

Ray shook his head. "Mindy hasn't mentioned him. And, more significantly, neither did you when you told your story."

Now he had me. "I've got my reasons," I said. "Mindy doesn't like him. I thought it best not to mention him. I didn't want to upset her."

"It's not whether you, or anyone else, likes or doesn't like him that concerns me."

"What concerns you? How do you know he's my friend?"

"I was at Louie's the night he played. I saw you talking with him. I saw your reaction to his music."

"I talked to him because Louie suggested we invite him to play for our wedding. My reaction was the same as the rest of the audience's. We loved him. He gave us a good time. He had us in the palm of his hand."

"He seems to have most everyone he meets in the palm of his hand."

I poured myself a glass of water. "Want some?" Ray declined. "So that's what concerns you? That he knows how to work a crowd?"

"I'll be totally up front with you, Tom. I've been keeping a wary eye on him for a long time. The way he's able to influence people is impressive. At first I explained it in terms of charisma or charm, the ability some people have to become the center of attention the moment they walk into a room. But it's more than that with him. It's almost as if he's able to, I don't know, harness power from somewhere else and use it to bend people to his will."

"Power from somewhere else?" I repeated. "From where? The Otherworld?"

"Perhaps. I've seen him cast a spell on people more than once. Let me ask you—how did you feel when you two were talking?"

"Alive? Energized?" I paused, then added, "I was also anxious because he seemed to know something about my brother, something he wouldn't come right out and say."

"That doesn't surprise me."

"Why not? Do *you* know something about my brother you're not telling me?"

Ray Dale shook his head. "All I know about Patrick is what we talked about today, and those are rumors that may or may not involve him. It wouldn't surprise me if Lodi knows more, though. Lodi seems to know more than he should about lots of people. You're not the first person he's left asking questions."

"What's that supposed to mean?"

"I've seen him play several times. I've overheard several of his conversations with others. I've interviewed people about their conversations with him."

"So you're stalking him?"

"I wouldn't put it in those terms."

"Does he know you're stalking him?"

"He knows I'm interested in him. He and I have even collaborated on a project or two. My guess is that he doesn't see me as any sort of threat."

"Should he see you as a threat?"

"Not yet."

"Did you overhear the conversation I had with him on Louie's back deck after the show?"

"No. I went home after the Woody Guthrie sing along." Ray sighed, removed his pince-nez and cleaned the lenses. I thought he was going to grill me about the after-hours conversation, but he put the glasses back on, brushed a lock of his white hair off his face and said, "Look, Tom, I don't have any type of specific warning to give you. I can't say that he's harmed anyone or done something illegal or anything like that. All I'm saying is that I think you should be careful around him."

"OK. Advice taken."

"Have you seen him since that night at Louie's?"

I exhaled and took a sip of water. "I saw him when I went to Delaware County."

"To Andes?"

"Yes. I saw him in the general store, where he works. I stopped by for a slice of pizza. Lodi gave me directions to the Earle farm, where I had my hallucin … odd experience. I was supposed to go back to the general store. I was planning to tell him everything I knew about Patrick and everything that had been happening to me and Mindy. But I didn't make it back to the general store. Like I said earlier, I blacked out and ended up back home in Clinton Falls." I took another sip of water. "Mindy thinks Lodi slipped some hallucinogenic mushrooms on my pizza."

Ray Dale laughed.

"What?" I said.

"I don't think he'd be that crude. But I also wouldn't be surprised if he was somehow involved in what happened to you. For example, you very well might have gone back to the general store without knowing it. You might have already told him everything."

I thought that over for a minute. "So you think I should be careful."

"I do. If you won't take my word for it, then at least trust Mindy's instincts, like I know you have in the past."

"There's one other thing," I said.

"What?"

"His fingernails creep me out."

"That doesn't surprise me, either."

"Why not?"

Outside, Martin Comstock honked the horn.

"Here." Instead of answering my question Ray Dale handed me a business card that he produced from the shirt pocket beneath his overalls. "My number's on there. Both my numbers, at home and at the office."

"Thanks."

"Please don't share it with anyone."

"I won't."

"Will you stay up here all summer?"

"More or less. Why?"

"Because I want you to call me when you get back to Clinton Falls." He smiled. "I think I owe you a tour of the Institute. There are a few things I'd like to show you. Important things."

I looked at the card and returned the smile. "I'd appreciate that," I said. "But I hope you're not expecting me to call you the next time I see Lodi."

"That's completely up to you. But if he does play for your wedding, you might want me here as well, just in case." And with that he said goodbye, walked out the door and climbed into the back seat of Martin Comstock's car. I watched the Cutlass back out and drive away, thereby bookending what had indeed been a very strange afternoon.

Chapter Thirty Five

Mindy's parents were scheduled to pay us a visit the next day. After Ray and the bishop and the River Rat Reporters left, I asked her if they might consider postponing their visit until the following week so we could spend some time processing what we had learned. No, she said, her parents could not postpone their visit because they were leaving for an Alaskan cruise a couple days after that. This would be their only opportunity to see us before the wedding.

I tried to strike up a conversation about Ostend's council, which went something like this:

"What do you think of Ray's work?"

"It's interesting."

"I wonder how many of your colleagues would find his work a legitimate field of study."

"Not many, I bet."

"He's fortunate that his work is privately funded."

"God bless the Ostends."

Mindy cut the conversation short at that point and went for a run. She returned home, showered and read her book for the rest of the evening. I puttered around the cottage and boathouse, not quite able to concentrate on any one activity.

The next day, Mindy's parents arrived just after lunch. The four of us spent the afternoon boating around the islands, swimming off the dock and watching the activity on the river from our lounge chairs. Mindy's parents were glad to see us, but it was obvious that they also sensed the tension between us. When Mindy and her mom went inside to change and prepare dinner, her father asked me point blank if I was ready to marry his daughter.

"Of course I am," I said.

"You've got everything in order, then?" he continued.

"We do," I said.

"Business going well?"

"It is. I've got more work than I can keep up with."

"That's a good name you've got for it."

"Upstate Historical Services. Mindy thought it up."

"She's a smart one," he said. "Finances are stable, then?"

I nodded. "Our checking account's fluid. Each of us has a growing retirement account. We're on Mindy's health insurance, which saves us a lot on both deductibles and premiums."

"State plan's a good one."

"Yes, sir."

"Mindy said you're done redecorating?"

"We are." I paused. "Well, we're almost done. The last bit of work is painting the living room trim. But I can go back to Clinton Falls anytime and knock that off in an afternoon."

"Can I ask you a related question?"

"Sure."

"Why come up here so suddenly? Mindy's not one to miss such an important obligation as undergraduate commencement, and all the while you insisted you'd finish the redecorating before you relocated for the summer."

"We kind of had to come up here," I explained, trying not to dig too deep of a hole for myself to fall into. "We had to get away."

My soon to be father-in-law sipped his iced tea. "I don't mean to pry," he said. "After all, it's your life and Mindy's life and the two of you have to find your own way. But I have a sneaking suspicion—and your last comment confirmed it—that you're running away from something. If that's true, I just hope it's not my daughter you're running from."

I considered what he said as we watched a Canadian tour boat pass by. We could hear the French voice of the taped tour guide through the boat's speakers. "It's more like I'm running towards something," I explained.

"And what is it you're running towards?"

"Last week, I got the best lead yet on the whereabouts of my brother. We came up here to follow that lead."

"Then let me amend what I just said. I hope that running towards your brother doesn't cause you to run away from Mindy. Especially at this juncture."

"No, sir. She's right by my side all the way. Always has been and always will be."

"I know that," Len McDonnell said, nodding. "I've always known that, despite your obfuscations."

"Obfuscations, sir?"

"I know what putting our lives together really means," he said. With that, he stood up and walked into the house to refill his drink.

Even worse, at dinner, Mindy and her mother both looked especially anxious. After taking a few bites of the delicious salad they had prepared, a salad loaded with asparagus, walnuts and dried cranberries, and topped with blackened chicken and a vinaigrette dressing, Len mentioned that he and I had had a talk, and that everything was OK according to what he could see.

"Everything is certainly not OK," Linda McDonnell said, dropping her fork onto her plate. "Something's very much wrong, Leonard, and I don't understand it."

I looked at Mindy, who hadn't eaten a thing and whose eyes were red from crying.

"I've never seen them like this," Mindy's mother added. "I've seen them together for over a decade and I've never seen them like *this*. Look at them, Len! They're about to be married! Look at the frowns on their faces! Look at Mindy's eyes! They should be happy! They are clearly not happy!"

"She overrates happiness," Len said to me. "She's never been able to understand the fact that happiness, especially in a marriage, comes and goes and that we have little, if any, control over its coming and going. What matters in marriage is to stay together and stay strong through both the good times and the bad."

"I agree," I said.

"You say that now, Len, but you didn't see the bruises on her arms!" Mindy's mother exclaimed. "I did see them, when we tried on her wedding dress!"

"Mom, stop ... " Mindy said between sobs. "Dad's right. Everything's OK."

"Don't say that just to placate my feelings!" Linda said. "I'm your mother! I know when something's wrong with you, and I can tell you right now that everything is definitely not OK!"

Len McDonnell slowly put down his fork and finished chewing a piece of chicken. He wiped the corners of his mouth with his napkin. Then he rubbed his beard and gave his daughter a long, stern look.

"Mindy, show me your arms," he ordered.

Tentatively, Mindy raised the sleeves of her shirt. The bruises, three of them on each side, were as visible as they had been the day before when she showed them to the River Rat Reporters, although they were more black now than blue. As I looked at the marks I had left on the woman I loved, I knew I had lost her parents' trust, perhaps irredeemably, and feared that I had lost her trust as well.

"Were you mugged?" Mindy's father asked. "Were you? If I've told you once I've told you a thousand times that you should not be living in the city and riding your bike to work." He looked at me and scowled. "You should have bought her a house in a safe neighborhood," he said. "You should have made her drive to work."

"She didn't get mugged," I said.

Mindy, with tears flowing down her cheeks, shook her head and tried to tell me to stop.

"What happened, then?" Len demanded. "Mindy, what happened?"

I took a deep breath and exhaled. "I did it," I said. "I did it in my sleep. It happened a couple nights ago. That's why we came up here in such a hurry. I was dreaming when I did it. When I woke Mindy up, she drove us here to get me away from … from I don't know what."

Linda McDonnell, crying, reached out and held her daughter in an all-encompassing hug. "No!" she sobbed. "No!"

"I was dreaming," I continued. "I dreamed that I was with my brother under the water, right out there, across the channel, right where my parents died." I paused as the McDonnells scanned the river. "I dreamed he tried to hold my head underwater and drown me. In my dream, I panicked. I reached forward and tried to grab my brother to keep myself above water. But it wasn't my brother's arms I had my fingers around. It was Mindy's. I had no idea what I was doing. I was totally out of control. I … "

"Have you apologized?" Len asked, barely containing his anger. "Have you said you're sorry?"

"He has," Mindy answered in a whisper. "A hundred times."

Chapter Thirty Six

THE REST OF THE EVENING with the McDonnells was awkward, to say the least. We sat outside for the sunset and picked at our dessert in silence. When the bugs came out we played euchre on the screened-in porch. Len and I won handily, not because we were particularly good at the game but rather because Mindy and her mom were distracted and morose through the whole match. Nor did Mindy's father say a word to me beyond what was necessary for the game. When Len and Linda wished us goodnight, Len added that they were leaving very early the next morning so they'd have plenty of time to finish packing for their Alaskan cruise. It was the first time they visited the Thousand Islands without the four of us enjoying a farewell breakfast at the little round restaurant on the mainland, which Mindy's parents loved.

Mindy got up before dawn to see them off. She did not wake me up, either when her parents departed or when she left on a day trip to Clinton Falls to explain to the dean why she had missed undergraduate commencement. She hadn't told me she was going. I discovered she was gone only when I read her note next to the coffee maker telling me all this, and that she'd pick something up for dinner on her way back north.

But then she called me later that afternoon and said she was staying the night at our bungalow.

"Why?" I asked, my anxiety rising.

"I want the living room done, like we said all along. I'm

going to finish painting the trim, hang the curtains and put the furniture back where it belongs. If I can do it quickly, I'll see you tomorrow, or maybe the day after that."

"Mindy, I'm not sure that's a good idea," I suggested.

"Why not?"

"Because everything that's happened to us started in the living room," I said.

Mindy mumbled something I couldn't make out.

"Is it still there?" I asked, anxiety edging into my voice.

"What?"

"Our word? Our ARIEL?"

"Yes, it's still here."

I sighed. "How do you feel about it?"

"What do you mean how do I feel?"

"You know, does seeing the word make you feel like you felt the night you were knocked out? Or like you felt the morning after?"

She hesitated before answering. "Honestly, Tom? What I feel right now is pretty pissed off."

"Oh," I said.

"The cutting brush you used is ruined because you didn't wash it or wrap it. I had to go out and buy a new one. The paint has a crust on top. You left the living room a mess. And I still have to meet with the dean about missing graduation. What am I supposed to say to him about that?"

"I'm sorry, Mindy."

Silence.

"You still there? Mindy? Hello?"

"Yes."

"What's really wrong?" I asked, holding back sobs. "Besides still having to talk with the dean?"

"The living room's a mess. We were supposed to go north this year only after everything was done. Including the living room. Including graduation!"

"I'm sorry. I tried to finish it, but then I noticed the similarities in handwriting and—"

"Stop, Tom. You've explained that already. There's no need to rehash it."

Another awkward silence.

"Mindy, why did you leave so suddenly? You could've woken me up."

Silence.

"Mindy? Why didn't you wake me up?"

She sighed. "I needed to get away, that's all. With everything going on … it's all too much for me to handle, Tom. I just needed to get away."

"That's why we came up north in the first place!" I said, my voice trembling and rising to a shout. "We came to Heron's Nest to get away from everything that happened back there! How can you think you can get away by going back to where everything happened? How … "

I could hear Mindy sobbing as I figured out what she really meant, and what was really wrong. Any anger I felt bottomed out into grief.

"What you mean is that you need to get away from me," I finally whispered.

Between sobs, she squeaked out what sounded like a yes.

"Are you coming back?"

"I'm sorry," she said. She hung up the phone.

I called her back a dozen times, alternating between her cell phone and our home phone. Her refusal to answer made me angry again, both at her for leaving and at myself for causing her to leave. When I remembered that I didn't even wish her good luck in her meeting with the dean, I got even angrier at myself for not considering what was important to her. I called her again, foolishly thinking that having a new question to ask would somehow cause her to answer. My anger rose to new heights when each call went to voice mail. Walking up the stairs to our bedroom, I punched right through the sheetrock and slammed my fist against a stud.

Chapter Thirty Seven

FOR THE NEXT THREE DAYS I did almost everything in excess. I drove my boat too fast. I drank until I passed out. I slept until late morning. I prayed until I ran out of words. I cried until I ran out of tears. I kayaked until my arms burned and my legs cramped. I swam until I could barely stay afloat, then swam home and drank some more. The only I thing I didn't do was eat. I knew in my gut that I had driven Mindy away for good. I knew that my recurring personality flaws of paranoia, obsession and inability to compromise—flaws I had vowed to change for my own well-being and for the well-being of our relationship—had once again caused pain and suffering in the life of someone I loved.

What was I to do? Mindy wasn't answering her phone and hadn't responded to my messages despite my filling up both our home phone answering machine and her voice mail. I couldn't drive to Clinton Falls and confront her for two reasons. First, I had nothing to say, and because of my excessive living was in no shape to say it even if I did. Second, Mindy had taken our car, and with the whereabouts of my truck unknown, I had no way to get to Clinton Falls. I didn't call any of the River Rat Reporters because all I wanted to do was forget about our so-called council and live a life free from otherworldly influence, at least for a while.

THE DAY AFTER MINDY LEFT I spent several hours in my father's crow's nest office, listening to his Beethoven records and looking through his files.

For a decade before my father died he wrote editorials for the newspaper he used to own. I had recently formed the opinion that these essays were some of his best writing —clearly argued, straight from the heart, unencumbered by how his arguments would affect the loyalty of advertisers. He was something of a left-wing museum piece, offering up caustic criticisms of Reagan's America while many others were busy reaping profits from the opportunities that the president's policy of deregulation provided.

Historically speaking his columns were about as far removed from the mainstream opinion as was possible. Rather than fawning over the Founding Fathers, he praised the men and women who stood against the Constitution as the true protectors of both individual liberty and, more importantly, the common weal. Without the Anti-Federalists, he argued, the Bill of Rights would not exist and America would suffer under the banker's tyranny that Alexander Hamilton dreamed of and the Reaganites tried to implement. Rather than condemning violence, he praised the rabble-rousers who, throughout American history, refused to obey those who would rule over them and instead took up arms against their social and economic betters. He cited as the most significant battles for freedom Shay's Rebellion, the Whiskey Rebellion, John Brown's raid on Harper's Ferry, the Coal Wars in Matewan, West Virginia, the Civil Rights protests of the 1950's and 60's and the Wounded Knee Resistance.

I was more than a little surprised to discover in one editorial a full assessment of the Anti-Rent Wars. The editorial was dated August 7, 1995—the sesquicentennial of Osman Steele's murder and just over a year before my parents died and my brother disappeared. I had no memory of reading the opinion piece when it came out, but then again my politics differed enough from my father's back then that I rarely appreciated what he wrote.

He placed the Anti-Rent Wars—"an under-appreciated furlong in the race to freedom"—in the tradition of Spartacus' slave revolt, the thirteenth century Albigensian resistance against Pope Innocent III, the October Days of the French Revolution, Nat Turner's attack on Harper's Ferry and the Swing uprisings in eighteenth-century England. He wrote of how the Anti-Rent Wars were the new world's last stand against old-world feudalism and a counterpart to the great uprisings of 1848 that spread across continental Europe like wildfire. He extolled the courage of men like Smith Bouton in the Helderbergs, who had also fought in the Canadian Patriot Wars, and William Brisbane in Delaware County. He lauded the Anti-Renters as heroes who broke the back of the aristocratic landlords and did more than any other group of patriots since the Anti-Federalists to secure freedom for common Americans. He quoted Jefferson's words about the tree of liberty needing occasional nourishment with the blood of tyrants. He wrote about how easily tyranny could spread among the people when it was fed by fear, and how people could overcome that fear by drawing upon their collective courage. Then, in a closing salvo that sent chills up my spine, he argued that Osman Steele's death, while unfortunate, "was a necessary and appropriate sacrifice to the angels of the Earth, angels who for too long had watched the children of men suffer under the cruel yoke of the Patroons."

What did he mean by that, I wondered. He knew about the undines and, presumably, about the other elementals as well. He was a practicing Roman Catholic. Did my father know that Ariel was the governing angel of the elemental beings? Did he share my suspicions that Osman Steele's murder had some strange, esoteric meaning that was justifiably overlooked by reasonable academic historians? Did he write the "ARIEL" on our wall from beyond the grave? Or was I foolishly superimposing occult meaning onto what was a nicely turned metaphor and nothing more? Then again, Raphael Ostend had told me more than once that metaphors, not straightforward facts, are the way of the Otherworld. Whatever the meaning of my father's words, it was clear that I could no longer escape from the new way of thinking that had been introduced to me in the days of Napoleon's gold and had reasserted itself a few days before at Ostend's council. I had to contend with this new way of thinking one way or another.

Chapter Thirty Eight

FINALLY, ON THE THIRD DAY of Mindy's absence, I decided to contend with it by calling my cousin and asking him if I could borrow his truck. He agreed without asking any questions and came over to Heron's Nest as soon as he finished the morning's work.

We sat down at the kitchen table and chatted for a few minutes about his parents, who were enjoying early retirement in Florida. Suddenly, he stopped talking and looked me over from head to toe. "You don't look good," he said. "You're nervous too, all twitchy and shit. What's wrong?" Then he went over to the kitchen closet and saw the recycling bin. "Oh," he said.

When I told him what was happening, he stood up, grabbed me by the shoulder and exclaimed, "Grow a pair, would you? She's a little confused, maybe even flummoxed, but nothing more than that. She needs your steady hand, cuz! She needs to know you're there for her. So go be there for her!"

"I am. That's why I asked to borrow your truck," I said.

"After three days? Seriously? Come on. I'm going with you." He read my expression and held up a hand. "Don't even try to argue," he said.

"Where's *your* truck?" he asked as we flew down I-81 well above the speed limit. The classic rock played loud and Andrew tapped the steering wheel in time to whatever song came on the radio. He was living on adrenalin. I felt like I was surviving on nervous energy.

"I don't know," I said. "I drove it to Delaware County and lost track of it when I blacked out. I ended up back home, but my truck didn't."

"You're in worse shape than I thought," Andrew said. "Losing a woman is one thing, but a truck?" He shook his head, but with a hint of a smirk. "Man, I don't know about you."

Once in Clinton Falls we turned the corner and approached our house. I saw that my truck still wasn't home. Mindy's Ford Focus was, however, a fact that set my heart racing.

"Just take it easy," Andrew advised as he pulled into the driveway behind the Ford. "Just tell her you're sorry, that you made a mistake. Don't try to explain yourself or defend your actions."

"OK." I took a deep breath and slowly exhaled.

"If she accepts your apology without argument, tell her how you can't live without her and all the rest of it. If she tries to argue, just repeat your apology and make an even stronger admission of guilt."

"I can do that," I said.

"Good. If I don't see you walk out that door in fifteen minutes, I'll leave you two alone. I'll be at Louie's if you need anything. Jeez, I haven't seen that guy in ages!"

"Wish me luck," I said as I got out of the car.

"You'll need more than that, cuz," Andrew replied.

I walked through the back door into our kitchen. "Hello," I said. "Mindy? Are you home?"

I could see as I walked through the dining room that she had finished painting the living room trim. I could also see that she had rehung the curtains and put the furniture back in place. It looked good, but I kicked myself again for not having completed the job myself, like I should have done, when I had the chance.

I walked into the living room and froze. There, on the wall opposite where the sage tint semigloss "ARIEL" still shone beneath three coats of teaberry green, three other words were written in sage tint semigloss, this time over the satin wall paint. "FLANAGAN—COME BACK!" is what I saw, written in the same beautiful script as the word opposite it and as the two messages delivered to Martha Radisson.

"Mindy!" I shouted, my voice heavy with panic. I ran upstairs. "MINDY!"

Andrew must have heard me, because by the time I came back downstairs he was already in the living room, staring at one wall, then the other, then back again.

"She's not here?" he asked, still staring.

"No," I whispered. "The bed's made. Only her painting clothes are in the hamper. I don't think she was here for long."

"Damn, this *is* weird," Andrew said, his finger within a hair-breadth of the angel's name. "And that." He turned and pointed at the new message, his finger shaking ever so slightly. "Come back where?"

"Delaware County," I said. "Andes. The Moses Earle farm."

Andrew turned to face me. "We're not going there until we're done looking for her here," he said. "We need to check her office. And Louie's. And the gym. And anywhere else you can think of."

"She's not at any of those places," I said.

"You think she went to Delaware County because of what your wall told you to do?"

"Trust me," I said.

Andrew considered what I said and nodded. "Well, we should check her office and Louie's place anyway, just to make sure."

"She won't be there."

"Can't hurt to make sure," Andrew said.

So we drove first to the university. Andrew parked in a handicapped spot and turned his truck's hazard lights on. I ran into Hammond Hall and back out just as quickly. Neither of us said a word as I jumped back into the passenger seat and Andrew reversed and peeled out of the parking lot.

We both went into the 357. Louie was there, as always, wiping down glassware. Ghedi was there too, chopping vegetables for the evening's cooking. Denise was at the bar, highlighting lines in a textbook.

"Tom!" Louie said as he slid a couple of wine glasses into the slats above the bar. "Where've you been? And Andrew! My God, it's been, what, five years?"

Louie put the rag over his shoulder and came out from behind the bar to give Andrew a hug. "Ghedi, Denise, this is Tom's cousin Andrew Hibbard. Consider this a treat because he rarely gets down this way."

Louie looked at Andrew then at me. He furrowed his brow. "What are you doing here, anyway?" he asked. "Is everything OK?"

"We're looking for Mindy," I said. "She came back home a few days ago and won't answer her phone. She's not at home. She's not in her office."

"Dammit," Louie said. He threw a wet towel at me. "You got into a fight with her, didn't you."

Ghedi and Denise made eye contact, then returned to what they were doing.

"We did fight, and I don't want to talk about it," I said.

"Well I haven't seen her," Louie said. "Ghedi? Denise?"

"We have not seen her either," Ghedi said.

"But she did call me," Denise admitted.

I moved towards her. "When?" I asked.

"Yesterday," Denise said.

I waited. "What did she say?" I finally asked.

"She made me promise not to tell you."

"Come on," I pleaded. "She's not at the house. I think she went ... I think she's in trouble."

"I don't think I should betray Mindy's confidence," Denise said.

"I think she's in big trouble."

"So explain to me what happened, and if she's really in trouble I'll tell you what we talked about."

"Fair enough," Andrew said, and sat at the bar.

I picked up Louie's towel and told our story much as I had told it to those who had gathered on our lawn for Raphael Ostend's council, adding some material that Ostend and Ray Dale had shared that day. I felt hesitant in telling it, but I was confident that my friends were listening without judgment, despite Ray's warnings to the contrary.

"That's insane!" Denise exclaimed.

"It probably is," I admitted.

"You're in pretty deep," Louie said. He looked at Denise. "Ghedi and I both saw the word on Tom and Mindy's wall. That 'ARIEL.' It's real, but it's not natural."

Ghedi came around the bar and put his arm around my shoulders. "Would you like me to contact my Uncle Nelson in Somalia? He serves as our village priest and may be able to help you, even from that far of a distance."

"Priest?" Andrew asked. "You're Catholic?"

"No," Ghedi said. "He is not that kind of a priest."

"I'm OK," I said to reassure Ghedi. "What I need is Denise's information."

"She asked me about the night Lodi played at Louie's," Denise said. "She asked me about Lodi."

"What did you tell her?"

"I told her about that night," Denise said. "I told her about his music, about the name-that-tune game, and about the conversation we had afterwards on the deck."

"And Tom, you didn't tell her all this?" Louie asked.

"I thought it best not to," I said.

Louie exhaled with a whistle.

"That seals it," Andrew said. "Aren't you glad we came here?"

"Seals what?" Louie asked.

"I suspect Mindy drove to Delaware County when she

saw the second piece of writing on our wall," I said. "Now we also know who she went to see."

Andrew was on his feet and turning towards the door when Denise said, "She told me she saw him in a dream."

"What?" I asked. "When?"

"I already told you, she told me yesterday. So she had the dream the night before last."

"Did she tell you what the dream was about?"

"She said she saw Lodi in her dream. She described him perfectly. She never saw him in person, did she?"

"No," I said. "She had graduation events the night he played here, and again when I went down to Delaware County. What happened in her dream, Denise? Did she tell you that?"

Denise looked away. "You know where she is. You know who she's looking for. Isn't that enough?"

"She's probably right, Tom," Louie said.

"What did Mindy tell you, Denise? What happened in her dream?"

"Come on, Tom—"

"What did she tell you?" I shouted.

Ghedi moved out from behind the bar, ready to defend his girlfriend if necessary. Andrew had a hand on my wrist.

"She said Lodi seduced her," Denise said softly. "She said he used music to do it. He used candles with the same scent that she smelled the night she got knocked out ... "

Chapter Thirty Nine

I WAS OUT THE DOOR in a flash, with Andrew right behind me. I beat him to the driver's side, took the keys from the sun visor and started the truck. Andrew hopped into the passenger seat just as I peeled out of Louie's parking lot onto the road.

"That can't be why she went to see him," Andrew said. "I know her as well as you do! There has to be another explanation. She'd never do that."

I turned toward my cousin and scowled. I did not want to parse my way through possible explanations. I knew Mindy had gone to see Lodi—that fact was enough for me. Feelings of anger, betrayal, guilt and revenge tore their way through my mind and my gut. I gripped the steering wheel tightly with both hands and clenched my teeth. I reminded myself to practice the mindful breathing that Andrew had spoken of in the kitchen at Heron's Nest, but I could only do it for a few seconds before the mindfulness was drowned out again by anger. Andrew tolerated the absence of radio music for the ride along the Thruway and down Route 28. He respected my silence as well, although he kept looking my way and, I thought, telepathically encouraging me to breathe. I only broke the silence as we began to descend the mountain.

"What is that?" I said, the fire of anger quenched for a moment by curiosity.

"That's one hell of a storm," Andrew added.

And it was indeed one hell of a storm. The clouds to

the south were layers of charcoal and battleship grey and were simultaneously billowing up into the sky and swirling earthward in the emerging shape of a funnel. Lightning flashed within the cloud; thunder boomed against the hills. Below the clouds and on either side of the funnel was a mist that hung in the air like a curtain. The line between the mist and the cloud above it was as clearly demarcated as the white and black squares on a chess board. Both storm and mist were moving south.

I pulled into a scenic overlook so we could watch the storm. Mesmerized by what we saw, we did not hear the flock of starlings until they were right over our heads. They flew in a tightly packed group and moved as one, zigging and zagging and looping, folding in on themselves and back out again. At one point they turned to the north and tried to fly away from the storm. But to no avail—like iron filings acted upon by a magnet they were pulled inexorably towards it.

"What did Comstock call that?" Andrew asked.

"Murmuration," I said.

"It all starts with the birds," Andrew said. "Same story here as in the Thousand Islands."

"I thought it started with fluctuations in the river levels?" I asked.

Just then a bright flash of lightning and a violent crack of thunder signaled an imminent transition from mist to rain.

"I think the river levels are about to fluctuate," Andrew said. "What is it down there, the Susquehanna?"

"Delaware," I said. "The West Branch is here, the East Branch starts on the other side of the Catskills." I gave my cousin an ironic smile. "Welcome to Anti-Rent country. We'd better get going before the rain starts."

"Yeah," Andrew said. "Mind if I drive?"

I gave him the keys as I got in the passenger side. "It's your truck," I said.

We sped down the mountain and into Delhi. The rain still hadn't come as we passed Osman Steele's obelisk, even as we entered Andes.

"Pull over here," I said as we approached the general store where Lodi made pizza, bread and soup.

Andrew followed me into the store. Lodi's cousin Emma was working the register again, but with no customers in the store her attention was directed to the impending storm.

"Come on in," she said cheerfully. "Start raining yet?"

"Not yet," I said.

"But when it does!"

"Where is he?" I asked.

"Where is who? My cousin?" Then she recognized me. "You're the guy who needs an OSHA refresher! The one who was looking for Moses Earle's old farm. Lodi's not here. He stopped in yesterday to get paid."

"Where'd he go? Was anybody with him?"

"He didn't say where he went. And yes, there was someone with him. Well, someone who came to see him and left with him."

"Who? A woman with light brown hair?"

Emma shook her head. "No. It wasn't a woman with light brown hair. It was a man. Tall, and with hair like yours."

"Was his name Patrick?" I asked.

"Lodi didn't introduce us," she replied. "But the guy didn't look too good. Kinda wobbly. Had a hard time keeping his eyes open."

"What's Lodi's number?" I asked as I pulled out my cell phone. "It's important that I find him."

"Service is out," she said just as the notification appeared on my screen. "Land lines are out too. And the internet, which is *really* weird. I told you, this storm's gonna be a bad one. Really bad. Can you feel the electricity?"

I could. "Do you have any idea where Lodi might have gone?" I asked.

"Back home maybe?"

"Where's he live?" I asked.

"In an apartment at the farm," Emma said. "He renovated the old barn after my uncle built a new one for the cows." She gave me directions.

Andrew turned to leave, but I told him to wait a minute. I moved towards the counter and asked Emma if she remembered anything about the day I stopped in for pizza.

"It was only last week," she said. "Of course I remember."

"What did Lodi do after I left? After he finished making that pizza? How long did he stay here after I left?"

"He stayed another hour, maybe more. After you came in he remembered he had to get some bread dough ready for the next day. So he finished the pizza, made bread dough and set it aside to rise overnight."

"Do you know where he went after he finished the dough? Do you know if he followed me up to Moses Earle's farm?"

"I know exactly where he went," she said. "He went to the same place where he probably is now, back to our farm to help my uncle plant the winter rye. They're doing a hundred acres of it this year so it would have taken them a while."

"Why'd he tell me to come back to the store after I visited the Earle farm if he knew he wasn't going to be here?"

"I don't know. Maybe he forgot about the planting when he told you that?" She pulled out her phone, touched the screen and scrolled. "Here it is. Look. He called me just a few minutes after he left and asked me to give you directions to the farm if you came back to the store."

"Did I?"

"Did you what?" she asked, confused.

"Did I come back to the store?"

"Uh, no."

"Do you remember if someone took my truck?"

"Your truck? Seriously? I have no idea if anyone took your truck. Have you tried the sheriff?"

"Let's go, Tom," Andrew said. "Let's get out of here."

"Well, thanks anyway," I said.

"Good luck!" she said as we left.

Chapter Forty

ANDREW DROVE CAUTIOUSLY, expecting the rain to start at any second. I rode with the window open, puzzling over why the rain hadn't started yet even though the asphalt sky now blocked every hint of sunlight.

"This is it," Andrew said as we turned onto the red clay seasonal limited use highway. "Hale Hollow Road."

"Bet Hale Hollow Road'll be a mud pit soon," I replied.

"So let's get in, get Mindy and get out," my cousin suggested, "just like we did with our G.I. Joe's as kids."

I laughed, but just for a moment. "And if Patrick's there?" I asked.

Andrew sighed. "Remember what we used to do with Big Jim?"

"Yeah," I said. "We used to leave him there. In the sandbox, tied to a dock piling, wherever he was."

"You remember why?"

"Because he was never part of the mission."

"I hate to say this, but I've been meaning to bring it up for a while now. I think it might be time to give up this search for your brother."

"Why?"

"Because your primary mission is Mindy."

"Did you hear what Emma said?" He gave me a look. "Lodi's cousin? The cashier back at the general store?"

"Yeah. So?"

"She said Lodi was there with a tall guy with hair like mine."

"Probably another cousin. Bet they come a dime a dozen down here in Delaware County."

"It was him," I insisted.

"OK," Andrew conceded. "But I think you should consider how you'll respond if you discover he doesn't want you to find him. Maybe there's a good reason you haven't heard from him in ten years. Besides, you and Mindy are already carrying a heavy enough load. Last thing you need is that." He glanced up. "And if we get stuck down here on Mud Hollow Road, you're the one who's gonna tell Mrs. Backlund of Tar Island why I don't have her porch done before her kids arrive for summer vacation."

"Fair enough," I said, "on both counts."

After driving past a mile of dense woodland dominated by maple, fir and ash, the latter of which was just starting to leaf out, we passed a hilly pasture where four beautiful Belgians grazed, their manes and tails tussled by the wind. The horses didn't seem the least bit concerned about the storm.

"Bingo," Andrew said as we approached a gable-roofed barn on our left. The barn had a fieldstone foundation and board and batten siding above that. On the end farthest away from the road, a wooden bridge led from a set of doors on the second story to a steep hill. Across the street from the barn was a freshly painted white farmhouse with a wraparound porch that would've made Mrs. Backlund of Tar Island jealous.

The sky billowed and raged at what was obviously the center of the storm. Water vapor extended downwards like arms trying to punch through the earth's crust.

"Does that count as rain?" I asked.

"I don't know," Andrew said. "I don't know what to think about what we're seeing. But look!" He pointed. On the far side of the house was my truck. "Got your keys?"

I jingled them, and for the first time in days I felt something other than gloom.

Returning my attention to the sky, I was reminded of

Mary Earley's mural in the Delhi post office, the print of which Professor McNally had given me when I visited him the week before to discuss the Anti-Rent Wars. The sky here looked like the sky in that painting, black and grey, swirling and menacing, a tableau of dread.

Lodi stood near the barn's gable-end doorway and watched us arrive. He wore jeans and a Carhartt jacket and a Mets cap pulled down tight. He didn't once glance at the sky, even though it seemed to concentrate its energy on him. Incongruously, he had something on the grill, the smoke from which curled up into and joined the mist above.

Andrew parked his truck next to mine. As I opened the passenger door gust of wind caught it and pulled it from my hand.

"Watch it now," my cousin said.

I tried to apply the lesson Andrew taught me after my encounter with the bishop. I closed the door. Slowly and steadily, mindfully breathing all the way, I crossed the road, walked up to Lodi and asked him where Mindy was.

He smiled and looked at the curled fingers of his left hand. He picked a hangnail and flicked it away. "You think she's here," he said. "You drove all this way with"—he looked past me—"with your cousin because you thought she came to me." Then his eyes widened. "Or you think I kidnapped her?" I made to answer but he quieted me. "Tell you what. Look up at the sky and tell me what you see."

"I came for Mindy," I said.

"She's not here, Tom. Now look up at the sky and tell me what you see." He looked me in the eye until I answered.

"A storm. Big, billowing clouds. Um, a twister too. Shouldn't we go inside? Maybe down to the basement? Those stone walls look pretty strong."

"You bet they're strong. They've been standing for almost two centuries. They've almost returned to the ground by now. But no, I don't think we'll have to take shelter."

"You don't?"

"Look again. Take a good long look at what's happening up there. See anything strange about that so-called twister of yours?"

"It's ... it's not twisting."

"No, it's not. Nor is it going to touch the ground."

"Are you sure?" I asked.

"It's been sitting over my house for three full days and hasn't come an inch closer to the ground. Weather's always strange around here, but this, as they say, is ridiculous. Come inside anyway. Not for shelter but because I've got something to show you. And someone for you to meet." He again looked beyond me and shouted. "Andrew, right? Come on in. It might not rain, but it might get a lot worse out here before it gets better, even without a twister."

I turned and pointed to my truck. "How'd that get here?" I asked.

"You don't remember?" Lodi, who seemed genuinely surprised, stopped at the door.

"I don't. I remember being on Moses Earle's farm when something weird happened. I ended up at home, where I woke up later during a pretty bad nightmare."

"Huh. Well, I found you on Moses Earle's farm all right after you didn't come here and didn't return to the store. I drove you home in your truck, then drove it back here. I almost had to carry you you were so out of it."

"Did I say anything? Tell you what happened?"

"You were mumbling something about your brother and a boat. You didn't say what happened up at the farm."

"Was Mindy home when you dropped me there?"

"Her car was there, or at least I assume it was her car. Ford Focus?" I nodded. "But it was late. You said you were fine and went inside. I told you to call me the next day and I'd return your truck. I never heard from you until now."

"What's cooking?" Andrew asked as he approached the grill. "Smells really good!"

"Lamb shank," Lodi said. "I'd offer you some, but it's not for us."

Suddenly, the sky darkened even more. I looked up and sensed a shadow cross either over or through the strange cloud formation. The shadow was there and gone in less than a second, but its cold presence seemed to linger beneath my skin.

"What the hell was that?" Andrew asked.

"Ask your cousin," Lodi said.

"What's that supposed to mean?" I asked.

Lodi shrugged. "It's on your wall."

"Ariel?" I whispered the word.

I thought I saw a flash in the cloud. But I told myself it was a storm after all, and storms do produce lightning.

But Lodi said, "Look, that's the second time you said that name in my presence. Whisper it if you must say it. Better yet, and at least for the time being, try not to say it at all."

My eyes followed the plume of smoke downwards from the mist to the large piece of lamb. I pointed to the grill. "Is that who you're cooking for?"

"You're learning," was Lodi's reply.

"Is it an angel?" I whispered.

"Angel. Demon. Daemon. God. Call it what you like. Categories lose their relevance with things like that. Come on," he said. "I need to show you this."

We followed him through the door and into a simply arranged open living space consisting of a small kitchen, an oak table with six chairs, a desk and three padded rocking chairs. He motioned for us to join him behind the desk. He opened a laptop and brought up a National Weather Service radar map.

"Guess the internet's back on," I said. I turned on my phone to see if I had a signal. Nothing.

"Service is still out," Lodi said. "Phone, internet, TV, AM, FM, everything."

"How come you've got service?" Andrew asked.

"Special network," Lodi said. Then he pointed to the screen, where the radar loop was almost finished buffering. "Where'd you come from? Clinton Falls?"

"Wellesley Island originally. We stopped by Clinton Falls to look for Mindy. We came here when we didn't find her."

"And like I said, you won't find her here either. OK. Look. There's clear skies over the Saint Lawrence. Nothing over Clinton Falls. Same with Cooperstown, Oneonta, Delhi." With a pencil Lodi traced the map in a southeasterly direction. He tapped the screen. "We're here."

"I don't get it," I said. "There's no storm, no cloud cover. Nothing."

Lodi clicked on a link that brought up the satellite view.

"Same thing," I said. "Clear skies all across the Northeastern United States. Is the radar broken? Or maybe the satellite's malfunctioning because of the storm."

Andrew shook his head. "The storm might affect the radar, but not the satellite. Satellites are far above all this. No clouds and no storms up where they are."

"Insightful point," Lodi said. "So why's there a storm, and an ostensibly severe one at that, over my house?"

Andrew shrugged his shoulders. I shook my head.

"Now come here," Lodi instructed.

He led us up a flight of stairs and down a hallway that traversed the length of the barn. At the end of the hallway was a window looking out at woods adjacent to the pasture where the four Belgians grazed.

"Take a look," Lodi said. "And I'll tell you right now, before you ask, that yes, you really are indeed seeing what you think you're seeing."

Andrew and I moved close to the window to get a good view. What we witnessed astonished us. Into the woods and up a hill the earth undulated like a wave. The rise and fall accelerated for a few minutes until the ground was split open by some huge invisible razor that upended trees, cut through root systems and left a deep scar of grass, soil and stone on its surface. The red clay exposed from beneath the topsoil looked like dried blood.

I heard the water before I saw it—a freshet growing into a stream widening into a creek strengthening into a torrent. Churning and bubbling, it followed the course of the gouged earth and flowed right towards Lodi's barn. There was no way the sills of the barn could hold out against this, I thought, even if they have been around for almost two centuries. I was about to turn and run for safety when the whole scene disappeared. The land, the grass, the trees—all of them shimmered for a moment before the process started again and repeated itself to the smallest detail and with the same endpoint.

"What the hell?" Andrew said, both fear and disbelief mixed into his voice.

"Just a minute," Lodi responded, squeezing between us. He moved his outstretched finger back and forth. "The next exhibit should start any second. Let me see ... there! Now! Ten o'clock!" We looked in that direction and saw the branch of a tree light up like a struck match. The flame just as suddenly disappeared, then appeared again on another tree. The flame jumped from tree to tree for about two minutes before the pyrotechnics stopped. None of the branches showed any signs of burn. The scene repeated itself again after a few minutes pause, with branches on other trees serving as tinder.

"What did we just see?" I asked, my heart pounding.

"I think you know," Lodi answered. "I think you both know."

Both Andrew and I were silent for a moment before I asked, "But why are they so angry?"

"You mean why are they so angry right here, right now?"

"I guess that's what I mean," I said.

"It's the cross I bear," Lodi said. "But let me show you

something else first, then I'll tell you the answer to your question." Lodi turned and we followed him to a closed room off the same upstairs hallway. He slowly opened the door. The room was illuminated with scented candles, not of the chemical variety but naturally and beautifully fragranced. I noticed right away that at least one of them, probably several of them, were lemon verbena.

Lodi grabbed a large candle that gave off a peculiarly bright, greenish flame. He turned towards us with a grave expression on his face and put his finger to his lips. He nodded to me and I nodded back. Then he moved the candle close to the face of the man laying on a bed. The man lay on his side. His muscles were rigid. His arms were curled under his head and a wool blanket covered the lower two-thirds of his body.

My brother had a strained expression on his face. He was thinner than he was when I last saw him ten years before. His hair was still dark, except for the temples, which were solid grey. I reached down and laid a hand on his brow. His skin was cold to the touch. My hand began to tremble. Tears welled up in my eyes and I felt my stomach drop.

"It's OK," Lodi said tenderly, placing a hand on my shoulder.

Only when he moved the candle right up to Patrick's mouth and the flame flickered did I know my brother was alive.

Chapter Forty One

"How did it happen?" I asked. We were back downstairs, gathered around Lodi's desk in the rocking chairs. "How did he get like that?"

"What exactly's wrong with him?" Andrew added.

"I don't know the answer to any of those questions," Lodi said. "My best guess, however, is that he traveled through time."

"He *what*?" Andrew asked.

"Time-traveled. Well, we both did, actually, several years ago. Patrick's condition seems to be one of the potential side-effects. When he and I did it together we slept twelve hours a day for three straight days. But this is worse. Much worse. I think he did it again and came back like this."

"He's catatonic," Andrew said.

Lodi nodded. "Catatonic indeed."

"Was he with you yesterday at the store? Emma said she saw him. She said he could barely stand or keep his eyes open."

"He was with me. He showed up at the store yesterday afternoon. Before that I hadn't seen him in about four years! He was able to keep going for some time, but he took a turn for the worse last night. He passed out completely on our way back here."

"Shouldn't we get him to a hospital?" I asked.

Lodi produced a sheet of paper from a desk drawer. He handed it to me. It was a handwritten, notarized statement that listed the conditions under which Patrick Flanagan was not to receive medical attention. Unconsciousness was one of them.

"He gave me that when he walked into the store," Lodi said.

I handed back the paper and asked, "So what's keeping him alive?"

"I'm wondering the same thing," Lodi admitted. He pointed his thumb upwards and whispered," Maybe it is."

Andrew said, "Back to how this all happened. This time travel. How'd you do it? You got a time machine back in the other side of the barn?"

"No. We store our farm equipment in there. Plows, furrows, rakes."

"How 'bout a tractor?" Andrew asked. "I didn't notice one outside."

"We don't own a tractor," Lodi answered. "Not the four-wheeled kind anyway."

"Isn't that the only kind?" Andrew asked.

Lodi shook his head. "We have a walk-behind two-wheeled tractor. It's a versatile machine. Italian. Lots of attachments. Ours runs on biodiesel."

"But that can't plow and seed, what"—Andrew waved an arm—"five hundred acres?"

"Five hundred fifty," Lodi said. "And no it can't. A walk-behind can do a lot, but it can't do that. For that we use the four Belgians you probably saw out in the north pasture. The equipment in the other end of the barn is for them. We do things the old way here on Hale Hollow Farm. The land likes it better that way, which is a very important consideration." He paused and looked at me. "So no, we do not have a time machine. Nor do we use a magical cave or standing stone. We ... well, your brother, with my help, learned to do it differently."

"Can you see into the future?" I asked. I was thinking about the bishop's story and was curious if Lodi somehow knew Patrick back when we were kids.

"No. When I met your brother he could though. He could predict and slightly manipulate the future. He'd been trying to manipulate the past for some time, but without success. He needed the help of the elementals to do it successfully. That's where I came in. I helped him summon the elementals and get their help. Without them, he probably wouldn't have made it through alive."

"He's catatonic," Andrew reminded us.

"And he might be dead if he tried to engage the past the same way he engaged the future."

I gestured to my cousin. "We know why he was trying to change the past," I said.

Lodi smiled. "Oh?"

"He was trying to save our parents."

"Ah, yes. I remember that story. I heard it from him first, then from you."

I swallowed before I spoke. "He succeeded?"

Lodi shook his head. "No, he didn't. You of all people should know that."

"Wait a sec," Andrew said. "He changed something else in the past?"

Lodi smiled, and without answering Andrew's question he stood up, went into the kitchen and poured three tall glasses of tap water, one for each of us.

Andrew drank half of his. "This is good water!" he said.

"Spring water," Lodi explained. "Flows down the hill behind the barn."

"Was that what we saw when ... when the ground gave way?" I asked. "The spring underneath the rock?"

Lodi nodded. "My family's been drawing from that spring for many, many years." He held his glass up to the light. "Who knows? Maybe the best time-traveling magic is in this water."

I took another sip of water. "What colors did you wear?" I asked. "What colors were your calico?"

"Well," Lodi said. He sat down. "Either that was a really

good guess or … well." He looked right at me and smiled. "Now I see why you were so interested in that particular topic of conversation on Louie's back deck. Mine was grass green and sky blue. My mask was thundercloud grey, with two bull's horns attached."

"And my brother wore purple and orange with stag antlers," I said.

"He did indeed," Lodi said.

"What help did Patrick receive from the elementals?" I asked.

"Do you know how difficult it is to summon one of them? To raise one of them up to our plane of existence?" Lodi asked. "Only the most talented adepts can do that. That's a once-a-century skill. It took me many years of practice and much heartache to summon even the most insignificant earth-being."

"Patrick did it," I said with more than a little pride. "Back in 2003 he successfully summoned a fire-being."

"He did?" Lodi asked, springing from his chair. "A salamander?"

"It was at the Genesee Country Village in Mumford, just south of Rochester. I heard the story from a blacksmith who saw it happen, a reliable witness if there ever was one. My brother summoned a salamander and kept it visible for several minutes."

"That's news to me," Lodi admitted as he paced the room. "Of course, we lost touch about a year or so before that. Wow. That's quite a game-changer."

"How?" Andrew asked.

"The important thing to remember about the elementals is that once you connect with them, all four types can do just about anything you want them to do, including take you through time. There are benefits and drawbacks to each one, especially for time travel. Earth beings, gnomes, can take you back quite successfully, but they might leave you there. Sylphs or fairies can do a lot more, including take you into the future. They might also trick you, however, and send you where you don't want to go. The water beings are able to take you far back into the past, but only for a brief time, a dip of the feet if you will."

"And salamanders?" I asked. "What can the fire-beings do?"

"They," Lodi said, "they are the most gifted and dangerous of all. They can burn away a whole aeon of the past just like that." He snapped his fingers. "But at the same time they can burn away your own past if you're not careful. That's why what he did in Mumford is a game-changer."

"Is that what happened to my brother?" I asked. "Did the fire-beings do this to him?"

"I'm not sure," Lodi admitted, "although this new bit of information makes me wonder."

"Did my brother kill Osman Steele?" I asked.

"Slow down," Lodi advised. "Don't get ahead of yourself." He paused for a moment, sipped his water and stared into his glass. "In fact, I think I'd better follow my own suggestion. All this talk about what it was like and where we went has put me ahead of where I should be. I need to go back. I need to tell you about about my family and me, and then about how I met Patrick and about how the two of us came to agree on taking the trip back to 1845." He walked over to the window and drew back the curtains. The funnel cloud was still about fifty feet from the ground and holding steady. "Looks like we've got time."

Chapter Forty Two

"My family cleared this land and built this farm," Lodi said. "They came here from Scotland in the 1790's, dirt poor and carrying all their possessions on their backs. But they made a little money in Boston and were able to put a down payment on this land and buy a few Herefords. I still have the original land contract stored away upstairs. It seemed like a good deal on the surface—minimal down payment, low interest, no rent for five years, partial rent for five years after that, full rent in perpetuity after ten years."

"What exactly was the rent?" I asked.

"For the second five year span it was ten bushels of wheat per one hundred acres, for the third five years it was fifteen bushels of wheat, and afterwards twenty bushels of wheat. Like I said, it seemed like a good deal on the surface, but there were more obligations in the fine print. In addition to the rent, the landlords owned all live and dead trees and all rough and cut lumber, all water courses and the mills built upon them, and the rights to all minerals laying under the ground. In return for using these resources, the tenants owed the landlords—I memorized this part—'yearly and every year the yearly rent of two fat hens and one day's labor, with a wagon, sled or plough with a yoke of oxen or pair of horses and a driver, at such time and place within ten miles as the party of the first part, his heirs and assigns shall require.' And this was rent paid in perpetuity, which means the rent could not be canceled, nor could the lease be terminated. In essence, my family was enslaved.

"But they paid their rent. They paid it faithfully and without complaint for years. Then the Hardenberghs sold the land to Charlotte Verplanck, who lived in a big townhouse on Wall Street and in an even bigger mansion in the Hudson Valley. Her lifestyle was expensive. Her land agents were much more aggressive in demanding payment of rents than the original owners' agents. When the lease matured and full rent was due, they relentlessly sought payment.

"Thing was, at the same time, my family, along with other tenant families, discovered that the landlords' claim to the land wasn't as clear as their collection agents made it sound. Copies of the original land grant, made by King George, said that the 1701 Hardenbergh Patent went as far west and north as the East Branch of the Delaware River, but the Hardenberghs and the families that bought their land claimed the patent included land as far west and north as the West Branch of the Delaware River. My ancestors' land, and the heart of the Delaware County Anti-Rent movement, was between the two branches. The Verplanck's had no clear title on the land. When we discovered this, we stopped paying the rent.

"We got involved in politics. We joined an Anti-Rent association. We wore the calico and donned masks, and our women signaled us with tin horns. We gathered with our fellow tenants on holidays and sang songs and listened to speeches and ate and drank. We grew confident. We knew we had influence, both locally, where Anti-Rent sentiments ran high, and in Albany, where politicians couldn't help but listen to our cries for freedom." Lodi paused and drank some water. "I don't need to recite the rest of the story, do I? From what you said on Louie's back deck, I'm pretty sure you know what happened next."

"I do," I said. "The sheriffs and undersheriffs rode out from Delhi to collect the rent. Many farmers refused to pay. The law and order men harassed them. The farmers harassed back. The conflict came to a head on August 7, 1845, when Osman Steele was shot trying to force a rent sale on Moses Earle's farm."

"That's right," Lodi said, and he repeated slowly, "Osman Steele was shot."

"Did your family know him?"

"My family had one encounter after another with Osman Steele. He'd come here trying to collect the rent, blustering and threatening, waving his papers with one hand and his gun with the other. He was drunk more often than not. My family knew he was all bluster, at least before August 7, 1845."

"Was anyone from your family there?"

Lodi nodded. "We were all there! Several men from my family were in the lower field near the road on reconnaissance duty. But let me pause my family story right there. Let me tell you how Patrick and I met. Then we'll go back to 1845 and hopefully I can explain what happened."

"Fair enough," Andrew said.

"OK, then. I met Patrick in Hamden at a Delaware County Historical Association immersion day for kids. I was working there part time that summer. He was doing Anti-Rent reenactments and was working with a group of town ball interpreters … you know what that is?"

"1848 rules baseball," I said. "He played that out in Mumford too."

"Patrick had a thing he did after the game ended. He'd come wobbling out of a barn in his full Anti-Rent costume, moaning and groaning like he was Frankenstein's monster. The kids loved it! They'd run around him and scream. Some of the bolder boys would tackle him and try to remove his mask. But Trick never let that happen. He'd always get back off the ground and return to the barn before they could reveal his secret identity.

"I saw him next at a gig in Oneonta. It must have been around 1999 or 2000, definitely before 9/11. He bought me a beer between sets and told me how much my music spoke to him on a deep, personal level. Later on, when he told me the story of what caused his suffering, he said my music was an early step in the healing process. I liked that. It affirmed what I'd hoped for some time, that I helped people heal through the power of my music. Patrick helped me identify and clarify that healing gift."

"He bought you a beer between sets?" I asked.

"Sounds familiar, huh? I thought exactly that when I met you at Louie's. And the similarities don't end there. Like you, your brother said he was looking for something he'd lost. Like you, he hoped I could help him find it. When you came to me that night at Louie's, I saw the similarities right away."

"What was he looking for?" I asked.

"You know what I think?"

"What?"

"The way I see it, you two were being drawn together, and I was meant to be the link between you."

"Could very well be true," Andrew said.

"Anyway, he was living in Oneonta at the time, working for George Pratchett, a local expert in old home restoration. They're the outfit that fixed up this barn when we built the new one for our cows."

"This is some fine workmanship," Andrew said, looking around and pointing out the rafters. "I've been meaning to tell you that. I'm glad you left some of the old beams exposed."

"George Pratchett's the best," Lodi said. "Costs a fortune, but he's worth it. And thank you for the compliment."

"It's fitting that Patrick worked construction," I said. "Our grandfather was a master. Andrew inherited the family business when his father retired and is known as the best contractor on the river."

"I'll even give him a job when he wakes up," Andrew said.

Lodi smiled. "While working we talked a lot about the

Anti-Rent Wars and Osman Steele's murder. He first knew about them from a column your father wrote, Tom. Then he experienced the Anti-Rent Wars in historical reenactments. As I mentioned, he was part of one, a group from Delhi. He traveled to living history museums all across the state. Mumford, of course, Hamden, Cooperstown, even out to Sturbridge a time or two. At first he was an extra, hanging out in the background and shouting insults at the sheriff and his cronies, including Steele. Eventually he got the starring role, the Anti-Renter who shot and killed Osman Steele—"

"So my brother was the killer!"

"Didn't you hear him?" Andrew said. "Patrick was the shooter in reenactments."

"May I continue?" Lodi asked.

"Sorry," I said.

"So Patrick played the role of Osman Steele's killer. After a few weeks he noticed something strange happening: it was getting easier and easier to complete the task."

"How?" I asked.

"All kinds of weird things would happen," Lodi said, "all kinds of minor irregularities would present themselves. A person in front of Patrick would move out of the way. The man playing Steele would position himself closer to Patrick and more in range of his gun. After a week or so, Patrick decided he'd intentionally try to miss, to *not* kill Osman Steele. Didn't work."

"Why did it matter?" Andrew asked. "He was firing blanks, right? And the reenactment was choreographed, wasn't it?"

"Yes and yes. Steele still fell to the ground dead because the actor playing him knew his part. But the glitches mattered quite a bit, at least to Patrick. The upshot is this: put simply, he gradually became aware that someone, *something* was trying to help him kill Osman Steele. And it didn't look good to the audiences. The glitches made the troupe look amateurish. Patrick almost lost the role. He was not happy.

"Then he and his troupe performed at the Delaware County Fair in Walton. By this time I was watching the reenactments closely to help Patrick discover what was going on. It was during their second night's performance that I saw it, out of the corner of my eye. Just to Patrick's right I saw the earth shift. Almost imperceptibly I saw the earth move and the air bend and pull a man standing in front of Patrick off balance. I knew what it was. And I knew how to catch it."

"Catch it?"

"Yes. I don't have time to explain the details of how I did it. Let's just say that I perfected a way to trap an elemental and prevent it from returning to it's original plane of existence. So we caught it. We talked with it. After a lot of wrangling and hemming and hawing it made us an offer. It told us if we released it it would help us go back in time to August 7, 1845. It would take us to Moses Earle's farm and put us front and center of the actual event. How could we pass up an offer like that? So we went back."

"Hold on," I said. "Why would an earth-being try to help my brother kill Osman Steele in reenactments?"

"Rule number one when associating with the elementals: do not, *do not*, try to guess their intentions."

"Why not?"

"Because you'll drive yourself nuts, first of all. And more significantly, just when you think you've figured out their intentions, or if they think you think you've figured out their intentions, they'll change course in midstream just to fuck with your mind. They're mercurial. The more damage they can do, the happier they are."

"Like up your hill," Andrew said.

"Exactly. Now let me get back to my story. Patrick and I were in the front ranks at the sale itself. You know the story. Steele blustered and threatened. The Anti-Renters raised their rifles, cocked and aimed. But then, when Steele moved forward to force the issue, Patrick did something surprising."

"He shot Steele!" I exclaimed.

"No. He shot at the ground next to Steele's horse and frightened it. The horse bucked, sending Steele to the ground. A half-second later another Anti-Renter's bullet grazed Steele's shoulder as he was falling. Steele got up from the ground and ran into Moses Earle's house, where Moses Earle's wife cleaned and dressed his wound. To his credit, Sheriff Moore ordered his men to stand down rather than open fire. One of the Anti-Rent leaders, probably Warren Scudder from Roxbury, told his men to do the same. The Anti-Renters lingered for a few minutes then went home. The law and order men joined Steele in Moses Earle's farmhouse and kept watch. A bloodbath was averted. From all his practice as an interpreter, Patrick knew exactly what to do and exactly when to do it. He saved Steele's life. He changed history.

"That night, Patrick and I partied with the Anti-Renters. We swore oaths to never put away our calico and masks. We drank good brandy and even better cider. We sang songs of victory and triumph, of tyranny overthrown and freedom gained." Lodi smiled. "It was quite a night.

"The following week Governor Silas Wright personally visited Delaware and Schoharie Counties and brought leaders from both sides to the negotiating table. More importantly, also the following week, Charlotte Verplanck sent notice to Moses Earle that she would sell him the land for which he owed the rent, thereby resolving the immediate issue that had led to the conflict in the first place. Other landlords gradually followed suit, and by 1880 most of Delaware County's land was owned rather than leased. The families that could afford large herds were also making a fortune selling the finest butter available anywhere in the nation. Butter and peace. Doesn't get any better than that does it?"

Chapter Forty Three

I WAS STANDING BY THIS POINT, standing right next to Lodi and breathing hard. "That's not the way it happened!" I shouted. "Steele was shot! He died! The end result was recrimination, persecution, tyranny! I researched it! You sang about it, like you said! What was it, that night on Louie's deck?"

"The song?"

"'The Fall Campaign,' that was it, or 'The Reign of Terror'!"

"Those songs shouldn't have been," Lodi said, meeting my dismay with calm.

"What do you mean they shouldn't have been?"

"Patrick went back to save Osman Steele, not kill him."

"What? How? I read about it! Studied it! What you're telling us is impossible! You can't change history like that! *That's not the way it happened!*"

"You historians change history all the time," Lodi said with the wave of his hand. "What do you call it? Revisionism?"

"But not like *that*! Tell me right now that what you're saying is a lie!" I balled my fist. "Tell me or I'll ... "

Andrew stood and slammed a hand against my chest.

"No!" I shouted, slapping it away. "Not this time!"

"Shut up and listen!" he said, pushing me back into a chair. "Listen to what I'm about to ask. OK," my cousin continued, turning back to Lodi, "so you went back in time and changed history? As impossible as it sounds, you did it? Osman Steele lived? It worked?"

"We did it. Well, Patrick did, just as I explained. He went back in time and reversed history." Lodi gave me a smiling glance. "And it seemed to work."

"Why would he do that?" Andrew asked.

"Practice."

"For what?"

I thought for a second. "He was practicing so he could go back and save Mom and Dad! And he must have tried that too! That's why he's passed out."

Lodi and Andrew both looked at me in silence.

"He's catatonic," I said quietly. "He must have failed."

"I'm sorry," Lodi said.

"Wait a minute," Andrew said. "You said your attempt to save Osman Steele *seemed* to work?"

"Yes. There were upsides to saving Steele's life and bringing resolution to the Anti-Rent conflict," Lodi said. "Ostensible peace and butter-based prosperity were foremost among them. But there were things happening beneath the surface—literally beneath the surface. Tom, I think you know what I'm going to say. I think you already know what forces the Anti-Renters inadvertently unleashed."

Andrew looked at me for an answer. I didn't have one at first, but then it came to me. "The costumes," I said. "It was like we were talking about on Louie's deck. By wearing the costumes the Anti-Renters inadvertently … I don't know, summoned the elementals?"

"Summoned, invited, paved the way for. The verb you choose doesn't matter so much as the effects. Maybe unleashed is the appropriate verb. In the course of events that your brother and I created, Osman Steele lived and the farmers of Delaware County had no reason to put away their calico and leather. Their wives did not silence their tin horns. They kept wearing them and blaring them, mostly in celebration of what they justifiably considered a hard-won victory. They found out only after it was too late that they were nourishing the earth-beings, feeding their strength. The people of Delaware County didn't know any of this, of course. Unlike the Iroquois and other Native American peoples, the Anti-Renters had no system of protection against the earth-beings, no way of channeling their energy. Unleashed is definitely the right word. By the time the people noticed what was happening—a rockslide here, a sinkhole there—it was too late. The end result was pretty much what you saw happening up the hill and in the woods, only worse. Unimaginably worse."

"The history books don't say anything about *that*," I said.

Lodi laughed. "Do you expect they would?"

"How was it worse?" Andrew asked.

"Do you know how New York City gets its water?"

"From reservoirs up this way, right?"

"Yes. The Pepacton Reservoir, right in the heart of Anti-Rent country, is the largest one and supplies a quarter of New York's water. In the timeline that Patrick and I created, the elementals found the pipelines that carry water down to the city. They followed them. They poisoned the water, not with bacteria or lead or any modern day toxin, but with a spiritual poison. With madness. Bedlam ensued in New York. Chaos that made that Kurt Russell movie look like kindergarten recess. That was the 1950's. Things got worse before they got better, and whether they even got better is debatable."

"Sounds like you and Patrick made a pretty bad mistake," Andrew said.

Lodi nodded. "We knew it the minute we came back. Once we understood what was happening, we knew we had to set things right. We went back again and returned Osman Steele to the dead, right where we should have left him in the first place."

"How'd you do that?" Andrew asked.

"Patrick let events proceed as they had before we intervened. He did not fire at the ground near Steele's horse. The bullet fired by another Anti-Renter hit its mark. Steele fell to the ground and died."

"Who killed him?" I asked. "The second time around? What did you see? Who was the Anti-Renter who fired the fatal shot?"

"I killed him," Lodi said. "That time I was standing in the second row of the left flank of the Anti-Renters. From there, from just over the shoulder of John van Steenbergh, I fired the shot."

So that was the answer to my question, I thought, the answer I'd been searching for despite myself and despite everything my quest had brought into my and Mindy's life together. I closed my eyes and breathed deep.

"But your hill," Andrew said, "and the fire in the trees …"

"Turns out, we couldn't undo *all* the damage. The earth-beings had become too strong. They were immune, or at least able to withstand, time changes that people cannot withstand. Remember the trap I mentioned earlier?"

"Yes."

"When we went back the second time, I used it to confine the earth-beings to our hill behind the barn."

"They've been there since 1845?" Andrew asked. "Well, since the second 1845?"

"Yes," Lodi answered. "And my family has managed them for over a hundred and sixty years. And that's what I do. Besides making pizza and bread, and playing the guitar every now and again, I manage them. Like I said, it's my cross to bear."

"Is there any way you can send them back to where they belong?" Andrew asked.

"We may soon find out," Lodi said. "And if there is a way to send them back, believe me, I will."

I shook my head and smiled. "Still, by going back again and shooting the sheriff, you were able to return the history books to say what they should have said all along."

"Re-revisionism, you might call it," Lodi said.

I couldn't help but laugh.

Lodi continued. "And that's when Patrick hit the road, after we got back. He traveled to historical villages all over the northeast, reenacting the murder. Yesterday was the first I've seen of him since then. By killing Steele again and again in his reenactments, he said he was able to maintain some semblance of the status quo. Meanwhile, by using my trap, I was able to contain the damage to my family's property, at least so far. Better here than New York City, wouldn't you say?"

The ringing of a phone, a land line, made me jump. Lodi excused himself and went into the kitchen to answer it. I watched and listened to his end of the conversation: "Yes, this is he. Hi! ... Wow ... OK, but why not here? ... No, I understand ... Yes, of course. I will ... I always do. I'll tell him right away." Then he said goodbye and hung up.

"We've got a solution and a problem," Lodi said as he returned to his desk.

"Who was that?" I asked.

"Professor Ray Dale of the Institute—"

"Yes, I know him. He's a former classmate." I recalled Ray's warning from a few days before. "Why's he calling you?"

"He's one of the people who's been helping me find a way to send my unwanted pets back to where they belong."

"Has he?"

"He thinks so. That's the solution. Now let me show you the problem. The problem's worse."

He turned his computer our way. He opened an e-mail sent by "rdale@sunycf.edu" and clicked on a link. My jaw dropped as he moved from one tab to the next, showing us a series of grainy, poorly focused photos taken in and around several Upstate New York cities. They looked like pictures from a traffic camera. In one of them, a wall of snow was moving towards Buffalo from the west. In another, the Genesee River had reversed course and was flooding downtown Rochester. Earthquakes were ripping apart the elevated highways that crossed through downtown Syracuse. Utica was the target of a fast approaching supercell. The sky above Watertown was darkened by thousands of crows. People in Albany were passing out because the oxygen level of the atmosphere had dipped precipitously.

"My God," Andrew said.

"Lodi, what are these?" I asked.

"Frightening, huh?" he answered. "They're from tech that Professor Dale has been trying to refine for about a decade. Looks like he finally figured it out."

"What does this tech do? What do those pictures show?"

"The tech reads Otherworld activity and predicts its results. Those pictures show what's going to happen in about a day and a half if we don't succeed."

"Succeed at doing what?" Andrew asked.

"At closing the gap." Lodi pointed to the screen. "Closing the gap might prevent that from happening."

"What gap?" I asked. "The one behind your barn?"

"No. The gap Ray's concerned about, the gap we need to close, is the one on the Saint Lawrence River. That one is emphatically *not* under control. If we don't close it in the next day or two, this—" he gestured towards the screen again—"this will all happen. It'll spread like a fungus, like an epidemic. And that's the last thing we want to see. But the good news is, if I can get my earth-beings up there, then we might be able to send them through the gap before closing it."

"So what are we going to do?" Andrew asked.

"You are going to drive me up to the river."

"Will do," Andrew said. "We'll be there in a few hours."

"No," Lodi answered. He pointed to the screen. "We're taking the long way around."

Andrew's face beamed. "We're going to trap them!"

"Not quite," Lodi answered.

"What about me?" I asked.

"You need to drive your brother to your apartment at Clinton Falls. Ray Dale will meet you there with someone who can help him. After that, you, Ray, Patrick and Mindy will meet us at your Wellesley Island cottage."

"Mindy!" I exclaimed. "Where is she?"

"She's in Clinton Falls," Lodi said.

Andrew smiled and punched my arm. "Told you we'd find her," he said.

I stood up. "Where in Clinton Falls? We looked everywhere!"

"Did you look at the Institute for Applied Philosophical Research?"

I shook my head.

"That's where she is."

"I'M TAKING YOU HOME," I told my brother as I followed Andrew's truck onto Hale Hollow Road and hit the gas. "You're going back to the Islands." I smiled as I spoke the words, despite a growing fear that I knew what awaited us when we got there.

Part Three

Clinton Falls
The Thousand Islands
Clinton Falls

As Iron at a Distance is drawn by the Lodestone, there being some Invisible Communications between them: So is there in us a World of Love to somewhat, though we know not what in the World that should be. There are invisible ways of Conveyance by which some Great Thing doth touch our souls, and by which we tend to it. Do you not feel yourself Drawn with the Expectation and Desire of some Great Thing?

—Thomas Traherne, *The Centuries of Meditations*
(1660s)

Chapter Forty Four

"AND TO TOP IT ALL OFF, Billy jumped in with an underwater blowtorch and cut the cable the Undees had wrapped around the *Ouroboros*' propellor! I hope you get a chance to see the *Ouroboros* someday. It's, I don't know, it's like a steel cloud floating on the water, one of the most extraordinary things I've ever seen! Anyway, when I heard what Billy did, I ran through the ship and leapt overboard myself. But I was too late. I couldn't save him. And when I jumped into the water I landed on ... I landed on *something* that kept me on the surface. Whatever it was, it also floated Billy back up to the surface. I pulled him onto a raft, but it was too late. Patrick, do you know what I'm talking about? Have you seen them? I guess it would be more accurate to ask if you've felt them. I'm assuming you have from what the bishop said. Before that, before Billy died saving the river, I felt them carry me to Magdalena Island, to the Sisters of Mercy. And once I got there they healed me—my broken leg, that I already told you about. It was, I don't know, it was weird."

I rambled on and on as I drove. I had no idea whether my brother could hear me. But it felt good to tell the story because it allowed me to share with him a foundational experience of my life. And knowing that we were on our way back to the river, remembering the dream I had had back on that warm, sunny May afternoon, talking helped me keep up my courage.

"Right after all that happened Martin Comstock ... Remember him? He was the bartender at Castello's that Mom and Dad used to go talk to after giving us quarters for the jukebox. Anyway, it was right after Billy died that Martin told me what happened to Mom and Dad and you. It probably won't surprise you to learn that I couldn't believe it. Fake your death? No way! No way anyone would do that!"

I paused for a mile or two and let the breeze from the open window refresh me. I was happy to be back in my own truck and, despite the memory of my dream, was happy to have Patrick alongside me.

"I still don't know *why* you did it. Were you trying to protect the gold? Trying to keep your knowledge of the undines and what they could do a secret? Billy told me once that the undines themselves were protectors of the gold. He said the gold itself came from heaven and was more precious than any metal drawn from the earth. If that's the case, then I see why you might want to keep everything a secret. There are a lot worse men than Walter Maitland out there. What could they do with the gold? What can we do with it? I guess we'll find out soon enough." I laughed. "Or maybe you were just doing what Dad told you to do. And maybe that's why Dad told all of us to leave you be."

We pulled onto the thruway, my EZ Pass paying the toll. I turned on the music about then because I was running out of things to say. But I realized after a few songs that I hadn't told Patrick anything about Mindy. I switched off the radio.

"Mindy McDonnell," I said. "Man, wait 'til you meet her! She's everything to me. Everything. We've been friends for a long time, a couple now for five years. We met at school, while we were classmates in the American history program. You can't imagine how happy I was when she said yes to marrying me! I think what I like most about her is how smart she is. Not book smart so much, although she *is* that. She's the youngest chair the history department's ever had, after all! What I mean is that she also has more common sense than most people, certainly more than I have." I paused for a moment and smiled. "I think she reminds me of Mom. You know, with that combination of academic intelligence and street smarts. They say you marry someone just like your mother, don't they?"

I was silent for the rest of the drive. I was thinking about Mindy. I was working towards an understanding of why she had left me, moving closer and closer to forgiveness. I was also anticipating the emotions I'd feel when we finally exchanged our vows. I was thinking about how much I looked forward to settling in to life with her as a married couple, as a new family.

Mindy's car was still in the driveway like it had been when Andrew and I had stopped by earlier that day. This time, though, she was home and came running outside before I cut the engine.

Any residual anger I felt was quickly matched by the joy of seeing her again. I closed my eyes and breathed. By the time I opened them she had the passenger door open and was holding Patrick's hand in hers.

"Who thought it would end like this?" she said. She looked at me, saw the bereft expression on my face and smiled. "Our search for him, I mean," she added to my immense relief. "We'd better get him inside. Ray really thinks he can help him."

I got out of the truck and closed the door. "How? Who's he bringing with him?"

"I don't know," Mindy admitted. Then she asked, "You were with Lodi?"

"Andrew and I both were. We were looking for you."

"Ray knows him," Mindy said as I walked around the truck.

"I gathered as much when Ray called. Lodi said they work together from time to time."

"Even so, Ray still doesn't trust him," Mindy said.

"Ray told me that himself, in our kitchen after the Council of Ostend."

Mindy smiled. "That's what you call it?"

I smiled with her. "That's what Andrew called it. He compared it to Elrond's Council in the Lord of the Rings."

"Pure Andrew," Mindy said with a laugh. "Where is he?"

"With Lodi. But don't worry, He's driving. He'll be fine. He knows how to take care of himself. You and Ray might not trust Lodi, but I'm pretty sure he's on our side."

"Ray said Lodi's always and only on Lodi's side."

"I'd rather not argue about it again," I admitted. I took her hands in mine. "Look at the bright side. I got my truck back."

"Yes, you did." She smiled again.

"How are your arms?"

"Getting better." She held them up and I could see that the bruises were almost gone.

"I'm sorry, Mindy … "

"Stop apologizing!" She slapped the truck's quarter panel.

"No, I'm sorry for bringing all this into your life. I'm starting to think I should've waited to propose until after I found Patrick, until I got my life completely back in order."

She ignored that bit. "You know what else Ray said about Lodi? He said Lodi's side probably corresponds with our side, at least for the time being. So, it's OK, Tom. For now I'll trust him. I'll keep an eye on him, but I'll trust him." She leaned forward and kissed my cheek. "Come on, let's get Patrick inside."

Chapter Forty Five

"I THINK I FIGURED OUT SOMETHING about you," Mindy said as we sat on the front porch swing, taking a much needed respite from everything that had wedged us apart. Ray had told Mindy that we should stay the night in Clinton Falls and that he would come over to our house early the next morning to help Patrick. Rest would be good for all of us, he said. But he still didn't say who he was bringing to help my brother.

"Finally! After all these years!" I joked, although I wasn't sure I wanted her to continue.

"Do you want to know what?"

"Go ahead."

"Put simply, you trust the past more than you trust the present."

"What's that supposed to mean?"

"Most people believe the world's going to get better. They're optimistic about human progress. Most people study the past either to inform the present or to find a better way into the future. You're different. You feel like something's missing from the present, but you don't think you'll find it in the future because you don't trust progress. You can't quite place your finger on what that something is. It's not just your parents or brother either. It's something bigger, something existential. It's something that would still be missing even if your parents were alive, and most assuredly is still missing even though your brother is only a wall away. And you think you'll find this missing something in the past.

That's why you study history. You don't want to inform the present or find a better way into the future. You long for a golden age, yearn for a lost paradise. But the problem is this: your golden age, your paradise, probably never even existed in the first place."

I thought about it for a minute and silently agreed that she was more or less correct. But I also felt something bubbling up within me, something painful, something from the past that I knew I couldn't escape.

"Now don't get me wrong," she continued. "I'm not being the least bit critical. In fact, your sense of historical idealism is one of the things I love most about you. It's infuriating, yes, but also lovable."

"Thanks. I think."

"You're welcome. What bothered me is that I couldn't place it, couldn't figure out for the longest time why you do the things you do, why you dig so hard! Now I see that it's more than being impulsive. It's your way of trying to chip through the wall that separates you from the past, from all that you believe was once good."

I blushed. Then I pointed my thumb over my shoulder. "Patrick would agree, you know."

"He would? Really? Why?"

"As it turns out, the bishop only scratched the surface of Patrick's story. My brother could do a lot more than see into and influence the future, Mindy. He took Lodi back in time, back to 1845. First they saved Osman Steele. Then Lodi killed him again because Osman Steele *not* dying was immeasurably worse than the alternative. Those Anti-Rent costumes almost ruined things."

"How so?" She held up a hand. "And by the way, just to let you know, I'm setting my incredulity aside only for the moment and only for the sake of this conversation."

"Wearing the costumes pulled the elementals from the Otherworld into ours. A ... I don't know, a horde of them.

A swarm. Have you seen what they can do? Did Ray show you his photos?"

"The probability photos? Yes, he did. But I'm not convinced they're not doctored."

"Lodi didn't tell me this," I said, ignoring her last point, "but I'm guessing that what's about to happen in our cities is also being caused by something in the past that went terribly wrong. Patrick and Lodi could only delay the inevitable for a little while ... well, just over a century and a half in this case. But ultimately they couldn't stop it from happening, and that's my point. The answer does lie in the past, Mindy, and we can't escape it."

My voice was trembling now. Whatever it was from the past was inching closer to the surface.

"Why'd they do it?" Mindy asked. "Why did Patrick and Lodi go back?"

"He was practicing," I said, tears starting to flow.

"Patrick was practicing? For what?" Mindy saw my expression. "Tom? What is it?"

"All I want is to see them again!" I wailed. "All I want is one more day! One more *minute*!"

I stood and began to pace. Mindy stood with me and took me in her arms. She held me tight, then tighter, as I lost muscle control and my shoulders heaved. My repeated cries of "I miss them so much!" were barely comprehensible through my sobs.

Mindy didn't say a word. I could tell she was crying with me; her empathy is what eventually settled me down.

"I'm so sorry," she said after a time. "I didn't know you had all that in you."

I shook my head and sat down. "I didn't either," I said. "It's been ten years."

"What do you want to do?"

I inhaled deeply and exhaled slowly. "We can't escape the past," I repeated.

Mindy looked at me for a long moment, then nodded as

if to confirm everything was OK. She say down next to me. "Ray thinks he knows a way to stop it," she said.

"Why didn't you tell me you came to see him?"

"I didn't come to see him. I came here to finish the living room and meet with the dean," Mindy answered. "When I got here, there was a message on my office voice mail from Ray, telling me to call him right away."

"How'd that go, by the way? Your meeting with the dean?"

"Slap on the wrist," Mindy said. "As punishment he's appointing me chair of the English department next year along with history. They have a nasty internecine war going on that the dean thinks I might be able to resolve."

"Blessed are the peacemakers," I said with a laugh, which felt good.

"You'll owe me back rubs," she responded. "At least three a week to relieve the stress of mediating the latest iteration of the English Civil War."

"Will do," I promised. We swung for a couple minutes. "You know, you don't have to go back up with me. You can stay here for a while see if things blow over. We've got a couple more weeks 'til we really have to get things together for the wedding."

"I have to go back up," she replied with a shake of her head. "I promised you I'd see this through and I have to keep that promise."

"OK," I said, feeling relieved.

"There's another reason I have to go back up," Mindy added.

"What?"

"When I returned Ray's phone call, he told me there was something in Lady Ostend's papers that I had to see, something Raphael Ostend had asked him to confirm after the group meeting on our lawn."

"What was it?"

"A mention of me."

"What did she say?"

"That I would be important." Mindy swallowed. "That I would have a significant role to play at the end of things. Those were her words, Tom: at the end of things."

"Did she mention you by name?"

"Yes."

I was silent for a moment as I did the math. "Mindy, Lady Ostend died in 1965, six years before you were born."

"I know."

"How could she have mentioned you? How could she have known you were important?"

Mindy didn't answer. Instead, she stood up and walked into the house. When she returned to the porch she handed me a large brown envelope.

"What's this?" I asked as she sat in a chair on the other side of the porch.

"My mother gave it to me while they were visiting. She said she found it in the attic during spring cleaning. I'd totally forgotten about it. Read it. I don't think it's reappearance was a coincidence."

I opened the envelope and removed an essay, stapled at the top left corner, titled "Borderland: A Brief History of the Thousand Islands." It was from Mindy's high school advanced placement English class and was written in April 1989. The essay began with a couple stories frequently told by tour boat operators having to do with a bright yellow line that marks the border between the United States and Canada. Then Mindy moved on to explain the political and economic complexities of a water border and the many places to hide amidst the islands. She wrote about the pirate William Johnston and explained the geological history of the Thousand Islands. Then she told a personal story about one final border present in the region. Mindy's story was written as follows.

We were on vacation (duh!) at Wellesley Island

State Park. I was playing with my doll, named Shelly, at the water's edge. She was the kind that closed her eyes when you tipped her backwards. I had her practicing her backstroke in the water—I remember that because her eyes were closed. Shelly and I were the only ones there. All the other kids had gone back to their campsites for dinner. My mom and I were about to go back to ours too because my dad was grilling hot dogs and my sister and brother had gone with him to help. I remember that because my mom had just given me my ten minute warning. We were also leaving the next day, so I really didn't want to get out of the water. I said this to Shelly.

"I don't want you to go, either," is the reply I heard.

I stood Shelly up. Her eyes opened. She was not the kind of doll with the string in the back who talked when you pulled it. I was playing in the water. My mom had warned me that playing in the water with Chrissy, the doll that talked, would ruin her, so I left Chrissy at home to watch over things.

I looked back at my mom. She waved. "Ten minutes, honey," she said. She obviously didn't want to go either and had decided to stop time. She was still in the same spot, still halfway up the hill, still reading her Good Housekeeping and gazing out at the river, probably thinking how little she wanted to get back to doing real housekeeping. She wasn't the one who said "I don't want you to go, either," either. I knew that much.

I held Shelly tight and walked out into the water a couple steps. Danny Channing, our across-the-street neighbor back home who also came up to the Thousand Islands, usually two weeks before we did, was fond of telling me about the eels that he saw in the water, here at Wellesley Island Park, in Alex Bay, in Clayton, on boat tours, while water skiing—listen to Danny Channing and you'd think the river was filled with eels and only eels. I hated eels. So for me to walk up to my thighs in that allegedly eel-infested water without either of my parents was a pretty big deal. But there were no eels. Nor fish. Only a voice that said again, "I don't want you to go, either." Small waves were coming in from the wakes of the boats that passed far away. To my eyes there were other waves happening too as the river spoke, waves going both with and against the natural ebb and flow.

The story has no real ending. My dad came back down to the swimming area and told us that the hot dogs were ready. My mom said, "Dinner time sweetie. Come on out of the water and dry yourself off." I obeyed. Both my parents knew something was up because I didn't want any s'mores. My sister and brother knew something was up because I didn't return their teasing. Thankfully, all of them assumed I was down in the dumps because we were going home the following day. I was, of course. But I was also kind of shellshocked. Numbed. There was no way I would have articulated it like this back then, but I knew I had just had a spiritual experience. I knew that the border between here and there had just been breached right before my eyes. It never happened again. Once was probably enough.

The border between here and there is the "substantially harder to pin down" borderland I mentioned earlier. I don't want to call it a supernatural border because that just gets too complicated. It's a liminal border, I guess, just below, or beyond, our conscious awareness. It's a border between here and there, between earth and heaven, between the seen and the unseen, between this world and an "otherworld," between what we can reach out and touch with our hands and what we can feel only with our hearts. Geology can't explain it, although we should keep in mind that in the Thousand Islands ancient rock shaped by fire is kissed, day after day, moment after moment, by the other two elements of air and water. Perhaps it's a spiritual Frontenac Arch, connecting what we know and do now with what's happening on another plane of existence.

History can't explain this liminal border, either, but it can help confirm that it's there. The original inhabitants of the Thousand Islands knew about this particular borderland. In fact, to them it was the only one that mattered since neither America nor Canada existed back then, and when the countries did exist the Native Americans didn't recognize their sovereignty anyway. They called the Thousand Islands "God's Garden." They said that the islands themselves were tears that fell from God's eyes at the rending of the world. They carved petroglyphs on the ancient cliff walls as a testament to what they learned from things they could not see.

There's a reason why tourist attractions spring up where they do. It's not only natural beauty or geography or ease of access. The reason why the Thousand Islands region was so popular in the Gilded Age and is again since the 1960's is that people want to be here. Why else would the Pullmans, Emerys, Bournes, Strausses, Boldts and so many other rich and famous families choose to build their mansions and castles here? They, and modern day sunbathers and water-skiers as well, might not recognize it consciously (hence liminal) but they do become drawn to a place because it offers them what ordinary, everyday life cannot. A Hindu swami understood it when he came to the Thousand Islands in the late 1800's and opened a retreat house that remains active today. Christians from all over the world understand it when, on Sunday afternoons, they worship in the water at Half Moon Bay, beside the Precambrian pink granite cliffs and beneath the open sky of the "world's tallest cathedral." Children, especially, understand it because they are still in tune with the unseen things around them.

I certainly experienced it on that summer day of my sixth year on this earth, as I stood on the edge of an ancient rock and looked down into the water shared by two great nations. I stood at three different borderlands at once that day—the historical, the geological and the spiritual. On that day, I experienced everything that the Thousand Islands had to offer.

I returned the essay to the envelope and handed it back to Mindy. "Mr. Farber's an idiot," I said. Then I gave a loud laugh.

"What?" Mindy asked. "You don't believe it happened?"

"No, no, not that." I was still giggling, "although I am relieved to see there's something to you other than your skeptical side."

"Then what? What are you laughing at?"

"The grade. The B-plus. The totally undeserved B-plus. You've forgotten about it because you only remember your A's!"

Mindy laughed a little with me. "You're probably right," she finally said.

"But seriously," I said after a moment. "You know what really happened, don't you?"

"At first I thought it was the undines."

"That's exactly what it was," I said.

"But Raphael Ostend thinks something different happened. He thinks it was his grandmother, communicating to me through an intermediary."

"The undines," I said again. "We already know she could communicate with them."

"But they can't talk," Mindy said, "at least not in a way humans can understand. Remember the story Raphael told about how the undines warned his grandmother and saved her life?"

"Yes. The time lightning hit the tree and knocked it into the river. The tree just missed the *Archangel* because the undines had told her to watch out." I paused and tried to recall more details. "The undines gave her a headache. They communicated in an extremely high-pitched sound, almost beyond human hearing."

"And I heard a voice. A clear voice, coming from the water. You see, that's what bothered me back when I was a little girl, and that's what still bothers me now. I *heard a voice*, darling. I *heard* it."

"Did Ostend say what he thinks the intermediary is?"

"He said Lady Ostend could also communicate with the dead. In particular, there was one dead man that she enjoyed communicating with quite often. A dead man we knew. A dead man who can travel through time."

"Billy?" I whispered. "Billy Masterson?"

Mindy nodded. "Yes. Raphael suspected as much. And I confirmed as much when I read Lady Ostend's journals. She and Billy communicated regularly. She communicated with Billy through the undines, through other intermediaries and directly. Billy performed certain tasks for her that she couldn't do herself."

"What tasks?"

"Well, they stopped a Nazi U-boat for one. They also protected Napoleon's gold, hid it so malicious people wouldn't be able to find it and use it for destructive purposes. And, for whatever reason, Billy contacted me."

I considered all this in silence for a moment before I asked, "Do you think it was Billy?"

Mindy slowly nodded. "Why not? Andrew saw him out on the river. You saw him in your dreams." Her face became stern. "Don't get me wrong, I'm still not OK with any of this. Rationally I mean. I have no way of explaining it, but yes, I think it probably was Billy Masterson's ghost who told me that the river didn't want me to go either."

"OK. So what's that supposed to mean? What's it mean that the river doesn't want you to go either?"

"I don't know."

"What are you going to do?"

"Both Ray and Raphael advised that I keep an open mind and remain flexible."

"Sounds like good advice to me," I affirmed. I held out a hand, which Mindy took. "Back rubs?" I asked.

"And maybe a little more," she answered.

Chapter Forty Six

I FELT MUCH BETTER the next morning, both from the mutual back rubs—and a little bit more—and from the mindful breathing that Andrew had taught me how to do before the council of Ostend. Ray Dale arrived early that same morning, as promised, looking exhausted and frazzled. I was just as surprised to see Ray's companion as I was to see Ray himself arrive at Heron's Nest a few days before with Martin Comstock.

"Ghedi!" I said as I met the two of them on the back porch. "Are you here to help my brother?"

"I am," he said.

"How?"

"My grandmother taught me how to cook more than stew, you know."

"But what ... "

"Something like that. I need to see him now. Where is he?"

"In our living room. On the couch."

Ghedi didn't even glance at the word written on one wall and the declaration written on the other as he moved into the room. He went straight to the couch, dropped to a knee and placed his hands first on Patrick's forehead, then his heart, then his abdomen.

Ray, however, showed great interest in both the "ARIEL" and the "FLANAGAN! COME BACK!" He returned to his car, carried a duffel bag full of instruments into the living room and set it on a side table. He measured the letters and took pictures. He illuminated them with ultraviolet light and examined them with night-vision goggles.

"These are amazing," Ray said, the goggles hanging from his neck. "When all this is over, can I send a team over to cut them out of your walls? Don't worry—I'll have them patch everything up as good as new." He returned his gaze to the "ARIEL." "I need this in my collection. This writing …"

I was about to agree to pictures only when Ghedi motioned for us to be quiet.

"In fact," he added with urgency, gesturing towards Patrick, "could you please leave me alone with him? I need to concentrate and I can do that best if there is no one else in the room."

"Can you help him?" I asked.

"I think so."

"What's wrong with him?"

"He's been soul-stripped."

"He's been what?"

"Soul-stripped. Yes. It happens when … well, when a shaman takes a trip into the Otherworld and is unable to completely return." Ghedi knelt at my brother's side. "Part of him is here, on your couch. Another part of him is missing. His condition is bad, but I have seen worse. Please, the sooner you leave us alone the better it will be for him."

"PATRICK'S A SHAMAN?" I asked in the kitchen a moment later.

"Apparently," Ray said. "If he traveled to the Otherworld he is, by definition, a shaman. Ghedi knows the type. But don't worry. He's the best there is at what he does. If anyone can help your brother, it's Ghedi Ali Gaal."

I looked towards the living room and saw a shaft of green and blue light under the door. I heard Ghedi talking in a language I could not understand. Ghedi, I thought. Ghedi Ali Gaal. I laughed.

"What?" Ray said as he and Mindy both gave me a puzzled look.

"Ghedi means sojourner," I said. "He explained that to us the night we were on the back deck of The 357 with Lodi."

"I wouldn't be surprised if both of them, Ghedi and Lodi, have sojourned down the same road as your brother."

"At least Ghedi and Lodi came back," I said.

Mindy checked her watch. "You should tell us about your plan," she said.

"You're right," Ray agreed. "We're out of here the minute Ghedi finishes his work." He sighed. "I've known for some time that pressure from the Otherworld was slowly building up and seeping into our world, especially on the river, but in other locations as well. Lady Ostend knew it too. She saw the telltale signs—war, cultural and intellectual confusion, the breakdown of societies. She studied past incidents of Otherworld intrusion and discovered a way to reverse the flow, to relieve the pressure on our side and return the Otherworldly beings to where they belong. What I was able to do that she wasn't was pinpoint exactly where the pressure was building up the most."

"Those pictures you sent Lodi … " I started to say.

Ray smiled and nodded, clearly proud of his work. "Yes. The ones that show what will happen if we don't succeed."

"What exactly do they show?" I asked.

"Concentrations of elemental beings. The river's the epicenter."

"They're at Lodi's farm too," I said.

"Lodi's farm is bad, but he seems to have that under control. The river's much, much worse. If we don't thicken the thin place there, then all hell'll break loose in a day or two. So the essence of my plan is to send the various and sundry elementals back where they belong."

"How?" I asked.

"First, by luring them up to the river. That's where the

boundary between here and there is currently the most fluid."

"Are Lodi and Andrew doing the luring?" I asked.

"Yes! Precisely! They are luring them there, as many as they can find, from the shores of Lake Erie to the Hudson River."

"How?" Mindy asked.

"That's Lodi's special talent," Ray answered. "That's what he does best, and that's why, Tom, I advised you to stay away from him when we talked after Ostend's council. Lodi can communicate with the elementals, summon them and, at least for a time, submit them to his will."

"His trap," I said. "The one behind his barn. He showed it to me, to me and Andrew."

"Most true magicians don't advertise their talents."

"Magician?" Mindy asked.

"Yes. A shaman travels from our world to the Otherworld. A magician brings beings from the Otherworld to here."

"Patrick's both," I said.

"He is," Ray confirmed.

"Lodi said that someone like Patrick, someone who can summon a fire-being, comes around about once a century."

"That's about right," Ray said. "But at some crucial junctures in human affairs two or even three might appear at the same time and in the same place. Fifth-century Greece was one of those times. Seventeenth-century Europe was another. Here and now seems to be yet another."

"So Andrew's driving Lodi around the state, and Lodi's forcing the elementals to follow him to the river."

"Not forcing. Enticing. As we said before, luring. And there should be quite a collection of them by the time they get here! If only I had the tech to see them in their full glory rather than just sense their presence or predict their effects—what a vision that would be!"

I thought about my dreams and shuddered. Would the

air- and water-beings cause the storms that had sent me seeking refuge in the cement-walled garage? Would the fire-beings burn away the river as I saw in another dream? Would the earth-beings swallow an entire island as the River Rat Reporters had dreamed?

"There's something else," I said. "Something Lodi told me he wanted to do."

"What?" Mindy asked.

"He wants to bring the elementals he has trapped at his place and send them through with the others."

"Oh," Ray said.

Mindy glanced my way before asking," Oh what? Is there a problem with that?"

"Releasing them from the trap could be a big problem."

"Why?" I asked.

"Because they'll be released from their trap. They'll be free. Who knows what'll happen then." Ray sighed. "I guess all we can do is trust that Lodi knows what he's doing."

"How do we close the thin place? Once Lodi and Andrew get the elementals up to the river and we get them back across, I mean?"

"That's where my work comes in," Ray said. "I'm going to close the gap with some tech I've been perfecting for years. I won't give you the details now. Suffice it to say that the Thousand Islands have proved an excellent laboratory for my research."

I looked at Mindy, who was suddenly pale. "Mindy? What's wrong?"

"I think I might know what my role is."

"What?"

"Well, I can't be sure, but what if I'm the bait? What if I'm Fay Wray?" Mindy whispered the last part.

"The *bait?*" I rose from the table. I turned back around and pointed a finger at Ray. "No way! We are not going to put Mindy out there as bait! You'd better tell us about this tech! What's it do? Will it put Mindy in danger? Any of us in danger?"

"My tech simply ... is supposed to widen the portal. Once Lodi and Andrew get the elementals there, my tech should provide enough energy to widen the doorway from our world to the Otherworld and then close it again."

"Is your tech dangerous?" I asked.

"The whole operation's dangerous," Ray admitted. "This entire situation is dangerous. But the purpose of my tech is to minimize danger by moving people further away from the portal than they would otherwise be. In that sense, whatever any of our roles are in the plan, we'll be safer than we would be using no tech at all."

WE WERE STILL DISCUSSING the details of Ray's plan when Ghedi opened the door from the living room and stepped into the kitchen. There was a darkness around his eyes that I had never seen before. He was weak too, and had a hard time standing. His hands hung limp at his side. I led him to the kitchen table and Mindy gave him a glass of water. He drank a sip and set the glass down.

"He is ready for you," Ghedi said to me.

Ray pointed to his watch. "Make it quick. I know it's important to you, but we need to get up to the river," he said.

"And I need to go home and recuperate," Ghedi said.

"You and Mindy can drive Ghedi home and drive up together," I said. "I'll drive Patrick." I turned to Ghedi, knelt down next to him and took his hand, which trembled as I held it in mine. "Whatever you did for him, thank you. A thousand times thank you."

Ghedi tried to smile. "I have not performed a recovery like that in a very long time. That was more difficult than I expected."

"I owe you big time. When we get back to Clinton Falls, I'll repay you however I can."

"I know exactly what that repayment will be," Ghedi said.

WHEN I WALKED INTO THE LIVING ROOM I found my brother with his palm pressed up against the "ARIEL." Neither Mindy nor I, nor anyone else for all I knew, had ever touched it. Was the word glowing? I thought so, but my attention shifted from the word to my brother when he turned and I saw his face. *It* glowed, of that I was certain. His green eyes were luminous. His smile was wide. His cheekbones were shining in the sunlight that came through the windows.

"Time to go, eh?" he said as he pulled his hands away from the wall.

Chapter Forty Seven

"How do you feel?" I asked my brother as we drove north. I kept taking my eyes off the road to look at him, kept hitting the Jesus strips as my truck veered to right. Despite the warnings that my dreams had given me, I was happy after the cathartic talk Mindy and I had had the night before. I was happy to be back in my brother's company, eager to be returning to the place where we had spent so much time together growing up.

Patrick was studying his hands. He turned to me and smiled, his eyes still bright. "Great! Really great! That Ghedi's a genius!"

"How'd you get like that?"

"Hmm." He kept looking at his hands, turning them over and looking at them.

"You're not going to tell me?"

"Not yet."

"What did Ghedi do to you? Did it have something to do with the word on our wall?"

"Hmm," he said again, smiling wider.

"Are you going to answer any of my questions?"

"Keep trying."

"OK then. Lodi said you just showed up in Andes. He thinks you traveled back into the past again."

"Does he now?" he said, still looking at his hands, still smiling.

"Well did you?"

"Lodi always takes things more literally than they need

to be taken. I did travel back into the past, as did he, but it wasn't like we did so physically. You know, in the flesh. I mean, if there *had* been cameras there and if someone *had* taken a picture, we wouldn't have been in it."

"But Lodi said he shot and killed Osman Steele."

"Oh boy," Patrick said.

"You're saying he didn't kill Osman Steele?" I was about to give Mindy credit for not trusting Lodi.

"It's not as simple as did he or did he not," my brother said. "It's not binary like that. When you go back like we did and things happen ... well, we experience things differently than we usually do. Did Lodi pull the trigger? Sort of. Did Lodi set in motion a series of actions and re-actions that looped back in time and led to the death of Osman Steele? Definitely yes. We both experienced the events of August 7, 1845, in the sense that they're as real as any other memory is real. Or better yet, they're as real as any dream is real." He sighed. "But please, ask me something else. Trying to explain how it happens gives me a headache."

I swallowed, wondering if I was confident enough in my emotional stability to ask the question I needed to ask. "Can you tell me about Labor Day 1996? Can you tell me about the day Mom and Dad died?"

"Ah, yes," my brother said. "We need to discuss that topic right away since that's when our roads diverged. I want to know more about the path your life took, by the way. But not now. Not until quieter times."

If they ever come, I thought. "So tell me about that day," I said.

He laughed softly. "The first thing I know about that day is this: the moment I hit the water, my life changed in ways I never could've imagined, in ways I still don't fully understand."

"Of course your life changed. Mine did too, irrevocably. Our parents died. It was tragic."

"That's not quite what I mean," he said carefully. "Experiencing the death of our parents is the way of the world. Most everybody goes through it. What's tragic is when it happens the other way around, when a parent watches a child die. No, what I'm talking about is a series of changes that is definitely not the way of the world, or at least not the way of the particular world that we know."

"What happened?" I asked.

"Well, first, as Billy was lifting Mom out of the water, *another* Billy appeared."

"His ghost," I said matter-of-factly.

Patrick was surprised. "You've seen him?"

"Only in dreams." I paused. "Patrick, one dream I had was about Mom and Dad's death. You were there. You prevented me from swimming to the crash. You told me twice that Dad was telling me to let you be. There was someone else there too, someone near the boat … "

"Probably Billy's ghost. Have you seen him in other dreams?"

"Yes. One was about a massive storm that destroyed Cape Vincent. Another was … well, never mind."

"No problem. I'm sure you'll tell me when you're ready. Ever see Billy while awake?"

"No. Andrew Hibbard did though, about a year after Billy died. He warned Andrew that a big change is coming, but that Andrew would be OK if he kept riding the wake."

"What's that mean?"

"I'm not sure, although I have a feeling that whatever big change Billy was talking about has already started."

"Could be," Patrick said thoughtfully. "But the more significant question is, how will it end?"

"I don't know," I said. "Mindy saw him too, only she saw him years ago when she was a kid."

"Interesting."

"What happened to you when Billy's ghost appeared?" I asked.

"He saved me. He got me out of there, away from the

wrecked boat and burning oil. He led me deep into the water, as the others were taking Mom and Dad out. I wanted to go back, but Billy Number Two convinced me it was too late to help them. He took me away."

"To where?"

"I don't know exactly. It was underwater, some sort of cave. Billy Number Two called it the 'Octopus' Garden,' like the Beatles song. I told him I didn't understand because there were no octopi in the river. He said this was still the river, but not quite the river I knew. He said this was The River, capital T, capital R. The strangest thing was that I could breathe, just like I could the whole time we were swimming. I asked him how that was possible and he told me to reach out and touch it. So I moved my hand forward, and something offered resistance. It was a barely visible, transparent membrane that held water out and air in. I asked him how long the air would last and he pointed up. I looked up and saw something tube-like extending all the way to the surface. I had an endless supply, it seemed. And the air was amazing! I couldn't begin to guess its chemical composition, but it tasted sweet and citrusy and tingled my sinuses when I inhaled.

"But Billy told me I couldn't stay there long. He insisted I had to go help people. He said I had to work for what mattered. He said I'd been given a gift, just like the undines had given him. The difference was that I could use my gift in this life as well as in the next. He told me to rest for a while, after which time the water beings would help me get to where I needed to be and help me start doing what I needed to do."

"Where did they take you?" I asked.

"That I do know. They took me to Magdalena Island, which is in the Admiralty Group, just downriver from—"

"I know," I interrupted. "A few years ago, I ended up on Magdalena Island myself after I escaped an attack on

Raphael Ostend's yacht. I was telling you about it on our drive down to Clinton Falls, but you were asleep."

"Really! How did you get there? Get picked up by another boat? Swim?"

"No. Well, I started swimming but passed out after a while. I suspect I got there the same way you did."

"The undines," he said. I responded with a nod. "That makes sense. Did they teach you how to do anything? Give you any abilities?"

I shook my head. "They healed my leg, which I'd broken a few weeks before when I crashed my truck. But no. No lessons. No abilities."

"They told me what I already knew," Patrick said. "That I could see through time and sometimes even influence the future."

"The bishop mentioned that," I said.

"The bishop? He's still around?" my brother asked, surprised.

"He and the River Rat Reporters came to Heron's Nest a few days ago for a group discussion. I couldn't believe it either when I saw him. I thought he was long gone. He told us about you and the Mets in '86."

"He remembered that? Wow, I'm impressed. He helped me out a lot when I was a kid."

"Did you cause Buckner to miss the winning grounder?" I asked.

Patrick guffawed. "The bishop told you *that*?"

"He intimated it," I said.

"Confusion comes with age," Patrick said. "But, like I said, he helped me quite a lot. He helped me after the crash. He picked me up from Magdalena Island and piloted me back to the mainland." Patrick laughed softly. "We saw you, you know, looking for your drunk speedboater."

I breathed before I spoke, remembering Andrew's advice about controlling my anger. "When was that?"

"A day or two after the crash."

"Why didn't you stop me? Why didn't you say something?"

"Because I had to wait to see if ... well, to see if it worked."

"If what worked?"

"The other reason I didn't say anything back then is because Dad gave me pretty specific instructions about what to do if he and Mom got into trouble. He told me to contact the bishop if I ever found myself alone and in need of help. I was alone and in need of help on Magdalena Island. I told the nuns what Dad had told me, and they called the bishop right away."

"That doesn't answer my question," I said. 'Why didn't you say something when you saw me hopelessly riding up and down the river looking for a drunk speedboater that didn't exist?"

"Dad also told me to leave you out of it, to not tell you about what happened and why. I think he feared for your safety. I think he wanted to keep you as far away from danger as he could. For his part, the bishop assured me that he would personally take care of you and see to it that you got what you needed."

"Good of him to assume he knew what I needed," I said. "What I really needed was closure, for Mom and Dad and for you. What I got, at least for you, was an empty casket."

"I'm sorry about that," Patrick said. "At first the bishop didn't agree with me on that. He insisted I should make sure you knew I was alive. But I couldn't do that."

"Why not?"

"I still had work to do, work that you could not know about."

"What work?" I asked.

His stare was stern. "Work that you could not know about."

"OK then," I said, frustrated. "The bishop told me

Mom and Dad didn't know you could see the future. He said you never told them. Is that true?"

"Of course they knew! How could they not? But they kept it to themselves."

"Did Dad use your gift of foresight for gambling?"

Patrick thought for a moment and laughed. "He would've never done that! I suppose his drinking buddies might have, but he never would've."

"Oh," I said, not wanting to detour into a defense of the Reporters. "There's something else I don't understand. Why did Dad want to keep only me as far away from danger as he could? Why not you?"

Patrick sighed and shook his head. "All I can say is that both Mom and Dad knew that you had to take a different path than any of us."

"They knew something was going to happen that day, didn't they?"

"They did."

"Because you told them?"

Patrick nodded. "But Mom sensed it before I told them. You know, she could almost do what I can do."

"See the future? Change it?"

"Definitely see the future. Could she shape it? I'm not so sure. But she knew something was going to happen." He made a quarter turn towards me. "Do you remember their favorite song?"

"Of course. 'Bridge over Troubled Water.' It was the last song they danced to, at Castello's a couple nights before they died."

My brother faced me and smiled. "How'd you know that?"

"I could give the same type of cryptic answer you do, you know."

"But you won't because you're a straight shooter. How'd you know that was their favorite song?"

"You're right. Here's your answer: I did my research.

When I came back up to the river five years ago I listened to the stories the River Rat Reporters had to tell. Martin Comstock told the story about the dance. It was also the story of how they died." I could hear Mindy citing exhibit A for her theory that I sought answers only in the past.

"Comstock probably didn't know the significance of the song. Ostend might have … what's his first name?"

"Raphael."

"That's it! Raphael Ostend. Of all the Reporters, he's the one who might've known what a bridge over troubled water really meant to Mom and Dad."

"You damn well better explain that," I said pointing a finger at him.

"Of course. They, and probably us, were the bridge over troubled water. The water was the river, obviously. The trouble was what they thought was inevitably going to happen, especially after the summer of '76."

I thought back to Jim Pembroke's story about how he encountered Napoleon's gold while piloting the CANCO-2000 to it's doom. "Environmental catastrophe?" I asked.

"That's what they feared would trigger it."

"Trigger what?"

"A wholesale rebellion of the river against humanity. A deluge, or worse. They knew the river was alive and they knew it was angry. They feared that the water-beings would … well, wage war on people. Mom and Dad meant to assuage the undines, to find as much of Napoleon's gold as they could and feed the water-beings to their content. It was a naïve, noble effort. And now, ten years later … "

I gave him a moment to continue. He didn't. "Ten years later what?" I asked. I thought for a moment. "Oh. It's not just the water-beings that are pissed off," I said.

Patrick pointed a finger right at me. "Bingo," he said. "They're all angry now, brother, and the only hope we have is to send them back."

"No more placating them?"

My brother shook his head. "The time for that has passed. Now, more or less as Lady Ostend foresaw, our only hope is to send them back to the other side." Patrick inhaled deeply through his nose and exhaled through his mouth. "Unfortunately, once we do that they'll remain on the other side for a long, long time."

"Why unfortunately?"

"I'm surprised Raphael Ostend or Professor Ray Dale didn't tell you."

"Tell me what?"

"You're the historian. Take the long view for a minute. For almost five thousand years the elementals have partnered with humanity to make this visible world of ours a magnificent place, filled with beauty and wonder. The orange glow of a setting sun, the deep blue of the ocean, the verdant green of a forest canopy—most of the beauty we experience is magnified by their presence. And once they're gone … "

I thought back to my dream about the scorched, dry river. "Once they're gone we've got nothing but rock, air, fire and water."

He reached over and touched my arm with a fingertip, a touch that sent a shockwave of heat and pain up my arm, over my shoulder, down my back and into my bowels.

"We're left with nothing but that," Patrick said.

Chapter Forty Eight

THE *ARCHANGEL* WAS MOORED at our dock. When Jim Pembroke saw us pull into the driveway he shot up from a lawn chair and motioned for us to join him.

He and Patrick shook hands. "My God, it is you. Patrick Flanagan! Welcome back to the land of the living." He doffed his captain's hat.

"This is Jim Pembroke," I said, "proud captain of the *Thousand Islands Queen*."

Patrick laughed. "The one who said the international border was a yellow line just under the surface of the water?"

"The very one," Pembroke affirmed.

"He invented that story," I said. "Now all the tour guides use it."

"How'd it feel crossing the bridge?" Pembroke asked. "Coming back home? Assuming you haven't been up here this whole time."

"No, this is the first time I've been on the river in about a decade. It felt good, actually. It was like coming home."

"Glad to hear it."

"Where are we going?" I asked.

"Ostend told me to get the four of you to his place as soon as possible. He'll take it from there. Where are the others?"

"Mindy and Ray should be here soon. They had to drive a friend home before they came here."

"Any sign of Andrew and Lodi?"

"No, not yet. Show Patrick what you've done to Heron's Nest," Pembroke suggested. "I'll send Mindy in for you when she gets here."

"THE PLACE LOOKS GREAT," Patrick said as we walked upstairs. "You've made some good improvements."

I let him pass me as we approached his old room. "Didn't change a thing in here," I said.

Patrick smiled as he opened the door and saw the Mets posters covering the wall on either side of the window. He went straight to his stereo. He opened the lid of his turntable and moved the arm.

"Wonder if the stylus is still good," he asked as the platform began to spin.

"Dad's got a few extra in his office," I said.

"Diamond?"

"Of course."

"You know what I want to do when all this ends? Sit back with the headphones on and listen to *The Dark Side of the Moon* over and over again." He returned the turntable arm and the platform slowed to a stop. "You didn't steal any of my Floyd albums did you?"

"Steal? Of course not. I borrowed. Whatever's not here is up in dad's loft."

He moved to his dresser. He opened the top drawer, then the two below that one after another. He took out a t-shirt and unfolded it.

"These new?" he asked.

"Some of them. I refreshed your wardrobe every year hoping you'd come back."

He smiled. "Thank you, brother," he said, and surprised me with a hug.

"Let me show you dad's office." I led him up the stairs.

"You haven't changed a thing in here either!" he said as we entered the crow's nest room.

Patrick sat down in our father's chair. I leaned against

the window. He pointed to a framed picture of the four of us on the Lyman. The photo was taken by our Uncle Jack on a beautiful July day a couple months before our parents died.

"I remember that day," Patrick said. "You were between classes." He spun around in the chair. "Was that the last time I saw you that summer?"

"No. I came up again when the August term ended."

"That's right! We went water skiing. Man, that was a good summer."

"Until it wasn't," I added. "Patrick, what were you holding back on the way up here?"

"I spent much of that summer hanging out with the Templeton twins. Lucy and Beth. They wanted me to tell them which one I'd marry. Were they at the funeral?"

"What aren't you telling me?" I persisted.

He paused, then stood up and began leafing through our father's albums.

"*Brain Salad Surgery*!" he exclaimed.

"Patrick. I need to know."

He slid the record back into the shelf. "And you will," he finally said. "But not now. Let me tell you when all this ends."

"Before you get lost in *The Dark Side of the Moon*?"

"Immediately when it ends," Patrick said.

"When? I need to know."

"OK. I promise I'll tell you everything. But you'll have to wait until after you and Mindy get married."

"You sound like Charles Darnay with Doctor Manette," I said. "That worries me."

Patrick laughed. "Mom's favorite book! I remember that. Jarvis Lorry sent the message that Manette was recalled to life."

"Like you," I said.

"And I'm not the only one!" Patrick exclaimed.

I heard a car door slam and turned to look out the window. "It's Mindy and Ray. Let's go."

MINDY AND RAY were already aboard the *Archangel* by the time we got outside. I joined them in the guest cabin. Patrick stayed with Jim Pembroke at the wheel, enjoying his return to the river. Jim piloted us through the American channel along Wellesley Island and under the American span of the Thousand Islands bridge, turned north around Boldt Castle and hit the throttle hard as we entered Canadian water. Boat traffic was still light, although there were more fishermen on the water than there had been just a few days before. A slight breeze blew from the south, bringing with it air that grew increasingly moist and hazy.

I sat with Mindy on one padded bench. Ray Dale sat opposite us, wearing his pince-nez, pencil in hand, concentrating on an open notebook. I could see drawings that looked vaguely circular and notes in the margins. Ray added a scribble or two and flipped back and forth to other pages in the notebook.

"Is that your plan?" I asked.

Ray didn't look up. "It is. Well, part of it. But I'd rather you see it firsthand than hear about it from me."

I leaned forward. Ray caught me and closed the notebook.

"Looks like some sort of loop?"

Mindy put a hand on my arm. "Tom. Stop."

"Have you seen it?"

"Not yet," she said, exasperated.

"I told her what Ostend told me," Ray said. "It's very important that we enter into the plan with as few preconceptions as possible. Right now only Raphael knows the plan in full."

"You don't?"

"I only know my part."

"Why do the rest of us have to go in blind?" I asked.

"That's an excellent way of putting it. The rest of us are going in blind so the elementals themselves will go in blind. The last thing we want is for them to know what we plan to do. The fewer of us who know what's supposed to happen, the likelier it is that we'll maintain the element of surprise." Ray smiled. "No pun intended, of course."

"They can read our minds?" I asked.

"With sufficient strength, yes," Ray said. He smiled at my expression. "Why does that surprise you? You already know they can visit us in our dreams. If they come in numbers as large as we expect them to come, they will no doubt have sufficient strength to read our waking thoughts."

"So how will you and Ostend keep them out?"

"Tin foil hats," Ray deadpanned.

Mindy looked at me, turned to Ray and burst out laughing. I joined her. Ray smiled and went back to his notebook.

VALHALLA, the Ostend family castle that dwarfed both Boldt's and Singer's constructs, loomed in the distance like a stone sentinel keeping watch over the thickening river mist. The castle was built on two adjacent islands and one side was connected to the other by an elevated walkway. American, Canadian, New York and Ontario flags flew from the castle's towers. The pink granite walls shone bright, even in the mist. After taking in the sight of Valhalla, I went to the back of the cabin and searched upriver for signs of Andrew and Lodi.

"I think we'll know when they get here," Mindy said as she wrapped an arm around my waist.

"I was in Cape Vincent in my dream," I said. "When things went bad."

"We're going in the opposite direction," Mindy said.

"We might yet end up there."

Mindy persisted. "The likelihood of that is shrinking."

"It was our wedding day."

"I know." Mindy spun around me and slid her arms up

and around my shoulders. Her smile was electric. "Let's change that."

"How?"

"By making today our wedding day."

"What?"

"I know it's crazy. But if we do it, if we get married today, we'll alter what happened in your dream. We'll be like Patrick and change the future."

"Mindy … "

"We're fifty miles away from Cape Vincent, right?"

"Yes."

"And you're not wearing your tux, are you?"

"No. But you're wearing jeans and a sweater."

"So what. There's no dress code. Let's get married now."

Mindy stepped away and produced a folded sheet of paper, our marriage license, from her windbreaker pocket.

"You brought that along?"

"I've been thinking about this since Raphael told me I'd have a role to play in Lady Ostend's plan. It makes perfect sense for us to do it now."

I considered telling Mindy about Patrick's promise, but I didn't want to make it seem like hearing his story was more important than our wedding.

"What about our party?" I asked. I was running out of questions.

"We'll still have it, just as planned."

"But … "

"People do it all the time! They elope and then they celebrate later with everyone. Come on. It'll be a day to remember!"

"Today or July eighth?" I asked.

"Both!"

I sighed. "Who'll perform the ceremony?"

"Mike Slattery."

Warming up to the idea, I smiled. "Mayor of Alex Bay," I said.

"Exactly. He's at Valhalla now, but when we get there we can all come out on the *Archangel*. Jim can pilot us into American water. Everything will be on the up and up."

"Rings?"

Mindy pulled the box from her coat pocket and held it up. I laughed, and we kissed on the lips. "But we can leave the blessing of the rings for our party," she said. "We wouldn't want to lose them."

"So much for our wedding planning!" I said. Then I frowned. "Your parents."

"I called them from Ray's office. I explained what was happening, without giving away the details, and I informed them that this might be a possibility. My dad's OK with it."

"But you're mom's not."

"Not quite. I'll have to wear my wedding dress on July eighth to placate her. And you your tuxedo. But she does appreciate us holding off on the blessing of the rings. That is her favorite part." Mindy kissed me again. "What do you say?"

"Guess it's my turn to say yes," I answered.

Chapter Forty Nine

AN HOUR LATER we were anchored in American water, just upriver from the Cross Island light. Mindy had obviously contacted Mike Slattery before we left Heron's Nest because Mike stood in front of us wearing a long rainbow stole over his shorts and golf shirt. He'd officiated hundreds of weddings in his many years as mayor of Alex Bay. We were both very happy to have him officiate ours.

Raphael Ostend and Martin Comstock served as our official witnesses. Ray Dale stood on Mindy's side and Jim Pembroke stood on mine. Patrick stood behind us a little way back, with the same enigmatic smile on his face that I had not yet gotten used to. What a way to be reunited with the family, I thought. I regretted that Andrew wasn't there, but he had told me more than once that he hated the ceremonies as much as he loved the receptions. Even though part of me hoped he would pop up out of the water and climb aboard, I knew that his arrival with Lodi would presage the appearance of the beings they were supposed to bring with them, beings I did not want to encounter.

Where were they? The sky above the river offered no clues. It was a grey sky, thick with clouds and with no breeze. The river was calm. The sky hung over the river like a curtain, perhaps protecting us from what was to come, perhaps shielding our vision from what we feared to see.

Later, Mike Slattery told us that he had adapted our wedding ceremony from the *New Zealand Prayerbook*, which he'd bought when he and his wife toured the South Pacific in 1999.

Here are the beautiful opening words Mike shared:

> We have come together to ask God's blessing on Mindy and Tom, to witness their marriage and to bring them our love and support.
>
> I ask you now to pray for them. Praying is an outlook, a sustained energy, which creates a marriage and makes love and forgiveness life-long.
>
> Those who marry are God's ministers to each other of reconciliation and change. As they grow together, wife and husband foster one another's strengths, they provide each other with the reassurance and love needed to overcome their weaknesses.
>
> From this beginning God draws them now to a completely new life. They become awake to each other, aware of each other, sensitive to each other's needs.

By this point Mindy and I both were crying. I wiped the tears off Mindy's cheeks, gave her a tissue and used one myself. I looked around at my friends and brother, all of them family to me, and smiled. I put my arm around Mindy's waist and held her tight. We returned our attention to Mike as he continued:

> May God's grace surround you and keep you all, and so we pray that the peace of God which is beyond our understanding keep guard over your thoughts and hearts.
>
> God keep you friends with one another, forgiving one another in kindness.
>
> May hope keep you joyful.
>
> Stand firm in trouble.
>
> Be strong in prayer.

> May God make you compassionate and brave.
> Above all, may there always be love to bind and keep you whole.

I turned to face Mindy and held her hands in mine. I looked into her eyes as tears moistened my smile. I saw love and trust and strength in her eyes. I hoped she saw the same in mine. With Mike's guidance I said these vows in as strong and clear a voice as I could manage:

> Mindy, I take you to be my wife. All that I have I offer you; what you have to give I gladly receive; wherever you go I will go.
> You are my love.
> God keep me true to you always and you to me.

Mindy tightened her grip on my hands and repeated the words to me. Her voice was loud and firm, although the tears continued to fall from her eyes.

> Tom, I take you to be my husband.
> All that I have I offer you; what you have to give I gladly receive; wherever you go I will go.
> You are my love.
> God keep me true to you always and you to me.

Our hands clasped tighter. Our eyes locked on each other. I could see the green flecks in Mindy's brown eyes dancing. I loved her more than ever, wanted nothing other than to remain joined together with her as we were right then, soul to soul.

Mike concluded the ceremony with this blessing, which stirred my heart and warmed me to the core of my being:

> Loving Spirit, grant to Mindy and Tom, that in

giving and forgiving they may receive from each other lasting joy.

Bind them together with cords that cannot be broken. Bind them together with love. Grant that they may always take delight in each other, and each remain the other's heart's desire.

May they reach such trust and confidence in each other as shall keep them from unnecessary distress.

May they find courage to meet the heartaches, disappointments and agonies life can bring.

Be their rock, their fortress, for they put their trust in you.

Help them to look beyond their own family and their own concerns to see the world, suffering and struggling, the world you have given us to share with one another. Open their eyes and their hearts.

Give them grace to accept that they are mortal, to face the possibility of death and the separation it must bring.

We ask this in the name of Jesus, who is the resurrection, who is eternal life. Amen.

At some point during Mike's final prayer, and just for a few seconds, a burst of sunlight speared through the clouds, illuminating Mindy's hair and making her eyes even brighter. It was only for a few seconds, but the light and warmth of that sunburst boosted my courage and gave me an eternity worth of hope.

Chapter Fifty

OUR WEDDING GUESTS CLAPPED and cheered when Mike concluded his prayers and services. Mindy and I shared a light kiss and held each other tight for a long time. Then we took turns hugging the others. Captain Pembroke produced a bottle of champagne from an ice chest, as he did so often at the end of romantic sunset tours. Martin Comstock, ever the bartender, popped the cork, and we passed the bottle around. By the time we finished it we were back at Valhalla.

"Why don't the two of you spend some time alone," Raphael Ostend offered as we disembarked. He glanced upriver and his lips parted in surprise. Mindy and I both turned around to see what he saw.

The horizon was thick with clouds from which bolts of lightning flashed in all directions. The clouds were growing horizontally, piling up into layer after layer of increasing darkness. The river raged with whitecaps that we could distinguish even at this distance. The storm was slowly moving our way. Valhalla stood firm in the face of its approach, however, and I trusted that it would keep us safe.

"Go to the eastern guest suite," Ostend suggested. "Take the time while you can."

"But keep it brief," Ray Dale said. "That storm's moving fast and right towards us. We've got to all be where we need to be before it gets here."

"There's time yet for that," Ostend said. "Some time anyway. Consider the next twenty minutes your honeymoon."

On a couch in Valhalla's eastern guest suite, I rested my head on Mindy's chest as she stroked my forehead and ran her hands through my hair. I could hear the beating of her heart and the rhythm of her breathing. We laughed and talked for a few minutes about how we didn't feel much different now that we were married. But we spent most of the time in silence, enjoying each other's company as we had so many times before. I was about to kiss her and see where it led when we were interrupted by a knock on the door.

"That would be Patrick," I said as I got off the couch and walked to the door.

Mindy gave me a worried look as I opened the door. She took my hand and held it tight.

"It's OK," I said. I gave Mindy a kiss and pulled away from her grip. "He and I have something to talk about. It shouldn't take long." I kissed her again. "Our real honeymoon hasn't even begun."

Patrick led me downstairs to Raphael Ostend's office. Ostend was there, at his desk, but rose and made for the exit when we entered. He gave me a look with even more worry in it than Mindy's.

"That was a conveniently timed wedding," Patrick said as he closed the door.

"Mindy's idea. She thought we might be able to change what's coming by doing things differently than how I saw them done in my dreams."

"Wise woman. Is being her husband really what you want?"

"Yes, it is."

"OK then. I'll fulfill my promise."

"Thank you."

"Don't thank me yet. And we'd better sit down," he added, which we did in two leather chairs near the fireplace, across the room from the desk.

"OK," I said. "Tell me."

"Do you remember where you were that day?"

"The day Mom and Dad died?"

Patrick nodded.

"Of course I remember where I was that day. I drove up to the river as soon as Louie Fratello told me what happened. When I got here I borrowed Uncle Jack's boat and searched for the drunk speedboater. I—"

"That was after the crash. Do you recall where you were exactly when the crash happened?"

"I was in Clinton Falls. Probably in my office at the university reading or preparing a lecture. That's when Louie called."

"Are you sure that's where you were? Are you sure Louie called you? Do you remember it clearly?"

I though for a moment. "I'm not sure. But Louie must have been the one to break the news. And I must have driven up here."

"When do your clear memories start? What's the first thing you recall about that day? Remember clearly, that is?"

"Crossing the bridge to get Uncle Jack's boat. I wanted more than anything to find that drunk speedboater."

"Uncle Jack kept his boat in Fisher's Landing, right? On the mainland?"

"Yes." I anticipated his next question. "I drove across the bridge from Wellesley Island because I must have driven to Heron's Nest first, then to Uncle Jack's boat on the mainland."

"I'll ask you again. Are you sure about that? Do you recall it clearly?"

"It was a decade ago."

"And people often remember the details of a life-changing event as if it happened yesterday."

"Tell me what you're getting at," I said. "Stop asking vague questions and get to the point."

"I'm trying to learn as much as possible about what you

remember from that day. Clouded memories seem to be one of the most common consequences."

"Of what?"

"Of what happened."

"OK. Rewind back to the conversation we had on the way up here. You said Dad knew something was going to happen. How did Dad know that? Did you tell him? Did you see something?"

A gust of wind from the approaching storm back-drafted down the chimney and caused the fire to flicker and pop. I snuffed out a spark with my shoe.

"We're wasting time," Patrick said. "Yes. Dad knew something was going to happen because I told him something was going to happen. In a recurring vision I saw Mom and Dad both die. There was water and fire in all my premonitions, so I knew it would happen on the river, probably while they were in the Lyman. Mom saw the same vision I did, but with less detail." Patrick hesitated and gave me a hard look. "You were there, brother."

"Me? What?" I remembered the shared dream that sent Mindy and me to the river. Did Patrick have the same dream? I was about to ask him when he continued.

"You were in my premonitions, Tom. You were on the boat. I saw you die that day. I saw you die with Mom and Dad."

My mind raced as I sorted out the implications of what Patrick had just said. Then I had an ah-ha moment. "You're not always right," I said. "Your premonitions don't always come true."

Patrick lowered his head. "They do always come true, at least in terms of showing the people about to be affected by whatever's going to happen. You were on the boat, Tom. I saw it six or seven times before the crash. And when it happened, it happened with you there. It happened just as I foresaw it. You were on the boat and, like Mom and Dad, you died."

"But ... "

"I'm sorry," Patrick said.

My head throbbed and my vision clouded over. "Then how am I here now?"

Patrick set his jaw, leaned forward and looked right into my eyes. "I changed it," he said, his mouth curling into a smile. "I was able to get you out of there, off the boat."

"How?" I asked, unable to believe what I was hearing. "How were you able to change the future?"

His smile widened. "I didn't change the future. I tried, but I kept seeing Mom, Dad and you on the boat. I tried to save you all, but for some reason I couldn't come anywhere close to changing what would happen. I couldn't change a single detail. I was blocked every time. And then it happened, and you were there."

The wind gusted again and rattled the windows. "What are you talking about?" I said.

"Like I said, you were there. You died in the crash."

"Then how ... "

"What I changed was the past, Tom. That's why your memories are so hazy. You can't remember what happened that day because I changed what happened."

I thought about that for a moment and felt my anger rise again. "And you didn't go back and save Mom and Dad?"

"I tried. Believe me, I tried. Over and over again, I tried to go back and save Mom and Dad. But I couldn't do it. Just like when I tried to change what I saw ahead and couldn't, I also couldn't change what was behind us."

"Except with me," I said.

"Except with you. And that's the real reason why I couldn't say anything when I saw you searching for the drunk speedboater. I discovered after my excursions back to 1845 that history has to be cured. It needs time to sort itself out and become solidified."

I nodded. "It needs time to stop being current events and start being history."

"That's a good way to put it. When I saw you on your quest, the new history I created, the one in which you were alive, hadn't yet cured. There was a pretty good chance you still weren't going to make it. The way you were tearing up and down the river on Uncle Jack's boat, I was convinced that you'd still die. I was convinced that history would not allow itself to be changed, that it would use your own recklessness to kill you again. After that, and after the bishop had gotten me to safety, I was convinced that I had failed. I avoided you and all mention of you for years. I knew about your search and did whatever I could to keep out of your way. Then that lady saw me in Mumford and thought I was you."

"Martha Radisson," I said.

"That's right," Patrick said. "She gave a talk at that conference. But she left town before I could ask her about you. That didn't much matter, though, because the more I thought about it, the more I knew you were alive and OK."

"How did you know that?"

"Because she knew you. She obviously knew you before 2003 and thought she saw you then. It was almost seven years after the crash, plenty of time for events to be cured. That proved to me you were alive."

"Patrick, remember the dream I told you about? The one where I saw Mom and Dad die and where you wouldn't let me anywhere near them?"

"Yes. The one where there was someone else near the boat."

"Was it me I saw?"

My brother nodded. "It was. In your dream, I was trying to keep you away from yourself."

Feeling light-headed, I searched for a tether in history, like I had done so often before when loosed from my moorings. "How am I different from Osman Steele?" I asked. "I mean, your attempt to save him failed. Well, you saved him the first time around, but the consequences were so unacceptable that you and Lodi went back and returned things to the way they originally were. How is it different with me?"

"It's not different with you," Patrick said. "You are no different from Osman Steele."

I had to breathe a few times before asking my next question. "So what are the consequences of me?"

"Look around you. Look at what's happening. Look at your dreams. All of it's the consequences of you."

I sighed. "When did you do it?"

"Don't ask me that."

"I just did. I need to know."

"You really don't."

"Was it two weeks ago?"

"Why then?"

"That's when Martha Radisson gave me the card and when the word appeared on our wall," I said. "It's also soon before you turned up at Lodi's and lost consciousness."

Patrick sighed. "Look, telling you when I went back doesn't matter. It's not relevant at all. What does matter is that you're here. One thing I will share with you is that you shouldn't be surprised if your life has seemed a little weird since September 7, 1996, and not just because you lost your parents."

"Actually, it has been," I replied, thinking back to my involvement with the Radissons and the Napoleon's gold adventure. "Let me ask you something else that might matter now. Did you use fire to bring me back?"

Patrick acknowledged my insight with a smile and a proud nod. "Yes. I applied what I learned at William Hamilton's forge in Mumford to the problem of how to bring you back. I used the other three elements as well. They were all there on the day you died, after all."

"So it was sometime between June 2003 and two weeks ago that you went back."

"Check," my brother said.

"You might as well just tell me."

"No. I'm not going to tell you. Believe me, that's not an anniversary you want to celebrate."

Especially now that Mindy and I had a new one of our own to celebrate, I thought. So I let it go, at least for the moment. "I understand the presence of fire, water and air at the crash," I said instead, "but where was the earth?"

"In the wood of the Lyman!" Patrick exclaimed. "That boat was more special than most, you know. It had ... it had a soul."

"How did you do it? It was me you brought back, after all, I should know how you did it."

"Believe me, if I got too far into the mechanics of it, you wouldn't understand. What matters is the aftermath. In the aftermath, there were ... there are some pretty angry elementals out there who do not appreciate what I did. They didn't want me to save you. They didn't want history to be changed. The elementals are vindictive. They're too angry to mollify and they want their revenge on you and on everyone around you. They're after you, brother."

"After *me?*"

"They're coming here right now because Lodi's luring them. But they'd be coming here regardless because you're here. They're coming here to hurt you and to hurt the ones you love."

"Mindy!" I shouted as I sprung up from the chair.

But Patrick had hold of me before I could reach the door. "They're coming for all of us," he said. "They're a lot angrier than they were in 1845. Look what we've done to them. Look what we've done to their water, their land, their air. Like I said on our way up here, anything we do now is too little, too late. Well, almost everything."

I slumped in my brother's arms. "So what do I have to do?"

"When I went back to 1845 the second time I went back to make things right."

"I know. We already talked about this. You and Lodi went back to set in motion a series of events that killed Osman Steele a second time. Definitively."

"Killing Osman Steele was not why I went back. I went back to meet Osman Steele at the tavern in Andes—"

"Hunting's Tavern."

"Yes, Hunting's Tavern. I met with him at the bar. We had a drink."

"The time he dropped the bullet in the glass and said that lead cannot penetrate Steele?"

Patrick led me back to the chairs. We sat. "Yes, right before the showdown on Moses Earle's farm. I met with him and explained to him what I knew would happen if he lived and if the Anti-Renters continued wearing their costumes and blowing their horns, feeding the elementals. I explained to him the anger and anarchy that would result. I explained to him, just like I explained to you a moment ago, how they will not be placated unless by death." My brother paused.

"And?"

"He was a good man, the undersheriff. He genuinely wanted what was best for the people he served and for his family. Deep down inside, he wanted to do what was good and right. His temperament might have led him astray now and again, but overall he was a good man."

"How was he a good man?" I asked, thinking back to what I'd learned about his hot-headed temper and his harassment of the Anti-Renters.

"He understood."

"He did?"

"He did. His life was messy, far more messy than yours is. He was dizzy all the time and couldn't think straight. He often had a difficult time walking and, sometimes, breathing." Patrick laughed.

"What?"

"Ironically enough, he blamed it on the Anti-Renters and their costumes. Before he encountered them, he told me, he felt fine."

"He chose to die," I said.

Patrick looked me in the eye and gave just the slightest of nods.

"At Moses Earle's farm, he positioned himself to take the bullet," I added.

"I told him where to position his horse to receive the bullet. I told him that if any of the others missed, I wouldn't."

"I need to make the same choice," I whispered.

"You do. And that's why I'm here." My brother leaned closer and put his hand on my shoulder. He and I both looked out the window, where the sky was darkening and rain was starting to fall.

"Keep her safe," I said, tears falling from eyes.

"Listen to me," he said. "I don't know what this plan is, and I don't know how much Lodi and that professor of yours or any of your friends can help. But I will do everything in my power to protect Mindy, especially now that she's my sister-in-law." He shook me by the shoulders and looked deeply into my eyes. "Everything in my power, brother."

Chapter Fifty One

WE FOUND THE OTHERS in the ballroom, some sitting, some standing around the large oak table that should have dominated the room. It didn't because of Lady Ostend's portrait, painted by Frederic Remington in 1892. The larger-than-life size painting hung over the mantle, and from it the great woman gazed down upon the entire room with equal amounts of wisdom and compassion. The exquisite painting was a testament to Lady Ostend's spiritual philosophy. In each corner of the canvas was a different color—green, brown, blue, red—each color representing one of the four classical elements. I stopped in the doorway and gazed at the portrait for several minutes. All four colors seemed to undulate and shimmer as if directly connected to their spiritual manifestations that slowly approached Valhalla from the west.

"You look like you've seen a ghost," Mindy said when she finally noticed me in the doorway. She moved around the table to embrace me. She held me for a moment, then pulled away and turned to Patrick, who raised an eyebrow and shrugged. Mindy held my hands and looked into my eyes. To my relief, she did not ask what Patrick and I had been talking about.

"Andrew and Lodi are moments away," Raphael Ostend announced. "Mindy, Tom, Patrick, come with me. Andrew and Lodi are meeting us in the boathouse."

"Why not the others?" I asked.

"Professor Dale and I are stationed in the tower," Jim Pembroke said, "Our job is to observe and record."

"Which reminds me," Ray said, "I left most of my instruments on your boat."

"Let's get them," Jim said.

"What instruments?" Patrick asked.

"I've got ultraviolet cameras, infrared cameras, sensors of several different types, electromagnetic meters."

"We'll help you set them up," Mike Slattery said.

"You're not coming?" Mindy asked.

"Martin and Mike are staying here with me," Ostend said, glancing up at his grandmother. "We're too old to participate directly, but we can watch and listen, and might even be able to offer support and guidance. Come, we need to hurry."

WE DESCENDED THE MAIN STAIRCASE to the lobby and, once outside, followed the curving cobblestone path to the boathouse. Thick grey clouds blew across the upper atmosphere at tremendous speed. The clouds were heavy and alive with electricity. The river was alive, too, roaring and roiling against Valhalla's breakwater, spilling over the rock and onto the well-manicured lawn.

Raphael Ostend gripped the boathouse door handle and paused. He looked at me and then at Patrick. He smiled. "Brace yourselves," he advised. "What you're about to see might shock you." He opened the door and let us through.

"It can't be!" Patrick exclaimed when he saw what was there. "It couldn't possibly be!" He looked back at me, his smile accompanied by a welling-up of tears.

What couldn't possibly be was my father's Lyman, named *No Name*, moored with rope to a red granite arch. It looked brand new, with polished wood, bright chrome trim and soft leather upholstery. Seeing the boat so lovingly restored gave my spirits a lift, lightening somewhat the burden of fear that had weighed me down for weeks.

I turned to face Ostend. "Did you do this?"

"I only paid for it. The work was done by several of the river's most accomplished craftsmen." He handed me the keys. "They made several enhancements, similar to those on the *Archangel*. This boat will keep you safe."

"It's beautiful," Mindy said, running her hand along the polished wood of the bow.

"Patrick's right," I said as I followed Mindy's lead and caressed the *No Name's* hull. "You showed it to me in storage at our first Ostend Ball. The boat was in ruins! This can't possibly be!"

"Nothing is irreversible," Ostend said. "Nothing is truly lost if it's soul survives. The *No Name*, like the *Archangel*, has a hearty soul."

Patrick caught my eye and smiled.

"Well thank you," I said. "No, I'm sorry, thank you doesn't even begin to express it." I opened the door. The handle pulled and the hinges turned with well-oiled ease. "Where are we taking it?"

"To Griffin Island," Ostend answered.

Mindy and I exchanged a look of shock. I stepped away from the door and it sprung closed.

Patrick noticed our reaction. "What's wrong with Griffin Island?" he asked.

"It … it disappeared in several of our friends' dreams," I replied. "In Andrew's dream, it disappeared with me and Mindy on it."

"And we took heed. You two are not going to be on Griffin Island," Ostend explained. "You two are going to stay on the *No Name* with Andrew. You're to deposit Patrick and Lodi on Griffin Island, then return to a point in the river at least fifty meters away until their work is complete."

"What are we supposed to do?" Mindy asked.

"You and Tom have the very important role of turning on the machine."

"Ray's machine," Mindy said.

"Yes. Professor Dale's machine must be switched on remotely," Ostend answered.

"What will Patrick and Lodi be doing on Griffin Island?" I asked.

"They will guide the elementals into the portal that the machine will open. Both of them have been to the Otherworld before and, presumably, know how to return. When they signal you that they are back, you will change the machine's setting to close the portal, hopefully for good. But you, Melinda, and you, Tom, must stay on the boat with Andrew. As I said, this boat, with its enhancements, will keep you both safe."

"I'm ready," Patrick said. He offered me a knowing look.

I was about to ask what happens if the machine doesn't work when we heard a voice yelling "Holy shit! Holy, HOLY SHIT!" over the sound of an approaching outboard motor.

Andrew, wide-eyed and wild, cut the motor of his flat-bottomed Crestliner just as he entered the boathouse. He tossed me the lanyard. I pulled it backwards, stopping him just inches from the Lyman.

"That's our cousin," I said to Patrick's laughter.

"I can't believe this is happening!" Andrew shouted even louder. His pupils were dilated. His hands were shaking. He was so unsteady that I had to help him onto the landing and support him for a moment as he regained his balance.

Lodi followed him with a nimble leap from the boat to the rock ledge. He walked straight to Raphael Ostend and held out a hand, which Ostend accepted.

"It's an honor to finally meet you face to face," Lodi said. "I hoped I would when Tom asked me to play for his and Mindy's after hours party. The circumstances have changed, obviously, but I am honored to meet you nonetheless."

"And I you," Ostend replied. "Professor Dale has told me quite a lot about you." Ostend motioned to the sky and then to the water. "You have enviable talents."

"No kidding!" interjected Andrew. "The whole way across New York he sat in the back of my pickup playing his … what's that thing called?"

"A pan flute," Lodi said, "or pipes."

"Playing his homemade pipes," Andrew finished. "And they just kept coming! They followed us, they cut us off from up ahead! They came at us from the side! Sometimes I could see them, other times I could hear them, other times I just *knew* they were there. Holy shit, that was amazing!"

"What did you play?" I asked. "What songs? That horn dance you played for us on Louie's deck?"

"A variation of a horn dance," Lodi said. "And many other songs, some old, some new. Each of the four types of beings is attracted by a different sort of song. I've learned them all over the years."

As if in agreement, the wind gusted and the river simultaneously surged.

"Andrew, you remember your cousin Patrick?" I asked.

"Of course!" The two hugged.

"I know you've declined my offers before," Ostend said, handing Lodi a folded sheet of paper, "but I'll extend it to you again as a courtesy."

Lodi unfolded the sheet of paper and glanced at it. "Generous," he said. "Thank you, but I work much more effectively as a free agent."

"Someday, perhaps, you'll say yes," Ostend said with a smile. Lodi handed him the paper and he returned it to his inside pocket.

"Where are the others?" Patrick asked. "The gnomes and salamanders?"

"You'll see them soon enough," Lodi answered. "Too soon if we don't get going."

"We're taking the *No Name*," Mindy instructed.

The second she spoke, Lodi's lips widened into a great smile. He gestured to her and looked at me. "Is this her?" he asked. "Is this your mysterious bride?"

"None other," I answered. "Lodi, this is Mindy. Mindy, Lodi."

"Charmed," Mindy said.

"Not nearly as much as I am," Lodi said as he bent to kiss her hand. "How's the wedding planning?"

Mindy looked at me and we both laughed. Lodi gave us a puzzled look.

"We're already married," Mindy said. "The mayor of Alexandria Bay performed the ceremony earlier today."

"Does this mean the July gig is cancelled?" Lodi asked with a frown.

"Not at all," Mindy answered. "We'll reaffirm our vows, exchange rings and party on as planned." She caught Andrew's eyes and turned to face him. "I'm sorry," she said, taking his hands. "I'm sorry we did it without you."

"Did I miss the cake?" Andrew asked.

"No," Mindy said. "And we'll make sure you get the first and biggest piece."

Andrew smiled. "Wait," he said, walking to the *No Name's* stern. "Is this what I think it is?"

"The Flanagan family Lyman," Raphael Ostend said. "It makes it's return to the river today, with you, Andrew Hibbard, at the helm."

Andrew smiled again, this time like a child who'd just been given a new toy.

Chapter Fifty Two

THE NEXT DAY, the newspapers and local TV channels reported that an unusually powerful supercell had formed over the eastern end of Lake Ontario and had moved northeast along the Saint Lawrence River at a surprisingly high speed. It had cut a swath across Wolfe Island and had skirted Cape Vincent, and had strengthened as it hit the deep water between Grindstone Island and Clayton. It had wreaked havoc on Wellesley Island, flattening houses and uprooting trees where it might have touched down and become a tornado. The American span of the bridge had been closed and was being investigated for possible structural damage.

The storm had intensified again as it crossed the most tourist-heavy section of the river at Alexandria Bay. It had torn a sculpted hart off Boldt Castle's arch. It had spun a freighter, the *Calliope*, a full one hundred eighty degrees. Unable to correct his ship's course before it slammed into Alex Bay's public docks, the captain, Ricky Reynolds, had purposefully ran the ship aground on the Rock Island Shoal, saving millions of dollars in damage and probably several lives. The storm had produced water spouts as it moved north of the Summerland Group and into Canadian waters. The microburst was at its strongest when it hit the Ostend Group, doing substantial damage to Valhalla's outbuildings, but leaving the main structure unharmed. The path of the supercell puzzled the meteorologists, who were used to seeing storms weaken as they got that far downriver and into cooler air. All told, the storm was dubbed one of the most severe to ever hit the Thousand Islands, a conclusion we could readily confirm.

The Weather Channel interviewed islanders who described wind that howled and gusts that sounded like a freight train. They obtained video of horizontal rain and of lightning that looked like fire. They compared the sizes of not-yet-melted hailstones to that of golf balls. One Tar Islander had in his freezer a hailstone the size of a croquet ball. When the report aired, they played over and over again a fifteen second cell phone clip of lightning striking an island cliff and causing an avalanche of rock to fall into the river. Another video, much more blurry but with disturbingly clear audio, showed a flock of ospreys being blown against a cliff wall. The Weather Channel compared the microburst to a severe tornado barreling through the flatlands of Oklahoma or Kansas.

What the local news stations and the Weather Channel failed to report, however, was what we noticed right away when we saw the storm brewing while aboard the *Archangel*: that the storm, as if by its own conscious decision, remained confined to the boundary of the river. The mainland on either side of the river was not affected at all by the storm, only the river and its islands.

THE MACHINE that Ray Dale had devised consisted of twelve powerful transmitters, spaced equidistantly along Griffin Island's perimeter, that broadcasted sound and emitted light. The sound, Ray said, was a combination of both ultra-high and ultra-low frequencies, neither of which could be heard by human ears. As I later discovered, however, the low frequency pulses could be felt in the trembling rock of Griffin Island. The light that pulsed from the transmitters was a combination of ultraviolet A and B, along with some infrared. According to Ray, the cumulative effect of sound and light would show more clearly what was already there, a doorway or portal to the Otherworld, and would act as a beacon calling the elemental beings through.

Griffin Island itself was, as Andrew had described it at the Council of Ostend, a rhombus-shaped piece of rock about three acres in size, set apart from the other islands of the Ostend Group by about a half mile of alternating deep and shallow water. It was a glacially-formed *roche moutonnee*, or sheep's back, with one shore gently sloping into the water and the other ending in an imposing forty foot cliff. The island was covered in larch and fir. It was a beautiful spot for kayakers and campers. There were no campers here on this day, only the twelve transmitters of Ray Dale's machine, set up on tripods around the island's perimeter.

THE WIND BLEW TO A GALE and the waves crashed against Griffin Island's cliffs and rocked us as we rounded the island's gently sloping side. Andrew carefully piloted the *No Name* alongside a flat ledge of rock that jutted out into the river. At Andrew's urging, Patrick and Lodi, each with a backpack, disembarked there. They reminded us to return in an hour, or sooner if they signaled us with a red flare.

"Are you going back in time?" I nervously asked before they started their trek around the island to check the transmitters.

"I'd love to!" Lodi said emphatically.

"Not intentionally," was Patrick's worrisome answer.

"And if you end up there anyway?"

"I know what you're thinking," Patrick whispered in my ear as Andrew tried to keep the boat steady over the waves. "And I hold to what I said earlier. I won't do anything to hurt you or to undo what I already did."

The inflated boat fenders scraped furiously against the granite. "Unless you want your Lyman destroyed again, we've got to get into deeper water," Andrew shouted.

"OK," I said. And to Patrick and Lodi, "Good luck."

Andrew piloted the *No Name* to a spot about fifty yards

to the southwest of Griffin Island and just over twenty five feet deep.

THE AIR-SPIRITS WERE THE FIRST to present themselves. Initially they came gently, a brief lull in the storm, bringing with them a clear, crisp breeze that, in a good year—any other year—could be enjoyed on many a July and August evening. Andrew cut the Lyman's engine as the gentle air hugged the river and the wind and waves calmed. The three of us sat down in the upholstered benches to give our stiff legs a rest. Mindy put her arm around me and rested her head on my shoulder. The sun, piercing through the clouds, was pleasant and warm.

Breathing deep, the air caressed my throat and lungs. It was fresh air, healing air, air tinged with the scent of pine and seaweed. It was exactly this air that had made the Thousand Islands such a popular destination for convalescents a hundred years before.

We discovered all too quickly that the storm hadn't actually left us; instead it had curled around to the south and west, as if to gather more moisture, more force. We felt the wind pick up after only fifteen minutes or so of calm. It gusted at first, leaving intermittent moments when the fresh air of healing could still be enjoyed. But then it blew steadily, accelerating by degrees until it was stronger and more menacing than it had been all day. The effects of the wind were all around us. The dark clouds returned, blocking the sun and taking away its warmth. The waves returned, eventually crashing over the transom and into the boat. Andrew started the engine to maneuver us between the waves. All three of us returned to our feet to better keep our balance. Eventually the wind made breathing difficult. Mindy and I held each other to keep from falling onto the boat's deck or, worse, out of it. Andrew stood like a linebacker waiting to make a tackle, perfectly balanced, intense, in complete control of the *No Name*.

The wind caused the pine trees on Griffin Island to sway violently. With increasing frequency, and increasing alarm, we heard loud snaps as branches and entire trunks broke off and fell to the ground.

Then something changed. At first the shift was almost imperceptible, like a slight drop in temperature or barometric pressure, or a minute shift in the wind's direction. After a moment the change was inescapable: the wind was mingling with the water, eroding the boundary between sky and river. Days like this were as frequent on the river as the days of beauty and healing. The air on these days was thick and oppressive, like living inside a humidifier.

After about ten minutes the balance between wind and wave shifted and the water started to move on its own, the waves rising in inverse proportion to the wind's deceleration. At the same time, the sky darkened as the heart of the storm reached the Ostend Group of islands. Rain fell, first as a mist and then as thick, dark sheets. The river rose, water beings pulled up from below by the force of a now vertical wind.

"We've got to get on land!" Andrew shouted. "Between the waves and the rain, we're taking in too much water!"

Hail started to mix in with the precipitation just as Andrew spoke the words.

"Great," he added. He turned to face me and shouted again, "We've got to get on land!"

"No!" Mindy shouted back. "Tom and I are not setting foot on Griffin Island!"

In the quietest of whispers, something told me I needed to be on Griffin Island anyway, despite the warnings of the River Rat Reporters, despite Andrew's dream, despite Mindy's insistence. But I didn't want to reveal that to Andrew and Mindy. So I said, "she's right," and left it at that.

"Raphael said the *No Name's* been enhanced," Mindy said into my ear. "Maybe with bilge pumps?" She leaned over the instrument panel and shielded her eyes against the rain and hail. "Aha!" she said, flicking a switch that set a motor running. Seconds later the water had drained through thin parallel slats that ran the length the floor. The motor quieted.

"Automatic," I said, impressed.

"Let's hope that's not the only improvement!" Andrew yelled.

After a few more minutes of intense rain, a strange feeling started to creep upon me. It was a heightened sense of concentration mixed with light-headedness and a tingling of my nerves. My vision seemed clearer, my hearing more acute. It was the feeling I'd been searching for when I went out in my kayak the day after our arrival on the river, the same feeling I had on Moses Earle's farm in Andes when I saw the buck transform into an Anti-Renter and I journeyed into the Otherworld. Now that it was here, and despite my desire to replicate it, the feeling scared me.

I heard Mindy talking in tones that became increasingly distant, saying something about there not being a switch to turn on Ray's machine. I saw through clouded eyes my cousin trying to control the boat's steering as the waves grew stronger and more menacing. I looked down into the water, deep into the river that had given me so much good, and some pain, for so many years. I heard the river whisper my name. I leaned forward, wanting more than anything to become one with the water, to join the spiritual beings that I now saw with a vision beyond my eyes and perhaps—yes!—to become one with them. My breathing was filled with the scent of lemon verbena.

Like Osman Steele, I was ready to give up myself for something bigger.

I slipped out of Mindy's grasp and fell into the Saint Lawrence.

Chapter Fifty Three

I FEEL MYSELF BEING EMBRACED by the river as I descend. I feel warmed and loved beyond the possibilities of human love. With my mind's eye I see the river's soul. It is gold, a soft gold, barely metallic, that suffuses the water around me with light and warmth. It caresses my body, seeps through my skin and fills my inmost being. It brings me joy and causes me to laugh out loud as I recollect all the goodness I've experienced in and around this water. It's more than memory, as Martha Radisson had explained it a few weeks before in my Clinton Falls office. I actually relive the joy of waterskiing and cliff diving with family and friends, the peace of solitude in my kayak, the family love at barbecues and bonfires, of hot dogs and Jiffy Pop and s'mores. Then, to my amazement, I start to see what brought me joy. There's my cousin Andrew laughing with me on a tube as his parents, Jack and Linda, pull us on the Chris-Craft. There's me and Patrick playing with our Matchbox cars and Hot Wheels on the road we made with our Tonka trucks. There's the three of us, diving off the public dock at Thousand Islands Park without a care in the world. There's my mom, reading *A Tale of Two Cities* out loud as we lounge together in our hammock. And there's my dad, his Yankees cap pulled way down, a can of Genny Light in his hand, teaching me how to grill a steak to perfection. Finally there's Mindy and me at the Boldt Castle New Year's Eve fireworks, holding each other close, laughing, promising each other we'll be together forever.

What the river shows me brings me to tears. They are tears of joy for all the happiness that these beloved people and so many others had given me. Yet they are also tears of regret for all those times I'd fallen short of expectations and had disappointed Mindy and my parents and the people I loved. Most of all, they are tears for my beloved Saint Lawrence. For years it had been a refuge from pain for me and many others. How much longer can it provide refuge? How much longer can it be a place where purity and wisdom, truth and tenderness are nurtured against the more base instincts of human life? My tears mingle with the tears of the river, which I can somehow differentiate from the ordinary water around me. I know that what my family has shared for generations in this water and on these islands is about to end. We cry together, as if saying a final goodbye.

Slowly, yet persistently, another feeling rises through the water and meets me near the surface. It wrenches my gut and pounds my mind, presses me from every direction. It's anger that overtakes me now, the rage of a hundred years and more of human abuse. It's anger against the garbage, oil, sewage and plastic thrown into the river by people who fail to care. It's an anger that, at the moment, seems directed towards me as an embodiment of all that's wrong with humanity.

Then the river shows me why it's angry. It shows me visions of oil seeping from the *CANCO-2000* as it scrapes across Pullman Shoal. It shows me the *Roy Jodrey*, which rests on rock ledges just offshore of Wellesley Island and still leaks fuel after all these years. It shows me the gasoline and batteries that careless boaters throw into it day after day. I see the toxic sludge pumped into the Saint Lawrence by the aluminum plant in Massena. The river shows me the sewage and transmits its stench to my nose. It shows me the dead fish and birds, the ruined ecosystems, the dead zones annihilated by the zebra-mussels that came on the hulls and in the bilge of tankers and freighters. It shows me tons upon tons of plastic in every shape and size. Much of the plastic is too small to see with human eyes, but it's still there, choking life from the river. I take measure of the river's anger—so hot, so immediate, quickly rising to a boil—and I shake with fear. I try to turn back to the Lyman.

But I'm stopped about fifty feet from the boat. I can see the *No Name's* hull and the churn of its propeller. I think I can see Mindy's hand extending down into the breaking waves, hopelessly reaching for mine. I can see them, but I cannot get to them. I feel myself surrounded. I feel myself cut off from everything around me besides the river's red-hot rage. I try to scream, but my breath is being choked out of my lungs. I try to turn, but an overwhelming force is pushing me ... where? Pushing me *inward* from all directions at once.

The heat I feel is no illusion. It's caused, I see, by tongues of fire that rise from the depths of the river floor and join with the flames that shoot down from the clouds like lightning. The river *is* starting to boil, I notice with alarm. I look down and see what looks like lava oozing from the river floor. Will the river gain an island rather than lose one, the opposite of what the River Rat Reporters dreamed? The geological and glacial history of the Thousand Islands seem irrelevant—the volcanism I'm seeing below me is utterly independent of what was or what should be.

The fire twists and twirls. The flames lick and curl around me, terrifying me. But I realize after a moment that the flames aren't burning my body. Somewhat relieved, I wonder what's happening above water. No sooner do I have the thought than I am carried upwards to the surface. I see that the flames above the water do indeed burn: they have engulfed the tops of the trees on the upper side of Griffin Island, causing the pines and larches to look like candles on a birthday cake. The sound of popping pinecones and hissing pitch is deafening. I think of Patrick and Lodi and try to swim towards Griffin Island's shore. My own effort gets me nowhere, but when I think "swim" I am moved swiftly across the water by an invisible force and end up face down in the rock and mud, with waves lapping against my aching legs and lower abdomen.

I roll on to my back and the sky grabs my attention. Tongues of flame hop from cloud to cloud. Water sprays upwards from the river into these same clouds like a downpour in reverse. The water doesn't quench the flame, only hisses in anger as the two elements meet in a blast of smoke and steam. Gusts of wind blow the clouds swiftly in a circular pattern, and sway the flaming trees like Bic lighters at a rock concert. I can see the *No Name* at a distance, bobbing up and down in the waves. I cannot tell if Andrew and Mindy are still aboard.

"Tom!" my brother shouts from about ten yards away. The wind buffets his clothes and he's ankle-deep in water. He anticipates a falling, flaming bough of white pine and hops out of the way before it crashes and sparks to his left. He moves forward and cups his hands around his eyes to see me better. "What the hell are you doing off the boat?"

I hear him as if I'm inside a cocoon. I cannot answer him. I try running to him, but I'm stopped just as I was when trying to swim back to Andrew and Mindy on the *No Name*.

Patrick cranes his neck and narrows his eyes in heightened concentration. "You don't have to do it! I think we found another way! Do you understand? *You don't have to do it!*" His eyes narrow and he scowls. "Dammit!" he says. "You're already there." He starts to walk away, then turns and points. "Don't go *anywhere!*" he shouts. "*Don't move!*"

But I do have to do it, I tell myself. I do have to follow the same path that Osman Steele followed, the path of self-sacrifice for the good of the many, perhaps for the very existence of the river. I remain still and try to control my breathing. I think about what's happening around me. I wonder what the others are seeing from Valhalla. I wonder if what's happening now is what Lady Ostend foresaw. I wonder if Ray Dale's machine is doing what it's supposed to do, is doing all this. Most of all I wonder about Mindy. Is Andrew keeping her safe? Is Patrick doing everything in his power to fulfill his promise and keep her safe?

I'm wondering about all these things when I see someone else on Griffin Island's shore. I turn slowly around and move a step towards the water, surprised that I can finally move at all. Her embroidered gown is immune to the wind and rain. Her blond hair is dry and in perfect order. She floats towards me and we meet. I can smell once again the minty freshness of her body and breath. I can see the curves of her shoulders, breasts and hips underneath the fabric of her exquisite gown.

"What is it you most desire?" she asks slowly and with a smile.

"Mindy," I say without a second's thought.

"Are you willing to give yourself up for her and for the others? Are you willing to let go?"

"Yes. I wouldn't be here otherwise."

Her deep stare transfixes me. I can't turn away, can't even blink. I feel her gaze burrow through my eyes and into my soul. She sees me, I know, all of me.

"The here and now that you and Mindy share is but a sliver of time," she says.

I swallow as I recall the words Mike Slattery spoke at our wedding.

Give them grace to accept that they are mortal, to face the possibility of death and the separation it must bring.

"I know," I say.

"Are you willing to leave her for a time so you can be with her forever? Even with all the pain and disappointment that might bring you?"

"Yes," I say.

"Then it may yet be so," she says as she glides a hand from the top of my head to my ear to my chin.

She smiles again, which brings a smile to my face, then turns and glides back towards the water, slowly fading from view and dissolving into mist herself as she reaches the border between island and river.

"But what do I do?" I pointlessly ask.

I know it's the end. I know whatever I do will bring to a close this chapter in my life. I only pray that what comes next will be what the woman hinted it would be.

"Tough call," I hear a familiar voice say right off my left shoulder.

"Billy," I say. "Am I ever glad to see you!"

"Sure 'bout that?" The cloud of cigarette smoke he blows hits me in the face.

"What happens if I choose ... you know, will I become like you?"

"There's only one of me. What happens is you'll become like them."

He gestures forward. I see a tree in the midst of Griffin Island's flaming larches and pines. This tree is unburnt and beautiful. Its silver bark is without blemish, its branches perfectly shaped. Its leaves are the deepest green I've ever seen. It's loaded with milk-white flowers that glow with life. It gives off a scent that I recognize right away, the scent of citrus and sweetness that overwhelms the smoke from the fires and from Billy's cigarette. It wasn't lemon verbena at all, I realize. On our bungalow's front porch with Mindy, in the hollow at Moses Earle's farm, here on the river right before I fell in—on all these occasions it was this tree that filled the air with freshness and life and love.

Next to the tree, on either side of it, I see two figures slowly materialize. A man and a woman walk forward and join hands. I know who they are right away. My sobs almost cause me to choke.

"They're waitin' for you," Billy whispers. "Mary and

Charlie were always really good at waitin' for you. Like I said, tough call."

"Dad?" I say. "Mom?"

"We love you, son," my mother says, her voice filled with beauty and joy.

"We're proud of the man you've become," my father adds.

Through my tears, I see their bodies brighten with a beautiful soft yellow light.

"And all manner of things shall be well!" they say together.

About to walk towards the center of the island, to walk right into the wind and flame and to the beauty and love waiting for me on the other side, I see another figure appear, this time on the ground, struggling to crawl out of the water and on to the shore. I blink my eyes against the wind and rain. The first thing I recognize is her long brown hair, which she was wearing pulled back into a ponytail but now flows out in all directions, lapped by the waves. I run to her. She raises her head and looks and me and smiles.

"Mindy," I say, in equal measure relieved and terrified by her presence.

"Atta boy!" Billy says as he disappears. "And don't worry. They'll stay good at waitin' for as long as it takes."

Chapter Fifty Four

"Where are we?" Mindy asks as she takes my hands and stands up.

"I think we're over there," I say, embracing her tightly and abandoning myself to her arms and to the smell of her hair and neck. "Or somewhere in between."

"Was that Billy?"

"It was. He came to help me. And that—" I turn to point out my parents but they, and the white-flowered tree, are gone.

"How did I get here?" she asks.

"I don't know. But I think it's like when you had the same dream I did, the one about the accident. Mindy, the woman was here. I think she's Ar—"

A series of obscenely loud snaps and crashes interrupts me. Somewhere on Griffin Island a whole swath of trees has fallen. Then, from the other side of the island, comes a rush of air and water, followed by a stream of flame that seems aimed right at us.

"Into the water!" Mindy screams as we already run together in that direction. Too late, I remember Patrick's instructions to not move.

Thigh deep, standing on rock, we hear another series of explosions that causes us to turn back towards the island. We see more flame, this time ascending skyward at regular intervals of about twenty or thirty yards. Then we see to our right explosions like fireworks and more flame.

"Ray's machine," I say. "The rods are exploding!"

Mindy holds me tighter. "Are they supposed to?" she asks.

"I don't know," I say. I see that the wind, water and fire seem to stop their forward movement at the shore. Maybe Ray's machine is supposed to explode. "There was no switch, was there."

"No there wasn't. I think it was Raphael's way of keeping us on the boat by making us think we had something to do."

"That's the last thing I heard you say before I fell in."

Mindy laughed.

"What?"

"Raphael's ruse didn't work," she said.

"No it didn't," I agreed.

"I think we're safe here," Mindy guesses.

I brush back her hair and look into her eyes. "Don't let go of me," I say.

"Never," she answers.

We're thigh deep in water, standing on rock. The water is splashing all around us, propelled by the wind and by its own inner momentum. But I notice that the water begins to ripple in a different way, as if in response to a deeper set of forces. Then the rock upon which we're standing abruptly shakes, causing me to stumble a bit, which causes Mindy to tighten her grip around my waist so I don't fall.

"What was that?" she asks.

"The earth," I say. "The only one of the four we haven't felt yet."

The rock we're on shakes again, but this time more violently. And the tremors are clearly not confined to our rock: the fiery trees on Griffin Island are shaking too, and shuffling, as they continue to sway in the wind.

"Swim!" Mindy shouts. "Swim back towards Valhalla!" I nod. I hadn't studied the charts of this section of the river, but I know from Andrew's commentary while piloting us around Griffin Island that there is a series a shoals between us and Ostend's castle. I hope and pray that the geography of the Otherworld is the same as ours.

Always the stronger swimmer, Mindy moves ahead of me and has to tread water for a moment as I catch up. When I do, she takes my hand and holds it.

"Don't wait for me," I say.

"Always have and always will," she replies.

"OK then. Let's go." I blink the water out of my eyes.

"There should be a shoal just up ahead," Mindy says, pointing. "Maybe a bit to our right."

We reach the shoal together and are able to get a good foothold on a narrow cut in the rock. The waves are chest high here, but at least the ground is not shaking.

Mindy takes my hand again. I slide it up her arm and around her shoulder. She puts hers around my waist.

We watch the trees continue to burn, the whole of Griffin Island continue to shake. The wind diminishes where we are, but fifty yards away it blows even harder. And it starts to blow in circles, concentrating its power on Griffin Island. Mindy and I both gape as the funnel cloud forms. We gasp as the funnel cloud pulls the fire from the trees and spins it too, causing the water vapor in the clouds and the water sucked up from the river to hiss and spit.

There's lightning and thunder over Griffin Island. The spinning cloud glows and pulses. A sudden loud crash sends my heart into my throat. A second later pieces of granite propel outwards from the island and splash into the river. A basketball size chunk lands just a few feet from the presumed safety of our shoal.

"My God," Mindy whispers.

Tears flow down her face. I can taste the salt of my own. Mindy buries her head in my shoulder and cries even harder.

"Patrick," I croak, barely able to verbalize his name.

Then a cloud of smoke and dust rises from Griffin Island's shore. It is a cloud very much unlike the angry, swirling one that seems bent on destroying the island. It is, I quickly realize, the same sort of cloud that Andrew and I had seen on our journey into Delaware County, the same sort of cloud that Mary Earley had painted in her magnificent mural of the Anti-Rent Wars.

And at the center of this cloud is a human-shaped figure surrounded by a blazing white light. The light comes from her, I realize when my eyes adjust to it. Although her billowing gown is still black, the jewels embroidered on it now shine like a thousand suns, and her face and hair shine even more brightly.

I see other figures slowly take shape in the cloud, figures of fire and water and of darker cloud, all circling around and following the woman. I gently lift Mindy's head and tell her to look. As I do so, large pieces of granite break away from Griffin Island with crunching, cracking purpose. As they shoot over the water they change shape. By the time I can see them through the haze and mist, they almost look human. Human, but with this difference: they are solid blocks of granite with seams of green and blue and orange and red, with heads shaped like sheepskin masks and with horns or large ears protruding from their temples.

"The costumes," I whisper to Mindy's disbelief and to my own astonishment. We share a wide-eyed glance. "The Anti-Renters modeled their costumes after the earth-beings."

And then we see Lodi. He's playing his pipes, carried forward to the front of the group by two massive pieces of rock that are more colorful than the rest.

He sees us and stops playing for a moment. The earth-beings of Griffin Island pause with him. I can see him smile, his eyes bright with purpose and thrill. He nods. He says something that I can't hear through the cacophony.

"Travel well," Mindy says, pointing to Lodi as he and the earth-beings start to enter the clouds and disappear. "He just told us to travel well."

Ten minutes later it's all over. The wind has settled down. The fire has been extinguished. The river is placid, except for a bubble or two where pieces of rock that were once Griffin Island finally settle below the surface. And then, once the last bits of stone submerge, Griffin Island itself is gone.

Chapter Fifty Five

ANDREW FOUND US. We were still standing on the shoal, but barely standing. Our feet were in pain from being squeezed into the cut. We were nearly asleep, resting our heads against each other with our eyes closed. Andrew had cut the *No Name's* engine and coasted up to our shoal. He surprised us, causing us to almost slip off the rock as we suddenly straightened.

"You guy's want a moment?" he asked.

"No," Mindy answered. "We've had enough time here."

We climbed aboard and sat, exhausted, in the second set of pilot chairs.

"What did you see?" I asked.

"After you jumped in?" he asked. I nodded. "Wind, waves, lightning strikes, flaming trees. Then things got foggy. Very foggy. I could barely see ten feet past the bow."

"And Griffin Island?"

"When the fog cleared it was gone, just like in my dream. Makes me wonder if it was ever there in the first place."

"It was there all right," Mindy said. "But we weren't on it at the time it disappeared."

"Thank God for that," Andrew said.

A thought leapt into my brain. "We need to look for Patrick," I said.

"I'm on it," Andrew said, "right after I get you two back to Valhalla."

"No!" Mindy and I both exclaimed.

Andrew saw our insistence and turned the boat around.

"How are we going to find him?" I asked.

"The *No Name* has pretty advanced radar," my cousin said, "along with several types of depth finders. I think it can pick him up wherever he is."

"One of the enhancements," I said.

"Want to hear another one? It's got these sensors that predict the depth of an oncoming wave and it's wavelength. Then it adjusts the pitch and haul accordingly. I've never seen anything like it!"

"You want it?" I found myself say.

Andrew turned and smiled. "You serious?"

I nodded. "Keep it docked at Hibbard Island. If I ever want to borrow it I'll let you know. You'll use it a lot more than I will."

Mindy, watching the radar screen, cleared her throat.

"Right," I said. "Is that OK with you?"

"Absolutely," she said. She pointed to the screen, where a small dot blipped in and out. "It's Patrick," she said.

We found him floating on a log in about fifty feet of water. He saw us and waved.

"We did it!" he shouted.

"And I'm still here!" I replied. Mindy and Andrew both looked at me suspiciously.

"Sit next to me," Andrew said after we hauled my brother aboard. "The seat's heated."

Patrick sat and let out a deep sigh. "It'll never be the same, you know," he said.

"I know," I said. "Nothing ever is."

Andrew turned the boat back towards Valhalla. He hit the throttle then just as quickly let off. "Wait. Shouldn't we be looking for Lodi?" he asked.

"Don't bother," Patrick said.

"Why not?"

"What was the last you saw of him?"

"When he got off the boat with you," Andrew said.

I turned to Patrick. "And you?"

"I saw him for the last time right after I left you on the shore. I hiked back up to the cliffs. I found him sitting up there, playing a slow, low-pitched dirge on his flute. That's when the rock started to shake. And that's when I got the hell out of there."

"What did you do?" I asked.

"I dove off the cliff into the river," my brother answered. "I found a piece of wood and held on for dear life. When did you last see him?"

"We saw him leading a band of earth-beings," I said. "They looked like Anti-Renters." Andrew gave me a look of suspicion mixed with shock. "We saw things differently," I told him. "We saw events from another perspective."

"So he ended up with the gnomes," Patrick said with a smile. "Good."

"How's that good?" Mindy asked.

"It's what he wanted. It's why he was here. He's been trying for years to get to the Otherworld."

"Will he ever come back?" I asked.

Patrick's smile grew wider. "With him, I wouldn't rule anything out."

Chapter Fifty Six

THE PHOTO ALBUM from our July wedding celebration arrived four months to the day after our official wedding, four months to the day after Griffin Island disappeared. We spent that early-autumn evening going through it page by page, enjoying the photos and reliving the day. There was the *Archangel*, polished to a golden-brown sheen that gleamed in the sun, caught on film from the bow and from the stern. There was the nineteen piece orchestra playing Handel's *Water Music*—we could almost hear those joyous melodies again as we turned the album's pages. There were Len and Linda McDonnell, dancing with each other, dancing with Mindy and me, the four of us dancing together. There was Patrick dancing with our aunt Nancy, Andrew's mom, bright smiles on their faces. There was Louie doing the YMCA with my Uncle Jack. There were Louie and Ghedi and Denise, the latter two on their first visit to the river. There were the River Rat Reporters, all dressed up in the same tuxedos they wore for the annual Ostend Ball in November. Together they lifted glasses of champagne in our honor.

And there were dozens of pictures of Mindy and me. In one we stood with Napoleon as he blessed our rings on the beautiful Cape Vincent shore. In another we shared our first dance, a waltz, to Strauss' *On the Blue Danube*. There were several photos of us kissing, of course. And there was one of us and Raphael Ostend, holding our hands in his as he shared with us his understanding of what happened on the day Griffin Island disappeared. A particularly poignant photo showed us arm in arm at the *Archangel's* bow as the sun set behind us. But our favorite was the final picture of the album, which showed us from behind, stepping off the gangplank of the *Archangel* back onto the mainland.

The final photo was a symbolic one because it marked the last time we were on the river. Before the ceremony started we had already packed our bags and had loaded them into Mindy's car. And I had already turned over the keys to Heron's Nest to my brother, who needed the place more than we did after all he'd been through. When the *Archangel* and the other wedding boats docked for the night, we said goodbye to our wedding guests and drove to Watertown, where we spent the night in a cheap, comfortable family-owned motel.

We honeymooned in the Poconos. We hiked up mountains and followed winding trails to spectacular waterfalls. We sat in a hot tub under the stars and sipped champagne. We watched old movies on cable TV and took naps. We made love in the morning and in the afternoon and sometimes again after dinner and before the hot tub.

One evening, after a particularly beautiful hike that culminated in a spectacular view of the Endless Mountains to the north and west, I told Mindy about my conversation with Patrick at Valhalla.

She listened carefully, then cried. She held me close and stroked my brow. She cried some more. Then she breathed deeply, wiped the tears from her cheeks and let out a loud sigh. "Well, if we've learned anything from all this," she concluded, "it's that it's hard to deny anyone their own unique perspective on events, however strange that perspective may seem to others."

I don't know whether her words were an attempt at a rational explanation or an emotional coping mechanism. I didn't press the issue. I just cried with her and held her as she held me. We never spoke about it again.

On our way back home we spent a day in the Catskills. We drove to Moses Earle's farm and I showed Mindy where I had taken my first journey to the Otherworld. We ate pizza at the general store in Andes. Emma recognized me, but she didn't ask if I'd seen her cousin. This puzzled me until I noticed a post card on the bulletin board, which was otherwise filled with business cards for contractors and firewood sellers, babysitters and farmers selling hay.

"Can I take a closer look?" I asked.

"Sure," Emma said. "The board's public."

It was a picture of a beautiful island, slightly rhomboid in shape, that sloped gently upwards from a sandy beach on one end to a dramatic cliff on the other. Rather than pines and larches, this island had palm trees and tall grass that swayed in the tropical breeze.

Mindy grabbed the card out of my hand. "It can't be!" she exclaimed.

"Turn it over," I said.

"I am indeed livin' the Dream!" Lodi had written.

I reached out and traced the beautiful script with my finger. The ink was blue, but it still looked eerily familiar. And there was no postmark. Emma said it had been delivered by the USPS, though, or at least by a guy in a light blue uniform, on Thursday of the previous week.

"Do you know where this is from?" I asked Lodi's cousin.

"The Caribbean I think? No!" She slapped the counter. "The South Pacific! He always said he wanted to visit the South Pacific!"

I photographed both sides of postcard, but I couldn't directly compare Lodi's handwriting to the handwriting on our living room wall because both the "ARIEL" and the "FLANAGAN! COME BACK!" were gone. The words had disappeared slowly over the summer, fading a little bit each day until the writing existed only as the shadow of a memory that became distant each day. By the time Labor Day came around and Mindy had returned to teaching, we wondered if the words had been there at all.

Ray Dale still had his photos, though. He had filed them away along with all the other evidence he had collected. When I visited him in mid-September for my tour of the Institute for Applied Philosophical Research, he said he was working on an article, but that it would take him many months, perhaps a year, to complete his investigation. Ray compared the writing on Lodi's postcard with his photos of the writing on our wall and deemed the similarities intriguing but inconclusive. Later, a handwriting expert at the university concurred.

And what of Martha Radisson's original note card and the card she'd given to Ray? That's best explained by yet another note card we received from her on the same day we received our wedding album. I read the card out loud to Mindy once we finished looking at our pictures for the umpteenth time.

"Congratulations on your weddings!" it said. "I hear they went well! And I'm very happy to hear that you found your brother and that he, too, is well. I received your note, Tom, but I find it rather odd. Why, I asked when I saw them, would you send me two blank note cards engraved with my name? Where did you get them? Are they meant to be a practical joke? Your reference to 'strange words of magic' especially puzzled me. But to be perfectly honest I'd prefer not to hear any more on the subject. I am very busy here in Cooperstown. If you need research assistance on a future project please call me. I thank you in advance for keeping our conversations strictly academic."

I set Martha's card on the table, then picked it up again and turned it in my hands.

"Sometimes it's best not to remember," Mindy said, looking me in the eye and taking the card.

"And other times ... " I started to say.

But Mindy enfolded my hand in hers, guided it to the

open photo album and placed it on our favorite picture, the one of us walking away and not looking back. We smiled together, and instead of finishing the thought I leaned forward and gave my wife a kiss.

Afterword

LIKE TOM FLANAGAN, I entered into this story via the straightforward yet unanswerable question, "Who killed Osman Steele?" The murder that marked the beginning of the end of the Anti-Rent Wars remains a mystery. The Anti-Rent Wars themselves, however, are a well-documented, if under-appreciated, episode in American history. Henry Christman's *Tin Horns and Calico* remains the definitive work. Christman was a great storyteller. In his words the tin horns can still be heard, the calico can still be seen and the people of Delaware County and the hilltowns can most definitely still be known and understood. Both David Ellis's *Landlords and Farmers in the Hudson-Mohawk Region* and Reeve Huston's *Rural Society, Popular Protest, and Party Politics in Antebellum, New York* offer some deeper scholarly perspective on events. Dorothy Kubik's *A Free Soil—A Free People* is a fine example of local history and a testament to the historical consciousness of Delaware County's people. Throughout the writing process, Nancy Cannon's *Voice of the People: Daily Life in the Antebellum Rural Delaware County New York Area* (*http://www.oneonta.edu/library/dailylife/acknow.html*) was an invaluable resource for understanding just what the web site's title says.

At the same time as I was reading about the Anti-Rent Wars and contemplating the mystery of Osman Steele's death, I was also developing a deep personal connection with the land. For ten years as of this story's publication I owned and worked a small farm in the foothills of the

Catskill mountains. Like Lodi, I tried to do things the old way, to respect the land as a living entity, as a partner in the constant art of creation rather than as an enemy to be overcome. I learned how to respect the land from many friends and neighbors, including Bill Hribar Sr. and Billy Jr., John Stucin, Tom and Julie Huntsman, Jim Atwell and a dozen other local farmers.

We fertilize our garden with horse manure. We practice rotational grazing. We get our drinking water from a natural spring. I found in the rock, soil and springs of our hills and vales what I had already found in the water of the Saint Lawrence River: a deep and abiding appreciation for the unseen, spiritual nature of existence. Our natural spring, for example, is a place where rock, water and air join together in a beautiful dance of life. I may not have seen any gnomes, fairies or undines there, but at certain times on certain days, when the fire of the sun heats up the imagination just so, I can hear their music and feel their invisible presence.

I found words to help me express these feelings in the poetry of William Blake, W.B. Yeats and T.S. Eliot, and in the deeply personal life stories of C.G. Jung and Kathleen Raine. The provocative thought and brilliant writing of Patrick Harpur helped shape my ideas into their current form. Harpur's *Daimonic Reality: A Field Guide to the Otherworld* is a masterpiece. His *The Philosopher's Secret Fire* is the perfect antidote to the epidemic of materialism that infects and thereby weakens contemporary Western culture. Having just recently resigned from college teaching to pursue other opportunities, I was ready to shift my perspective on history from pursuing and interpreting just the facts to appreciating the spiritual complexities of human life that no social science can measure.

One part of that spiritual complexity is our experience and understanding of time. History pulls and pushes us into a linear way of thinking that also restricts our natural capacity to connect with the unseen, spiritual world. I decided in writing *Ariel's Gift* to unshackle at least a couple of the characters from the confines of time and thus from the bounds of history. Larry Dossey and, a century before him, J.W. Dunne both thrilled me with their research and speculations on the malleability of time.

Finally, there's family. My own family is quite unlike either Tom's or Mindy's. Yet all families share certain patterns, a truth I discovered through studying family systems theory. One of the most inescapable patterns in family life is the way we arrange ourselves in threes. Triangles are everywhere, and it didn't take me long to conclude that the Tom/Mindy/Patrick triangle would be the frame around which *Ariel's Gift* would be built. And within their family triangle, as within so many others including, blessedly, my own, is to be found a Great Thing that touches our souls and draws us onward, an invisible World of Love.

Bibliography

Apaleius. *The God of Socrates.* In *The Works of Apueius*, translated by Mrs. Henry Tighe, Hudson Gurney, Mary Blachford Tighe. London: George Bell and Sons, 1902, pp. 350-373.

Christman, Henry. *Tin Horns and Calico: A Decisive Episode in the Emergence of Democracy.* New York, NY: Henry Holt and Company, 1945.

Delaware County Historical Association. *Two Stones for Every Dirt: The Story of Delaware County, New York.* Fleischmanns, NY: Purple Mountain Press, 1987.

Dossey, Larry. *The Power of Premonitions.* New York, NY: Dutton, 2009.

Dunne, J.W. *An Experiment with Time.* London: A.C. Black Ltd., 1929.

Ellis, David Maldwyn. *Landlords and Farmers in the Hudson-Mohawk Region, 1790-1850.* Ithaca, NY: Cornell University Press, 1946.

Fort, Charles. *The Book of the Damned.* New York, NY: Boni and Liveright, Inc., 1919.

Harpur. Patrick. *Daimonic Reality: A Field Guide to the Otherworld.* Ravensdale, WA: Pine Winds Press, 1994.

———. *The Philosopher's Secret Fire: A History of the Imagination.* Somerset, England: Squeeze Press, 2002.

Hildegard of Bingen. *Mystical Visions,* translated by Bruce Hozeski. Rochester, VT: Bear and Company, 1986.

Huston, Reeve. *Rural Society, Popular Protest, and Party Politics in Antebellum, New York.* New York, NY: Oxford University Press, 2000.

Jung, Karl. *Memories, Dreams, Reflections,* translated by Richard and Clara Winston. New York, NY: Vintage Books, 1965.

Keel, John. *The Mothman Prophecies.* New York, NY: Tor, 1975.

———. *Our Haunted Planet.* Lakeville, MN: Galde Press, 2010.

Kubik, Dorothy. *A Free Soil—A Free People: The Anti-Rent War in Delaware County, New York.* Fleischmanns, NY: Purple Mountain Press, 1997.

Raine, Kathleen. *Autobiographies.* San Rafael, CA: Coracle Press. 1998.

Ariel's Gift Playlist

1. *Take Shelter*, Ben Nichols
2. *Roll With the Changes*, REO Speedwagon
3. *Drift Away*, Dobie Gray
4. *Turn Back the Hands of Time*, Tyrone Davis
5. *People Get Ready*, The Impressions
6. *Travelin' Man/Beautiful Loser*, Bob Seger
7. *Good Times*, Sam Cooke
8. *Lodi*, Creedence Clearwater Revival
9. *You Angel You*, Bob Dylan
10. *This Land Is Your Land*, Woody Guthrie
11. *Lindbergh*, Woody Guthrie
12. *Jarama Valley*, Woody Guthrie
13. *Do-Re-Mi*, Woody Guthrie
14. *Dreams*, Van Halen
15. *Blinded By the Light*, Manfred Mann's Earth Band
16. *Water Music Suite #2 In D, HWV 349*, Handel

About the Author

THOMAS PULLYBLANK has served as a college history professor and a United Methodist pastor. *Ariel's Gift* is his third novel, which completes the Tom Flanagan historical mysteries. He followed the first two novels of the trilogy, *Cornflower's Ghost: An Historical Mystery*, and *Napoleon's Gold: A Legend of the Saint Lawrence River*, with a collection of short stories related to *Napoleon's Gold*, titled *The Ghost of Billy Masterson & Other Thousand Island Tales*.

In addition to Upstate New York historical mysteries, Pullyblank is also the author of *For None Can Rank Above Thee: A History of Cal-Mum Red Raiders Football*, a chronicle of his legendary high school football team in Caledonia, New York.

Pullyblank now works as a conflict mediator, and lives with his family in Fly Creek, New York. As he did as a child with his parents, he still spends time with his family every summer in his beloved Thousand Islands.

Also available from
Square Circle Press

**The Ghost of
Billy Masterson & Other
Thousand Island Tales**

by

Thomas Pullyblank

A collection of short stories supplemental to *Cornflower's Ghost*, *Napoleon's Gold*, and *Ariel's Gift*.

The beautiful Thousand Islands often seem like a magical place and in Thomas Pullyblank's new book of short stories they actually are magic—a place of underwater spirits and time travelers. ... [As] I read this book, I imagined sitting next to Pullybank on a cool summer night at an island campfire. As he spun out his tale, the mighty river pulsed along the shore, its water filled with secrets.
—*Betsy Kepes, North Country Public Radio*

To read the full reviews of the novels and short stories of Thomas Pullyblank and to view our full catalog, please visit www.SquareCirclePress.com

CPSIA information can be obtained
at www.ICGtesting.com
Printed in the USA
LVHW110710060820
662303LV00005B/651